ABOUT THE AUTHOR

One of the most neglected American writers and also one of the best loved, Nelson Algren wrote once that "literature is made upon any occasion that a challenge is put to the legal apparatus by conscience in touch with humanity." His writings always lived up to that definition. He was born March 28, 1909 in Detroit and lived mostly in Chicago. His first short fiction was published in *Story* magazine in 1933. In 1935 he published his first novel, *Somebody in Boots*. In early 1942, Algren put the finishing touches on a second novel and joined the war as an enlisted man. By 1945, he still had not made the grade of Private first class, but the novel *Never Come Morning* was widely praised and eventually sold over a million copies. Jean-Paul Sartre translated the French-language edition. In 1947 came *The Neon Wilderness*, his famous short story collection which would permanently establish his place in American letters. *The Man with the Golden Arm*, winner of the first National Book Award, appeared in 1949. Then came *Chicago: City on the Make* (1951), a prose poem and *A Walk on the Wild Side* (1956), possibly his greatest novel. Algren also published two travel books, *Who Lost an American?* and *Notes from a Sea Voyage*. *The Last Carousel*, a collection of short fiction and nonfiction, appeared in 1973. He died on May 9, 1981, within days of his appointment as a fellow of the American Academy and Institute of Arts and Letters. His last novel, *The Devil's Stocking*, based on the life of Hurricane Carter, and *Nonconformity: Writing on Writing*, a 1952 essay on the art of writing, were published posthumously in 1983 and 1996 respectively.

THE NEON WILDERNESS

NELSON ALGREN

SEVEN STORIES PRESS
new york

Copyright © 1933, 1934, 1941, 1942, 1943, 1944, 1947 by Nelson Algren
Copyright © renewed 1974 by Nelson Algren.
All rights reserved.
First Printing, 1986

Acknowledgment is made to the following magazines for permission to reprint the stories indicated: to *American Mercury* for "He Swung and He Missed"

Seven Stories Press
140 Watts Street
New York, N.Y. 10013
www.sevenstories.com

In Canada:
Publishers Group Canada, 559 College Street, Suite 402, Toronto, Ontario M4B 3E2, Canada

In the U.K.:
Turnaround Publisher Services Ltd., Unit 3, Olympia Trading Estate, Coburg Road, Wood Green, London M6G 1A9

In Australia:
Palgrave Macmillan, 15–19 Claremont Street, South Yarra, VIC 3141

Library of Congress Cataloging-in-Publication Data

Algren, Nelson, 1909-1981
    The neon wilderness/Nelson Algren—1st Seven Stories Press edition
    p. cm.
    ISBN: 978-1-58322-550-9
    1. Chicago (Ill.)—Social life and customs—Fiction. 2. City and town life—
Illinois—Chicago—Fiction. I. Title.
PS3501.L4625N36 1997
813'.52—DC21
                                 96-40151
                                 CIP

Printed in the USA

10 9 8 7 6 5

contents

introduction
by tom carson

The Neon Wilderness, first published in 1947, is the pivotal
book of Nelson Algren's career—the one which bid a subdued
but determined farewell to everything that had earlier made
him no more than just another good writer, and inaugurated
the idiosyncratic, bedevilled, cantankerously poetic sensibility
that would see him ranked among the few literary originals of
his time. With *The Neon Wilderness,* Algren turned into one of
the few American writers, increasingly uncommon since Dreiser, in whom compassion for the dispossessed does not involve
a sort of mental portage to reach them. The great revelation for
him had been that deprivation was not an abnormal social
category but a human absolute, and the pressure in *Neon
Wilderness* comes from a writer trying to measure up to the
people he's writing about.

He had begun as a Depression novelist, albeit one whose
conventionally patterned outrage at social injustice felt more
like a fence around his material than a key to its meaning.
Traces of the attitude can be found in some of the earlier pieces
in this collection. But while a novel can be written to back up a
thesis, the short story is more resistant to that. Its equivalent

tendency is toward parable—a harder version of the truth, poetic and ineluctable rather than sociological and circumstantial. So even "A Bottle of Milk for Mother," included here, is in some ways more resonant than the novel (*Never Come Morning*, Algren's second) for which it provided the seed. In this version, he doesn't have to explain the interlock of events leading up to Lefty Bicek's arrest for the most useless imaginable homicide, much less stage-manage them into spelling out any acceptable sort of message, either of pity or condemnation. He can simply present Bicek, in all his terrified terribleness, as a random window on humanity.

There's an implicit condescension in most fiction about the lower depths, starting with that term for them. The writer's typical rejection of artfulness, of all literary lilt and sensuality, however manfully meant as an indictment, ends up slipping you the hint that beauty and grace are qualities somehow beyond the class of people in question. Not so for Algren, once he'd found himself. He cultivated every quicksilver ravishment of language that he knew, flinting it with a colloquialism no longer merely mimetic—although Algren could be a fictional ventriloquist of unusual attentiveness and tact, as several stories here display—but metaphorically charged, because he knew that nothing less multilayered and fine-tuned would do justice to the complicated nuance and subtle play of inner awareness that his characters were otherwise presumed to lack only because they were unable to articulate them. The best mature stories in *Neon Wilderness* move on a river of such openness to the details of experience, and perception so unmarred by preconception, that pigeonholing them according to their subject matter ends up seeming like a form of evasion.

Which is why the style is one of the few genuinely poetic prose styles that can also be called genuinely accurate. Once he'd learned to fly, Algren took chances with his material that no conventional proletarian writer would dare. When his people con outrageously, or blunder into the same emotional manhole they've blundered into a hundred times before, he derides them like the wised-up bar-keep down the block; and the intimacy telegraphed by his humor makes those fouled-up barterings with existence painful in a way that neither he nor his readers can exclude themselves from. And it's another mark of Algren's singularity that though his characters' destiny may be tragic, the best ones' behavior isn't always seen as pathetic. Trapped they may be—but their various delusions, eccentricities, addictions and other skewings of reality are often made to appear not as symptoms but active responses, survival strategies, necessarily inventive ways of coping and sustaining some sense of self in the trap. This is understanding on a uniquely humane and unmediated level.

It seems fitting that two of the most striking stories here anticipate crucial elements of Algren's two enduring novels. In plot, "The Captain Has Bad Dreams" is no more than a circumstantial account of the nightly lineup in a Chicago precinct house. A recidivist procession of burglars, drunks, junkies, and would-be rapists, never more haunting than in their sly awareness of their own failure, play out ritualistic maneuvers of chicanery and bluff before the captain, as if in a chess tournament where each piece equals a new game. In meaning, the story is a set of freeze-frames of a man trying to make logical what could only be expressed as inchoate despair: the tension between the captain's struggle to deny that he is as much part of the wreckage as the debris before him, and his yearning to give in like them to a nihilism that seems less compromised than his own existence, has made him near to mad. It's Dostoevsky shorn of metaphysics, and all the more monstrous for being mundane. And the captain will reappear in *The Man With the Golden Arm*, the book acknowledged as Algren's idiosyncratic masterpiece—obsessed, by then, by a furtive lust to write his own name on the list of the guilty, even as he stalks the junkie Frankie Machine.

Meanwhile, *A Walk On the Wild Side*—a masterpiece so idiosyncratic that it's never been properly acknowledged at all—is foreshadowed in "The Face On the Barroom Floor." The story's Railroad Shorty, like the novel's Legless Schmidt, is an ex-fighter who's been cut in half by a train, and now wheels himself around on a leather-strapped handmade platform. Under either name, he's a great creation—a cripple that you can't feel sorry for. His massive self-sufficiency commands only apprehensive respect; it's the most massively admirable quality he has, and yet it's what turned him into the monster that his deformity alone never could. A younger man (the novel's hero Dove Linkhorn, in the story a bespectacled bartender nicknamed "Fancy"), as determined to break free of callowness as the cripple is of ever being seen as weak, challenges the latter's authority by attempting to sever his one human link, the hooker whose bed he shares while refusing to do the same with her money. In the brutality that ensues, Fancy is beaten to a pulp, and the cripple loses his human connection anyway—he recoils, not in disgust but in self-disgust, from the woman's delight in the reason for the beating. But none of them could have acted in any other way—at least not without relinquishing their struggle for an identity of their own, the only battlefield where the outcome is still open for them. Futile, and awful, it may be; but meaningless—no.

But the claim for *Neon Wilderness* doesn't rest only on the preludes it offers to Algren's subsequent work. Look, for instance, at the desperate, wondrously written "Design For Departure." A rather ordinary young woman slips, less down than sideways, into hooking and addiction—dreamily, but her dreaminess long outlasts her hopes. Finally, she comes to see herself as the Virgin Mary, and her lover-connection as Christ. But her insanity, instead of being characterized as pathetic, is merely witnessed: it's the thing that lets her go on living in an unbearable situation. Or else read, in "Depend On Aunt Elly," about another woman submitting to a scheming jailer's black-mail in order to regain her freedom after being unjustly sent to prison, and fatalistically accepting her lover's leaving her when he finds out about it; and notice how, in Algren's telling, even anger ultimately gets subsumed within a sense of all-abiding mystery. There is, in this book, a great deal of wonderful writing; and a number of people, places, feelings, and truths that you may never have met, seen, or known, but that you'll never be able to stop yourself from recognizing once the book is closed.

—TOM CARSON
New York, June 1985

for
my mother
and the memory of
my father

Children of the cold sun and the broken horizon,
O secret faces, multitudes, eyes of inscrutable grief,
great breath of millions, in unknown crowds or alone,
rooms of dreamers above the cement abyss,—and I,
who all night restive in the unsleeping rain,
awake and saw the windows covered with tears.

noon, and dark twilight, and night with argon peaks,
matchless city, terrible . . . and all, all
I see are innocent; not walls, nor men
brutal, remote, stunned, querulous, weak, or cold
do crimes so massive, but the hideous fact
stands guilty: the usurpation of man over man.

The City, BY DAVID WOLFF

the captain has bad dreams

or who put the sodium amytal in the hill & hill?

They come off the streets for a night or a week and pause before the amplifier with a single light, like a vigil light, burning high overhead. Each pauses, one passing moment, to make his brief confessional:

"Leo Cooney. Fraud'lent perscription. It's a bad bang, Captain."

Life is a bad bang for Cooney: a bum rap and no probation.

"What do you use when you can't get morphine sulphate?"

"Paregoric."

And steps back into the shadows. You won't see Cooney in the light again.

Yes, and he'll drink starch too. His nose didn't get white from blowing it.

The thin-featured Negro beside him is trying to look like an M-G-M Mexican: broad-brimmed hat and sideburns so deep and dark they look like cords fastening the foolish hat under the chin.

"What you in here for, Sugar-Cure?"

"Walked off with a dolla' 'n fo'got to bring a man his change."

"You mean you forgot to bring him his marijuana. Where'd you come from?"

"Chillicothe, Ohio."

"Didn't the Chamber of Commerce know you were coming in?"

"I didn't tell 'em. I was in the House of Correction."

"Turn around and face the back wall. Take off that hat."

The pseudo-Mexican removed his hat, faced the wall a moment, and turned back to face the darkened rows where a hundred victims of recent crimes watched silently. The Captain explained: "We just wanted to see the back of your head. So when they turn you over we'll know who you are. Next man."

The man with the midnight complexion and the Ogden Avenue eyes steps forward.

"You still here from last week, Irving? Or is this a new charge?"

"From Friday night, I still don't know."

"Didn't you ask the officer what he was arresting you for?"

"No sir."

"You always did before."

"It wasn't none of my business, I figured."

"Did you knock her down or was she pushed?"

"Captain, that I *wouldn't* do."

"You'd do anything. The complaint is signed against you."

"She fell down. I went to help her up, so her pocketbook opened up. I was helpin' her to pick up the t'ings."

"You're always helpin' women pick up their things, somehow. We got six stop warrants for you from New York for helpin' out there."

"New York can't touch me."

The Captain looked down at Irving's record and shrugged helplessly. "He won't work and you can't gas him," he sighed. "Next man."

"Ah was talkin' to a lady on the street under the impression it was mah wife."

"Tell that to a mule and he'll kick your head off. Next man."

"I beat up my tenant."

"Does that come under sports?"

The fellow is left looking bewildered as the amplifier is moved on. The Captain didn't always have the heart to point the unwavering finger of guilt.

He saw the dispossessed ones come and go, the twisted and the stunted ones, and felt equally indifferent to all: all the litters spawned in the city's unpoliced corners, when no one was watching to make them spawn in someone else's back yard; all the ones for whom no ordinance provided. You couldn't drown them because they weren't cats, and when you drove them off they found their way back home anyhow. The Captain could never quite understand why it had always to be him to turn on the lights overhead, why it had always to be him to trap them in their lies, why it had always to be him to call: "Next!"

"What's your name?"

"Duffy. I do everythin'."

"If I catch you lyin' with a name like that——" The Captain consulted the record. "Right you are. You're the devil's own boy." The Captain is proud of Duffy. "How many times you been arrested, Duff?"

"Every time I got out of jail."

The Captain's pride in Duffy faded as he eyed the next man, a willowy youth in a black slouch hat and black coat, with a face as white as his collar.

"Don't even tell me your name," the Captain warned him. "I know what you are—but I don't use that kind of language." The youth in black, as though dismissed, started toward the steps.

"Watch him or he'll waltz away!"

An officer waved the boy back and the women witnesses tittered. The women loved it.

"What's your profession?" the Captain asked the willowy one innocently.

"I *work*, Captain."

"What do you work at?"

"Why, Captain, at my *profession.*"

"What's your profession?"

"Oh, Captain."

"I'm glad we cleared that up. Did you ever do time, Sweet-lips?"

"Yes sir—210 days."

"What for?"

"I don't *know.*"

"They just locked you up and let you out 210 days later?"

"Yes sir."

"A man don't forget what he goes to jail 210 days for."

"Oh my *goodness,* Captain, that's so long ago, it just seems to pass my mind."

The Captain gave up. "You'll end up in a ditch with your little toes turned up. Next."

An old stewbum, with a pinched-up face the color of the West Madison Street pavement, squints out at the darkened rows painfully, like a half-squashed beetle.

"Fer stealin' half a poun' o' peas."

"You ought to be ashamed of yourself. Half a pound of peas. Next time take a fifty-pound sack and do it right."

The next was a half-pint with his cap on backward.

"Are you coming or going?" the Captain asked.

"I always wear it that way. I'm an exercise boy. I gallop horses."

"I see. You started out bangin' the horses 'n now you're bangin' yourself. Is that your trouble?"

"No sir. Too many taverns is my trouble. I go 'n drink forty 'r fifty beers 'n then the bubbles go to my head."

"What kind of beer?"

"Any kind with foam on."

"Ever try working?"

"I'm waitin' for a contract to do labor—like cookin'."

"You couldn't cook water for a barber. You're a loose bum

livin' off the weaker bums until Hawthorne opens, that's all. We'll get a jacket for you one of these days."

The line filed off disconsolately, and the next line was held back while a matron hustled a young Mexican girl in to face the crowd.

"What was the needle and eye dropper for, Juanita?"

"For have *good* time."

"How long you think you'll live, Juanita?"

"Maybe die tomorrow."

"I think you'll die in an institution."

"I think too."

And the men come on again: the flashy and the penitent, the beaten ones and the wise guys, the hangdog heel thieves and the disdainful coneroos, walking, half crouched, through a downpour of light like men walking through rain. The frayed and the hesitant, the sleek and the bold, the odd fish and the callow youths, the good-humored bindle stiffs and the bitter veterans.

And the simple everyday bottle-boy, who fights when he drinks, and he drinks all the time.

"Irresisting an officer is all," says Bottle-Boy, and adds half to himself, wistfully, "Seems every time I get drunk I take a joy ride in a Checker cab."

"Good thing you don't get drunk every half hour. You'd have traffic blocked."

Next is a bald and pious-looking runt.

"I induced a little girl."

"Did you have a license?"

The warm weather brought this kind in. "Where was this, Non Compis?"

"In a tee-*ay*-ter. I was disposin' myself."

"That's not a bad idea. Why don't you take a good belt of cocaine and jump out a twenty-story window?"

"Sometimes I feel like it."

"Here—I'll open the window for you."

The runt was on the verge of tears. "I wasn't thinkin' of nothin' wrong," he pleaded.

Such men haunted the Captain. In sleep he saw their pale lascivious faces; watched them moving like blind men beneath the thousand-columned El, where a calamitous yellow light filtered downward all night long. In this tragic and fluorescent dream they passed and repassed him restlessly, their faces half averted, forever smiling uneasily as though sharing some secret and comforting knowledge of evil which he could never know.

They lived in an unpossessed twilight land, a neon wilderness whose shores the Captain sometimes envisaged dimly; in sleep he sought that shore forever, always drawing nearer, like a swimmer far out at sea; yet never, somehow, attaining those long, low sands. He would awaken feeling unnatural, dreading the evening and the yellow showup's glare.

"What kind of work you do?"

"I'm a garment presser."

"You mean you press some sucker's pockets till there's nothing left in 'em. What about that watch?"

"A friend of mine put it in my pocket to keep hisself from gettin' robbed by some crook."

"You stick to that. You crumb-elbowed dead-picker. You tell that one to the court. You stuffed stewbum. You're an habitual." The Captain waved the man's record across the mike to taunt him. "Wouldn't you give a lot to have this thrown away? Wait till we get universal fingerprinting and some of you birds try going to work. You'll find out then what it means to have a record. We'll have you dead to rights in three days flat and we'll rearrest you every time the gates open up for you. What were you doing with that .38 Special? Don't you know only officers can carry those?"

"I wasn't nowhere near it. It was just on the premises."

"You would of used it."

"My feets in my shoes but they ain't movin', are they?"

"They'll be movin' on wheels one of these days though. You'll only need one more white shirt then." The Captain quieted himself, wondering what had made him lose his temper over such a tramp.

"What do *you* do, next man?"

"I'm a millwright—I make rubber."

"Rubber checks, you mean. Next, what for?"

"Relief fraudery 'n not havin' my restoration card."

"How about mopery with intent to gawk?"

"I don't remember doin' *that*."

"Do you remember that sodomy charge?"

"That's in the past."

"What about the future?"

"Oh, I'm a nice fella now."

"I'll bet you're an angel—by the clock."

The Captain eyed the next man critically. A Texan in an outdated mail-order suit with the collar slipping toward the small of his back and the shoulders loose as though he had no shoulders.

"Is that the suit you walked out of Sears, Roebuck with?"

"Ah was willin' t' pay for it."

"But they just didn't give you the time?"

"Naw sir, I couldn't git in a word."

"For wearin' that thing they ought to pay you. Ever carry a gun?"

"Just a little ol' piece o' cow-gun. Couldn't get a bullet in 'er if ah'd tried."

"What did you pull up lame in the Box Elder County Jail for?"

"We were just playin' cahds 'n a man jumped out the window."

"Did you have a little ol' piece o' cow-gun that time too?"

"Naw. Just a little ol' piece o' pinknife was all."

"You could've brought down a moose with that switch. I bet it stuck out of his back so far you could've tied a ribbon on it. Next man, what's your trouble?"

"Late hours. Previously, I was always out late."

"Previously you were a big stuffed bum and you still are. What were you doing around that hotel?"

"Waitin' for a woman."

"On the fire escape? Is that where you usually do your courting?"

"I wasn't courtin'. I was just gonna sell her some old cotton stockin's."

"I see. You came all the way from Wood Street to hide on a fire escape to sell a woman a pair of cotton stockings."

"Well, it wasn't just that. I was in that neighborhood lookin' for work."

"What kind of work?"

"Oh, just an odd job for the night."

"And you got caught doing the odd job. Next."

"I was takin' a short cut through an alley."

"You took a short cut when you saw the squad car, you mean. What were you doing at 2 A.M. with a screwdriver and a sledge hammer?"

"I didn't have no screwdriver."

"Who did?"

"My buddy."

"Where's he?"

"In the morgue."

"That's a damned good thing. Too bad you didn't run too. Are you crazy?"

"Ask the doctor."

"He's crazier than you are to let you out of Menard in the first place. You're lucky you're not charged with murder again."

"I wish I was."

"Why?"

"It's an easier death."

"Have you tried gas?"

"No. But I hear it's pretty good."

The Captain turned wearily toward the listeners. "That comes from not wearing boxing gloves when he goes to bed. Next."

A middle-aged Negro in a woman's dress and a woman's castoff hat.

"Skip him," the Captain directed. "All he needs is medical attention. Or the gas chamber. Look at those eyes. He ought to have a bullet between them. Next."

Some nights the Captain was all for hanging the lot of them at 11 P.M. On other evenings he advised them to take turns throwing themselves under the El, which roared regularly past. Once he offered a forger immediate freedom if he'd promise to shoot himself in the lobby downstairs. "I'll loan you the gun," the Captain offered. Tonight he was advising gas.

"I fell asleep in the back room of a tavern," the next man explained. "I was tryin' to get out."

"Get out with the profits, you mean."

"I'm going straight now."

"Straight back to the pen, you mean. You're through now."

"Not if I break out."

"You couldn't break out of a wet paper bag, brave guy. You had a gun when the officers dropped in on you—why didn't you shoot it out?"

"I got better sense."

"You mean you were too yellow."

"I'm not yellow."

"No? It's coming out of your ears, Mr. Rat. Look at him," the Captain appealed to the audience. "He's twenty-two and doesn't look a day over forty. What's next?"

Four of the last five in line were underage, undersized Italians, all in for the same series of currency-exchange jobs. Only the fifth was talking.

"I'm s'posed to testify up against them guys," number five confessed sheepishly, nodding toward his pals. The four looked straight ahead while the Captain eyed the fifth steadily.

"You better make it stick, Carl," he counseled gravely. "You'll be better off in Statesville if you don't."

A fat boy with glasses and a face the color of a raw oyster was next.

"You the guy who writes them funny letters?"

"Yes sir. To the girl in the bakery. I trade with her."

"She don't want to trade with *you*. Next."

This was a youth of twenty, a tousled, good-natured, and careless-looking Pole wearing a sweater upon which a winged roller skate had been engraved in red, white, and blue.

"Tell us what you told your mother when we arrested you, Chester."

"I told her, 'Mother, you've worked for me for twenty years. Now go out and get a job for yourself.' "

"What she have you brought in here for?"

"I put the bread knife into the old man."

"Are you going to the funeral?"

The boy raised one casual eyebrow toward the Captain. "Certainly. If there's free booze." And yawned.

The Captain went white. "Look at him!" he shouted, as though all eyes were not already pinned on the boy. "Look at him up there! He thinks he's going to get the D.S.C.!"

The boy looked bored. He knew what he was going to get.

"All I do is drink 'n fight," the next fellow explained confidently, and wore a bandage about his temples to bear him out.

"What was 180 days in '39 for? Walkin' down the wrong side of the street?"

"All I do is fight."

"Who's Turner Grady?"

"That's my alias name."

The Captain read: "Turner Grady, strong-arm robbery; Turner Grady, assault to do great bodily harm——"

"Must be some other peoples. All I do is fight."

"Speeding a car without the owner's consent," the next youth admitted brightly.

"That wouldn't come under auto theft, would it? Where were you going so fast?"

"To meet my wife."

"She's better off that you didn't get there. Next."

"I was very drunk 'n clothing disarranged," the old boy next in line confessed, with the blunt-nosed leer of a hyena in heat.

"You mean you're a cannibal 'n they should of drowned you when you were three. You're a dangerous man to have on the streets. Your roof is leaking. What do you do, next man?"

"I'm a sort of mechanic. I fix juke boxes."

"The hell you do. Your partner grabs a man's arms and you kick his legs out from under him. That's the kind of mechanic you are. What was that stretch in the Shelby County Penal Farm for?"

"Pickpocketin'."

"Wrong again. You couldn't get your hand in a rain barrel. You're a common neck-stretcher. That's my opinion."

"That's just *your* opinion."

"You'll find out my opinion. You're under the lights now. Next."

The last man in line stood against the lighted wall as though impaled, an agonized Jesus in long outgrown clothes. He clenched his knuckles about the horizontal bar behind him, twisting this way and that, writhing with the effort of staying within the boundaries assigned to him by the number over his head. When he spoke it was in a scream suppressed to a whisper.

"Gave myself—up—voluntarily—addict."

And with each jerked phrase his whole body strained on the bar as though he were chained to a torture rack.

"Quit squirming up there!" the Captain demanded.

"It's—crowded—up—here," the addict explained piteously.

"Take him off before he takes a header. He'll never make work scarce. Next."

"A smart copper thought I was drunk. He was automatic'lly

mistook. I got high blood pressure, that's why I was stagger-in'."

"And you staggered into a beauty parlor?"

"Lookin' for my wife was all."

"At 4 A.M.?"

"She goes to work early."

"Ever try goin' to work yourself?"

"Can't find anything I *like* to do."

"If somebody laid down in bed beside you with a job," the Captain inquired mildly, "would you take it?"

"Yes sir. I'd take it."

"But you wouldn't get up to get one. And if that officer hadn't had a conscience you'd be in the morgue—some of the cowboys on the force would've gotten themselves a seven-hundred-dollar raise."

"I just had a major operation."

"When the right officers operate you *will* hit the morgue."

"I got high blood pressure."

That seemed to explain everything. The Captain eyed him quizzically. "Why didn't you say that in the first place? We thought you were guilty. Case dismissed."

The next youth looked like Hollywood Boulevard: a good-looking young husky in a natty tan topcoat.

"What's your name, Lady-Killer?"

"I wouldn't know that."

"What's the extent of your education?"

"None."

The Captain referred to the record: "Kelly Costello—1941 —robbery by night; Kelly Costello—1942—larceny from the person; Kelly Costello—1944—larceny by bailee———"

"Don't forget 1943," the youth advised him. The Captain corrected himself. "Kelly Costello—1943—destruction of property———"

"Get it right. It was safeblowing."

"How do you know? You don't even know your name."

"You just read 'em. I'll tell you when you're wrong."

"I'll tell you something too, Brainstorm: You're going to be in so long this time you'll think you're the warden. Next."

This was a nervous little five-foot wretch, bobbing his head around in front of the amplifier and trying to say six things at once.

"I was workin' nights 'n——"

"I don't care what shift you were on. What you *here* for?"

"I was comin'. down the street on suspicion——"

"It was an alley. You were tailing a milkman——"

"No sir. I was in a drunkard's stupidness. I was lookin' for the labratory——"

"What—with a whole alley? How many drinks you have?"

"Just one."

"From a water glass or a bathtub? Tell us about it."

"Well, I went down to the County Building with my buddy to enlist in the Marines, 'n he didn't pass, so he says let's wait, we'll enlist in the Navy Air Corps instead."

"Well?"

"Well, he couldn't pass that neither, so we tried the Regular Army, 'n he flunked that too."

"So you both went out 'n got drunk?"

"No, just me. I felt so bad for him."

"You ever been arrested before?"

"No sir. This is my first time."

"The first time this week, you mean."

"Oh, I been arrested in Michigan. I thought you meant in Illinois. I never been arrested in Illinois. I never did no wrong in Illinois."

"What good does that do you?"

"It don't. It's just that I love my state so much I go to Michigan to steal," he explained with an expression almost beatific.

"I wish you'd stop posin' for holy pictures up there," the Captain wished wistfully—and seemed to remember something. "Aren't you the kid they picked up that time on his way to put a flower on his mother's grave?"

"That was me." Proudly.

"They should've buried you with her. Next."

"Who stole those coats?" the Captain asked the next man.

"Nobody."

"Are they missing?"

"Certainly *not.*" With indignation at the implication.

"Where are they?"

"At the police station."

"I guess that covers everything."

"It covers everything except I didn't do it."

"Have you paid your income tax?"

"I ain't made five hundred dollars in five hundred years. The police keep me too busy."

"Where you're going you'll have time on your hands. Next."

As the line of men filed off a middle-aged redhead was hustled in by a matron.

"What you here for this time, Ginger?"

"I don't know, Captain."

"I'm sure I didn't send for you. Did you drink with that man?"

"We lifted a couple."

"You think he'll ever wake up?"

"I didn't know he'd gone to bed."

"What was the hundred days and a hundred dollars for in '44?"

"I didn't pay the fine."

"I didn't pay it for you. What did you steal that time?"

"I didn't steal anything. I was trying to buy a house dress, that was all."

"A *house dress?*" The Captain couldn't believe his ears. "What would *you* want with a house dress? You're never at home." And then, before she had a chance to explain this contradiction, the Captain let her have it: "Who put the sodium amytal in the Hill & Hill?"

Something like the shadow of a half-seen horror passed across her broken face; she had stood here before, in her cheap coat and frowsy little hat and her slip showing; so tonight must be the same as any other night. Only, tonight a man was dead.

"You've been acting mighty funny since 1921," the Captain told her thoughtfully. "Now you're just a piece of trade. Try taking a long walk on a short pier one of these days. Next."

It seemed to the Captain that the lines would never stop coming. Out of the curtained brothels, out of the padlocked poolrooms, the lines came on forever. His life was no longer measured by the days of the week, but only by the monotonous monotones of ragged men offering threadbare lies: "I was tempted t' rob 'n rape." "A man put a gun on me 'n said I broke his window." "They suppose I rob somebody—I suppose I didn't." "I'm accused of arsony 'r somthin'." "Just out of the Army 'n decided to take matters in my own hands." "I walked off with the man-I'm-workin'-for's money. My family needed it." "I contributed to a minor."

When he got the last one the Captain always asked, "What did you contribute?"

"Why, I contributed some candy."

"You're always giving little girls candy. How come you never give *me* any?"

That's how tired the Captain was.

"What were you in the post prison at Presidio for?"

"Fer false pretenses."

"What do you mean—false pretenses?"

"Somethin' I didn't do."

"I see. And what was that rap in the Allegheny County Workhouse for?"

"Fer fishin'."

"You're talking fact there all right; for trousers through a window. You got to have a license for that in this state.

You're so crooked when you die they'll have to screw you in the ground. Next."

"Ah got three threatenin' phone calls one evenin' tellin' me to come down to the El at Thirty-first Street, a man down there wanted to kill me with a knife."

"So naturally you went."

"Yes sir. Naturally."

"That was shrewd. Tell us what happened."

"Nothin' happened. Ah cut him, that's all."

"Did you tell him to shake his head then?" The Captain didn't stay for an answer. He only sighed heavily and gestured for the next speaker.

"I was drunk 'n hollerin' around the house."

"You were beating your mother, you mean. You started out tapping a gas main in '33 and now you're beating your mother. You're a brave guy. What you go down for in '43? Somebody tell you there was a war on?"

"That was for wresslin' with a girl on the sidewalk 'n talkin' to a guy through a door."

"What were you discussing? How to dispose of the body?"

"He said I was askin' for a guy name of Murphy 'n I don't even know no Murphy."

"So they sent you up for six months just because you don't know any Murphy?"

"That was the size of it."

"You're a victim of circumstances. They should've hung you. Next man, where were you arrested?"

"Right alongside my wife."

"That means something—when they come to your flat for you, doesn't it? Isn't that bad?"

"They were lookin' for somebody else."

"And they got you. That's even better. What were those rubber gloves in the dresser for?"

"They belonged to a doctor friend."

"What was the tape for?"

"To mend the windows."

"What were the masks for?"

"They was from a Halloween party."

"Were you in a hot car earlier in the evening?"

"A couple friends gave me a ride. I didn't know what they was gonna do."

"What do you think they had you in the car for—ballast? Next." The mulatto with the heroin still wandering curiously about the corners of his brain stood silently before the mike, his eyes on that unpossessed twilit shore. Till the mike was moved on and the last man in line had been questioned and the Captain was asking wearily, "Anyone who can identify any of these men please step forward."

The mulatto reacted at last. He took a single step forward. "I want—to—i-dentify—you," he announced, looking straight ahead.

"What did *I* do?" The Captain seemed taken a little aback.

"You—throw money at me—all the time."

"Put the mike back there," the Captain ordered. "Did you ever do time in an institution?"

The youth's voice came forth in an uncontrolled scream, so . that the metal base of the amplifier rang faintly.

"Fifty-five years!"

The Captain spoke quietly, trying to calm the torment in the tortured brain.

"You did a year and a day, Oliver. It only seemed like fifty-five. Was that for peddling or possession?"

"Add a hundred 'n ninety to *that* one! And JUMP— JUMP—JUMP for joy, children—JUMP for joy!"

"What the devil *are* you taking?"

And now the voice was the faintest of horror-struck whispers:

"Gage."

"Gage don't make you holler like that."

The voice was coy, cool, and inviting, yet still verging on a scream: "Peppermints, Captain—they makes me just JUMP for joy."

"What were you sentenced in Memphis for?"

The voice returned in a laughing shout:

"Only a co-incident!"

"What was that no-bill 'for murder for? Another coinci-dent?"

"Only a coincident!"

The Captain gave up sadly, as though giving up forever. The lights were dimmed overhead and the evening's last long line shuffled off: old rogues and wagon grifters, shakedown artists and coneroos, heel thieves and strong-arm merchants, extortionists and drunks, cat burglars from Brooklyn and live wires from nowhere. They filed off with the hophead still croaking hollowly from far back in the cell block, like an insane parrot, over and over, "Only a coincident! It's all a silly coincident!"

Till only the Captain was left with that echo, and a single light like a vigil light burning feverishly far overhead.

That light would burn all night for him, he knew. It would be waiting for him there, in the secret shallows of sleep, shining from that far-off shore.

Or beneath the thousand-columned El it would light their pale, lascivious faces.

The Captain had bad dreams.

But would never attain that twilit shore.

how the devil came down division street

Last Saturday evening there was a great argument in the Polonia Bar. All the biggest drunks on Division were there, trying to decide who the biggest drunk of them was. Symanski said he was, and Oljiec said he was, and Koncel said he was, and Czechowski said he was.

Then Roman Orlov came in and the argument was decided. For Poor Roman has been drunk so long, night and day, that when we remember living men we almost forget Poor Roman, as though he were no longer really among the living at all.

"The devil lives in a double-shot," Roman explains himself obscurely. "I got a great worm inside. Gnaws and gnaws. Every day I drown him and every day he gnaws. Help me drown the worm, fellas."

So I bought Poor Roman a double-shot and asked him frankly how, before he was thirty, he had become the biggest drunk on Division.

It took a long time, and many double-shots, for him to tell. But tell it he did, between curses and sobs, and I tell it now as closely to what he told as I can. Without the sobs, of course. And of course without any cursing.

When Roman was thirteen, it seems, the Orlovs moved into three stove-heated rooms in the rear of a lopsided tenement on Noble Street. Mama O. cooked in a Division Street restaurant by day and cooked in her own home by night.

Papa O. played an accordion for pennies in Division Street taverns by night and slept alone in the rooms by day.

There were only two beds in the tiny flat, so nobody encouraged Papa O. to come home at all.

Because he was the oldest, Roman slept between the twins, on the bed set up in the front room, to keep the pair from fighting during the night as they did during the day. Every day Teresa, who was eleven and could not learn her lessons as well as some of her classmates, slept with Mama O. in the windowless back bedroom, under a bleeding heart in a gilded oval frame.

If Papa O. got in before light, as happened occasionally early in the week, he crawled uncomplainingly under Roman's bed until Roman rose and got the twins, who were seven, up with him in time for Mass.

If Udo, who was something between a collie and a St. Bernard and as big as both together, was already curled up beneath the front-room bed, Papa O. slugged him with the accordion in friendly reproach—and went on into the back bedroom to crawl under Mama O.'s bed. In such an event he slept under a bed all day. For he never crawled, even with daylight, into Mama O.'s bed. Empty or not. As though he did not feel himself worthy to sleep there even when she was gone.

It was as though, having given himself all night to his accordion, he must remain true to it during the day.

For all manner of strange things went on in Papa O.'s head, as even the twins had become aware. Things so strange that Teresa was made ashamed of them by her schoolmates, whenever they wanted someone to tease.

This, too, was why no one, not even the twins, paid Papa O. any heed when the family returned from Mass one Sunday forenoon and he told them someone had been knocking while they were away.

"Some*body* was by door," he insisted. "I say 'Hallo.' Was no*body*." He looked slyly about him at the children. "Who plays tricks by Papa?"

"Maybe was Zolewitzes," Mama O. suggested indifferently. "Mama Z. comes perhaps to borrow."

That Sunday night it was cold in all the corners. Papa O. was gone to play for pennies and drinks, Mama O. was frying *pierogi,* the twins were in bed, and Teresa was studying her catechism across the table from Roman, when someone knocked lightly twice.

To Roman it sounded like someone at the clothes-closet door; but that was foolish to think, since the twins were in bed. Yet, when he opened the hall door, only a cold wind came into the room from the long gaslit passage.

Roman, being only thirteen, did not dare look behind the door. Far less to speak of the clothes closet.

All that night a light snow fell, while Roman O. lay wakeful, fancying he saw it falling on darkened streets all over the mysterious earth, on the pointing roof tops of old-world cities, on mountain-high waves of the mid-Atlantic, and in the leaning eaves of Noble Street. He was just falling off to sleep when the knocking came again. Three times, like a measured warning.

The boy stiffened under the covers, listening with his fear. Heard the hall door squeak softly, as though Papa O. were sneaking in. But Papa O. never knocked, and Papa O. never sneaked. Papa O. came home with the accordion banging against buildings all down Noble Street, jingling his pennies proudly, singing off-key bravely, mumbling and laughing and stumbling. Papa O. never knocked. He kicked the door in happily and shouted cheerfully, "What you say, all peoples? How's t'ings, ever-body?" Papa O. pulled people out of bed and rattled pans and laughed at nothing and argued with unseen bartenders until somebody gave him sausage and eggs and coffee and bread and hung the accordion safely away.

Roman crept, barefooted, in the long underwear Mama O. had sewed on him in the early fall, to the hallway door.

The whole house slept. The windows were frosted and a thin line of ice had edged up under the front window and along the pane. The family slept. Roman shoved the door open gently. The tenement slept. Down the hall the single jet flickered feebly. No one. Nothing. The people slept.

Roman looked behind the door, shivering now with more than cold.

No one. Nothing. All night long.

He returned to bed and prayed quietly, until he heard Mama O. rise; waited till he knew she had the fire going in the big kitchen stove. Then, dressing with his back to the heat, he told Mama O. what he had heard. Mama O. said nothing.

Two mornings later, Papa O. came home without the accordion. It did not matter then to Mama O. whether he had sold it or lost it or loaned it; she knew it at last for a sign, she had felt the change coming, she said, in her blood. For she had dreamed a dream, all night, of a stranger waiting in the hall: a young man, drunken, leaning against the gaslit wall for support, with blood down the front of his shirt and drying on his hands. She knew, as all the Orlovs knew, that the unhappy dead return to warn or comfort, to plead or repent, to gain peace or to avenge.

That day, standing over steaming kettles, Mama O. went back in her mind to all those dear to her of earth who had died: the cousin drowned at sea, the brother returned from the war to die, the mother and father gone from their fields before she had married.

That night she knocked on Mama Zolewitz's door. Mama Z. sat silently, as though she had been expecting Mama O. for many evenings.

"Landlord doesn't like we should tell new tenants too soon," Mama Z. explained even before being told of the knocking, "so you shouldn't say it, I told. It was a young man lived in this place, in your very rooms. A strong young man, and good to look at. But sick, sick in the head from the drink. A sinner certainly. For here he lived with his lady without being wed, and she worked and he did not. That he did not work had little to do with what happened, and the drink had little to do. For it was being unwed that brought it on, at night, on the New Year. He returned from the taverns that night and beat her till her screams were a whimpering. Till her whimpering became nothing. A strong young man, like a bull, made violent by the drink. When the whimpering ceased, there was no sound at all. No sound until noon, when the police came with shouting.

"What was there to shout about? I could have told them before they came. The young man had hanged himself in the bedroom closet. Thus it is that one sin leads to another, and both were buried together. In unsanctified ground, with no priest near."

Mama O. grew pale. Her very clothes closet.

"It is nothing to worry," Mama Z. told her neighbor sagely. "He does not knock to do harm. He comes only to gain a little peace that good Christian prayer for him may give. Pray for the young man, Mama O. He wishes peace."

That night after supper the Orlovs gathered in prayer about the front-room stove, and Papa O. prayed also. For now that the accordion was gone, the taverns must do without him. When the prayer was done, he went to bed with Mama O. like a good husband, and the knocking did not come again.

Each night the Orlovs prayed for the poor young man. And each night Papa O. went to bed with Mama O. for lack of his accordion.

Mama O. knew then that the knocking had been a sign of good omen, and told the priest, and the priest blessed her for a Christian. He said it was the will of God that the Orlovs should redeem the young man by prayer and that Papa O. should have a wife instead of an accordion.

Papa O. stayed at home until, for lack of music, he became the best janitor on Noble Street. Mama Z. went to the priest and told of her part in the miracle of the poor young man, and the priest blessed Mama Z. also.

When the landlord learned that his house was no longer haunted he brought the Orlovs gifts; and when the rent was late he said nothing. So the priest blessed him equally, and in time the Orlovs paid no rent at all, but prayed for the landlord instead.

Teresa became the most important person in her class, for it became known that a miracle had been done in the Orlov home. Sister Mary Ursula said the child looked more like a little saint every day. And no other child in the room ever had her lessons as well as Teresa thereafter.

The twins sensed the miracle and grew up to be fast friends, doing all things together, even to wearing the same clothes and reading the same catechism. Udo, too, knew that the home was blessed. For he received no more blows from the accordion.

Only one sad aspect shadowed this great and happy change: Poor Roman was left bedless. For with Papa O. home every night like a good husband, Teresa must sleep between the twins.

Thus it came about that the nights of Roman Orlov became fitful and restless, first under the front-room bed and then under the back-room bed. With the springs overhead squeaking half the night as likely as not. The nights of Roman's boyhood were thereafter passed beneath one bed or the other, with no bed of his own at all. Until, attaining his young manhood and his seventeenth year, he took at last to sleeping during the day in order to have no need for sleep at night.

And at night, as everyone knows, there is no place to go but the taverns.

So it was, being abroad with no place to go and the whole night to kill, that Roman took his father's place. He had no accordion for excuse—only lack of a bed. He came to think of the dawn, when the taverns closed and he must go home, as the bitterest hour of the day.

This is why he still calls the dawn the bitterest hour: he must go home though he has no home.

Is this a drunkard's tale or sober truth? I can only say he told it like the truth, drinking double-shots all the while. I only know that no one argues about who the biggest drunk on Division is if Roman O. is around.

I only know what Mama O. now tells, after many years and Papa O. in his grave and the twins scattered: that the young man who knocked was in truth the devil. For did she not give him, without knowing what she did, a good son in return for a worthless husband?

"I'm drownin' the worm t'night," Poor Roman explains, talking to his double-shot. "Help me drown the worm t'night, fellas."

Does the devil live in a double-shot? Is he the one who naws, all night, within?

Or is he the one who knocks, on winter nights, with blood rying on his knuckles, in the gaslit passages of our dreams?

is your name joe?

I hate t' see the spring 'n summer come so bad. I just don't seem so good as other people any more. Sometimes I'm that disgusted of myself I think: "Just one more dope, that's me." I won't set up there in that room another spring alone, thinkin' stuff like that. It just starts goin' through my head as soon as I come in that door. Like someone who lives there I can't see, somebody who knows better, tellin' me: "Just one more dope, that's you."

It used t' be, last spring, some Joe guy'd drop up every night. That's when I started in like this, afraid to think. He talked so smart I'd think whatever I could say'd be all wrong. He'd kind of snicker sometimes, funny-like. He don't drop in no more. He liked the lively kind, he said. But still it keeps on goin' through my head. You figure maybe somethin's wrong with me?

If somethin's really *wrong,* I'll see a croaker. I'll tell him, "Doc, this ain't my fault, don't start in blamin' *me*—but somethin's *wrong.*" Then he'll fix it up somehow, he'll take my pulse. So's I won't go on thinkin' I'm the only dope on earth. You think so too? About I'm one more dope, I mean. You think so too?

You wouldn't tell me straight about it anyhow. You ain't no doc. You're wearin' specs awright, but you're no doc. If

you was I'd fix you up for free. Then you'd fix me. How's
that? Say, Specs, why don't you just pertend you are a doc?
Make off you are, I mean. "Why don't I go to County 'n get
fixed?" Specs says. I'll tell you, Specs, I won't go near that
place. They give you the black bottle there is why. They cut
up little dogs for medicine. I know, my first husband that I
married he went there. They fixed him up so's he lost all his
healt'.

You come from out of town or you live here? You look like
city stuff, but sort of simple. I wish I'd meet some really
simple guy, he wouldn't give me no fast stuff at all. Just talk
natural; so's I c'd talk straight back. It wouldn't matter then
if I said such wrong things all the time. He wouldn't mind at
all. No cheatin', nothin' phony, everythin' in the clear. All the
guys these days, though, they offsteer you. They're goin' scrooly
faster than the dames. You think I'm goin' scrooly too? Are
you a doc? Ain't nobody talked straight stuff to me in years.

Specs, I'll tell you what I think. I think I'm just the girl that
men forget, that's what. My first husband that I married, that
was another Joe. I sure am hard on Joes. That's two I had.
He musta been a German, he kept on sayin' "Gawd." "Gawd
this" 'n "Gawd that." Just scrooly about "Gawd." The one
who lost his healt', that's the Joe I mean. He bought a picture
of "Gawd"—when "Gawd" was a boy—'n bring it home. All
he'd do was talk about that picture 'n tell me how I'm no
good. I told him I *know* I'm no damn good, I'm good for nuts
awright, quit *blamin'* me. Why just keep rubbin' *that* in all
the time? 'Cause he wants that I should be like "Gawd," he
says. "You're strictly scrooly, Joe," I told him then.

One night he was perspirin' pretty bad. That Joe, he sweated
all the time. I told him stay in bed, keep warm. But no, he
has to get up. So I told him, "Go to hell, I don't care if you
croak under a fence. Get back in bed 'n croak there." That's
when he gimme one—right in the teeth, for sayin' that. He's
cursin' me for that right now. I'm hiccupin' is why. When you

hiccup it *means* somethin', Specs. It means that Joe is cursin' me. If it gets worse that means he's comin' nearer. Like when your ears burn someone's talkin' about you. That's for *true*.

I hope I hiccup worse 'n then he finds me. I hope he got a gun 'n finishes me off for keeps. But maybe it ain't *that* Joe at all; maybe it's that Joe that talked the fast stuff all the time. The second Joe, I mean, the smart one. The hell with Joes.

You know what he done once, the scrooly Joe, I mean? When I was sound asleep? He taken my Heart-of-Jesus locket off my neck. I wasn't fit to wear it, what *he* says. We went around that night. We went to battle then for true. All night long, would you believe it, Specs? God oh God, when I was down 'n he was kickin' me—how can a man do that to a woman 'n tell her how he loves her afters? Tell me *that,* you know so much. You shoulda seen him when the coppers bust it up. You couldn't see his puss for blood. The Polaks 'r good fighters, that's why. They never give a inch. Look at me, I'm a beat-out flower now but still I don't give in. That Joe, he beat me to a blood-soup twenty times—you think I give in t' him 'n "Gawd" fer that? I hit him with the iron board instead. Then I hit him with the iron. "I'm fightin' fer Poland now," I told him.

"She fights like a damned man," he told the court that time, 'n ever'body laughed. They laughed at me that time like I wasn't even natural. That's why I keep on thinkin' I'm no good. They're always laughin' at me, all of 'em, behind my back.

That's why I fight so hard, I guess. I ain't *that* bad. *Nobody's* that bad, Specs.

Once I come in at four o'clock 'n he tells me, "Get into bed." "I'm not sleepy," I told him. I was scared. "You got a bottle on you?" he asks me. I told him no.

So then I was prayin' t' St. Terese like everythin', he shouldn't find the bottle. She's my helper, she keeps me out of harm. Joe shouldn't find no bottle, what I prayed.

He found it though awright. That's when I scrammed. He kicked me out that night. I shouldn't come back no more, he says, he'll have me arrested if I come back. I just went to a all-night show instead. I knew he didn't mean it about not comin' back. Only, in the show I fell asleep 'n some other rat taken my Heart-of-Jesus locket off my neck. That goes to show you, stay out of shows. I knew Joe'd say I sold the locket if I come back without it. I was scared to go back. I could take the beatin', that'd do me good. But gettin' arrested, I ain't never been, except for drunk. Nobody in my family been arrested yet but me. I just hung around beer taverns after that.

I been goin' back to Joe two years. I ain't back yet. Can he do that? Get me arrested, I mean, for losin' a holy locket? You can't stay in taverns *all* the time. You got to go some other place sometimes too. So I went around to all the places I used to work, the baker 'n Goldblatt's 'n the hamburg stand. But taverns is the best. It's where they never kick you out is why.

I lost my birdstone ring in a tavern too. Some fella said, "Just let me see it once." 'N then he wouldn't give it back no more. I think he must of been another of them Joes. That's why I can't go back. Joe's ring is gone. He wouldn't stand for that. He'd say I sold it. *You* know I didn't sell it, *don't* you, Specs?

I'm American-born, I'm an educated girl, I got a good Polish education—you just don't know. But when I was down 'n he was kickin' me, 'n then the name he said. I couldn't stand for that. That was worse than kickin' even. He said I was a whore once, when I wasn't. I didn't mind him sayin' *that*. But what he called me then—I couldn't go back now.

So now I'll tell you somethin', Specs: Watch out for Joes. That's two I had 'n look where I am now.

That Joe who used to come up here last spring, he was a no-good Joe for true. He was the first guy I picked up on the street my whole damned life. I told him so. I thought he'd be nice to me then. You know what he said when I told him that? "There's always a first time," he says, "for everythin'," 'n laughs.

Why ain't there no last time, then, for anythin'? I mean, ain't there no last time, *never?* For the same old thing?

Last night I dreamed. I dream up somethin' scrooly every night. The guys is chasin' me, all night. All the guys is Joes. I go into a tavern 'n the place is full of Joes, I'm the only woman there, they all look at me. 'N then I look at them, the door is locked, 'n every one of them is Joe.

But last night—this was different. I never dreamed no dream like *that* before. I was eatin' a potato 'n a skinny white snake come out. He just keep comin' out, all night. You think there's somethin' goin' wrong with me?

I'll find out by the time it's spring again. That's why I hate to see the spring 'n summer come so bad. I must be the girl that men forgot awright.

depend on aunt elly

There wasn't anything to the case, to start with. Just the routine thing, in routine weather. A couple ordinary-looking cops on a hotel beat, making a Sunday morning checkup, the way they do around small hotels in Arkansas on some Sunday mornings.

When they walked in the Pfc was shaving and this girl, this Wilma, was sitting by the window smoking, waiting for him to take her to breakfast.

"You don't have to worry," the older officer assured the soldier. "We'll only hold you for a witness. Your folks won't find out."

"Ain't my folks I'm worryin' about," the boy blubbered, "it's my C.O. I'll lose my stripe for this."

He had to make Monday reveille, and there wouldn't be a trial judge around before Monday forenoon. By the time he got back to his barracks he'd be a full day overdue.

He was nineteen or so. The girl was, perhaps, twenty-three.

" 'N I don't want to testify up against her anyhow," the boy added as though he liked her. The girl put out her cigarette and stood up.

"Let him go," she told the cops. "You won't need him. I'll cop a plea."

"That'll save trouble all around."

When they let the Pfc go, on the courthouse steps, he tried to kiss her cheek; he was that green. She stalled him with a handshake, wishing he'd scram.

"I'll make it all up to you, Wilma," he assured her, while she wondered just how. And walked off without looking back. She never saw him again.

"It's what I get for playin' the streets," she thought resignedly in her cell that night. "I'd be better off in a house." But she'd never seriously considered such a step: it was too final.

She'd come to Texarkana to work in a defense plant the year before; when the plant closed she had a small car and a savings account besides. Home had been a railroaders' boardinghouse, at a whistle stop called Dustland, in the Oklahoma sand hills. In Texarkana she'd grown fond of her freedom and careless of her love. She had decided to stay on. The car had come in handy then.

"They got a room waitin' for you at the Roxy over on Fourth," one of the older hands had once apprised her. Wilma was disdainful. She was planning, indolently, to get out of the racket. "I don't want to get in that deep," she'd told the old hand. "I'm just in this game temporary."

In the morning she paid a fifteen-dollar fine and fifteen in costs, and returned to her room to get some sleep. "Sufficient unto the day is the evil thereof," she remembered her mother saying as she drifted dreamily toward sleep.

She was wakened by a knocking as abrupt as machine-gun fire; only soldiers and police knocked like that at such an hour. She glanced at her watch. Six A.M. on the nose.

"Judge Nix wants to see you again. We'll wait downstairs," they told her through the door.

"If they keep this up I'll have to go over to Fourth Street just for the protection," she reflected irritably. She dressed lazily, looking out at the first metallic glint of day on the roof of the hay, feed, and grain store next door. Another scorcher.

At the curb the driver opened the rear door for her. He was a red-necked Okie from the Indian dust lands who could have been her uncle Ollie. Never said much, but had always been half friendly in an embarrassed hick sort of way.

When Judge Nix came out of his anteroom he had to be assisted to the bench by a matron: a pallid old man with a shake in his head and in his voice, supported by a tidy-looking middle-aged blonde with a full figure and hair done in a neat bun. It was the first time Wilma had set eye on Elly Harper and it wasn't to be the last. She came around and stood beside Wilma as though Wilma were long-expected company, one hand touching Wilma's elbow too familiarly; while old Nix read something about being escorted somewhere by a woman. She didn't get it. But heard Elly's throaty voice by her side.

"Don't worry about a thing, Sissie. All you got is a little dose. You'll be back on the hustle in two weeks. You depend on Aunt Elly."

Another matron piled in the car beside them, and she was being squeezed tightly by the two big women. Wilma didn't like being touched and squeezed.

She knew she wasn't ill, but felt too indifferent to argue over something it wasn't going to do any good to argue about anyhow. I guess what she means is I need a good rest, she hoped vaguely as the car was wheeled south.

"I got my own car," she offered. "I could drive my own car if we got far to go."

Neither woman replied.

"Where *are* we going?" she demanded at last.

"Alexandria."

That seemed a long way to go for a rest.

"That's a good girl," Elly reassured her after another long minute of silence. And Wilma felt the older woman's hand on her knee when she said it.

In the fields, on the cottonseed-colored road to the main building, Wilma glimpsed barefoot women, in long blue denim dresses, cutting Johnson grass with sickles. Their hair had been clipped and they worked aimlessly, like mad women. Wilma had a mute panic, all to herself, that she was being taken to an asylum.

The main building looked like a long, low-lying field hospital, hastily erected on some alien plain: women were living in tents around it. These—minor offenders and trustees—turned their heads toward her with something of resentment, Wilma fancied, at the intrusion. Elly Harper left her in a small office to have her clothing checked.

She'd put an extra pair of oxfords in her bag, which she'd been planning to give her mother up in Dustland. But then the old lady went barefoot most of the time, so she told the checker she could have them.

"You'll need them yourself, Sis," the girl answered. "You'll be goin' barefooty yourself without them."

"That's all right," Wilma told her with confidence. "I'm only here for the two-week treatment and a little rest."

"You're here for three years at hard labor, Sissie," the girl answered softly, without raising her eyes. " 'Less you got cash in the bank."

That evening Wilma had her hair clipped and was assigned to the vats. The next morning she fell out in front of a matron and asked to be taken off.

"You any good with a sickle?" the matron asked, eyeing her head to toe. "You look too small to me."

Wilma had never seen a sickle. But she said yes, she was pretty handy with a sickle. That's what she thought of the vats.

She found out what a sickle was all right. Cutting the Johnson grass out of the sweet-potato patches, without gloves, taught her that in two strokes.

"I believe in bein' good at whatever you are," Wilma's cell mate, Katherine, said one afternoon when they were working side by side in the field. "I told the judge I was a hustlin' gal 'n a damned good one 'n if he give me a conviction I'd be a damned good con. But what I don't see is how could anyone be good at bein' a sheriff. He'd have to arrest his own mother to be a *real* good one, I guess.

"I'll tell you now," she confided to Wilma, "I don't know what's happenin' to me. My dad was a Christian man, but when he died he didn't leave a cryin' dime. I found the easy way to live, because we'd always lived easy when he was alive; but this place is more'n I bargained for with that judge. I feel like somethin's happenin' to me inside."

Two nights later Katherine tried to climb the bars. "The gang's comin'," she warned Wilma. "They're after us all."

In the morning she was put in solitary, and came back subdued three days later. She didn't have another spell until she'd been visited by her common-law husband. When he left, Katherine paid a matron to bring her benzedrine.

In the night she wakened crying that searchlights were shining into the cell, that someone kept staring at her out of the little unshaded night bulb of the corridor. A tiny bulb-face, pale and unblinking, hung there to watch her all night long. When Wilma soothed her she held a muttered conversation with her brother, who had been killed over Cologne: he was overhead in a helicopter, trying to find a place to land.

Ten cigarettes a week to the well-behaved, and minor illness was considered bad behavior. Wilma had to see Katherine hauled bodily out of the cell and carried out to the sweet-potato patch: to be left lying with the sun beating mercilessly upon her till dusk. She wasn't turning out to be as good a con as she'd thought she'd make.

What is it to them or Christ above that we sweat and hope for freedom? Wilma thought fretfully. It made no difference, she perceived, either to God or Aunt Elly.

Wilma had been at Alexandria twelve days when she was assigned to an ironing board at the laundry. The laundry came in every night from the men's prisons at Tucker and had to be gotten out by noon of the following day. Heavy, backbreaking labor. On Okie stew, without pepper or salt. On Sundays a slab of side-salt bacon two inches long.

"I did the two weeks," she reminded Aunt Elly. "I got the treatment."

"Your treatment is just starting, Sissie," Elly assured her.

"Two more weeks 'n I'm going over the hill." Elly looked at her to see if the little one meant that; and must have been convinced, because, on the day before her fourth week was up, she leaned over Wilma's ironing board.

"You got a car, Sissie. It ain't doing you much good in here. How much you got in cash?"

"I got 750 in the bank in Little Rock," Wilma boasted.

"For that much you can get a real break—with the car, of course."

"For that much I'll take a commitment of sentence," Wilma said, meaning a commutation.

"I can't do nothing for you about a commutation."

"And I can't do nothing for you about a car."

That Elly Harper. She had fifteen lifers furloughed to all parts of the country, and every blessed woman of them sending her fifty dollars a month just to stay on furlough.

"Business is business," Aunt Elly would say. "It's worth it to them to stay out 'n it's worth it to me to keep 'em out. Saves the taxpayers the cost of keeping them too. *Every*body benefits."

Five minutes after the morning bell Wilma suddenly pulled the plug on the iron. "I don't know to this day why I did that," Wilma wondered later. "I never did that till I was through for the day and I'd only been workin' five minutes. I looked up *after* I pulled it, with the plug still in my hand, and Elly was hookin' her finger at me in the door. I never been back to that iron board since."

Elly drove her up to Little Rock and she got a change of ownership for the car and withdrew her 750.

"Now," Wilma said cautiously, before handing Elly a dime, "I want mine."

Elly handed her the paper and Wilma handed her the money and the change of ownership.

In the hotel in Texarkana the Okie cop stood brooding over the paper: it wasn't right. He shook his head hopelessly as he handed it back.

"You ain't got no commutation, Sissie," he told her. "All you got is a furlough."

Wilma sank on the bed. What next? she wondered weakly.

"If she don't get that half a bill on the first of the month she'll get old Nix up in the middle of the night to get it. She won't stop at nothin', that one won't," the Okie warned her sympathetically. "You can depend on Aunt Elly."

"I said seven-fifty," Wilma told herself wistfully, with slow realization. "She would of took a hundred if I'd said a hundred."

And at that moment Wilma seemed to feel, ever so faintly, the lingering touch of Elly Harper's hand upon her knee.

It was in the house on Fourth Street that Wilma met this flat-faced clown, this Cherokee lush called Baby Needles. He used to come into town for fights in the Arena, and was billed for just what he was: a ring clown, an aging pug who made up for everything he didn't know by invariably falling through the bottom strand when coming into the ring, after preparing for a light spring over the top rope. When he'd catch a stiff one he made a point of applauding the blow with his gloves and grinning whitely with his mouthpiece. And when fighting a Negro he got laughs by scrubbing the fellow's poll in the clinches.

Paris was a dry town because of the army camp there. So, win or lose, every time he fought there he'd grab a bus and get over to Texarkana before the bars closed. A hundred miles wasn't a long jaunt for Baby for a bottle. He'd gone ten rounds, more than once, just for the drinks.

Yet he always visited her cold sober; and so regularly that she decided to put a stop to it. She stood in the middle of the room, in a flowered and faded kimono, a frowsy little bleached blonde with bad teeth and bloodshot eyes. She'd cry every time he came to see her.

"Quit yer bawlin'," he'd tell her. "You got a loaf of bread under yer arm 'n yer bawlin'. Look at the beatin's I take 'n *I* ain't bawlin'."

"I take a beatin' every time you see me here," she confessed. "I can't stand for you to see me here, I don't know why."

"Then whyn't you get out 'n go to work?"

"Because it's too late, stupid. I'm good for nothin' now. I'm a piece of trade. Where else could I make what I'm makin' here?" She didn't mention the reason she had to be making it, and he couldn't tell her where else. Just stood there looking at her as if he'd never seen a woman before, till she had to turn from his gaze.

"I don't want you to come to see me no more," she told him. "I got enough troubles already. I got more troubles than Dick Tracy." He had an easy smile all right; she had to look out the window to keep from crying.

Heard him pause in the doorway, trying to decide whether she meant it. "I mean it all right," she told the window. "If you come again I won't see you." She could see his reflection, blurred and wavering, with the hall light burning dimly behind it.

"Get your hat," Baby Needles said. Just like that. "Get your hat."

She lit a cigarette, the flame trembling with her fingers, and watched the reflection burn to a charred ash in the pane. "You don't get paid for clowning in here," she told him, looking him up and down as though to ask who did he think he was anyhow. He opened the clothes-closet door and flung her hat and coat across her lap.

They were married in a tourist camp outside of Dustland: she was going to show her old lady a legal husband. But the sand hills weren't much for a honeymoon, and two days was all she could stand. On the night that they returned to Texarkana she looked up the Okie cop with another piece of paper in her hand. She had the idea that she was free of Elly Harper.

The Okie shook his head in that hopeless, lop-eared way. "Gittin' married don't git you out of no con-viction," he drawled, handing her back the license. "Sissie, I jest can't see no way out of payin' that Elly fifty a month 'cept by doin' three years at that iron board." He paused. "Does that pug know about this deal?"

"He knows nothin'," Wilma admitted. "I was afraid to tell."

"I guess he wouldn't like fer you to be makin' any change of yer own on the side now, neither," the Okie suggested artfully.

Wilma shook her head. "No. He ain't like that. He clowns a lot. But he wouldn't clown around about a thing like that." She felt strangely proud of him in that moment, realizing, for the first time, that she was a respectable woman married to a respectable man.

Baby Needles was a slow-moving, slow-thinking, slow-mannered sort of devil who'd always taken his time and, until he'd met Wilma, had never wanted anything very much outside of a flop and a bowl of beer. He'd been born on a reservation, a quarter-blood Cherokee with a little Mex tossed in. He came of a long line of ne'er-do-wells and was strictly in the family tradition. He didn't know who his old man was, but it was a cinch it wasn't anybody who worked for a living. The little he knew about fighting he'd picked up around East Texas oil country, when money had been easy and opposition wasn't too tough.

Because the Baby didn't like to be hurt. He liked to dish it out. But he didn't like taking it. He'd been through six managers in ten years of pugging, and each had given him the go-by because he couldn't come from behind. You couldn't make him mad.

What he had in the trade was a wheeling left hand that was neither a hook nor a jab, but the slanting blow of a man with a scythe: it cut up or down, but always sidewise like a scythe.

For fifty bucks, when he wasn't on the bottle, he could be dangerous.

For a hundred, it developed suddenly—and sober—he was murder.

Perhaps it was fear that put him out in front the first time he fought for a century note: he had plenty of that in him. But he got out in front at the bell, and it was over before the faint clanging of the bell had died away.

That was in the little open-air arena on the outskirts of Paris, the week after they came back from Dustland, against a kid from the 99th Division at Camp Maxey. The kid was one of those soldiers' champions who'd looked like a comer around the camp PX. It was the first time he'd fought for folding money.

Baby got to him at the bell, when the boy fell away from Baby's right. He fell into the left, and Baby brought his elbow up to clinch it while his other glove braced the nape of the boy's neck, to keep the shock from being cushioned by a roll of the head: held with rigid stealth, the brain took the full brunt and Baby stepped back. The boy went face forward as though he'd been blackjacked. One minute and twenty-nine seconds of the first round. And the easiest hundred Baby had ever earned. He could do it when he wanted to all right.

"That wasn't no white man's punch," Wilma heard some soldier complain.

"Well, he ain't no white man," another threw in. Wilma turned on the pair of them.

"He's the whitest man who ever breathed," she told them hotly.

The pair had just looked at each other and grinned. Some white man.

That was the first time Wilma had seen Baby in the ring: he looked strangely different there than he had under the little naked bulb of the room on Fourth Street. His shoulders jutted like wind-bitten rocks; and when that ridged left hand had cut downward, the right had come up and the jutting elbow had come with it. His hands, that had always been so gentle with her, and had always felt rather small, were, she saw as the gloves were being cut off, as large as a heavyweight's.

His brows had been almost beaten off, leaving two thin red wires of scar tissue over the eyes: but the eyes were protected by the Indian cheekbones; the pupils themselves were as flat and black as his Indian hair. Without light as they were without depth, and half concealed by the loose and naked lids, they were the eyes of any Arizona sand turtle staring up at some ancestral sun.

For the Baby had one thing few fighters possess: he never blinked. Close up or from the opposing corner, whether he was hit or whether he was dishing it out: the picture of his opponent was never blurred for a moment in his brain by that involuntary snap of the lids which can cost a fighter a critical advantage. That's something a fighter either has or doesn't have: you can teach a man almost anything, but you can't teach him not to blink.

In the ring he fought leanly now, on his toes, like an aging tomcat. And wouldn't stand to be billed as a clown any more. Baby Needles was getting pride.

After his fifth straight win in Paris some newspaper bird in Dallas called Baby's left a bolo punch. He said that Baby even looked like Garcia. Maybe he did. But that left didn't look like Garcia's any more than Wilma looked like Jane Russell. You could tell them apart all right.

Baby could get by for a Garcia against the Post Exchange champions, but Fort Worth was tougher. Yet in his first fight there he gave away fourteen pounds against some farmer and cut him down in eight rounds. Fought him the following Saturday and beat him in two.

He was getting better. The papers said so. He was the best thing in middleweights in ten years. The papers said. He reminded one writer of Mickey Walker. He reminded another of Leo Lomski. So right away somebody had to write in and

remind everybody that Lomski had been practically a heavyweight. He reminded everybody of somebody.

But he only reminded Wilma of Elly Harper. She wrote
Wilma twice and Wilma tore the letters up without opening
them. She didn't have a dime of her own to send and she
couldn't bring herself to tell Baby and spoil everything.

He won twice in Dallas, repeated in New Orleans, and
hadn't had a drink in eight months when the telegram came
from Chicago, guaranteeing five hundred dollars and expenses.
Two hours later the pair of them were on a Chicago-bound
bus. Wilma made him sit next to the window. She was always
getting between him and other people, protectively. She was
afraid of the jokers who always wanted to hand Baby a bottle.

They took a room in a second-rate hotel around the corner
from the bus depot and a reporter phoned up from the lobby.

"Ain't nobody here to talk to you," Baby told the reporter.

"What's the matter with your manager?"

"I fired him," Baby answered. "He was bad luck." Tele-
phones were bad luck too. And reporters. He didn't know
about Puerto Ricans. He'd never fought one before.

But the reporter caught Wilma in the lobby, and the morning sport page carried a little item about how Baby Needles'
blonde bride was also his manager.

Baby didn't mind. And Wilma was tickled pink; it didn't
take much to tickle her.

"It's funny to think of *me* managin' *you* though," she confessed. She hadn't thought of it that way before. As though
anybody ever managed a man like Baby. He fought as he felt
like, for as long as he felt like, in the manner he felt like. He'd
never fought two fights alike, even against the same man. He'd
forget how he'd done it the first time.

Now he stretched out on the bed with one great copper
hand shielding his eyes as though from an anticipated blow.
He'd never wanted a drink so badly in his life.

Wilma wandered aimlessly about the little room, hanging up

their clothes; stood a long minute at the window watching the unfamiliar street below.

Then went wandering the unfamiliar streets all the long forenoon, just to let him be alone. In a dime store she bought a charm: a ten-cent rabbit's foot, for luck. And returned to the room proud of her purchase.

She laid the little foot beneath his hand, so he'd be certain to see it upon wakening and be pleased.

He wakened sullenly, without saying her name, and apparently without even seeing the lucky foot at all. She was in for one of his sullen moods, she saw. It was the Indian in him coming out right before a fight, she had once thought; only now she knew better: it was his thirst for the booze she wouldn't let him have, that was all. She picked the paw off the floor and put it in her purse, and when she opened it she saw the letter from Elly: he had opened it. She didn't say a word. She didn't even ask when it had arrived.

He should have had more sleep, she thought, walking beside him, carrying his bag down Wabash toward the Coliseum. She kept hold of his arm when they passed the suckers lining up for tickets. As though they might mob him.

They didn't even know who he was.

He came into the ring for the semi-windup looking ragged.

"Win, Baby," she pleaded with him silently, from the fifth row center. "Win, Baby." And in her mind was a nightmarish picture of a tiny, bright, and barren room containing nothing but a huge ironing board and a woman, strangely like herself, bent across it in a flowered and faded kimono. "Depend on Aunt Elly," a throaty voice whispered in her mind.

At the end of the round Baby's Negro bucketman murmured, "You out in front, Baby." Wilma had told him to keep telling Baby that, regardless; just so he'd think so.

"He ain't bleedin'," Baby contradicted him flatly, and spat in the bucket.

"He's just a big front-runner from the sticks," somebody

behind her observed. But she didn't even turn her head. All kinds of people got in on free passes, people not worth noticing at all.

In the middle of the fourth round someone hollered, "Pull up yer sock the next time yer down there, Chief!" Just because Baby was crouching a little while using his weight, and as it was shouted Baby brought that loving shoulder up. The Puerto Rican's cheek split like a melon and courage rose in Baby like a tide. He wheeled in fast with the sickle left: over the eyes was best. Blood. And the bell.

"Don't tell me," he cautioned the bucketman. It was bad luck to be told you were winning when you knew you really were. He watched the Puerto Rican's handlers taping the eye; the blood looked black beneath the lights. "All them Chinks got black blood," Baby thought without surprise.

"Needles is right," Wilma heard the critic behind her observe. "He uses more shoulder than glove, that devil."

"They call him Needles because that's the town he comes from," she said over her shoulder, with contempt. But between the warning whistle and the bell the same sure voice spoke quietly.

"It's his real name all the same."

Wilma knew better. A good, kind man. And a real clean fighter too. A little superstitious, that was all.

At the bell Baby took two rights to the button that buckled him back on his heels; in a half-rolling clinch along the ropes the Puerto Rican's eye tape hung loosely, like a bloody little horn. In close, Baby slashed it off with the crosscut left and the rest of the round looked easy. He was coasting in. And two seconds before the bell coasted straight into a driving left: his gloves hung loosely and his head waggled in shock. He came to his corner drooling. The bucketman had all he could do to bring him around.

It didn't seem possible. Not from the fifth row center. It wasn't possible to lose after having it in the bag. Only there it was, with the crowd grinning as though they'd expected something like it all along: Baby on a bicycle, his gloves trying to get something out of his eyes and his head snapping back, back, and his heels rocking; trying to hold to something and nothing to hold onto and no heart left in him at all. The Puerto Rican drove him half across the ring with the left, doubled him up with the right in his own corner, straightened him out with the left again, drove the right to the body, cupped Baby's chin in his gloves one split second, and tore the button off with the left. It didn't seem possible. But there it was.

"You've had it, clown!" someone chortled.

He had it all right.

She saw him going down to his knees like a stuck sheep; then face forward, with his head buried in his gloves, in an agony of exhaustion, while the bell clang-clanged like a 4-11 alarm and they were standing up in the rows to watch the sweating bucketman pouring ice water over Baby.

He sat sprawled, and started a little when the ice water hit him. Then put his right glove, slowly, on the back of his neck and rolled his head, slowly.

"Is it still on, Baby?" someone shouted.

"Don't roll it too far, Chief," another warned, with the buzzer's warning.

There was rubber in his legs, but he made it, and held until the ref wrestled him off—Baby didn't want a clean break now. He hadn't learned his stuff in gymnasiums. With his left still tying up the Puerto Rican, he hooked his elbow into the navel, drew off, and drove back in with his shoulders behind it and his feet almost off the ground. The Puerto Rican went green, then white, reaching feebly for Baby, and, failing to find him, slid slowly onto the seat of his pants with his arms holding his belly. At six he rolled over, got one knee beneath him, came up at nine with his back to Baby, and was half turned about when Baby threw the right from behind his man, between the half-raised arm and the shoulder. Baby stepped aside to let him fall.

"Somethin' must have made the Chief mad," somebody murmured doubtfully.

In their room she hovered over him; but her nearness seemed to tighten something in him now.

"They can't never say you don't come from behind no more," she flattered him timidly. "I never seen you get mad before. How come you got mad, honey?"

"I dunno. I just got mad, like. He didn't really hurt me. He didn't even touch me, the way I feel. I just got mad is all."

"The way I feel, I ain't touched you neither," she said boldly.

"I don't feel like fooling around," he warned her. "I ain't mad at nobody—I just don't like for anybody to touch me no more."

Just like that.

"Am I just anybody, Baby?"

"You're my luck is all."

Outside the slow rain stopped, and began again.

"Why don't you say what you're tryin' to say?" she asked.

"All I'm tryin' to say is I need a drink." He didn't even want to talk about it.

"That ain't all you're tryin' to say."

"*You* tell *me*."

"What you're tryin' to say is why didn't I tell you about how I was at Alexandria."

"That's your business."

"You mean you'd rather go back to the sticks where you got paid for fallin' through the ropes twice a week 'n live on the bottle like you done before you started comin' over to Fourth Street."

"You don't have to go back *there*," he told her, measuring every word.

"That's right, Baby. I can stay right here 'n go over to Twenty-second instead."

"Your best bet is to go back 'n do your time," he told her. "We'll start all over when you get out." But didn't sound like he meant it at all.

"It'll be too late then, Baby. You ain't got three good years left in you. 'N neither have I."

"It's too late awready," he conceded brutally, weary of pretending. "If you would of told me right off it would of been all right. Now I feel like I'd be a sucker to go on takin' beatin's from punch-drunk Chinks just to keep a dame in the clear."

"I thought you said he didn't hurt you."

"It's startin' to hurt now. All over." Then he dead-panned on her and shifted his eyes just a little. "I want a drink," he mumbled after a minute.

"Is it all right if I stay here tonight?" she asked.

He nodded. It was all right. "Just go down 'n get a bottle first."

She bought the best in the house. "Is this the best you got?" she asked, to make sure it wasn't just the second-best.

When she went to bed she left him sitting with his fancy bottle under the light. She wakened only once during the night and saw him still sitting there, talking to himself, holding his glass to the light and inspecting it gravely. Later his head fell heavily forward on his arms, and she had to get up and drag him onto the bed.

All that night the slant rain tapped, through the darkened hours, at the lightless pane: cold mockeries, for her alone, that tapped, and ceased, and tapped again.

Toward morning she rose. The rain had stopped in the night. And crept quietly about the room: he needed his sleep, and he slept softly: a good sound for her to hear. Abruptly, without interruption in his breathing, she knew he had wakened, though he had not opened his eyes.

"He's waitin' for me to go now," she thought.

When the door had closed behind her he rose and went, head swinging, to the dresser. She had left a note for him there, with the little lucky paw on top of it. It looked as though she had written it in the dark, the way it was scrawled; although the light had been on when she'd written it:

BABY, you can use this lucky foot instead of me. I hope it makes you lucky all the time. I hope you always come from behind.

Love, WILMA

Standing unsteadily in his striped fighter's trunks, swaying slightly from side to side, he touched the lucky foot tentatively. But it felt like bad luck between his fingers, and he crumpled it into the note as though it were a squashed roach and tossed it into a corner. Dames were bad luck too. It felt like everything, from here on out, was all bad luck.

He put his head behind his chin, sparred drunkenly with his shadow: a giant's shadow across the wall, elusive and threatening. Came in close and wheeled that left in, heavily. Then felt, suddenly, more tired than he'd ever felt in his life before; as though the bottom had dropped out of something inside him. And winning or losing or whether he ever came from behind again or whether he were drunk or sober didn't make any difference after all.

He went to the corner where the lucky foot lay and picked it up wearily, then stretched out on his stomach on the bed, with the furry little foot clutched in his hand, the great knuckles showing white and helplessly through the copper skin.

And slept at last, with the pitiless city sun beating in all day as though the dark and the rain and the cold, and the all-night tapping at the darkened panes, and the winds that blow forever away from home, might never, never, never come again.

Slept. And dreamed love-dreams.

stickman's laughter

Banty Longobardi trudged up his own back steps; his cap was in his hand and his pay on his hip. He'd take the old woman to the Little Pulaski—triple horror feature with blue enamel ovenware to the ladies and community singing.

But the door was locked and the woman was out, so he went down the steps again. She ought to know better than to go visiting on a community-singing, free-ovenware night.

He came to the alley beneath the El, where Punchdrunk Murphy so patiently watched, before the gamblers' door. Punchdrunk let him pass by raising one arm, and he stood at the dice table just to watch. The stickman pointed the stick at Banty; but Banty kept his pay in his pocket.

"I'm cold," he explained, when the dice came by again, meaning the dice didn't yet feel right to his hand. He opened his collar, the place was so warm, and unbuttoned the pocket where the week's pay hid. When they came by again he felt a bit warmer. Bought two chips for a dollar and bet them both on the field. Saw the dice turn a five and watched the banker making two chips four. Let the four ride, without betting on a pass, and saw a ten come up. So he pinched his little package and let some spook beside him finish his hand.

"Four soldiers to the good," he assured himself, "that's got it over community singin'. That's eight double features, any night of the week." She could go by herself or take Mrs. Prystalski some evening when he was putting in overtime. He felt them coming his way again as though bringing him money from home.

At half-past eight Banty had forty chips. At a quarter of nine he had ninety and had torn the top button off his shirt. At ten after ten he cashed in for forty dollars, and the stickman pointed jokingly with the stick while Banty tried buttoning a button that wasn't there.

"Tell 'em where you got it, Shorty," he advised Banty Longobardi, " 'n how easy it was."

Banty left through Murphy's door. He picked his way down the littered tunnel of the El, seeing the places where the gray cats lived and smelling the tar-wagon smell where someone's roof was being repaired in the summer weather. He heard the rush of city waters, beneath the city streets, and the passionate passing of the day's last express. So came again to his own back steps and trudged up a flight with a pay roll clutched in his bumpy, toughened little palm. And the old pay roll still on his hip.

But the door was locked and the woman was out, and Banty stood alone in the yellow kitchen. He stood beneath an unshaded bulb, the yellow light on his broken face, and walked into the tiny bedroom as into a stranger's place. There was nothing to see in there, however, but a disheveled bed with a chemise among the covers. He felt done in for a moment and sat on the bed's very edge, rubbing the nob of his nose. He had had the bridge of it removed ten years before, at a promoter's urging, when he wasn't yet twenty and had won four professional bouts. The promoter's theory had been that Banty would have earned enough, by the time he retired, to buy a wax bridge. The theory hadn't worked out: Banty sat swinging a pavement-colored cap between his knees without any bridge at all and tired enough for any two men. But when his head touched the pillow he felt alone all over again, and rose.

He left the bedroom light burning.

"To show her I been in here too," he considered sulkily, and pulled a half-gallon empty from under the kitchen sink—an empty was good for a sixteen-ouncer by Bruno the bartender any time.

He sat in the abandoned tavern before a schooner of winter beer. Why couldn't she have been home the one time he'd won? Once he'd lost his check at blackjack and had mumbled that he'd been jackrolled. She'd caught him in the lie, and he'd tried to convince her that she'd misunderstood: he hadn't said "jackroll," he'd said "blackjack." That was when she'd started laughing, he'd sounded that silly. But the way she'd laughed— it had let him laugh with her. That was how that one had ended. Some old woman.

Once he'd dropped ten dollars on something called Harp Weaver at Boston and she'd been home then too.

But this time, when he'd put them two months up on the landlord, she was gone for hours. And he didn't want to gamble any more. Banty felt he didn't want to gamble again the rest of his life. "A man's got to quit it sometime, and when he's thirty and a working stiff, then that's as good a time as any," he assured himself.

It didn't matter to him where his girl was. Wherever she was, she was taking care of herself. But he wanted her by his side, to take care of him now.

" 'What is life without a wife?' " he hummed idly, tapping the sweating glass with his stubby fingers. He had jammed the knuckles of the hand in his last bout, and in moments like this the knuckles ached a little: tapping them relieved the ache.

Then he had three shots, to relieve the ache further, and began wondering how long he'd been gone. He didn't want to drink up too much of the extra pay roll; but he'd give her plenty of time to get home and miss him a spell too.

Knowing that she was at her mother's didn't make the minutes pass any faster. And to her mother's was the only place she ever went that Banty didn't want to come along too. Her people didn't trust wops. They said things in Polish about Dagos that made Banty wish, sometimes, that he was a flannelmouth Polak too.

The bartender was a flannelmouth. Everyone in the ward was a flannelmouth. Banty threw two slugs down his throat in rapid succession, waited till they hit his stomach, then wandered idly over to the bar.

"C'mere," Banty commanded.

Bruno the bartender bent an ear over the pretzels. Banty leaned over, his pudgy palms gripping the bar's edge, and whispered confidentially:

"Can I say somethin'?"

"Go ahead."

"I wanta say somethin'."

"Okay, okay, go ahead and say something."

"What should I say?"

The bartender turned away, but Banty caught his sleeve.

"God *damn,* what kind of man are you, tellin' me t' say somethin'?"

Bruno the bartender brushed Banty off his sleeve, folded his arms on the bar, and leaned toward his customer with huge patience.

"Look, I not tell *you* what to say. *You* want to say something by *me.* Okay. Free country. I'm wait. You say."

"Okay," Banty said suddenly, "I'll say it! Chickory-chick-chala-chala—how's *that?*" He was proud of himself.

Bruno the bartender studied him one long moment. "Now I'll tell *you* something," Bruno said. "Your old lady just went by. You go home by her."

"Let her wait," Banty answered. "Let her wait till I'm good 'n ready."

"You lose your money," Bruno warned him.

Banty put his hand across his eyes because a light was in them. He saw a string attached to the light and stood up to pull it, to make everything dark like everything should be.

Everything got dark all right, and got dark with a roaring; the dark was a roaring in his head and he came to hearing the thunder of the Garfield Park local overhead and seeing the littered places, between the beams, where the gray cats lived. He heard the local slowing toward Damen. Saw Murphy opening a familiar door.

"It don't mean a thing if it don't cross the string," someone intoned warningly. But added hopefully, "Double your money 'n beat the banker."

He edged to the table, as curious as though he'd never seen a dice game in his life. A nice little package for anyone's starter, and he made an effort to remember whether he'd paid for them yet. Banty didn't want to cheat anyone.

"It ain't hard—nobody's barred . . ."

When he looked at the package again it was smaller. But in a moment it was almost as high as before. He wanted to ask them what he was doing and when she'd get home. But if he asked them something like that they could tell he was drunk and would start cheating, he thought cunningly. He fitted the table's edge into his palms to keep from falling backward onto his skull.

"When I'm in a public place," he explained obscurely, "that's where I am."

But no one was listening any more, and Bruno had told him something and now he'd gone and forgotten it.

The pile grew again. And grew a little more. Until, all of a sudden, it was the smallest pile he had ever seen and everyone was smiling, because it wasn't there at all. He felt the dice between his fingers and knew there was something he'd just forgotten to do. He shook absently and remembered at last: he'd forgotten to pinch his package. The stickman touched Banty's hand: the boy was shaking, but nothing was riding.

"What goes?" the stickman asked.

Banty reached uncertainly to his hip, pulled out the pay roll he'd worked for and slapped it down with the flat of his palm on pass. He saw one dice cross the string and turn up an ace while the other rolled endlessly on—bounced against the table's guard and hurried anxiously back toward its resting mate. An inch away from the ace it wavered between a deuce and a six, then rolled wearily over on its back. Double ace. Snake-eyes.

The aces looked up at Banty with such sober reproach that he felt his own head clearing. He returned their stare, pleadingly, and they looked back as though saying, "Sorry, pal, we done our best." And the stickman pointing his mocking stick:

"Tell 'em where you got it, Shorty, 'n how easy it was."

"Where's my pack-age?" Banty demanded, wanting to be drunk again so badly that he pronounced each word distinctly and too politely.

"Where at is my pack-age?"

"You put the pack-age on, friend."

"The whole pack-age?"

"The whole pack-age."

Banty swayed. They'd done it again.

"How do I feel?" he asked hopelessly. And then he began getting mad.

"I don't know," the stickman answered solemnly, "but you look like the wrath of God."

Banty rolled up his left sleeve to the shoulder. The muscle was tattooed with a pair of boxing gloves. He flexed the gloves in front of the stickman.

"What's that for?" the stickman asked.

"That's the Army," Banty explained.

He stood a moment, thinking it all over, rolling up the other sleeve to expose the right muscle. That one was tattooed with a broken heart.

"What's *that* for?" someone that sounded like Punchdrunk Murphy asked on his other side.

"That's the Navy," Banty explained. But his voice sounded intimidated to his own ear when he felt Murphy's fist grip his arm, urging him through the shadowed door, and he went humbly.

When Banty tried his own back door, the knob turned easily. The light he had left in the bedroom was out. He sensed her lying awake in the dark, worrying about where he'd been with the rent. Knowing that she did not speak because she did not want him lying to her, knowing that she could tell where he'd been, by his movements, without making him lie like a schoolboy. Sometimes he almost wished she'd ask foolish questions like other women did. And get fooled by the answers, too.

He undressed in the kitchen, wishing that there were a front room with one of those fancy red plush sofas in it so he could crawl onto it on nights like this and pretend to her, in the morning, that he'd been too drunk to know where he was lying down, he couldn't remember a thing. "I'd like to set on plush anyhow," he thought wonderingly. "I never set on plush in my life. I bet she'd like settin' on plush too."

"Banty!"

As though she'd read his mind. As though they had a plush couch and he'd been planning to evade her for a few hours with it. He did not reply. Maybe she'd ask him something foolish just this once, and he'd give her an answer as mocking as the stickman's laughter.

"You went out of the house 'n left all the lights on and the back door wide open."

"I thought somebody'd come in 'n leave us somethin'——— Ha! Ha!"

His laughter broke. It hadn't sounded like the stickman's after all.

He stood in the bedroom doorway in his long workman's underwear, shifting on his naked feet. She sat up and pulled on the light.

"What's the matter with you? Quit disguisin' your eyes. There. Look at me. You look drunk. Come over here."

She certainly had her own way of putting things, the old

woman. He took his hands off his eyes, ceasing the pretense of shielding them from the light, and wished humbly again that he were a Polak, feeling somehow that that would fix everything. He tried to think whether Punchdrunk Murphy were a Polak, but couldn't decide. If he just wasn't a wop, things like this wouldn't be happening to him week in and week out.

Every time you saw in the papers that some guy was going to the chair, it was a Dago. Why didn't they fry a Greek or a Swede for a change?

"Are you coming to bed or are you going to stand there on one foot all night?"

When she saw him shuffling toward her she switched off the light and lay back waiting for him in the dark. When he reached the bed he had only to wait for her to take his head on her breast.

That's the kind of old woman Banty had himself.

"My fault," she assured him softly, like a storyteller making up stories to put a child to sleep. "I knew it was payday but I went out just the same. No supper for poor Banty either. Poor Banty. Lost all his money and no supper either. Wanted to go to community singing and got hisself drunked up instead."

She felt his tenseness lessening. Felt his tears between the shadowed valley of her breasts. And knew they were for her.

His body jerked a little, once, as it relaxed toward sleep. She held him so, watching the dim carnations of the wall, till his breath began coming regularly and untroubled. When his hand clutched at hers in sleep she smiled a little: she could feel the place in the hand where the knuckles had jammed.

So nothing important had been lost after all.

a bottle of milk for mother

I feel I am of them—
I belong to those convicts and prostitutes myself,
And henceforth I will not deny them—
For how can I deny myself?

Two months after the Polish Warriors S.A.C. had had their heads shaved, Bruno Lefty Bicek got into his final difficulty with the Racine Street police. The arresting officers and a reporter from the *Dziennik Chicagoski* were grouped about the captain's desk when the boy was urged forward into the room by Sergeant Adamovitch, with two fingers wrapped about the boy's broad belt: a full-bodied boy wearing a worn and sleeveless blue work shirt grown too tight across the shoulders; and the shoulders themselves with a loose swing to them. His skull and face were shining from a recent scrubbing, so that the little bridgeless nose glistened between the protective points of the cheekbones. Behind the desk sat Kozak, eleven years on the force and brother to an alderman. The reporter stuck a cigarette behind one ear like a pencil.

"We spotted him followin' the drunk down Chicago——"
Sergeant Comiskey began.

Captain Kozak interrupted. "Let the jackroller tell us how he done it hisself."

"I ain't no jackroller."

"What you doin' here, then?"

Bicek folded his naked arms.

"Answer me. If you ain't here for jackrollin' it must be for strong-arm robb'ry—'r you one of them Chicago Av'noo moll-buzzers?"

"I ain't that neither."

"C'mon, c'mon, I seen you in here before—what were you up to, followin' that poor old man?"

"I ain't been in here before."

Neither Sergeant Milano, Comiskey, nor old Adamovitch moved an inch; yet the boy felt the semicircle about him drawing closer. Out of the corner of his eye he watched the reporter undoing the top button of his mangy raccoon coat, as though the barren little query room were already growing too warm for him.

"What were you doin' on Chicago Av'noo in the first place when you live up around Division? Ain't your own ward big enough you have to come down here to get in trouble? What do you *think* you're here for?"

"Well, I was just walkin' down Chicago like I said, to get a bottle of milk for Mother, when the officers jumped me. I didn't even see 'em drive up, they wouldn't let me say a word, I got no idea what I'm here for. I was just doin' a errand for Mother 'n——"

"All right, son, you want us to book you as a pickup 'n hold you overnight, is that it?"

"Yes sir."

"What about this, then?"

Kozak flipped a spring-blade knife with a five-inch blade onto the police blotter; the boy resisted an impulse to lean forward and take it. His own double-edged double-jointed spring-blade cuts-all genuine Filipino twisty-handled all-American gut-ripper.

"Is it yours or ain't it?"

"Never seen it before, Captain."

Kozak pulled a billy out of his belt, spread the blade across the bend of the blotter before him, and with one blow clubbed the blade off two inches from the handle. The boy winced as though he himself had received the blow. Kozak threw the broken blade into a basket and the knife into a drawer.

"Know why I did that, son?"

"Yes sir."

"Tell me."

" 'Cause it's three inches to the heart."

"No. 'Cause it's against the law to carry more than three inches of knife. C'mon, Lefty, tell us about it. 'N it better be good."

The boy began slowly, secretly gratified that Kozak appeared to know he was the Warriors' first-string left-hander: maybe he'd been out at that game against the Knothole Wonders the Sunday he'd finished his own game and then had relieved Dropkick Kodadek in the sixth in the second. Why hadn't anyone called him "Iron-Man Bicek" or "Fireball Bruno" for that one?

"Everythin' you say can be used against you," Kozak warned him earnestly. "Don't talk unless you want to." His lips formed each syllable precisely.

Then he added absently, as though talking to someone unseen. "We'll just hold you on an open charge till you do."

And his lips hadn't moved at all.

The boy licked his own lips, feeling a dryness coming into his throat and a tightening in his stomach. "We seen this boobatch with his collar turned inside out cash'n his check by Konstanty Stachula's Tonsorial Palace of Art on Division. So I followed him a way, that was all. Just break'n the old monotony was all. Just a notion, you might say, that come over me. I'm just a neighborhood kid, Captain."

He stopped as though he had finished the story. Kozak glanced over the boy's shoulder at the arresting officers and Lefty began again hurriedly.

"Ever' once in a while he'd pull a little single-shot of scotch out of his pocket, stop a second t' toss it down, 'n toss the bottle at the car tracks. I picked up a bottle that didn't bust but there wasn't a spider left in 'er, the boobatch'd drunk her dry. 'N do you know, he had his pockets *full* of them little bottles? 'Stead of buyin' hisself a fifth in the first place. Can't understand a man who'll buy liquor that way. Right before the corner of Walton 'n Noble he popped into a hallway. That was Chiney-Eye-the-Princinct-Captain's hallway, so I popped right in after him. Me'n Chiney-Eye 'r just like that." The boy crossed two fingers of his left hand and asked innocently, "Has the alderman been in to straighten this out, Captain?"

"What time was all this, Lefty?"

"Well, some of the street lamps was lit awready 'n I didn't see nobody either way down Noble. It'd just started spitt'n a little snow 'n I couldn't see clear down Walton account of Wojciechowski's Tavern bein' in the way. He was a old guy, a dino you. He couldn't speak a word of English. But he started in cryin' about how every time he gets a little drunk the same old thing happens to him 'n he's gettin' fed up, he lost his last three checks in the very same hallway 'n it's gettin' so his family don't believe him no more . . ."

Lefty paused, realizing that his tongue was going faster than his brain. He unfolded his arms and shoved them down his pants pockets; the pants were turned up at the cuffs and the cuffs were frayed. He drew a colorless cap off his hip pocket and stood clutching it in his left hand.

"I didn't take him them other times, Captain," he anticipated Kozak.

"Who did?"

Silence.

"What's Benkowski doin' for a living these days, Lefty?"

"Just nutsin' around."

"What's Nowogrodski up to?"

"Goes wolfin' on roller skates by Riverview. The rink's open all year round."

"Does he have much luck?"

"Never turns up a hair. They go by too fast."

"What's that evil-eye up to?"

Silence.

"You know who I mean. Idzikowski."

"The Finger?"

"You know who I mean. Don't stall."

"He's hexin' fights, I heard."

"Seen Kodadek lately?"

"I guess. A week 'r two 'r a month ago."

"What was *he* up to?"

"Sir?"

"What was Kodadek doin' the last time you seen him?"

"You mean Dropkick? He was nutsin' around."

"Does he nuts around drunks in hallways?"

Somewhere in the room a small clock or wrist watch began ticking distinctly.

"Nutsin' around ain't jackrollin'."

"You mean Dropkick ain't a jackroller but you are."

The boy's blond lashes shuttered his eyes.

"All right, get ahead with your lyin' a little faster."

Kozak's head came down almost neckless onto his shoulders, and his face was molded like a flatiron, the temples narrow and the jaws rounded. Between the jaws and the open collar, against the graying hair of the chest, hung a tiny crucifix, slender and golden, a shade lighter than his tunic's golden buttons.

"I told him I wasn't gonna take his check, I just needed a little change, I'd pay it back someday. But maybe he didn't understand. He kept hollerin' how he lost his last check, please to let him keep this one. 'Why you drink'n it all up, then,' I put it to him, 'if you're that anxious to hold onto it?' He gimme a foxy grin then 'n pulls out four of them little bottles from four different pockets, 'n each one was a different kind of liquor. I could have one, he tells me in Polish, which do I want, 'n I slapped all four out of his hands. All four. I don't like to see no full-grown man drinkin' that way. A Polak hillbilly he was, 'n certain'y no citizen.

" 'Now let me have that change,' I asked him, 'n that wasn't so much t' ask. I don't go around just lookin' fer trouble, Captain. 'N my feet was slop-full of water 'n snow. I'm just a neighborhood fella. But he acted like I was gonna kill him 'r somethin'. I got one hand over his mouth 'n a half nelson behind him 'n talked polite-like in Polish in his ear, 'n he begun sweatin' 'n tryin' t' wrench away on me. 'Take it easy,' I asked him. 'Be reas'nable, we're both in this up to our necks now.' 'N he wasn't drunk no more then, 'n he was plenty t' hold onto. You wouldn't think a old boobatch like that'd have so much stren'th left in him, boozin' down Division night after night, year after year, like he didn't have no home to go to. He pulled my hand off his mouth 'n started hollerin', '*Mlody bandyta! Mlody bandyta!*' 'n I could feel him slippin'. He was just too strong fer a kid like me to hold——"

"Because you were reach'n for his wallet with the other hand?"

"Oh no. The reason I couldn't hold him was my right hand had the nelson 'n I'm not so strong there like in my left 'n even my left ain't what it was before I thrun it out pitchin' that double-header."

"So you kept the rod in your left hand?"

The boy hesitated. Then: "Yes sir." And felt a single drop of sweat slide down his side from under his armpit. Stop and slide again down to the belt.

"What did you get off him?"

"I tell you, I had my hands too full to get *anythin'*—that's just what I been tryin' to tell you. I didn't get so much as one of them little single-shots for all my trouble."

"How many slugs did you fire?"

"Just one, Captain. That was all there was in 'er. I didn't really fire, though. Just at his feet. T' scare him so's he wouldn't jump me. I fired in self-defense. I just wanted to get out of there." He glanced helplessly around at Comiskey and Adamovitch. "You do crazy things sometimes, fellas—well, that's all I was doin'."

The boy caught his tongue and stood mute. In the silence of the query room there was only the scraping of the reporter's pencil and the unseen wrist watch. "I'll ask Chiney-Eye if it's legal, a reporter takin' down a confession, that's my out," the boy thought desperately, and added aloud, before he could stop himself: " 'N beside I had to show him——"

"Show him what, son?"

Silence.

"Show him what, Left-hander?"

"That I wasn't just another greenhorn sprout like he thought."

"Did he say you were just a sprout?"

"No. But I c'd tell. Lots of people think I'm just a green kid. I show 'em. I guess I showed 'em now all right." He felt he should be apologizing for something and couldn't tell whether it was for strong-arming a man or for failing to strong-arm him.

"I'm just a neighborhood kid. I belonged to the Keep-Our-City-Clean Club at St. John Cant'us. I told him polite-like, like a Polish-American citizen, this was Chiney-Eye-a-Friend-of-Mine's hallway. 'No more after this one,' I told him. 'This is your last time gettin' rolled, old man. After this I'm pertectin' you, I'm seein' to it nobody touches you—but the people who live here don't like this sort of thing goin' on any more'n you 'r I do. There's gotta be a stop to it, old man—'n we all gotta live, don't we?' That's what I told him in Polish."

Kozak exchanged glances with the prim-faced reporter from the *Chicagoski*, who began cleaning his black tortoise-shell spectacles hurriedly yet delicately, with the fringed tip of his cravat. They depended from a black ribbon; he snapped them back onto his beak.

"You shot him in the groin, Lefty. He's dead."

The reporter leaned slightly forward, but perceived no special reaction and so relaxed. A pretty comfy old chair for a dirty old police station, he thought lifelessly. Kozak shaded his eyes with his gloved hand and looked down at his charge sheet. The night lamp on the desk was still lit, as though he had been working all night; as the morning grew lighter behind him lines came out below his eyes, black as though packed with soot, and a curious droop came to the St. Bernard mouth.

"You shot him through the groin—zip." Kozak's voice came, flat and unemphatic, reading from the charge sheet as though without understanding. "Five children. Stella, Mary, Grosha, Wanda, Vincent. Thirteen, ten, six, six, and one two months. Mother invalided since last birth, name of Rose. WPA fifty-five dollars. You told the truth about *that,* at least."

Lefty's voice came in a shout: "You know *what?* That bullet must of bounced, that's what!"

"Who was along?"

"I was singlin'. Lone-wolf stuff." His voice possessed the first faint touch of fear.

"You said, 'We seen the man.' Was he a big man? How big a man was he?"

"I'd judge two hunerd twenty pounds," Comiskey offered, "at least. Fifty pounds heavier 'n this boy, just about. 'N half a head taller."

"Who's 'we,' Left-hander?"

"Captain, I said, 'We seen.' Lots of people, fellas, seen him is all I meant, cashin' his check by Stachula's when the place was crowded. Konstanty cashes checks if he knows you. Say, I even know the project that old man was on, far as that goes, because my old lady wanted we should give up the store so's I c'd get on it. But it was just me done it, Captain."

The raccoon coat readjusted his glasses. He would say something under a by-line like "This correspondent has never seen a colder gray than that in the eye of the wanton killer who arrogantly styles himself the *lone wolf of Potomac Street.*" He shifted uncomfortably, wanting to get farther from the wall radiator but disliking to rise and push the heavy chair.

"Where was that bald-headed pal of yours all this time?"

"Don't know the fella, Captain. Nobody got hair any more around the neighborhood, it seems. The whole damn Triangle went 'n got army haircuts by Stachula's."

"Just you 'n Benkowski, I mean. Don't be afraid, son—we're not tryin' to ring in anythin' you done afore this. Just this one you were out cowboyin' with Benkowski on; were you help'n him 'r was he help'n you? Did you 'r him have the rod?"

Lefty heard a Ford V-8 pull into the rear of the station, and a moment later the splash of the gas as the officers refueled. Behind him he could hear Milano's heavy breathing. He looked down at his shoes, carefully buttoned all the way up and tied with a double bowknot. He'd have to have new laces mighty soon or else start tying them with a single bow.

"That Benkowski's sort of a toothless monkey used to go on at the City Garden at around a hundred an' eighteen pounds, ain't he?"

"Don't know the fella well enough t' say."

"Just from seein' him fight once 'r twice is all. 'N he wore a mouthpiece, I couldn't tell about his teeth. Seems to me he came in about one thirty-three, if he's the same fella you're thinkin' of, Captain."

"I guess you fought at the City Garden once 'r twice yourself, ain't you?"

"Oh, once 'r twice."

"How'd you make out, Left'?"

"Won 'em both on K.O.s. Stopped both fights in the first. One was against that boogie from the Savoy. If he woulda got up I woulda killed him fer life. Fer Christ I would. I didn't know I could hit like I can."

"With Benkowski in your corner both times?"

"Oh no, sir."

"That's a bloodsuck'n lie. I seen him in your corner with my own eyes the time you won off Cooney from the C.Y.O. He's your manager, jackroller."

"I didn't say he wasn't."

"You said he wasn't secondin' you."

"He don't."

"Who does?"

"The Finger."

"You told me the Finger was your hex-man. Make up your mind."

"He does both, Captain. He handles the bucket 'n sponge 'n in between he fingers the guy I'm fightin', 'n if it's close he fingers the ref 'n judges. Finger, he never losed a fight. He waited for the boogie outside the dressing room 'n pointed him clear to the ring. He win that one for me awright." The boy spun the frayed greenish cap in his hand in a concentric circle about his index finger, remembering a time when the cap was new and had earlaps. The bright checks were all faded now, to the color of worn pavement, and the earlaps were tatters.

"What possessed your mob to get their heads shaved, Lefty?"

"I strong-armed him myself, I'm rugged as a bull." The boy began to swell his chest imperceptibly; when his lungs were quite full he shut his eyes, like swimming under water at the Oak Street beach, and let his breath out slowly, ounce by ounce.

"I didn't ask you that. I asked you what happened to your hair."

Lefty's capricious mind returned abruptly to the word "possessed" that Kozak had employed. That had a randy ring, sort of: "What possessed you boys?"

"I forgot what you just asked me."

"I asked you why you didn't realize it'd be easier for us to catch up with your mob when all of you had your heads shaved."

"I guess we figured there'd be so many guys with heads shaved it'd be harder to catch a finger than if we all had hair.

But that was some accident all the same. A fella was gonna lend Ma a barber chair 'n go fifty-fifty with her shavin' all the Polaks on P'tom'c Street right back of the store, for relief tickets. So she started on me, just to show the fellas, but the hair made her sicker 'n ever 'n back of the store's the only place she got to lie down 'n I hadda finish the job myself.

"The fellas begun giv'n me a Christ-awful razzin' then, ever' day. God oh God, wherever I went around the Triangle, all the neighborhood fellas 'n little niducks 'n old-time hoods by the Broken Knuckle, whenever they seen me they was pointin' 'n laughin' 'n sayin', 'Hi, Baldy Bicek!' So I went home 'n got the clippers 'n the first guy I seen was Bibleback Watrobinski, you wouldn't know him. I jumps him 'n pushes the clip right through the middle of his hair—he ain't had a haircut since the alderman got indicted you—'n then he took one look at what I done in the drugstore window 'n we both bust out laughin' 'n laughin', 'n fin'lly Bible says I better finish what I started. So he set down on the curb 'n I finished him. When I got all I could off that way I took him back to the store 'n heated water 'n shaved him close 'n Ma couldn't see the point at all.

"Me 'n Bible prowled around a couple days 'n here come Catfoot Nowogrodski from Fry Street you, out of Stachula's with a spanty-new sideburner haircut 'n a green tie. I grabbed his arms 'n let Bible run it through the middle just like I done him. Then it was Catfoot's turn, 'n we caught Chester Chekhovka fer *him,* 'n fer Chester we got Cowboy Okulanis from by the Nort'western Viaduct you, 'n fer him we got Mustang, 'n fer Mustang we got John from the Joint, 'n fer John we got Snake Baranowski, 'n we kep' right on goin' that way till we was doin' guys we never seen before even, Wallios 'n Greeks 'n a Flip from Clark Street he musta been, walkin' with a white girl we done it to. 'N fin'lly all the sprouts in the Triangle start comin' around with their heads shaved, they want to join up with the Baldheads A.C., they called it. They thought it was a club you.

"It got so a kid with his head shaved could beat up on a bigger kid because the big one'd be a-scared to fight back hard, he thought the Baldheads'd get him. So that's why we changed our name then, that's why we're not the Warriors any more, we're the Baldhead True American Social 'n Athletic Club.

"I played first for the Warriors when I wasn't on the mound," he added cautiously, " 'n I'm enterin' the Gold'n Gloves next year 'less I go to collitch instead. I went to St. John Cant'us all the way through. Eight' grade, that is. If I keep on gainin' weight I'll be a hunerd ninety-eight this time next year 'n be five-foot-ten—I'm a fair-size light-heavy right this minute. That's what in England they call a cruiser weight you."

He shuffled a step and made as though to unbutton his shirt to show his proportions. But Adamovitch put one hand on his shoulders and slapped the boy's hand down. He didn't like this kid. This was a low-class Polak. He himself was a high-class Polak because his name was Adamovitch and not Adamowski. This sort of kid kept spoiling things for the high-class Polaks by always showing off instead of just being good citizens like the Irish. That was why the Irish ran the City Hall and Police Department and the Board of Education and the Post Office while the Polaks stayed on relief and got drunk and never got anywhere and had everybody down on them. All they could do like the Irish, old Adamovitch reflected bitterly, was to fight under Irish names to get their ears knocked off at the City Garden.

"That's why I want to get out of this jam," this one was saying beside him. "So's it don't ruin my career in the rope' arena. I'm goin' straight. This has sure been one good lesson fer me. Now I'll go to a big-ten collitch 'n make good you."

Now, if the college-coat asked him, "What big-ten college?" he'd answer something screwy like "The Boozological Stoo-dent-Collitch." That ought to set Kozak back awhile, they

might even send him to a bug doc. He'd have to be careful—
not *too* screwy. Just screwy enough to get by without involving
Benkowski.

He scuffed his shoes and there was no sound in the close
little room save his uneasy scuffling; square-toed boy's shoes,
laced with a buttonhook. He wanted to look more closely at
the reporter but every time he caught the glint of the fellow's
glasses he felt awed and would have to drop his eyes; he'd
never seen glasses on a string like that before and would have
given a great deal to wear them a moment. He took to looking
steadily out of the barred window behind Kozak's head, where
the January sun was glowing sullenly, like a flame held steadily
in a fog. Heard an empty truck clattering east on Chicago,
sounding like either a '38 Chevvie or a '37 Ford dragging its
safety chain against the car tracks; closed his eyes and imagined sparks flashing from the tracks as the iron struck,
bounced, and struck again. The bullet had bounced too. Wow.

"What do you think we ought to do with a man like you,
Bicek?"

The boy heard the change from the familiar "Lefty" to
"Bicek" with a pang; and the dryness began in his throat
again.

"One to fourteen is all I can catch fer manslaughter." He
appraised Kozak as coolly as he could.

"You like farm work the next fourteen years? Is that okay
with you?"

"I said that's all I could get, at the most. This is a first
offense 'n self-defense too. I'll plead the unwritten law."

"Who give you *that* idea?"

"Thought of it myself. Just now. You ain't got a chance to
send me over the road 'n you know it."

"We can send you to St. Charles, Bicek. 'N transfer you
when you come of age. Unless we can make it first-degree
murder."

The boy ignored the latter possibility.

"Why, a few years on a farm'd true me up fine. I planned t' cut out cigarettes 'n whisky anyhow before I turn pro—a farm'd be just the place to do that."

"By the time you're released you'll be thirty-two, Bicek—too late to turn pro then, ain't it?"

"I wouldn't wait that long. Hungry Piontek-from-by-the-Warehouse you, he lammed twice from that St. Charles farm. 'N Hungry don't have all his marbles even. He ain't even a citizen."

"Then let's talk about somethin' you couldn't lam out of so fast 'n easy. Like the chair. Did you know that Bogatski from Noble Street, Bicek? The boy that burned last summer, I mean."

A plain-clothes man stuck his head in the door and called confidently: "That's the man, Captain. That's the man."

Bicek forced himself to grin good-naturedly. He was getting pretty good, these last couple days, at grinning under pressure. When a fellow got sore he couldn't think straight, he reflected anxiously. And so he yawned in Kozak's face with deliberateness, stretching himself as effortlessly as a cat.

"Captain, I ain't been in serious trouble like this before . . ." he acknowledged, and paused dramatically. He'd let them have it straight from the shoulder now: "So I'm mighty glad to be so close to the alderman. Even if he is indicted."

There. Now they knew. He'd told them.

"You talkin' about my brother, Bicek?"

The boy nodded solemnly. Now they knew who they had hold of at last.

The reporter took the cigarette off his ear and hung it on his lower lip. And Adamovitch guffawed.

The boy jerked toward the officer: Adamovitch was laughing openly at him. Then they were all laughing openly at him. He heard their derision, and a red rain danced one moment before his eyes; when the red rain was past, Kozak was sitting back easily, regarding him with the expression of a man who

has just been swung at and missed and plans to use the provo-
cation without undue haste. The captain didn't look like the
sort who'd swing back wildly or hurriedly. He didn't look like
the sort who missed. His complacency for a moment was as
unbearable to the boy as Adamovitch's guffaw had been. He
heard his tongue going, trying to regain his lost composure by
provoking them all.

"Hey, Stingywhiskers!" He turned on the reporter. "Get
your Eversharp goin' there, write down I plugged the old rum-
pot, write down Bicek carries a rod night 'n day 'n don't care
where he points it. You, I go around slappin' the crap out of
whoever I feel like——"

But they all remained mild, calm, and unmoved: for a moment he feared Adamovitch was going to pat him on the head
and say something fatherly in Polish.

"Take it easy, lad," Adamovitch suggested. "You're in the
query room. We're here to help you, boy. We want to see you
through this thing so's you can get back to pugging. You just
ain't letting us help you, son."

Kozak blew his nose as though that were an achievement in
itself, and spoke with the false friendliness of the insurance
man urging a fleeced customer toward the door.

"Want to tell us where you got that rod now, Lefty?"

"I don't want to tell you anything." His mind was setting
hard now, against them all. Against them all in here and all
like them outside. And the harder it set, the more things seemed
to be all right with Kozak: he dropped his eyes to his charge
sheet now and everything was all right with everybody. The
reporter shoved his notebook into his pocket and buttoned the
top button of his coat as though the questioning were over.

It was all too easy. They weren't going to ask him anything
more, and he stood wanting them to. He stood wishing them to
threaten, to shake their heads ominously, wheedle and cajole
and promise him mercy if he'd just talk about the rod.

"I ain't mad, Captain. I don't blame you men either. It's

your job, it's your bread 'n butter to talk tough to us neighborhood fellas—ever'body got to have a racket, 'n yours is talkin'
tough." He directed this last at the captain, for Comiskey and
Milano had left quietly. But Kozak was studying the charge
sheet as though Bruno Lefty Bicek were no longer in the room.
Nor anywhere at all.

"I'm still here," the boy said wryly, his lip twisting into a
dry and bitter grin.

Kozak looked up, his big, wind-beaten, impassive face looking suddenly to the boy like an autographed pitcher's mitt he
had once owned. His glance went past the boy and no light of
recognition came into his eyes. Lefty Bicek felt a panic rising in
him: a desperate fear that they weren't going to press him
about the rod, about the old man, about his feelings. "Don't
look at me like I ain't nowheres," he asked. And his voice was
struck flat by fear.

Something else! The time he and Dropkick had broken into
a slot machine! The time he and Casey had played the attention racket and made four dollars! Something! Anything else!

The reporter lit his cigarette.

"Your case is well disposed of," Kozak said, and his eyes
dropped to the charge sheet forever.

"I'm born in this country, I'm educated here——"

But no one was listening to Bruno Lefty Bicek any more.

He watched the reporter leaving with regret—at least the
guy could have offered him a drag—and stood waiting for
someone to tell him to go somewhere now, shifting uneasily
from one foot to the other. Then he started slowly, backward,
toward the door: he'd make Kozak tell Adamovitch to grab
him. Halfway to the door he turned his back on Kozak.

There was no voice behind him. Was this what "well disposed of" meant? He turned the knob and stepped confidently
into the corridor; at the end of the corridor he saw the door
that opened into the courtroom, and his heart began shaking
his whole body with the impulse to make a run for it. He

glanced back and Adamovitch was five yards behind, coming up catfooted like only an old man who has been a citizen-dress man can come up catfooted, just far enough behind and just casual enough to make it appear unimportant whether the boy made a run for it or not.

The Lone Wolf of Potomac Street waited miserably, in the long unlovely corridor, for the sergeant to thrust two fingers through the back of his belt. Didn't they realize that he might have Dropkick and Catfoot and Benkowski with a sub-machine gun in a streamlined cream-colored roadster right down front, that he'd zigzag through the courtroom onto the courtroom fire escape and—swish—down off the courtroom roof three stories with the chopper still under his arm and through the car's roof and into the driver's seat? Like that George Raft did that time he was innocent at the Chopin, and cops like Adamovitch had better start ducking when Lefty Bicek began making a run for it. He felt the fingers thrust overfamiliarly between his shirt and his belt.

A cold draft came down the corridor when the door at the far end opened; with the opening of the door came the smell of disinfectant from the basement cells. Outside, far overhead, the bells of St. John Cantius were beginning. The boy felt the winding steel of the staircase to the basement beneath his feet and heard the whining screech of a Chicago Avenue streetcar as it paused on Ogden for the traffic lights and then screeched on again, as though a cat were caught beneath its back wheels. Would it be snowing out there still? he wondered, seeing the whitewashed basement walls.

"Feel all right, son?" Adamovitch asked in his most fatherly voice, closing the cell door while thinking to himself: "The kid don't *feel* guilty is the whole trouble. You got to make them *feel* guilty or they'll never go to church at all. A man who goes to church without feeling guilty for *something* is wasting his time, I say." Inside the cell he saw the boy pause and go down on his knees in the cell's gray light. The boy's head turned slowly toward him, a pious oval in the dimness. Old Adamovitch took off his hat.

"This place'll rot down 'n mold over before Lefty Bicek starts prayin', boobatch. Prays, squeals, 'r bawls. So run along 'n I'll see you in hell with yer back broke. I'm lookin' for my cap I dropped is all."

Adamovitch watched him crawling forward on all fours, groping for the pavement-colored cap; when he saw Bicek find it he put his own hat back on and left feeling vaguely dissatisfied.

He did not stay to see the boy, still on his knees, put his hands across his mouth and stare at the shadowed wall.

Shadows were there within shadows.

"I knew I'd never get to be twenty-one anyhow," Lefty told himself softly at last.

he couldn't boogie-woogie worth a damn

At first he did not dare to venture out on the streets at all in daylight. She would bring him *pizza* and wine from the shop downstairs, saying she had company upstairs. Since she often had company there, there was nothing unusual in this. But with him in the room she had no means of bringing other soldiers there, and the *pizza* and wine cost many francs.

At first he had had plenty money. He'd been lucky all through Africa and Italy, and he had no one to send money to at home. But now the francs were almost gone and he would have to put on his uniform and take his chances.

She had put a blazing shine on his boots and wasn't satisfied even after he'd laced them up and the little bulb overhead was reflected in the boots like two tiny underwater moons tethered in each toe. She had to kneel to give them a final gloss.

When he was quite ready she gave him a final inspection, while he stood rigidly at attention, eyes forward and palms along his thighs. Then she kissed him on each cheek as though she were de Gaulle, and he kissed her on the mouth as though he were exactly what he was: Pfc Isaac Newton Bailey, U. S. Army, unattached, unassigned, and whereabouts unknown.

She went down the narrow stair well before him and stood blinking into the white Mediterranean light a moment in the narrow door. The door opened onto an off-limits street and he waited in shadow behind her until the ubiquitous jeep, bearing two MPs and a gendarme, came rolling, gently and alertly, down the ancient street. When it turned down the Rue Phocéens he gave her hand a final squeeze and she watched his slender back until it got safely around the corner. No more hide-and-seek today, she thought sadly, with a child's sadness. She had come to enjoy the game of hiding him.

For she'd been playing hide-and-seek on her own since she'd been fourteen in Algiers; and it was more fun when there were two to play. Then there was always something for which to cry warning: an American jeep or the white belt of a French MP. The Americans never walked, they'd drive the jeep up a staircase if they could. Always the jeep, the jeep; but the ones with the white belts and the cross of Lorraine on their helmets walked, slowly and sadly, like shamed men, wherever they went.

In the dark one could spot the French helmets half a block away, and they were easier to talk to than the Americans. Perhaps the Americans were afraid because they were in a strange land; for they always spoke with contempt, like conquerors. And to Michele they were all conquerors: the Americans, the French, the British, as the Germans had been before them. As the Italians had tried to be, but had seemed more like gypsies instead. With all of them, one must never laugh, for conquerors felt that all laughter, save their own, was directed at them. She liked this dark hiding one because he laughed with her, and the pair of them laughed at them all.

The dark hiding one was losing himself in the noonday crowds along the Rue Cannebière, not walking too fast, not loitering, a little glad that he was a Negro because, among so many Negro GIs and French colonials, it was easier for the MPs to spot a white awol than a black one.

He ate at the transient mess, slyly pocketing a piece of cake for Michele, and walked over to the PX line. This was the riskiest angle of all, because the N.C.O. at the door checked ration cards against dog tags, and Bailey wasn't wearing his own dog tags any more. He'd stolen the ones he now wore at the Red Cross showers and had made out the ration card to correspond to the tags.

He bought a carton of Pall Malls and a mess of soap, candy, and toilet articles. The stuff cost almost nothing, so he bought all the odds and ends of unrationed supplies he could stuff into his pockets: shoe polish, hair oil, bath towels, and razor blades. He earmarked a pack of chewing gum and two packs of cigarettes for Michele in a side pocket, and disposed of everything else except the razor blades and a small bar of soap in a barbershop half a block down the street. Then he strolled east down the Cannebière to the Columbia Red Cross.

Here the showers were unheated, but the danger of being spotted by anyone from his own outfit was less than at the Rainbow Red Cross. He'd decided to postpone making a break for the States until he was certain that his outfit was already back there. It would be just his luck, if he didn't, to creep on board some tank and wake up looking at his old C.O. He went across the Cannebière, feeling better for the shower, to the GI movie, entering without pausing to see what was playing. It turned out to be *GI Joe,* and halfway through he knew he was going to be sick and got out just in time.

Along the outdoor GI bar quite a crowd had gathered. GIs were helping an old Frenchie to get drunk. He'd drink half a can of GI beer and pour the rest over his head to show his gratitude. His head was shaven, wet and shining in the sun; sweat and beer mingled down his cheeks and soaked the front of his shirt. He'd do a little jig while giving himself a beer shower and daubed himself delicately under the armpits, like a woman in a bath.

The French watched solemnly. When one can was emptied, there would be another waiting. The GIs crowded the fence bordering the bar, shouting encouragement, calling to their buddies to come over and watch, and demanding that the old man dance, that he box, that he sing, that he make a speech and take another drink.

The French waited curiously. The old man, in a pair of trousers covered with grime and grease, his sockless feet in a pair of American tennis sneakers, lifted one trouser leg daintily, pointing one toe, to indicate that he was now a ballet dancer.

"None of that fancy stuff, Pop! Jitterbug it!"

The old one understood. He wiped sweat and beer off his forehead, drained half of a can, poured the remainder into his ears, and went into a kind of cancan with Gilda Gray variations, ending by pivoting in a Virginia reel beneath the beer can, held by two fingers against his skull. And the white light beat on his skull while dust rose under his feet. He licked at the sweat coming off his temples with his tongue and came forward slinking, arms dangling in a kind of senile boogie-woogie, until the crowd gave back; it surged back as he retreated, his mouth agape as though to catch raindrops on his tongue. The GIs applauded crazily. But the French only watched with blank, unpitying faces, looking from the soldiers to the dancer to see what was so funny.

To Isaac Bailey the performance seemed pathetic, and he felt curious about the old man; but most of all it seemed insane: the open mouths of the GIs on the fence, like inmates of an asylum applauding a fellow having a fit. The French looked like visitors to the State Asylum, where all aberrations were uniformed, regulated, and made presentable to the public eye; but were no less insane for having been made presentable. These visitors watched their demented cousins behind the fence emotionlessly; saw the open mouths of brainless laughter, the ecstatic gesturing and the manic persistence of madmen exalting each other's madness.

The old one announced abruptly, in gravel-voiced French: "*Le Carpentier contre Le Dempsey,*" and went immediately into a wild exchange of blows against the air, ducking unseen

gloves, countering a jab by leaping straight up in the air and
batting himself in the eye. He was Dempsey, he was Carpentier,
he was Luis Angel Firpo, he was the winner, the loser, the
second, the referee, he was down on all fours, then up to shove
the imaginary ref aside and kick his opponent, now prostrate,
à le sabot, squarely in the teeth; he sat on his imaginary victim's
head and banged it against the sidewalk. In the white heat the
whole business had a routine, street-corner sort of insanity,
about as funny as a sun-struck newsboy tearing up the late
editions and tossing the paper about like confetti.

Isaac Bailey walked off, feeling depressed, wondering
whether it was himself or the soldiers with whom there was
something missing. He didn't know. All he knew was that, suddenly and certainly, he felt that he'd never feel homesick for
Memphis again.

The main business was yet to do and must wait for night.
His Algérienne needed a dress, and you couldn't even buy a
decent scarf for under a thousand francs. Money came easy,
but didn't go far. Yet down by the docks overcoats were piled
to the rafters in the supply depots. They were worth five thousand francs each on the market—the price of a dress. He
strayed into the Bar Odéon and drank *vin rouge,* slowly,
already feeling squeamish about what he had to do.

In the corner booth five GIs were heckling a tart, giving her
the come-on and then telling her to scram, bum, till, like an
obedient dog that comes when called and runs when it's kicked
at, the girl didn't know whether she was being accepted or
rejected. She stood uncertainly in the middle of the room, her
head cocked like a puppy's to one side, not knowing whether
to laugh with them or be insulted, to sit down with them or go
far away.

Bailey saw the first lights of the night coming on along the
boulevard, and with their coming the eager, seeking, searching
faces of the wandering sidewalk thousands became anxious,
pallid, and fearful. Along the bars and down the alleys, beside

the docks and in the shadowed corners of these ancestral streets, he was haunted by these Mediterranean faces. The whole city, somehow, wore a mask of such impenetrable grief, after the thousand years of battle and defeat, that he was reminded of a woman's face after a loss so profound that she knew herself to be forever beyond tears. Yet it was not an unhappy face, for it possessed the wisdom of having known joy, of being possessed by joy while realizing that, at the end, there was no joy.

A thousand years of lust and poverty and war and the degradation of war. He saw not only the women whose men had died in Italy and Africa and Germany and Spain: it was also for those who had fallen before Syracuse and Rome; for the thousand forgotten campaigns in which they, the people of the narrow places, had always, and would always be, the everlasting losers.

And always the children who had never been children, the ancient, innocent wiseacres with the light of old Egypt in their eyes and American slang on their tongues.

There were also the great sea fogs, gentle as sleep itself, moving through the thronging streets to announce the morning and lifting in the forenoon to let the bronze sun see: then for a few hours the bars were gay, the loud-speakers of Vieux Marseilles shook the walls with the "Marseillaise" and canned speeches, the GIs came in loaded with the day's quota of black-market supplies, and the red-fezzed Moroccans sold *cigarettes assyriennes* while smoking Camels themselves. Then the night came down and the little bars were darkened and the GIs rode home drunk and far and over the sea a great bronze bell began tolling the long sea hours.

A city with a face as tragic as a human face: the composite face of all humanity, foolish and arrogant and humble and patient and lined by greed and fear and the perpetual search for the moment of swift joy, with always in the eyes the resigned waiting for the last great bell, tolling the last sea hour.

It was also a workers' city, a dirty dockside mechanic sprawling, in a drunken sleep, his feet trailing the littered sea.

In a doorway a chicken was tied by one leg with a piece of string, and a dog's howl came in spirals down a darkened stair well. And everything had the gaunt and shrouded look of dead Egypt: the stone ways, the barbarian terraces, and the clean ancestral light, giving a freshly tanned smell to the girls and a ring to the voices of the people and a copper-colored hue to the night.

He looked in the faces of the children and saw: Hun and Spaniard and Basque and Moor; Gaul and Levantine.

And whenever he heard the great sea bell he felt it must have tolled so when Egyptian legions held this shore: to those mercenaries, he realized, the lion-colored hills of Africa must have looked like home.

He spent a pleasant few moments fancying himself just such a soldier, of such a time: only the uniform had changed. The allegiance had been no stronger then than now. It had always been somebody else's war, so everything was really the same. Except, of course, for the American radios, and the American dances, the American jeeps. And the American transports in the harbor, waiting restlessly, like all things American.

At the corner of the Rue Petits Puits, where you duck under the Restaurant Verdi sign, through the arch and up the stone steps to Old Marseilles, he saw the Moroccan. He was standing very erect in the shadows, the top of his hat almost touching the top of the door against which he leaned. When he turned his face, Bailey saw the tribal markings, like a cat's scratches, blue-black, down either side of the face from the cheekbone to the corners of the mouth, as cruel and innocent as a child's.

"Hey, you, Joe," he heard the Moor call. "You speak, Joe—how much?"

How much for anything, that was. You name it, he'll buy it, a hat or a Hershey bar or a gun or a toothbrush. They made two hundred francs a month and would peel off five hundred for a carton of Pall Malls without even making a dent in the roll. They were easier to deal with than the French and had more money, because they were bolder. If it was dark enough they didn't bother to bargain; they took what they wanted. Bailey fished out a pack of razor blades.

"Cinquante."

The Moor whistled. *"Trop cher."* And nodded toward the bar, to suggest retiring, like gentlemen, to a booth to talk "beesness." Bailey knew better. The bar was all right for the Moor but was off limits to English and Americans. When they got you inside, with your rations on the wood, they'd start stalling. Then, because you'd realize suddenly that you were under the double pressure of dealing in black market and of being off limits, you'd take anything just to get out. You couldn't blame them. It was the Americans who'd started the *caveat-emptor* business by selling them cigarette cartons wadded with newspaper.

Bailey threw in a stick of chewing gum, a bar of Red Cross soap, and his necktie.

"Cent francs." The price was going up.

"Trop cher." At seventy-five they reached an agreement. Then he fingered Bailey's trousers. Ten bucks for the pants.

Bailey laughed good-naturedly, and the African laughed with him, but without dismissing his hope for a sale. *"Vous,"* he said, fingering his own trousers, "I geev."

That was a hot one. Ten bucks and the guy's own pants thrown in. As he walked off he realized, abruptly, how much safer he'd be in the other's clothes, if it wasn't for the need of his own to crash the transient line and the PX. But then, in a few months, there wouldn't be any transient mess and the PX would be closed for keeps and he'd have to get rid of the GI suit. He laughed to think of how Michele would greet him in such an outfit. Hell, Bailey thought disgustedly, I'd be her countryman then for sure. If he was he might as well go back

to Algiers with her. That's where she was going anyhow, when
the soldiers left, she'd said.

And what, he asked himself abruptly, did he have to go
back to Memphis for anyhow? He couldn't sing, he wasn't a
pug, he wouldn't shine shoes, and he couldn't boogie-woogie
worth a damn. He couldn't play an instrument, he never
clowned, and making up berths for the Pullman Company had
the same warm appeal for him as shining shoes. He wondered
whether he really wanted to go back at all. Maybe he only
thought so because everybody else had always been moaning
for home.

He felt homesick all right. Strangely homesick: for the lion-
colored hills he'd climbed in Africa. Even now, it seemed, he
could hear the far-off and sorrowful sound the sea had made
every night, when they'd been waiting for the green light to
Italy. Then stopped in the middle of the street with the sudden
realization that there was nothing to stop him from going
back: no one, nothing in the whole wide world, on land or
sea or above those hills.

On the Rue Petits Puits he began avoiding the lights, and
when he saw the long, low-lying shape of the GI garage, he left
the road and got through the hole in the wire he'd made on
his last raid.

Once inside, he didn't sneak any more. He slapped his feet
down like he owned the place and hurried down the middle
of the depot importantly, like any Pfc scurrying to report to
his N.C.O. He glanced at his watch to see if he were late: it
was ten minutes of ten. The colored guard eyed him without
curiosity as he passed, and at the end of the depot he walked
boldly into supply and switched on the light.

The overcoat on the top of the heap was too big. He had
to have one at least approximating his own size to make it look
legit. The third one was about right, and he tossed it out of
the supply window, standing on a desk to do so. Then he
walked out, leaving the light burning as though he'd be back

in a minute, and didn't look back to see whether he was getting away or not. The last time he'd been here he'd worn the overcoat out; but that had been in February, when he'd first snuck into town.

He didn't start sweating till he had the coat over his arm and was out of the light and halfway back to town. Then he decided, "That's the last time I pull that. *Positively* the last." Bailey knew about pressing one's luck. He'd already pressed it once too often.

At the Columbia Red Cross he checked the coat and went around the corner, to sit on a bench on the little street lined by birches that goes uphill along the car tracks. He waited till a spare, wispy little middle-aged Frenchie came and sat innocently beside him and whispered, *"Combien?"* For five thousand francs, Bailey assured him with gestures, his overcoat was a bargain. *Combien* rose and led him a quarter of a mile toward a bombed-out building. They would meet there in half an hour, it was agreed, Bailey with the coat and he with the francs.

When Bailey returned there with the coat, and the bargain had been achieved, he pulled out a ten-dollar bill, American, that he'd won on the boat coming over. It was a sort of good-luck bill that he'd never used, even when hard-pressed. "That's Memphis money," he used to tell the boys, when they'd offer to buy it off him just because it was American money. He sold it now, by flashlight, to *Combien,* getting two and a half for one because it was the blue-seal bill instead of the gold-seal invasion currency. Why the blue seals brought two and a half, while the gold seals only brought two was a mystery he'd never been able to understand.

When he got rid of the bill he knew he was saying good-by to Memphis.

At the Red Cross he got the farewell feeling all over, and fell into the night's last coke-and-donut line as a sort of good-by gesture. His mind was made up so firmly he was surprised at himself, as though something had been done for him without his consent. Just like the time he'd told the lieutenant to take the patrol out himself, he wasn't drawing any more fire for officers that night. Some devil of fool's courage had gotten into him at such times, and he'd had to obey or feel like a sucker.

"Let's see the pass, soldier."

He came to himself, realizing, for the first time, that the line was being ushered into the Red Cross by an MP. That's a hot one—a pass to get a coke and a donut. He turned away in disgust. "You know what you can do with that coke," he told the MP.

"You don't have to drink no coke," the MP told him, "just show the pass."

He found a pass with a month-old date, flashed it mechanically, and the MP turned the flashlight on it.

"That's the wrong one, Jack. Look again."

"I guess I lost the other," Bailey said carelessly. "The hell with the coke."

"I can't let you go, Jack. Look again."

"No use looking, I ain't got one. I left it in my coat at the Rainbow."

"Okay. I'll go with you."

They sauntered, as leisurely as the MP would permit, down the Cannebière. Down the alley, Bailey thought, pushing back the rising tide of panic. Of all the luck. Of all the MPs in the Delta Base he had to catch the one joker who was still bucking.

"The war's over," he told the joker.

No answer. Bailey stopped.

"What the hell, Sarge. I took a run out from St. Vic to see my girl, that's all. That's all, Sarge. Give me a break. I'm on shipping orders. I just wanted to say good-by, you know how that is. I'll go back in. Maybe I can do something for you sometime back in the States. Jeez, us vets got to stick together —you can put me on the truck yourself."

"You're not on no shipping orders. Not from St. Vic you ain't."

As in a dream Bailey saw him reaching for his whistle, swung and felt his knuckles crumple against the jaw; the whistle popped out of the mouth in a jolt of surprise and down the alley it was, heard the whistle at last and he was out on the slanting Rue Capucines, going uphill. His feet were weighted all the way up, and at the top he ducked into the railroad station, got across the tracks in front of a line of switching boxcars, and raced hell for leather, half crouched, across the darkened stubble between the bombed-out tenements where the gypsies lived.

He paused in a crevice, like a rat. Sweat was tickling his sides from his armpits to his belt. If no one had seen him duck in here he was all right. Wow. He'd never hit anyone so fast and so hard in his life. He was laughing and shaking with fear and relief, trying not to breathe too hard, and clenching his palms into his fists, all at once. It was ten minutes before he regained his breath and control. Then he waited another half hour, to be sure the MP would be off duty.

It was past one when he crept across the stubbled field toward the docks. He took a chance on an off-limits street in order to keep out of the light, and cut across the park where the Moroccans sold each other cigarettes in daylight. It was only half deserted now, even at this hour, and as he hurried past he heard a familiar whisper: "Hey, you, Joe! You speak —how much?"

When he got into the room he took off his shirt; it was stiff with perspiration. His Algérienne was sleeping, with the light still on and a cigarette still smoking in a water glass beside the couch. She was careless that way; but she couldn't have been sleeping long.

He turned out the light and she wakened; he felt her groping sleepily for him like a child. Still half asleep, she sensed something in the dark.

"You have fear, yes?"

"You damn right I got fear. I took off ten pounds. But it's all right now." He wondered at his trust in her. It felt absolutely implicit. Was that because his need was for such a trust, or because she was really that trustworthy? He didn't know and it didn't make any difference. That's how it was, and he wouldn't have it changed.

"You have fear of *bastille?*"

"*Oui.*"

But it wasn't just having to do a stretch that had scared him so. Not altogether. It was also the fear, he realized now, of losing her. It was having to do time and then be shipped back to Memphis without her that had given him the panic. "No wonder I slugged the MP," he thought.

"We'll have to hole up real still for a couple days," he told her. "Then we'll get out fast. To *Espagne.* Then *Afrique.*"

She sat up like a child being promised a trip to the circus.

"In *Espagne* we see *los toros?*"

"The hell with *los toros.* We're going to get on a tanker. You think I can pass for *algérien?*"

"You pass fine," she assured him. "In Algérie I have many friends. You will be my Algérien."

And across the waters, slowly, far-off and faintly across the waters, borne full of sorrow over the sounding sea, he heard the great bell tolling, tolling, from the lion-colored hills of home.

a lot you got to holler

It's a Barnum and Bailey world
Just as phony as it can be . . .
                                    Popular Song

I think I started stealing right after the old man threw Aunt
out of the house. I was about eight, and used to look forward
to her visit all week. She would dangle me on her knee, kiss me,
and give me small coins: pennies and nickels and dimes. I
remember her smell, the leather touch of her purse, and the
warm touch of her hand when she pressed the coins into my
hand. That smell, that purse, those kisses, and those coins were
all something that belonged peculiarly to her, as she belonged
peculiarly to me; for I never received, nor ever expected, those
things from anyone else.

The last time I heard her voice was in the hallway, and
sensed that she was pleading to kiss me good night. But the
old man was in a high-wheeled huff and made her leave without saying good-by. Years later I learned she didn't even have
a place to stay that night.

It must have been the next morning that I saw a neighbor
woman's purse on a dresser and put it down the front of my
shirt without even opening it. They found me sleeping under
the back porch with the purse under my cheek like a pillow.

The old man gave me a sound whaling for stealing; but
all the while he was slapping me around I had the conviction

that I hadn't really done what I was being slapped around for.
I felt that, if Aunt were there, she would say I hadn't done
anything wrong. I felt, for the first time, that everything was
wrong, all wrong.

I first began to believe, about that time, that Aunt was really
my mother. It was a screwy, kid's sort of hope, and a hope
that finally came true: I must have been about twelve when
I learned that the old man had left her and married her
younger sister. Don't ask me what he was thinking of, but
that's what he did. When I was born, and Aunt had no way
of taking care of me, he and the younger sister took me in. I
guess the old man figured that was the cheapest way out. He
always figured the cheapest way, no matter how much it cost
in the long run or who had to pay off. That's how it was that
I grew up remembering my mother as "Aunt" and calling my
aunt "Ma."

And everything, in remembering her, was hooked up with
the smell of her purse and the small coins of love it had carried:
I didn't grow up thinking of pennies and nickels and dimes as
such; I thought of them always, without fully realizing it, as
love-pennies, love-nickels, and love-dimes. When I saved them,
as a kid, I wasn't really saving money. Because when I'd realize
that money was all they came to I'd break the bank and get rid
of them at the nearest candy store as fast as I could spend. If
the candy store was closed I'd give them away.

It wasn't always stealing either. Once, when I was about
nine, I was going down Division Street flipping a dime. It
slipped through my fingers and rolled off the curb into the
gutter. When I stooped to pick it up I saw a quarter lying
beside it. I looked to see if it had Aunt's picture on it: it was
years before I really ceased to believe that the woman's head
on a quarter wasn't hers.

And for the next two weeks all I did was walk down Division
flipping that lucky dime. I couldn't tell you yet whether I was
looking for Aunt or another quarter. When I didn't find either

I tried new sidewalks and strange streets. I got to know the whole Near Northwest Side that way. Then I lost the dime. And that, in a small way, was like losing Aunt all over.

But I began dreaming up other ways of finding quarters. Toward spring I decided that lots of kids must have lost money skating on the pond at Eckert Park during the winter. I went over there on the first day that the ice was melting and surveyed the slush inch by inch, although the soles of my shoes were paper-thin. I found four pennies, three dice, and a tin of Prince Albert tobacco. The tin was rusted but the tobacco tasted interesting.

I was sick by evening and, in a fever, confessed about chewing the tobacco. That's the only time I remember admitting doing something wrong without getting whipped. I was too sick to whip.

But sick as I was, I didn't squeal about the four pennies. They were hidden. I was going to return them to Aunt, and I would have died before telling. I remember having a vague and feverish conviction that they were hers, because all the pennies and nickels in the world, somehow, really belonged to her.

By evening the doctor had to come: it wasn't the Prince Albert entirely. I'd caught cold from wading in the slush and it had gone into flu. That was the epidemic of 1917, I guess. Something has always happened to ruin my get-rich-quick schemes.

Toward the end of that summer I was coming home from a swimming pool in Little Italy, about a mile away, where kids could swim for a penny. I remember that my swimming suit was still wet under my clothes and that I took a short cut across the Northwestern tracks. There was a long board fence bounding the coalyard there, in those years, and as I passed a place where a board was missing a kid poked his head out and hissed, "Hey, you, c'mere," as though he'd been expecting me. I'd never seen the kid before. He was about seven, I guess.

He squatted down in the weeds and came up with a green bandanna in which lay eight singles and some small change. "That's your part," he tells me, and gives me half the bills and half the change. He'd taken it all out of a Northwestern caboose, and he knew it was stealing as well as I. That was why he'd called me: to share his guilt.

Only, I didn't feel guilty. I'd already had my beating for stealing, so what I had in my hand had been well paid for. I felt as though somebody, maybe God, had owed me this for a long time and it was only in the natural run of things that it should come my way at last. And as I stood there the warmth of the coins, that had been lying in summer sunlight, spread from my palm through my whole body; for Aunt's warmth was in all coins. When I closed my fist over them I was enclosing her hand, and in that moment they became so precious to me that my fingernails dug into the flesh as if I never wanted to open my hand again. Then I thought of the old man and flattened the bills and stuffed them into my rolled sleeves. I don't know where I got the idea to do that, but kids raised on crowded corners get cunning pretty early.

I wandered around looking for kids I knew and found half a dozen ragged strays lagging beer corks on the corner of Ellen Street. With a prissy-looking eleven-year-old blonde watching in solemn disapproval. I knew her. She lived next door and spent half her life, it seemed to me, on the alert for me to do something wrong in order to report it to the old man. If I spent a penny a mile away she'd learn of it and I'd become entangled in such a web of lies, trying to duck another beating, that I wouldn't know myself what the truth was.

So I stood there, with the most money I'd ever had in my life and just as unable to buy anything with it as though all the ice-cream parlors had closed for keeps. My bathing suit began to itch.

Kids are sly all right. There wasn't any use waiting for her to leave. She'd find out anyhow. So when no one was looking

I dropped a dollar in the dirt and hollered, "Oh boy! Look what I found!" The lagging stopped.

"Augie found a dollar! We were all here'n nobody seen it but Augie! Augie the lucky eagle-eye!"

So here we all go to the ice-cream store, with the kids crowding around me and the prissy blonde following like a little Pinkerton. I bought two cones for myself first and alternated at licking them—one chocolate and one vanilla. I didn't like strawberry even then.

I don't think all the kids got cones, because there must have been at least forty swarming into the store by that time.

The blonde got one though. A strawberry double-header.

When the lagging was resumed and the excitement had subsided I felt a crying need for more ice cream. It was getting toward suppertime but I hated going home, even to rid myself of the itching bathing suit; I felt a couple more cones would keep me going to all hours.

This time I played it safe. I only used a half dollar, which seemed then only half as wrong.

"Look! A halfer! Am I lucky today you!"

"Is he lucky today you. Lucky Augie the eagle-eye!"

And so back to the ice-cream store.

When I came out of the house the next morning half a dozen kids were waiting for me. Kids I'd never seen before, from way over on Chicago Avenue. They didn't say anything, but they followed me so closely it was impossible to lose a penny without being seen in the act. And, of course, the twenty-four-hour Pinkerton, the eye that never slept, a little taller than any of the other kids, still shadowing me and still as grave as ever.

The sprouts followed my very eyes: if I glanced toward a telephone pole they would race there and search the alley for yards around. The blonde didn't search. She was hep. She just watched my pockets and my hands.

It didn't do her any good, because I started lagging beer corks with the other kids until her interest wandered to other suspects on whom she was keeping book. And that evening I *earned* seventy-five cents selling the *Saturday Evening Blade* on the corner of Milwaukee Avenue and Ashland.

The same kids were waiting for me the next morning, and I spent every dime of the *Saturday Evening Blade* money on them before noon, to maintain my far-flung reputation as an easy spender. Six bits in a single morning broke all local records for loose living. And you can guess the rest: as soon as she'd finished another strawberry double-header the Pinkerton raced to Ma. "Augie steals money every day," she told the old lady.

"A lot you got to holler, Sissie," I told her. "You helped me spend it." I knew it wasn't any use saying I'd earned it selling the *Blade*. It was a beating either way.

Every time I was whipped unjustly I became lonely for Aunt, and the next morning I started out looking for her, to tell her how it was that nobody bothered you when you spent stolen money, except to help you spend it; but that the pay-off came when you were caught spending money you'd earned honestly. I couldn't figure that out, beyond feeling that my mistake had been in going to work at all. If I'd gone searching around that broken board in the coalyard fence, it seemed to me, instead of fooling around with the *Blade,* I might have done better. At least I wouldn't have been licked.

I had no idea where she lived, and so just wandered around looking at houses and occasionally ringing a doorbell in some blind hope that that might be the place she lived. I knew better than to ask Ma where Aunt lived, because all Ma did when I mentioned Aunt was to bawl.

It got so late that I was afraid to go home without some excuse. I'd been up and down streets and alleys the whole morning and most of the afternoon. And now the red headlines of the *Blade,* which had been featuring kidnap stories, came to my mind. Toward dark I stopped in an alley, found a piece of glass, and gave myself a long scratch down my right arm.

The kidnapers had done that, I would tell Ma, when I was struggling to get away.

That's one you'll have to figure out for yourself; but I don't think I really did it to pass myself off as a kidnaped kid. Nor entirely to get out of a beating, either. I think that, at bottom, I had the hope of getting sympathy out of the old man.

It turned out to be the worst beating I'd ever had, and I know I never tried for anyone's sympathy again. After that, I'm sure, I was entirely on my own. After that, so far as myself and the old man were concerned, it was strictly warfare.

But I still feel that, if I could, somehow, have seen Aunt that day, things might have turned out different. I think she might have kept things from getting mixed up, at least until I was grown enough to figure them out for myself. But I didn't see her, and when things got mixed up that day they stayed mixed for keeps.

We grew out of the beer-cork stage into lagging for ten-for-a-penny pictures of baseball players. Like the beer corks, some of these had a larger value than others: I remember trading an entire strip of ten to get just one of Joe Jackson. And a month later, when Jackson had been kicked out of organized baseball, I had to give one of him, one of Buck Weaver, and two Happy Felschs just to get one Ray Schalk—who'd been on the original strip I'd traded for Shoeless Joe in the first place.

When we started lagging for pennies we forgot about the baseball players, and nobody cared any more whether Ray Schalk was a good guy or a bad guy anyhow. The feeling grew that he may have been a sucker.

Who'd gotten the pay roll? that's what we wanted to know now.

We drifted into the crap games behind the Anderson School, and when the cops started breaking them up the attraction became irresistible. Once a dozen of us spent an afternoon in

the Racine Avenue Station because the kid we'd set up as a
lookout had wandered off to match nickels with the corner
newsie. It was a hot afternoon, and our numbers gave us
courage. We heckled the cops, and were really proud of being
jailbirds. How did we kill the afternoon when the cops ignored
us? You guessed it again. I lost forty-six cents.

When I got home Sissie had already told my old man where
I'd been. But the whipping was nothing at all compared to
the sense of manhood attained by an afternoon in the clink. It
was the most exciting thing that had ever happened to us. For
days we bragged to each other about our various parts in the
escapade: who was the most scared, who wasn't scared at
all, and whose brother, right now, was doing ninety days in
County. For us the kid whose brother was doing a stretch was
as distinguished as a kid in another neighborhood whose
brother was a college football star.

This was all in the days when newspapers were a penny
apiece and we had a lot of dodges around the stands. When the
race-track and baseball fans handed you a nickel, they'd grab
the sheet and stare at the results, with one hand held out blindly
for their change. The dodge was to lay a penny in the waiting
hand, click a second penny on the first and the third on the
second; but the last penny you just clicked, without dropping
it. The fellow would shove the change in his pocket and never
know he'd been gypped.

Sometimes, if a customer didn't have anything smaller than
a nickel or a dime, we'd plead that we had no change and go
into the nearest saloon to get it. Then we'd duck out the
Ladies' Entrance, leaving the sucker waiting in front.

When a streetcar was waiting for a red light we'd run up
alongside the car and some guy would stick his hand out for a
paper. If he offered a nickel or a dime we'd fumble and dig for
that change until the car started, and then run beside the car
with the change trying to reach the fellow's hand but never,
somehow, quite making it. That only failed me once. A guy

got off at the next stop and came back for the change. A tin-
horn.

Around Christmas the big paper guys had cards printed
and sold them to us little paper guys for a nickel apiece. The
cards read, if I remember rightly:

> Christmas comes but once a year
> And when it comes it brings good cheer
> So open your purse without a tear
> And remember the newsboy standing here.

Sometimes that one was good for as much as a quarter. But
this was the pay-off: we had to ask for the card back, because
it cost us a nickel, and the customer would be thinking it was
his, that he'd bought it. We called the big paper guys the
Knothole Wonders, I don't remember why.

There were no stands in those days; the papers were just
piled on the corners with stones on them, and every corner pile
was run by some big guy. If a little guy sold a paper, it had to
be in the middle of the block. But I remember selling a paper
to a woman on the corner of Robey and Division, right under
a big guy's nose.

I never tried that again. I had to buy the paper back from
the big guy—and got a kick that was positively terrific. It lifted
me off the ground and scattered my papers for yards. I didn't
even take time to howl while gathering them up in the rush of
noontime traffic—I was so afraid of losing those papers. But
when I got home it really began hurting, and I cried all night.

And every time I saw the big paper guy, for a year after, I
would still feel that kick. Sometimes I can still feel it.

And sometimes one of the big guys would make a deal with
one of the little guys. He would say, "Hey, sprout, you want to
buy me out tonight?" That meant buying him out around midnight, when the final lull began, at the wholesale price.

I made a deal like that once, but along about 1 A.M. it turned
bitterly cold, and I had more papers left than I could sell in a

week of Saturday nights. I was stuck. So I started to bawl, too
cold to stand still and too afraid to go home. Just wandered
around, wiping my nose on my sleeve and bawling, making
people pause to ask what the matter was. I sold out, bawling
the whole time. And had enough tears left over to help one of
the other kids get rid of his papers too. I must have been nine
or ten by that time.

If there wasn't anything in the headlines to yell about we
just hollered, "Big Whitehouse scandal! Big Whitehouse scandal!" I thought the Whitehouse was the Derby Hotel, where
the big guys went to see the big girls. It had white doors and a
long white marble desk.

One afternoon when I was about thirteen I delivered a
couple papers up there, to the third floor, and saw a woman in
a kimono come down the hall whom I took for Aunt. I said,
"Hello, Aunt," with such a hope of happiness in me I've never
felt since. I don't think I'll ever come that close again. But she
didn't answer and she didn't look around, and I had to believe
it wasn't her after all.

But in later years I figured it this way: if it really *hadn't*
been her, she would have turned when I called. She would
have turned her head to see who'd called her. I figure now she
was afraid to turn her head.

I went up there a number of times after that, under the
pretense of delivering a paper, and wandered the long plush-
carpeted hall listening to the laughter of women behind many
doors, hoping always to hear Aunt's laughter. It was dark in
the hallway, that was why she hadn't recognized me, I had
decided. It had been so long since I'd seen her, I'd grown so
much taller, that was why she hadn't recognized me. I spent so
much time up there that the desk man made me leave the
papers at the desk. He thought I was up to something else.

That's how it's always been: I was always in the clear so
long as I was truly guilty. But the minute my motives were
honest someone would finger me.

Another way we used to raise money was to go to the market and get those big empty barrels—not the casks, the barrels. The bigger guys could carry them, but we little guys rolled them. They rolled easy, and the meat packers paid us a nickel each for them. We couldn't find enough of them, naturally; so we'd steal them from one packer and sell them to another.

I must have been about fourteen when I made sudden friends with a kid who had a nice home. I don't remember the kid, but I remember the home, which was clean and bright all day, and his mother, who was handsome. It was a third-floor flat somewhere, with lots of plants in the front room with the sunlight on them. He had a puppy and we used to play with it up there. It's the first memory I have of being happy, playing with that pup in that pleasant place.

We must have been making a lot of noise, because this kid's mother walked past and said jokingly, to make us be a little quiet, "Why don't you kids just throw that dog out of the window?" I was so happy at just being there, so overwhelmed with an eagerness to please, that I picked up the pup, walked to the window and threw it out. Just like that.

I can still see that poor damned pup sprawling and turning and pawing for a foothold in mid-air on its way down to the pavement. And felt, suddenly, that I was falling too.

I was falling all right. But I was sixteen before I hit the ground. It happened the week after the old man told me that Aunt was dead, and I guess a kid still has a right to tears at that age. But I didn't shed one. I had some twisted idea that that would give the old man some sort of satisfaction. I just dummied up on him.

He was so puzzled because I didn't bawl, or even look like I felt bad, that he followed me out of the room to tell me that she was really my mother.

"I knew that eight years ago," I told him straight. "I knew she was my old lady the night you threw her out. But you were never my old man." Of course he was all right. I was just trying to make him feel like he was trying to make me feel.

He started blowing up and told me to get out. I knew he didn't mean it, because I was bringing him the rent. "If I left now," I told him, "you'd have me locked up. I'll wait till I'm of age. Then I'll see you in hell with your back broke."

"I'll be glad to get rid of you now," he tells me. "You're going to go bad, you might as well go now and get a good start."

"And you won't have me locked up for running away?"

"Why should I?" he asks. "All you been to me is trouble."

"What do you think you've been to me?" I asked him then. "A father? A lot you got to holler." And I grabbed my cap and left.

I took a room with Little Johnny Polish over on Western Avenue. Johnny called himself a juke-box mechanic, and he had a car. We went around fixing jukes whenever we got on the shorts. We really fixed them, too. Only, sometimes we'd make a mistake and hit some juke we'd already fixed once. We did that once in a bookie, of all places.

A tavern with a bookie in the back. I thought it looked familiar, but Johnny didn't say anything so we went right ahead. On the way out the bartender, who knew Johnny, called him over and said something, looking a little white. When we got in the car Johnny looked white too and I really wheeled out of there.

"They're gettin' tired of us in there," Johnny said after a while. "That's a syndicate box."

We didn't go near that joint again and were more careful altogether. We operated out of the neighborhood until the syndicate cooled off. And sometimes we'd have so many dimes, nickels, and quarters up in the room that we wouldn't even bother to divide them. We got a scale and weighed them. I remember we figured eleven ounces to the dollar.

The first time I took a fall I was alone having coffee at a

restaurant on Damen and Division. They sat down, one on either side of me, and the first thing that popped into my head was that they were syndicate men dressed like coppers. Something like that had happened in the neighborhood before.

They were real cops though. I had to sweat it out at Eleventh and State overnight and stand the showup before I found out that all it was was the old man. He'd reneged on his word to me, just as he had with Aunt. He'd given me out as a runaway and I had to put in twenty days at Juvenile.

All I remember of that stretch is this: when we came in we were given a copy of the rules, told to make the best of things, and that was all the interest any of us received there.

The night I got out I slugged a peanut machine—one of those El platform jobs. It was in the dark, at the far end of the platform, and all I went up to the thing for was to get a handful of peanuts. But when I put my hand on the lever I felt the warmth of the day still trapped in the metal, and the warmth of Aunt's hand pressing pennies into my hand—before I knew what I was doing I'd slugged the glass with my naked fist.

It was absolutely crazy and I don't understand it myself to this day. I cut the hell out of my hand and the woman at the cashier's cage heard the tinkle of the glass. I would have been a lot smarter to have slugged her instead of the peanuts.

That was the only time I used raw-jaw methods. Rip-and-tear is all right for kids, but there's no future in it.

Johnny Polish laughed his head off over that one when he came up to see me at County. Then he had the ward superintendent put in the fix and all I got was thirty days. I was paroled to my old man. What a laugh.

I've never figured out to myself why I pinned everything onto the old man. Sometimes I think I started blaming him before I was born almost. It wasn't anything I tried figuring at all, it was just the way I *felt,* so deep down that it was beyond all figuring.

I used to wake up nights thinking of the night he'd given her the bum's rush when she didn't have a place to go. Except, perhaps, the Derby Hotel. When I thought of *that* I think I could have killed him as quick as stepping on a roach. And that easy.

And yet by that time it wouldn't have done me any more good than stepping on a roach. When I came out of County I had him where I could have stepped on him any time. Like it says in the song, I had him in the palm of my hand.

All I did was lay around the house smoking cigarettes and playing the radio loud and never letting the old man tune in the Polish hour, because that was the one program, I knew, which he understood and enjoyed. In fact it was the only thing he enjoyed and the one thing he'd bought the radio for. I'd turn on Spike Jones and he'd sit in the kitchen and drink and take it out on Ma. That was their business, so long as they stayed in the kitchen. He wanted me home, he'd told the police. So now he had me there. He wasn't in much of a position to tell them he'd changed his mind.

Some nights I'd have half the neighborhood in the front room. Little Johnny'd bring up a couple neighborhood tramps and the joint would really jump. One night, just to get his goat, we started a strip-poker game. The old man lost his head and called the squad.

Little Johnny asked them in, and they saw who was there beside the tramps: the ward super, two precinct captains, Little Johnny, a Jew mouthpiece we called Noseberg O'Brien, and a bailiff from the Criminal Court. They asked us to be a little quiet about it and we slipped them a fin apiece, and they backed off. With all the writs and corpuses Noseberg O'Brien had in his hat, they were lucky to get out with their jobs, coming into a private home without a warrant like that.

After the party broke up I told the old man, polite-like, in Polish, that if he ever did a thing like that again they'd find him under the sink with his little toes turned up. Under the sink, with the rest of the pipes. But letting a roach go don't make you like him any more the next time you see him come crawlin'.

He *begged* me to leave then, and promised he wouldn't have me brought back.

"What's the use?" I said. "You'd have me locked up all over again is all."

"This time I won't," he said. And that time I knew he meant it at last. He had a stomachful of Little Augie by then.

I stayed home that night, and when I was packing, in the morning, he stuck his mug in the door and watched awhile, to see that I wasn't taking anything that belonged to him.

"You gonna die in jail, Augie," he tells me after a while, just to say something.

"You never cared where I lived," I told him, "a lot you got to holler where I die."

And I remembered how she had wanted to say good-by to me one night in this same house and he hadn't let her.

I didn't even say so long.

poor man's pennies

It's hard to understand what some women will see in some men. What Gladys, for example, could ever see in Sobotnik. Yet the bigger the lies he told, the tenderer she became with him. She'd call him her poor Rudy; but we neighborhood fellows just called him Hundred Per Cent.

You know: Hundred Per Cent bull. Always trying to prove he isn't a bum at heart before anyone even says he is.

He started out that way with her, from their very first conversation, and she's still listening to him. No, I couldn't tell you why. All she ever said was, "Lies are a poor man's pennies." Just as though she meant something about Rudy by it.

Their first conversation was in a drugstore, when Gladys remarked to her girl friend that she'd been seeing that little guy with the glasses around the neighborhood most of her life. Sobotnik overheard, but he didn't come in saying, "Yeh, that's me, I lived here all my life 'n seen you around lots of times too." Not Sobotnik. Not Hundred Per Cent. With him it's the hard way.

"I don't come from this crumby neighborhood," he tells her. "I'm from Kentucky. My people got four 'r five plantations down there. All I know is race horses 'n mint joolips."

Then he names her some of the hides he's bet fifty cents on to show. He was just in Chicago to straighten out some details about opening a new track in Florida, he explains, and has to catch a midnight plane to—— "Well, I ain't allowed to say where to."

"Ain't it almost time for you to be hopping it then?" Gladys asks, glancing at her watch. "You'll just have time to make it."

"For your sake I'll put it off till tomorrow," he decides grandly, warming up to her.

"For my sake you don't have to," she tells him.

He just brushes that off and starts on a new line. "I'm a Harvard man," he persists. "I guess you can tell awright."

"Oh, did you go to school too?" Gladys asks brightly. "How about droppin' in the chop-suey joint for a while then?" Gladys wasn't that hepped on chop suey; she was just trying to give him an out.

"Anyplace you say," he assures her, with forty-five cents in his pocket. "And a show afters."

In this neighborhood, with only forty-five cents, you're a bum. But Sobotnik, even with two dollars, he's still a bum.

So in the chop-suey joint he orders the best and leaves a twenty-cent tip where Gladys could see how much he was leaving and was careful to have her walk out well in front of him. He wasn't taking any chance of having her block the single exit. "There's a bill on the table, Sam," he tells the cashier sort of low. "Keep the change."

The cashier catches the waiter's eye, and the waiter comes out after Sobotnik on the run, a pint-sized Chinee.

"No bill on table," he informs Sobotnik.

"You shouldn't have the kind of customers that steal money off tables then," Sobotnik says, and turns to walk off.

"No bill on table," and he holds Sobotnik's sleeve.

"You lookin' for a couple bruises, Jack?" And he takes off his specs. Southern honor is a pretty touchy thing. "Get lost before you get 'em," he adds. "I'm Sobotnik."

"Maybe you Bling Closby too. No bill on table."

"Say that again 'n I'll splatter your brains."

"No bill on table."

And then Gladys, upon whom he was depending to restrain him, starts helping him off with his coat.

He took off his vest too, to gain a little time. A small crowd gathered while he rolled up his left sleeve. The Chinee waited impassively. When he had the right one rolled up the Chinee yanked him forward by his shirt front and sent him backward with a poke in the teeth all in a single movement.

Sobotnik stretched out flat on his back in the snow. Gladys laid the coat and vest under his head for a pillow while she paid off the waiter out of her own purse.

When it was safe to get up he rose with dignity, but without gratitude. "That's a nice trick to play on a fellow, the first time you meet him," he accused her, "takin' the dollar I leave for the waiter 'n almost gettin' me killed account of you."

"You don't have to worry about that buck," she assured him. "You don't owe me nothin'."

A girl like that. She could have had any one of a dozen of the neighborhood regulars, she was so regular herself. But she has to keep straightening this stuffed bum up and smoothing the hurts in his vanity every time he falls over himself.

She helped him, too, the time he was put on probation just for sitting in a tavern drinking a couple beers. Some fellow came in, pretending to be drunk, and bought Sobotnik a couple shots. Sobotnik got afraid that some crook might roll his pal, so he let the fellow put his watch in Sobotnik's pocket for safekeeping. Then they had another drink and sure enough, the jerk begins hollering that someone stole his watch.

"It all just goes to show you, don't try to do things for people or you'll wind up on the short end of the funnel," he told Gladys after that one. "That's my one weakness—helpin' people."

She kept him out of trouble until he was off probation. Then he slipped on the ice one night, and that was the worst rap of all. The sidewalk was like a dance floor; anyone could have fallen. And have their elbow go through a store window. In the dark a thing like that could happen to anybody. A jewelry-store window. But just try to tell the police anything.

She got that charge changed to drunk and disorderly, but he got another two years' probation. The only time in those two years that the police persecuted him was when he took a short cut on his way to put a flower on his mother's grave. He took the short cut through an alley, minding his own business, on the way to the florist about 3 A.M., when the police picked him up. He had a little trouble explaining what the bathtub he was carrying on his back had to do with the florist; because it was, he conceded, a little clumsy for carrying violets. It appeared, then, that it had been left lying out in the middle of the alley and he'd merely been doing his duty as a good citizen in hauling it out of the way so that some milkman's horse wouldn't stumble over it in the dark and break a leg. There were a few other minor items missing from the plumber's, such as a flashlight and a crowbar; but the plumber dropped charges when Gladys took care of him, and the court let it go as malicious mischief.

He did ninety days, and when he got out he and Gladys announced their engagement at a neighborhood dance. There was a lot of drinking, and Gladys lost sight of him for a while. She didn't even know he'd left until she saw the flatfoot in the doorway. They had him over at the Racine Street Station, two blocks away, and a couple of us went with her.

Sure enough, there he was, threatening to bring a $100,000 suit against the Royal Cab Company, and a Royal Cab driver signing a complaint. All Rudy had done, he told her, was to blow the driver's horn to call attention to the fact that he wanted a cab. But the driver insisted that he was inside the cab, behind the wheel, and that it was only by accident he'd leaned on the horn.

The charge should have been tampering, but he got off with a misdemeanor. Gladys told the judge they were getting married the next Sunday morning. Well, Rudy didn't slip on the ice again until the Saturday night before the wedding.

That was down in Gold's Department Store, and a goodly crowd was there.

Sobotnik has been stealing little stuff down Gold's aisles since he was in short pants. He knew that the only gun in the place was an old secondhand cow-gun carried by the old man who runs the freight elevator. The elevator man is older than old Gold himself; all he does is to lean against the elevator, half asleep all day. It's like a pension.

Sobotnik got the notion that he could get the gun off the old man without getting himself killed. The rest, he figured, should be easy. He began drinking on the notion, next door to Gold's, and, as the afternoon wore on, the more natural the notion seemed. He wondered why he hadn't thought of it years before.

But when he swung out of the tavern and saw that Gold's lights were on already and the long street was darkening, he went cold sober and had to return, in a hurry, to the bar; without knowing whether it was the lights or the darkness that had frightened him. He got drunk all over again on Gladys's credit. It wasn't until after eight, with her credit exhausted, that he realized dimly that he'd been brooding too long on the notion. Now he had to do it, drunk or sober. He'd never drunk so much in his life; nor ever been so sober.

"I'll show her 'n all of 'em this time," he assured himself. And swung into the store without looking at the lights at all.

He walked straight down the middle aisle—Ladies' Hose and Hardware—to the freight elevator where the ancient house dick lounged. And shoved his finger hard into the small of the old man's back.

"Into the elevator, copper." He grabbed the fellow's gun, shoved him into the lift, and shouted shrilly, "Into the base-ment—*fast!*"

His glasses had clouded up, but he heard the elevator door crash shut and the whine of its cables as it started down. And saw the dozen-odd customers turning slowly toward him, like people in a slow-motion movie. Then there was something stuffy between his teeth and he realized it was his handkerchief and couldn't remember when he'd put it there. He saw himself then, a sallow-faced shrimp with spectacles, a green tie, and a mouthful of dirty handkerchief, waving an oversize cow-gun; he spat out the rag and heard his own voice, going far away down endless aisles. Like an endless echo carried forever by the thudding overhead fans.

"Face the wa-als. Everee-*body!*"

He saw them turning by ones and twos, old Gold with a steel washboard under his arm and an oversize janitor with a clothesline clutched in his paw. He saw them all turn slowly. Saw the cashier's small white face, white as a split apple against the parched black line of her brows and the red of her mouth. Saw the split apple of a face disappearing slowly, going down like the elevator had gone down; heard her fall and knew she had fainted.

He leaned far over the counter and banged the cash drawer open and saw bills piled there just for him. Tens and twenties and singles and fives rubbing rawly against the cold sweat of his palm—and then the shining dimes and quarters and halves in the last drawer over! He reached over, so far over that he was tottering, and the liquor began coming up in his throat. His lips moved as he leaned, drunk with greed. Heard a coin go tinkling along the floor, saw it was a quarter rolling toward the men's goods department, and followed it anxiously.

He recovered the quarter, while sixty pairs of eyes followed his antics, in front of a rack bearing spring topcoats. With-out hesitation Sobotnik pocketed the quarter, pulled the

brightest coat of all off the rack, and was struggling into it
when old Gold's nose appeared above the cosmetics counter.
He was three feet behind Sobotnik, and he held the steel
washboard in his hand: the momentum of his swing carried
him half across the counter and the washboard caught Sobotnik spam behind the ears. He went down as though he'd
been shot, and the cow-gun went clattering down the aisle.

Then half the crowd was shoving each other aside for the
distinction of sitting on Sobotnik while old Gold bound him
with clotheslines. In his haste and nervousness old Gold got
himself tied with Rudy. In the middle of the tying Sobotnik
raised his head once, wearily—and immediately got beaned
again with the washboard. Old Gold was still trying to free
himself.

In front of the store the whole neighborhood waited. They
cheered as the cops loaded Rudy, dragging old Gold, into
the wagon; but only Gladys recognized him, by his shoes,
for which she'd paid. All you could see of Rudy, in the yards
of clothesline, was the tip of his nose like a nose sticking out
of a giant beehive.

At the station it took the officers ten minutes to unravel
Sobotnik from old Gold and another ten to bring Rudy
around. When he finally came to and sat, dripping with the
ice water they'd poured on him, the first thing he saw was
Gladys. His glasses had been lost in the fray, and he blinked
at her with his shortsighted eyes, as though waiting impatiently
for her to explain this one to him.

It was the cops who wanted *him* to explain, but he didn't
care what any cop wanted. He ignored them. "Ask him what
he thought he was trying to do," the bewildered cops urged
Gladys.

"What made you think you could get away with a crazy
stunt like that, Rudy?" she asked gently, putting an arm about
his frail shoulders.

"I wasn't trying to get away with a thing, honey," Rudy

told her. "I went in there to try on a topcoat for the wedding, because I wanted to look real nice for you. I just took the gun along for protection was all. But when I was trying the coat on, all of a sudden they wouldn't even give me a chance to pay for it. If they'd just give me a chance to pay, that was all I wanted. You know as well as I do, honey, I'm not the kind who wants something for nothing."

The cops looked at Gladys and Gladys looked at the cops. She sighed.

"We'll have to get a lawyer instead of a priest now," she told him. "It looks like our honeymoon'll be in the House of Correction."

"I'll defend myself," Rudy announced. "I know my rights. I'll plead the unwritten law. It was self-defense. It's double jeopardy, 'n then I'll sue for false arrest." He couldn't get that false-arrest idea out of his head.

"If you don't button up I'll sue *you* for breach of promise," she warned him, getting mad for once. "You're going to cop a plea 'n do your time—every day of it. 'N when you get out you're going to be paroled to me 'n put on probation the rest of your natural life. You'll do all your lying at home hereafter, 'n when you're not at home you'll be at work."

Rudy didn't say a word. As though he was beginning, dimly, to realize something at last.

I guess it's been a good ten years since Rudy finished that stretch, and he hasn't been in trouble since.

But what Gladys meant by saying that about a poor man's pennies, that I still can't figure out.

the face on the barroom floor

or too much salt on the pretzels

A long generation ago, back in the twisted twenties when Chicago was still a dangerous city, a mild-mannered youth called Fancy used to tend bar in a dingy speak-easy on the wrong side of Van Buren Street. He pleased the women of the third-rate burlesques, as well as those of the curtained brothels, by mixing flattery with easy credit. When asked for a shot on the cuff he would answer reflectively, "I wouldn't want such a good-lookin' girl like you to be goin' down State Street thirsty," and would pay for the drink himself.

To this lopsided shambles, where the lighting was so dim that all faces looked alike, no police ever came. For Brother B., whose speak-easy it was, avoided police attention by locking the doors and drawing the shutters whenever a fight began. So although there were frequent brawls, they were never accompanied by the sort of excitement which might attract passers-by: only the steady thudding of the fans overhead and the desperate scuffle of the fighters' shoes would be heard when two thieves fought along the floor.

Suddenly it would be done, and the half-muted babble of voices would rise over the fans' steady thudding. Brother B. would be pulling up the shutters and the mild-mannered youth would be unlocking the doors. And everyone, victor and vanquished, would be having a shot on the house. The juke would begin again and everyone would feel that something had at last been achieved that day.

"Let's see what them damned rum-dums are up to at Brother B.'s tonight," the peep-show cuties would say after the last show. "I'd rather see a fight than a floor show any time. Maybe there'll be a *good* fight tonight."

If a man were hurt so seriously that he could not rise even to drink, Brother B. poured a shot down his throat personally, hoisted him like a potato sack over his shoulder, and would leave by the rear entrance, if no one else volunteered to take charge of the hurt one. There, secretly beneath the curved steel of the El, beneath the endless ties, Brother B. would deposit the fellow, upright and gently, in the alley entrance of Greek Steve's Bar. For Steve paid for protection and Brother B. did not: let Steve put it on his account with the law, and Brother B. would perjure himself for Steve the next time Steve got in trouble by himself.

That was how it was. That was the way it had always been. "And so," Brother B. explained to Fancy, "that's how it's always going to be."

Yet all the fights were unnecessary, except in so far as they saved Brother B. the money he might otherwise have had to spend for entertainers; and not one of them ever solved anything. The rum-dums of Brother B.'s speak-easy fought, it appeared, solely for their honor: because Polak Frank had called Dago John the worst cannon on the street. "You couldn't get your hand in a flour barrel," he had declared. Or because Nick Zingo had said outright, before everyone, that Jew Schiffo's girl friend was a worn-out tramp. They fought for their self-respect. For Jew Schiffo's tramp, as he proved on the spot, with his bare hands and the help of a broken salt shaker, was not even nearly worn out. "And she'll bring in more on a Sunday afternoon in Oak Park than your Mrs. could hustle right here on the street in a month of Saturday nights."

Actually, they fought to fill the emptiness of their lives as they filled their empty glasses. They fought—not because the liquor was in them, but because it did not fill them enough. Because there wasn't enough whisky on South State to fill the emptiness of a single lost man of them all. The twisted, bitter taste of defeat parched their throats, and they blamed it on Brother B.'s pretzels.

"Too much salt on the pretzels, Brother B.," they claimed.

"That's what gives the boys a thirst," Brother B. explained. "That's why the mustard bowls is always full too."

Nobody *had* to eat the free lunch, that was true. But no one was going to eat it without getting a raging thirst out of it; not so long as Brother B. was in business.

Therefore it was only when a man stood up unassisted to the bar, while the fallen one was being supported there from the floor, that he tasted the sweet and fleeting taste of victory. Sometimes it seemed that a man who, ordinarily, would need a pint to get high needed only a couple double-shots and a triumph to be drunken.

To be drunken, to be forever drunken; when the unlabeled whisky failed a man, a conquest could quicken his blood instead.

The worst brawl of all was the most unnecessary, and the least expected. It involved the two men seemingly least equipped, of any thereabouts, to fight anybody. And when it was done Brother B. put the chairs on the tables, drew the shutters for the last time, sprinkled a little sawdust along the floor, and closed his doors for keeps.

It began in the forenoon heat of the hottest mid-August the city had ever known, in a joking conversation between Fancy and a round-shouldered little peep-show peeler, from the Peekholes of Paris across the street, who called herself Venus Darling.

"Some duke was just in askin' for you, Venus," Fancy teased the girl. "Name of Rudolf somethin'—Valentino, I think he said—how'd I remember it? Said you'n him had a little quarrel 'n he wanted to patch it up. Had two messenger boys carryin' flowers. Said he'd be back in a half hour."

"Tell Rudy not to bother me no more when he comes back," Venus requested modestly, "tell him we're quits." And added seriously, "What would I want a oil-hair spook like that for anyhow, Fancy? Ain't I got the best man breathin'? What's any of them movie creeps got that Railroad Shorty ain't got?"

Fancy could have answered, "Two legs." For among the women of the brothels and burlesques Venus enjoyed a unique distinction: Railroad Shorty was a legless man. Her distinction was as great as though she had been a murderer's mistress.

"You know what they say about bein' lucky in love," she coaxed Fancy now. "How's my credit today, Honey-Hush?"

"You call me 'Honey-Hush' when you want credit," Fancy complained, "but when you got the price all I hear is 'One double-shot comin' up, Four-Eyes.' How is *that?*"

"I'm just fickle, Honey-Hush," she told him. "One day I feel one way 'n the next I feel just the opposite. I never know, one day to the next, what kinda person I'm gonna feel like I am tomorrow."

"It's all right," he assured her softly, dropping his eyes as though she had said something he had had no right to hear. "We're all wrong around here. It's the life we live, the life we all live." Then, to bring the conversation back to a kidding level: "I understand Railroad is a pretty good man with the women," he suggested, and leered heavily.

"You guys with legs ain't even in the same league with him," the girl answered coolly, adding salt to the beer.

"Is that where he gets his money then?" Fancy asked with mild wonder, thinking half to himself.

"Ain't you askin' a lot for a single beer?"

Fancy wiped his hands on the bar towel and apologized weakly, "I was only kiddin', Venus."

"I hope to Christ you were," she said—and sloshed the beer deliberately over the bar he'd just wiped, and was gone.

"What got into *that* one?" Brother B. asked.

"She's in a high-wheeled huff about somethin'," Fancy answered vaguely, drying the bar deliberately, wishing she hadn't come in at all.

"People just don't know my Shorty," Venus was complaining to the ticket taker at the Paris. "He don't take a cryin' dime off *any* woman, he ain't built like that. 'N people who go around sayin' he does, they just don't know how sensitive my Shorty can get. They don't know how high-strung my Shorty is. They don't know what *pride* that man got. I'll tell you what, Honey-Hush, right there is the proudest man on earth, that's all."

The ticket taker did not appear to hear. She was sixty cents over and was being dimly pleased with herself for having short-changed somebody without realizing it.

But she heard all the same.

The legless man had no need of any woman's money. He was a person of endless versatility and unfailing resources. He was a cardsharp of such cunning that not a dive on the street would hire him to deal, for the suckers pushed their chairs back when Shorty mounted himself to the table with anybody's deck. He had never been detected slipping a card; but nobody is quicker than a sucker at sensing something wrong even when he can't put a finger on what it is.

"You know your business too good," Brother B. once advised him. "I don't want to catch you on the con in here—not even matching pennies. I got to pertect my customers. They come here to drink 'n fight 'n eat them good old pretzels." And to show there were no hard feelings, he pushed the pretzel bowl, freshly salted, toward Shorty, and even lowered it to save the cripple the effort of rising off his platform.

"I know it's tough, Shorty," Brother B. acknowledged. "You're too small to cannon the street cars 'n too little to reach a damper. Maybe somebody could boost you through a transom though—you ought to be all right at snatching twists' purses too."

"I got no use for a purse-snatchin' man," Shorty affirmed proudly. "That's plain dirty *stealin'*."

Thus he was a man of singular virtue, and to this single virtue he held fast: no man could accuse him of taking a dime from any woman, by guile or strength or seduction.

But he was a competent mechanic and a good hand to overhaul a hot car in a hurry.

He could preach salvation in a voice so gentle that the mission stiffs would linger on after the doughnuts were passed; he could roar hell-fire at those working toward the doors so fearfully that they returned sheepishly to their seats.

He could mix a drink capable of knocking a man out in a minute or fix one that wouldn't take effect for five hours.

He could sell a tip on a burned-out horse and sell the same sucker again, an hour after the horse had run out.

He never glanced anxiously about for a clock, for he always knew the time. Although he carried no watch, he could tell you the time within two minutes, any hour of the day or night, rain, sun, fog, or snow.

He could guess a man's weight within two pounds merely by touching his clothes lightly once. He was seldom in need of money, and he spent so freely that, on those rare days when he ran short, the tavern boys felt he was holding out on them. "Shorty *always* got money," they assumed, and would throw spittoons at him in resentment. He would duck cheerfully, secretly flattered by their anger. But if one of them tried to kick him he would catch the offending foot and twist it mercilessly in his great hands until his man lay on the floor wriggling helplessly.

"Look at him now, boys!" Shorty would chortle, rolling in a semicircle on his platform, at a safe distance from his victim's hands. "Wrigglin' like a pig!"

And there would be no more spittoon-tossing for a while.

For on the floor he was murderous. His shoulders belonged to a professional strong man—as indeed he once had been. "I had an act with Strangler Lewis in the old days," he asserted. "All it was was him gettin' a strangle on me 'n me gettin' out of it 'n then me gettin' a nelson on him 'n him not bein' able to get out of it. Zybysko couldn't get out of my nelson, in the old days."

At night he would unstrap his hips, leap onto the bed in a single jump, and toss money about him like chicken feed. "Count it, boys!" he would shout. "Count it all!" He earned ten to twenty dollars a day selling a perfumed water which he bottled himself. And the women of the burlesques preferred it, because it was his, to Schiaparelli's finest.

He took an odd pleasure, too, in passing up men on crutches, or men with a limp. "Watch me pass up that peg-leg gimp," he would boast—and off he would scoot past the other cripple, almost brushing him off the walk. Then he'd stop the platform as abruptly as though it had brakes, wheel about, and wait challengingly, to see what, if anything, the gimp cared to do about it.

"I can do anythin' an able-bodied man can do," he warned all able-bodied men. "I'll outdrink 'n outfight any man of you. You name it 'n I'll do it better." His single fear seemed to be that others might regard him as handicapped. He was so devoted to proving his powers that every dawn was an open challenge to prove himself anew, to himself and to all men, in all things, before night.

Smoking the first bitter cigarette of the dawn, he would resolve fiercely, in the breaking day, to yield to no man and to give no quarter: as none had been given him.

"Don't you go getting into no trouble over that girl," his housekeeper warned him on the evening of that sultry August day, fumbling with her keys. "That boy got a big mouth but he's only a boy and he don't mean nobody harm."

"What boy? What girl?"

"Don't pertend you ain't heard a word when the whole hotel is talkin'."

Shorty wheeled himself toward her and she backed involuntarily toward the door. Her hand was on the knob when he caught her by the wrist and twisted the keys out of her hand into his lap.

"You don't have to get rough. Gimme my keys. Venus told him she pays you off to stud her, that's what she told *me*." She slammed the door behind her.

Venus was resting. She was due to put on her strip act in fifteen minutes downstairs, and was lying alone in the dark when she heard him scratching like a cat at the door. He wheeled in before she had time to rise; she yanked on the little bulb above her bed. Shielding her eyes from the light, she feigned anger at his rudeness; at heart she was always happy to see him. He wheeled to the bed's edge until his great shaggy head rested on her pillow and she lay back to look directly into his eyes. They were lion's eyes, lit by yellow flares.

"How long I been takin' money off you?" he asked.

She saw he was serious and shook her head dubiously; yet oddly wishing, somehow, that he really had. She sat up.

"First you come bargin' in here like a damned tank 'n then you insult me." She glanced nervously at the door left ajar behind him, as though sensing trouble coming through it soon.

He was unfastening the straps to his platform. He wasn't one for half measures. Fear came up in her throat in a long dry burning there.

"You got somethin' awful wrong, Honey-Hush," she told him. "It was that Fancy said that to *me*." She sniffled, dabbing at her eyes. "I told him he better not let you hear him sayin' anything like that."

He studied her a long moment. Then wheeled, slowly and mechanically, across the uncarpeted floor and down the long and dim-lit corridor, leaving the door swinging a little behind him.

Sitting on the edge of the bed, she heard the platform clumping down the stair well and glanced at her watch: she'd have just time to get downstairs for her act.

That night the mild-mannered youth dreamed of the legless man. Lying on his rented bed, he heard a slow and heavy clumping, down some endless gaslit stair well. The legless man was coming. The light was on and he was sitting upright, paralyzed with an unnamed terror, watching the doorknob turning slowly, hoping uselessly that it would be too high for Shorty to turn all the way. He still had time to lock it—the key was still in the lock. Moving like a man wading in a slow-motion sea, stiff with dread, it was almost too late, almost too late, and saw, as the door opened slowly, slowly, that there was no one there. No one down a long and fog-lit hall. No one—he knew for sure—in the whole vast hotel. In an access of terror, his fingers fumbled, weak as water, at the key. And wakened at last with the light still burning and the key still in the lock, glinting a little from the light's reflection.

He rose shakily and glanced at his watch. It was hours before his usual time to rise. And so sat on the edge of his rented bed and asked himself what harm, after all, a halfy on a box could do to an able-bodied grammar-school graduate like himself. He sat on the disheveled bed, watching the lights of State Street blazing on and off, red and green, red and green; blowing brave smoke rings from cheap cigarettes; till the signs were darkened and the dawn came on and traffic picked up at last.

Fancy was untying his apron, at noon, preparing to run across the street for coffee, when Shorty coasted in. He wheeled himself, on his ball-bearinged platform, like a shattered statue. A man of overweening vanity, he enjoyed nothing so much as posturing on his stage, turning this way and that, if there were women near, to exhibit his classic features, his overdeveloped biceps, his torso as lean as a lifeguard's, and his neat little pointed brown beard. As he coasted past the bar he pointed mockingly at Fancy and called out, "Where'd you get them ears, Four-Eyes? Boys! Pipe the ears on Four-Eyes!"

No one had ever noticed Fancy's ears before; there was nothing particular about them to notice. Fancy leaned bleakly over the bar, trying to smile. It was a fine time to go for coffee.

"Your own ears ain't so little, Shorty," he replied, showing he knew a joke when he heard one.

Shorty wheeled back.

"You say something about *my* ears, fellow?"

Fancy fumbled with the apron; it had become knotted and his fingers were as numb as they'd been in his dream. The metal echo of the juke rang faintly once and died forever.

"What's the *matter* with my ears, Four-Eyes?"

Half a dozen derelicts gathered in a restless semicircle behind Shorty, fearing that the incident might end in a handshake. One, with his cap shading his eyes, cupped his palms to Shorty's ear and whispered in a whisky bass:

"Fancy was just sayin' he'd go fer you, boots 'n shoes, if you tried gettin' rough with him."

Another advised Shorty's other ear:

"He ast Venus why she has anythin' to do with a stinkin halfy."

"He said she paid you off."

"He said that's where you get your dough."

Railroad Shorty kept his great voice low. "Whyn't you come out on the floor 'n talk it over, Four-Eyes?" he asked softly.

"We can talk it out over the bar, Shorty. I got nothin against you."

"He's jealous," the shadow-capped voice put in, " 'cause he can't take Venus off you. He makes up dirty stories about you 'n her. He draws dirty pitchers of her 'n you too."

Railroad spoke with finality. "Come out of there 'r I'll come 'n get you."

Fancy waited for Brother B. to tell Shorty to blow. Instead he heard Brother B. locking the doors.

Fancy waited until he heard the shutters being pulled. Then he laid his glasses carefully on the cash register and noticed that the sign above the register read: No CREDIT.

The jackrollers and derelicts moved back against the wall, urging each other like men with the public welfare uppermost in mind.

"Give the men room now, fellas."

"Get them tables back, Zingo, so's nobody gets hurt."

"Let them have it out, fellas, that's what they want."

"No interferin', a square shake fer everybody."

"Make 'em shake hands first, so's there won't be no hard feelin's."

"No, after they're through is better, then it's just a mis-understandin' sort of. They're *both* good fellas."

"Then let's see which is the best," Brother B. put in impatiently.

Railroad wheeled to the end of the bar, to meet Fancy head on. Fancy leaned over with an iron spittoon in his hand.

"Back off 'r I'll bean you," he warned, making his voice almost tough. He waved the spittoon. Shorty backed the platform a foot.

"Farther. Back to the door."

Shorty wheeled backward reluctantly, his hands holding the little wheels in order to reverse them in a split moment; he rolled back an inch at a time, until the back of his head touched the knob of the washroom door. Fancy came out from behind the bar with the spittoon in his hand. Shorty wheeled forward slowly, one arm protecting his head. When the platform was almost upon him, and Shorty's arms were reaching, Fancy slammed the spittoon, like a discus, into Shorty's chest and rocked him like a stump in a storm; but his platform came on without wavering, his great arms reaching.

Fancy's fleeing heel slipped off Shorty's fingers but sent the boy stumbling; he recovered himself and came up, in the same motion, with a long swinging kick that caught the halfy squarely between the eyes. Shorty banged blindly into the bar, bounded back, caught his wheels, and covered his head with both hands. Fancy clambered onto the nearest table and squatted there miserably, trembling in the limbs like a puppy and listening for the sound of the shutters being raised. But heard only the steady, relentless whir of the fans overhead. And saw Shorty wiping the blood out of his eyes. He held his bandanna down to the cripple.

"Better brain him while he's blind," Fancy heard a low voice advising, and realized he must or be brained himself.

For they all knew that he didn't have it in him to do what he had to do. They knew to a man that he couldn't.

Shorty cleared his eyes deliberately. He too knew, folding the bandanna neatly and returning it back up to the boy.

"Thank you," Shorty said.

And hurled the table over with a single twist of his fingers, sending Fancy sprawling comic-strip fashion, all arms and legs. Shorty held him then, face down to the floor, steadying the floundering youth; then twisted once, like winding a coiled spring, and spun him halfway across the room, head over heels and skidding. Shorty scooted swiftly beside him, dragged him back to the middle of the floor by the collar, and the crowd closed in.

This was *it*.

Pale with pleasure, their faces in the half-light looked dimmed and bloated and blurred, like faces seen under water. Somewhere toward the back a woman giggled like a nervous girl. Then Shorty got Fancy's head beneath his shoulder, and the room seemed to smoke with blood.

Shorty rolled the boy over on his side, straddled the one arm by riding over it with the platform, and lifted the arm that lay protectively over the boy's eyes. He lifted it carefully and laid it aside, and the boy lay deathly still. As though hoping that by complete defenselessness he might, at this final moment, gain mercy.

"He looks done in, Shorty."

Shorty, arm upraised like a club, looked down at the small white face, so helpless now that it looked more like a child's than a man's.

"He's cold, Shorty."

And it was true: they crowded in to see. The boy was cold; the eyes, bright and unseeing with shock, were dilated. As the arm came down, with a soft and soggy sound.

It rose in a full swing back to the floor, till the knuckles touched the platform's edge, and swung forward and down, like a stone-crusher, in a full and crushing arc.

"Oof."

Someone was getting sick.

When he raised it again the men watched for it to falter; they drew back a little, as from a mechanical device, and it did not falter. Till, with each fresh blow, each man felt redeemed for the blow his own life had been to him. Till the face on the floor was a scarlet sponge, and Shorty's teeth were chattering as with a chill.

With each animal groan from the floor each man breathed more freely.

"I like t' get up close t' accidents," the woman's voice remarked. They turned, and it was Venus, her lips full and red with pleasure and her eyes alight. Kneeling, she put her arms about Shorty and kissed him full on the mouth.

Shorty looked around like a man in a lifting daze, saw the girl and the men and the bar and Brother B., and the drawn shades. Then he looked down.

And flung the girl from him with a low moan of disgust.

For the face on the floor was no longer a face. It was a paste of cartilage and blood through which a single sinister eye peered blindly. The broken mouth blew minute bubbles of froth and blood.

"He had it comin'," Venus assured her man. "You done just right." His head turned slowly toward her; and as it turned she drew back, twisting her fingers before her and looking, of a sudden, like a debauched old woman. Shorty tightened the straps of his platform, speaking in a confidential, hurried whisper to the face on the floor.

"Yer carpet rags from now on, son," he mourned, "carpet rags before yer time, like me'n all the peoples." And his voice was so melancholy that only its depth made it familiar. Then he heard Brother B. raising the blinds, and stroked his little pointed beard reflectively, blinking at the late sun that blinked back at him from the rising shutters. Then wheeled swiftly down the long aisle between the tables and the bar and out into the pavement-colored light.

Wheeling fast and noiselessly down the long, unlovely street, the little beard pointing in the wind, the derelicts watched him go and wondered what he had meant.

"Like Jesus Christ ridin' his cross 'stead of carryin' it," someone observed as though resenting such a variation.

"He looks more like the devil t' me," Venus Darling said bitterly.

"He'll look more like twenty to life if he don't keep on wheelin'," Brother B. added threateningly.

"You put too much salt on them pretzels, Brother B.," someone complained. "They made Halfy so thirsty he didn't know when to stop."

Brother B. carried Fancy to the rear of Greek Steve's Bar, and returned to sprinkle sawdust along the floor. Then he bought a drink for everyone in the place, but did not drink with a man of them; and when they had drunk he sent all of them out onto the street for keeps.

He locked the door, poured himself a shot, turned on the juke, and sat alone beside it, among the empty chairs, thinking of his own life and of all the days to come.

When morning came he was still sober, but the juke had

long stopped playing. Although he had drunk steadily all night, he had never felt soberer in his life. Moving like an old man, though he was barely forty, he put the chairs on the table and his cap on his head. Then he went to the register, punched out No SALE, and closed his doors forever.

the brothers' house

It was not I that sinned the sin,
The ruthless body dragged me in.
Whitman

All that day David lay on his bunk, thinking of a different place—a glad, bright place. Eyes closed, he saw the great prairie once more. He saw the quiet old house in which he was born, the house where his mother had worked and prayed. He saw the shadowed porch and the trim green lawn. He saw the sunny dooryard where tall lilacs grew. He saw the pleasant meadow where the great oak stood. He saw the sloping corn-land that rolled to the running sky and he seemed to smell the windy smell of clouds across the earth. He remembered how as a boy he had played in the sun in the summer; how the wind had gone wailing through the white nights of winter; how dead leaves had drifted in brown months of autumn; and how in the springtime all things were so fair, so tender and green, so young and unspoiled, so strange and so sweetly troubling. He opened his eyes. The cell was gray as death. The stench of a thousand imprisoned men hung in the air like a low gray pall. David thought, "I want to go back."

All that night David lay wakeful, remembering, regretting, hoping. In five months he would be free once more, free to breathe again and to live. Should he then return to the city? Of a sudden he hated the city, its manifold faces and narrow streets, the dark ways and the shouting. He hated the men who had used him more intensely than ever he'd hated his brothers. Should he beseech those brothers that he might return? Or should he go back without supplication—merely go back, merely come to a house that he had known, to a door that once had stood wide? Would they embrace him? He wondered. They were all four strong men. They were all four hard.

All that winter David went about his duties with the thought of freedom in his heart. All that sad winter he lived in hope. The desire for home sharpened. He began counting the hours of the slow days; then the minutes of the slow hours; and before the end he numbered the very seconds passing.

For David sensed that he stood at the gate of a different life —that these days and hours and seconds were the last unclean fringe of the old way.

Then it was April, and his time was up, and his life was beginning again. One sunny forenoon all the windows of the great courthouse were opened. All the long winter they had been locked, but now they were flung wide. And the morning when that happened was the morning David was again given freedom. He stood before the judge with his cap in his hand, with the clean breeze from the newly opened windows in his hair; and he promised then to live hereafter as heretofore he had not. Thus three times had David stood before. Three times in the past had he promised what he promised now.

He came out on the sunny street, blinking. How strange it was to walk in the open! How sweet it was just to breathe! He could not walk fast enough, could not breathe deeply enough. So he ran. Ran just a little way, he could not run far, he was not a strong man. And for twenty months he had been where the good sun never pierces, in the place where no man runs.

He slept in a field that night a dozen miles from any town. Once, toward morning, he woke suddenly, with a fear like a hand at his heart: he felt he was back on his prison bunk with the stench of caged men hanging, as a cloud suspended, in the

gray air about him. He sat bolt upright, fear shaking his heart
loosely about under his breast. It was a full half minute before
he realized; then he saw a small light from a farmhouse or a
barn shining to him from far in the distance, and he was reassured. But the little light went out as he watched—and before he fell once more to sleep he felt afraid of something; he
did not know quite what.

He was up with the sun, swinging along in the first faint blue
of day. And all that day joy kept him. All about him was so
beautiful that he wanted to sing; yet David knew no song. In
his life had been little of laughter. He wanted to sing, yet something hurt all the while. It was as though outwardly his spirit
rose and rejoiced, yet to itself sorrowed secretly.

Eighteen days David walked the way, feeling that now, at
last, he was going home. On the afternoon of the nineteenth
day he came to the great oak; and because he had rested in its
shade so often in his youth, he lay down beneath it now. The
small bent grasses pricked his palms and pressed themselves
among his fingers. Long shadows trembled in the light.

Once, when he was not quite twelve, David had run away
from home for a full day, and his brothers had found him
asleep beneath this very tree. He remembered how his mother
had cried over him when they brought him home all tears. This
time she would not be there. She would not be there tonight.
He fell to sleep remembering, and when he awoke it was dusk.

For a moment he felt uneasy, as men who have been often
mocked and shamed sometimes feel upon waking. Then he
jumped to his feet and shook the feeling off, for he had now
but a little space to go. Yet, somehow, the uneasiness within
remained.

As he walked through the dusk he passed a young orchard,
and the odor of cherry blossoms came fainting to him. Somewhere to his left a drowsy dove was calling low and patiently.
The great moon came over the edge of the prairie and it was
night.

O sweet maytime, O deep good air,
O prairie night so darkly fair,
O lilacs growing by the stair,
Shall no far April heal my pain?
Shall no spring make me whole again?

It was misting moonlight when he came in sight of the
house. How quietly it waited there! It looked like a dark-
cowled nun kneeling in prayer beneath great stars, the moonlight a halo about her bent head. How quietly it waited there!
The memory of his last night in it came upon him. He had
stood in the dooryard that night with his brothers about him,
like a caught thing. Jesse had beaten him, the brothers watching in a dark wolf-circle. How shameful that had been!

Now a lamp burned in the kitchen. Men were talking there.
He leaned on the gate, he listened intently: their voices came
to him in a slow curving murmuring, in a wave that broke and
fell, never falling quite to silence, never rising quite to clarity.
They perhaps had been plowing all day. Plowing the brown
earth.

Suddenly something was unfamiliar. Suddenly something
unseen was changed. Something was suddenly strange and
hostile. He felt he did not wish to go home after all. He felt ill.

The walls are bare within,
The brothers sit in a row,
There once was a woman here,
But that was long ago.

When the tall lamp flickers yellowly
And the gibbous moon rides low,
I see her face in the windy dark,
And I long for the long ago.

Someone was coming toward him. It was Jesse, he knew his
stride; David clung to the gate in his weakness. How strong,
how kind Jesse looked! Love for the brother choked him, his

love closed his throat. Jesse was speaking to him, and he could not reply.

"What do you want?" Jesse asked.

David could only raise his face to be recognized. Jesse saw.

"Well, what do you want?" he repeated.

please don't talk about me when i'm gone

You know what I was thinkin' when that crowd moved back a little to make room for me to get into the wagon? I was thinkin', my whole life it's the first time anyone made room for me. And now just look what for.

The boy never would've made a pass at me, because he was the innocent kind 'n figured me 'n Doc for man 'n wife.

"This lad is regular as rain," Doc would say to some bookie. "Anythin' he bets I stand back of." They're all used to Doc's line, they know it's all bluff. But the boy'd blush 'n be so tickled he wouldn't know how to thank Doc enough. He thought he was on his way to the big-time for sure.

Doc'd buy him a beer 'n interdoos him to some M.C. 'n the boy'd bow from the waist, like I guess he must of done in the old country, 'n say, "How-dee-doo, I'm interested in the tee-ayter also." He'd say each word real plain, like he'd memorized it.

'N sometimes the way he just *said* things, makin' his eyes so wide-like behind them glasses, he reminded me of a little kid peekin' over the edge of the table at what the big folks is eatin' before he's bare able to walk by hisself. Eyes big as saucers. 'N just as friendly, 'n natural-like. But he could say things out of books me 'n Doc wouldn't even understand, even though Doc always made off like he did anyhow.

"I can't swallow that lingo," Doc'd tell me. But I kind of *liked* hearin' him talk in that slow Dutchy way. His people was still in Holland, he said, they'd shipped him across with the family bank roll before the Germans come in, when he was only fourteen, him 'n uncle 'n aunt. He hadn't heard from his folks since the war ended 'n the uncle was supposed to be holdin' the bank roll until the boy became of age. When that happened, he said, he was going to take his money 'n go to Hollywood 'n be like Charles Boyer. Doc never asked me what I thought about the boy's story, and I never did make up my mind about how much of it was true and how much wasn't—what he was leaving out and what he was putting in.

I showed the rookie the aquarium one afternoon 'n another time I took him out to see the new baby hippo at the zoo. It was like takin' a kid around; I felt like his mother even though I was only four years older. He was surprised at somethin' new every minute, wherever I took him. And I was that dead sick of Doc it made me happy just to look at the rookie.

Doc, he'd follow him one night to the Y.M.C.A. on Wabash 'n the next to some cheap hotel on Harrison. He never stayed in the same place two nights runnin', Doc said, 'n never registered under the same name twice neither. One night he stayed up all night out by the airfields in Cicero watchin' the big planes comin' from California 'n fancy fellas in knickers gettin' out of them with their fancy dames. Me 'n Doc set in a tavern acrost the way keepin' a eye on him, 'n Doc was that scared the boy was gonna take off in one of them things he couldn't hardly set still.

"We got to get him now, Rose," he says. "It's time to put the hooks in. 'N we're gonna break it off in there when we do." And there was the rookie in a college-cut coat gogglin' up at the sky 'n Doc in a army overcoat a size too big for him fumblin' with a dime beer. If I could've been alone with that sprout two minutes I would've tipped him off right then 'n there to hop into one of them Hollywood planes. I bet he would have took me along too. I bet if I would've just asked he would of took me up in one of them over-the-Loop rubber-neck spins they have. That boy was kind enough for anybody.

But that Doc. I could hardly wipe my chin them days but I have to ask him can I first.

"Doc is going to Cleveland on a business trip tomorrow," I told the rookie. "I'm going to be awful lonely." I hated to do it, with Doc settin' behind the curtain to be sure I said it right. But that rookie, he was grateful as a pup. When I started lettin' him stay nights he'd spend half the night plannin' on how I should go about gettin' a divorce. I never had the heart to tell him that'd be a hard thing to do without bein' married to somebody first. Then, just when it was all set that I was to leave Doc, I'd have to decide that I was too old for the rookie, and everything'd be off again. We wasted an awful lot of time that way.

Then we got him drunk in a black-and-tan hot spot 'n the waitress brought him back change for a twenty, 'n Doc covered the change with his hand.

"You stole it," Doc tells him, "you stole every cryin' dime layin' here."

The boy just sort of hung on me, scared stiff, 'n Doc had the hooks in then for fair. And I was that dead sick of the whole lousy racket I pushed back my chair 'n shoved the rookie off.

"Cry on somebody else's neck," I told him.

Doc helped me on with my coat 'n tucked my scarf in around my neck; I felt his fingertips through the silk and they were cold, so cold. I felt his hand on my hand 'n a bill in it 'n I took it 'n set down again.

Doc had me take him to the Dreamland then, a tea joint with a cigar-store front on South Dearborn. The stuff just made him sick to his stomach 'n headachy at first, till he didn't know what he wanted no more. Only Doc knew what was good for him then; 'n it was him give the boy the needle, while he was drunk, for the first time. After that I kept him full to the gills. Don't blame me too much. I know I done all wrong.

The last night we went to the Dreamland we went there alone, just me 'n the rookie. I stuffed the crack under the door 'n plugged the keyhole, 'n it had been six years since I'd fooled with the stuff that serious. When he felt hisself goin' under he begun cryin', awful hoarse-like, 'n I just held him. I didn't mind holdin' him no more by that time. I didn't know what else to do no more but hold him. When he'd cried hisself out he come out with it all at once:

"I can get more cash, Rose. Lots more. I can get all we want."

I didn't think there was any more cash in the world than just what he was carryin' around loose on him every day. I thought it was just the junk gettin' to him. And I wanted the business over 'n done, one way or another, any way at all. I had the old feelin' I used to have, when me'n Doc first started keepin' comp'ny, that I was wadin' in a lake late at night up to my chin 'n the water gettin' deeper all the time 'n tryin' to push me off my feet, 'n not knowin' where the shore was any more in the dark. 'N I was that scared of Doc, 'n for all the stuff he had on me that he'd put me up to in the first place, I hardly knew where to turn.

He stood up slow-like 'n took off his coat 'n vest 'n tore the vest linin' up the back 'n it was stuffed with foldin' money.

"I ain't begun to spend, Rose," he says, like sayin' it in a dream, 'n I seen he hadn't. I never seen that much money in my life. And it was all stole. Every dollar there was stole.

"Put it back, Dutch," I asked him, 'n I never wanted nobody to do somethin' for me as bad as I wanted him to do that. I was that scared 'n there was that much of it. There was too much. I wasn't up to that much money. "Hide it somewheres till you're older," I told him. "Hide it under a pillow." And a wave pushed me over so easy-like 'n gentle backwards till there wasn't no more shore no more nowhere.

"Take it, Rose," he says. "Buy yourself a woods violet. Buy yourself a sunflower. It's to remember me by." And he begun that awful hoarse cryin' again 'n I felt him huggin' my knees. But I couldn't think, for the smell of the junk 'n for bein' that sick of Doc.

"I'll take it to the tailor myself," was all I could think of, 'n I didn't know what I meant myself till I seen the vest tore in two on the floor. I knew then I had to start thinkin' of somethin' else before Doc showed.

But for the life of me I couldn't. My feet'd go out from under me 'n the whole dirty world'd slip clean away. I'd forget I was a couple years older'n him—but I couldn't forget, even then, how different me 'n him really was, as much as we liked each other.

"Run downstairs 'n get a needle 'n thread," I told him. "I'll sew it up with all but one fifty inside—that'll be enough for us to get out of town on. Do you want to take one of them big planes to Hollywood 'n take me along?"

But I didn't say it—it was too late to say it then. It just went through my head like I wished it was still time to say it. And when I looked up he was standin' over me, lookin' down with that bucktoothed kid grin. "Do you really think I look like Boyer?" he asks me. 'N when he said it he looked so helpless 'n foolish 'n kind, I didn't want no bad thing to come to him ever, 'n my head cleared a little.

"Take them glasses off once, Dutch," I asked him. "I want to see what color your eyes are. To remember you by."

He took them off and they had the snowbird look in them sure enough. Even his nose was white.

"Put them back on now," I told him. "We're goin' back 'n tell your uncle you're sorry for what you done. We'll bring him his money back for a nurse for you. You're going to need one for a couple months." I got my own clothes on 'n shoved the bills under the pillow 'n opened the window 'n unplugged the keyhole. The street was clear 'n there wasn't a sound nowheres,

like the El had quit runnin' a year ago 'n all the cabbies had
died. "Get your things on 'n get hold of yourself," I told him,
unlocking the door. "We're clearing out of all this filth."

But his eyes was just points. He just set on the bed scrapin'
the back of his left hand with the fingernails of his right 'n
makin' a little grinding sound with his teeth. And the knob
turned in my hand.

There he was, in a spanty-new topcoat 'n new tan shoes 'n
a green-stripe tie. And playing the outraged husband for fair.

"I was just on my way to phone you, Doc," I said. But he
didn't even look at me. He just locked the door behind him 'n
went over to the bed 'n lifted the rookie's head 'n pulled the
eyelids back till only the whites showed. Then he slapped him,
hard, with the other hand. And the boy grinned like he hadn't
felt a thing.

"Good enough," says Doc. "Now what about you?"

"It's all under the pillow," I said, 'n knew I'd just done the
smartest thing of my life in puttin' it there, 'n the luckiest. And
the sorriest.

"He can get more, too," I told Doc. "He got stuff he ain't
even counted."

"You damned right he'll get more," Doc said, like the rookie
owed him more. "Now get his clothes back on him. Me'n
Dutch got to have a man-to-man talk."

When I'd dressed him Doc took him by the arm, 'n out the
door 'n down the stairs they went, like the closest pair of pals
you'd ever hope to see drunk together. Last I seen of them
was from behind the curtain. The rookie was gettin' into the
cab lookin' like somebody else had dressed him all right 'n it
went south down Dearborn. I was that glad to be rid of Doc,
after all them years, I would of felt happy, kind of, except for
losin' the rookie. And for thinking whatever would he think of
me someday when he'd realize what we'd pulled on him. It
made me so blue, for what he'd think of me when that day
came, I couldn't start to tell you.

Must of been almost a month 'n me thinking, hoping, that Doc was all in the past. I was still feeling blue as ever over the rookie though, passing the time getting plastered at McCoy's place, behind the Rock Island viaduct off Federal Street. I was about half stiff when Doc came in the door, and I got clear as a bell the minute I saw him. I hope I never get that clear again.

"You been gone some time, Doc," I said. "You look like you ought to sober up 'n start all over on a big one."

"I ain't been drunk in a month," he says. But I could barely hear him say it.

I'd seen him wear sporty clothes before, but nothin' like what he had on now: it was loud green checks and a zoot cap so wide it flopped over his ears and made his face so shadow-like I thought all of a sudden how his fingertips was so cold on me that time.

"I been tryin' to find you so long, Rose," but he didn't have no voice left hardly at all. "We're all set now." And he pulled out a wad he could have bought the tavern with.

"You got a sore throat, Doc?" I asked him; but he just shook his head sad-like, No. But he didn't talk no louder. I shoved my shot glass 'n the bottle toward him 'n he set the bottle aside. Like he just wasn't hisself no more. I felt a little sorry for him then, just for a minute.

Then I remembered the trusting sort I was when I met him 'n how if it hadn't been for him I never would of knew the life I've had at all 'n I didn't feel sorry no more. I felt glad. I thought of the rookie 'n poured myself a stiff one. He sat lookin' down at my shot glass till I got all tight inside. Then the juke began Ella Fitzgerald singin' "Please Don't Talk About Me When I'm Gone."

"Play me that again, Doc," I asked him before it stopped, 'n he fished a nickel out of a five-'n-dime change purse, a buffalo one; just like he didn't realize what he was holdin' at all. The little blue light went on when the nickel hit bottom 'n lit up his face all blue-like; then the light went off 'n the record started.

If you could have seen him, though, you might not think no husky little Irish blondie like me could get scared of a underfed little shoneen like that, all wore out 'n mossy-toothed like he looked. He sort of leaned against the box like he was restin' on it 'n it begun Tommy Dorsey doin' "On the Beach at Waikiki."

"You still go for that Hawoyun swing, Doc?" I asked him when he set down again. "They got that 'Moon of Manakoora' on number 'leven." I poured him a shot but he let it stand 'n I knew it was comin' then.

"He almost give me the slip, Rose. He was halfway to the Coast before I caught up with him. He won't see no more Boyer movies. I guess his ticker was bad. I only hit him once."

Only once. And he didn't say with what.

He didn't say a thing for so long that I put my hand over my mouth. I knew if I didn't I'd start screamin' 'n never stop.

"So we got to be more careful, Rose," he says, watchin' me close while I drank his shot, 'n his lips didn't move when he said it. "From now on we got to be careful *all* the time. You know how careful that is, Rose? That means say you're asleep, I got to be careful for you while you're sleepin', so's you don't start jabberin'. I got to be careful for both of us. I come a long way, I been tired a long time, just to be careful about you. You liked that boy too much, that's why things went wrong. The neighborhood is awright but cops is cops all over 'n they get a dame like you talkin' just as easy."

He tried to drink then, but he couldn't make it. It was like his throat had sort of closed up on him. "We got to lay off this joint. We got to quit shootin' the bottle altogether till things blow over. You might get stiff 'n start jabberin'."

"You shouldn't ought to of told me. You shouldn't ought to of come back at all. I was hopin' to Jesus you wouldn't. I was hopin' I'd never have to lay eye on you again." If I would of said another word I would've started bawlin'. It was the first time I'd talked back to him my whole endurin' life, and I didn't do it just for the rookie. It was for myself too. And for throwin' myself away on a sewer rat 'n knowin' I'd never be free of him ever now.

"I didn't want to come back, Rose. I know for a long time how you feel. But that's just why I had to come back, knowing how you feel. You know too much about me 'n I know too much about you 'n the cops know too much about the both of us."

I wanted to hear that Ella Fitzgerald doin' "Please Don't Talk About Me" just once more. I felt like I wasn't gonna hear no more juke music no more, never.

"Look," Doc says, just like he hadn't got through sayin' it all, "say you're not careful just once, say you're sleepin' 'n just your trap starts talkin' 'n it ain't me you're sleepin' with— you see my point of view?" And I seen then what he come back for all right. I seen it plain as the egg stain on that fancy green-stripe tie.

I set up with him four nights in that room, tryin' to catch a little sleep daytimes so's I wouldn't fall asleep of nights. I couldn't even go downstairs to the grocery. That's how far he trusted me. 'N him settin' on the edge of the bed noddin' under that zoot cap, 'n wakin' up 'n starin' at me, tryin' to get his courage up 'n his strength back, to do what he had to do. Noddin' 'n wakin' up, till I couldn't stand it another hour. I'd get all tight inside, like I'm gettin' ready to scream and I can't even scream. Then he sent the housekeeper's boy-scout kid downstairs for a dozen eggs, 'n didn't take his eyes off me the whole time I was cookin' them.

They was to settle his stomach, he says. But I knew it was me he was gettin' ready to settle. I knew it was almost time.

I was asleep in the rocker when he come at me from behind. He had the boy-scout kid's ball bat 'n I just opened my eyes 'n seen it swingin' down at me 'n got my hands up 'n the rocker went over backwards.

I remember seein' him layin' face down then across the rocker, like he was prayin' almost, 'n I looked around fer the ball bat 'n it was in my hand. I walked around to where the light hit his face, 'n there wasn't no face. And still I couldn't let go of the ball bat. 'N still I couldn't scream.

Then I seen the hall door been open the whole time.

I closed it soft-like, as though it made any difference if I slammed it then. I set the rocker up right 'n pulled his cap down over his eyes. Then I set in the rocker 'n just rocked 'n waited. You won't believe it, but I fell asleep holdin' the ball bat. I don't know how long I slept but I heard the bat clatterin' down a million steps, gettin' louder every time it hit, all the way down a million steps, 'n just before it hit bottom I woke up 'n someone was knockin' on the hall door.

All I done was say, "Come in."

It was the boy-scout kid come up to get his ball bat. He was wearin' the boy-scout suit 'n chewin' a candy bar with the paper peeled back like it was a banana. Then I heard him runnin' two steps at a time downstairs 'n knew he was on his way to do a good deed.

It was how them people moved back to let me in the wagon I won't be forgetting. Not that it was the first time I'd had to climb into the wagon. It was just the first time my whole life people was makin' a little room for me.

And now just look what for.

he swung and he missed

It was Miss Donahue of Public School 24 who finally urged Rocco, in his fifteenth year, out of eighth grade and into the world. She had watched him fighting, at recess times, from his sixth year on. The kindergarten had had no recesses or it would have been from his fifth year. She had nurtured him personally through four trying semesters and so it was with something like enthusiasm that she wrote in his autograph book, the afternoon of graduation day, "Trusting that Rocco will make good."

Ultimately, Rocco did. In his own way. He stepped from the schoolroom into the ring back of the Happy Hour Bar in a catchweight bout with an eight-dollar purse, winner take all. Rocco took it.

Uncle Mike Adler, local promoter, called the boy Young Rocco after that one and the name stuck. He fought through the middleweights and into the light-heavies, while his purses increased to as much as sixty dollars and expenses. In his nineteenth year he stopped growing, his purses stopped growing, and he married a girl called Lili.

He didn't win every one after that, somehow, and by the time he was twenty-two he was losing as often as he won. He fought on. It was all he could do. He never took a dive; he never had a setup or a soft touch. He stayed away from whisky;

he never gambled; he went to bed early before every bout and he loved his wife. He fought in a hundred corners of the city, under a half dozen managers, and he fought every man he was asked to, at any hour. He substituted, for better men, on as little as two hours' notice. He never ran out on a fight and he was never put down for a ten-count. He took beatings from the best in the business. But he never stayed down for ten.

He fought a comer from the Coast one night and took the worst beating of his career. But he was on his feet at the end. With a jaw broken in three places.

After that one he was hospitalized for three months and Lili went to work in a factory. She wasn't a strong girl and he didn't like it that she had to work. He fought again before his jaw was ready, and lost.

Yet even when he lost, the crowds liked him. They heckled him when he was introduced as Young Rocco, because he looked like thirty-four before he was twenty-six. Most of his hair had gone during his lay-off, and scar tissue over the eyes made him look less and less like a young anything. Friends came, friends left, money came in, was lost, was saved; he got the break on an occasional decision, and was occasionally robbed of a duke he'd earned. All things changed but his weight, which was 174, and his wife, who was Lili. And his record of never having been put down for ten. That stood, like his name. Which was forever Young Rocco.

That stuck to him like nothing else in the world but Lili.

At the end, which came when he was twenty-nine, all he had left was his record and his girl. Being twenty-nine, one of that pair had to go. He went six weeks without earning a dime before he came to that realization. When he found her wearing a pair of his old tennis shoes about the house, to save the heels of her only decent pair of shoes, he made up his mind.

Maybe Young Rocco wasn't the smartest pug in town, but he wasn't the punchiest either. Just because there was a dent in his face and a bigger one in his wallet, it didn't follow that his brain was dented. It wasn't. He knew what the score was. And he loved his girl.

He came into Uncle Mike's office looking for a fight and Mike was good enough not to ask what kind he wanted. He had a twenty-year-old named Solly Classki that he was bringing along under the billing of Kid Class. There was money back of the boy, no chances were to be taken. If Rocco was ready to dive, he had the fight. Uncle Mike put no pressure on Rocco. There were two light-heavies out in the gym ready to jump at the chance to dive for Solly Classki. All Rocco had to say was okay. His word was good enough for Uncle Mike. Rocco said it. And left the gym with the biggest purse of his career, and the first he'd gotten in advance, in his pocket: four twenties and two tens.

He gave Lili every dime of that money, and when he handed it over, he knew he was only doing the right thing for her. He had earned the right to sell out and he had sold. The ring owed him more than a C-note, he reflected soundly, and added loudly, for Lili's benefit, "I'll stop the bum dead in his tracks."

They were both happy that night. Rocco had never been happier since Graduation Day.

He had a headache all the way to the City Garden that night, but it lessened a little in the shadowed dressing room under the stands. The moment he saw the lights of the ring, as he came down the littered aisle alone, the ache sharpened once more.

Slouched unhappily in his corner for the windup, he watched the lights overhead swaying a little, and closed his eyes. When he opened them, a slow dust was rising toward the lights. He saw it sweep suddenly, swift and sidewise, high over the ropes and out across the dark and watchful rows. Below him someone pushed the warning buzzer.

He looked through Kid Class as they touched gloves, and glared sullenly over the boy's head while Ryan, the ref, hurried through the stuff about a clean break in the clinches. He felt the robe being taken from his shoulders, and suddenly, in that one brief moment before the bell, felt more tired than he ever had in a ring before. He went out in a half-crouch and someone called out, "Cut him down, Solly."

He backed to make the boy lead, and then came in long enough to flick his left twice into the teeth and skitter away. The bleachers whooped, sensing blood. He'd give them their money's worth for a couple rounds, anyhow. No use making it look too bad.

In the middle of the second round he began sensing that the boy was telegraphing his right by pulling his left shoulder, and stepped in to trap it. The boy's left came back bloody and Rocco knew he'd been hit by the way the bleachers began again. It didn't occur to him that it was time to dive; he didn't even remember. Instead, he saw the boy telegraphing the right once more and the left protecting the heart slipping loosely down toward the navel, the telltale left shoulder hunching— only it wasn't down, it wasn't a right. It wasn't to the heart. The boy's left snapped like a hurled rock between his eyes and he groped blindly for the other's arms, digging his chin sharply into the shoulder, hating the six-bit bunch out there for thinking he could be hurt so soon. He shoved the boy off, flashed his left twice into the teeth, burned him skillfully against the middle rope, and heeled him sharply as they broke. Then he skittered easily away. And the bell.

Down front, Mike Adler's eyes followed Rocco back to his corner.

Rocco came out for the third, fighting straight up, watching Solly's gloves coming languidly out of the other corner, dangling loosely a moment in the glare, and a flatiron smashed in under his heart so that he remembered, with sagging surprise, that he'd already been paid off. He caught his breath while following the indifferent gloves, thinking vaguely of Lili in oversize tennis shoes. The gloves drifted backward and dangled loosely with little to do but catch light idly four feet away. The right broke again beneath his heart and he grunted in spite of himself; the boy's close-cropped head followed in, cockily, no higher than Rocco's chin but coming neckless straight down to the shoulders. And the gloves were gone again. The boy was faster than he looked. And the pain in his head settled down to a steady beating between the eyes.

The great strength of a fighting man is his pride. That was Young Rocco's strength in the rounds that followed. The boy called Kid Class couldn't keep him down. He was down in the fourth, twice in the fifth, and again in the seventh. In that round he stood with his back against the ropes, standing the boy off with his left in the seconds before the bell. He had the trick of looking impassive when he was hurt, and his face at the bell looked as impassive as a catcher's mitt.

Between that round and the eighth Uncle Mike climbed into the ring beside Young Rocco. He said nothing. Just stood there looking down. He thought Rocco might have forgotten. He'd had four chances to stay down and he hadn't taken one. Rocco looked up. "I'm clear as a bell," he told Uncle Mike. He hadn't forgotten a thing.

Uncle Mike climbed back into his seat, resigned to anything that might happen. He understood better than Young Rocco. Rocco couldn't stay down until his knees would fail to bring him up. Uncle Mike sighed. He decided he liked Young Rocco. Somehow, he didn't feel as sorry for him as he had in the gym.

"I hope he makes it," he found himself hoping. The crowd felt differently. They had seen the lean and scarred Italian drop his man here twenty times before, the way he was trying to keep from being dropped himself now. They felt it was his turn. They were standing up in the rows to see it. The dust came briefly between. A tired moth struggled lamely upward toward the lights. And the bell.

Ryan came over between rounds, hooked Rocco's head back with a crooked forefinger on the chin, after Rocco's Negro handler had stopped the bleeding with collodion, and muttered something about the thing going too far. Rocco spat.

"Awright, Solly, drop it on him," someone called across the ropes.

It sounded, somehow, like money to Rocco. It sounded like somebody was being shortchanged out there.

But Solly stayed away, hands low, until the eighth was half gone. Then he was wide with a right, held and butted as they broke; Rocco felt the blood and got rid of some of it on the boy's left breast. He trapped the boy's left, rapping the kidneys fast before grabbing the arms again, and pressed his nose firmly into the hollow of the other's throat to arrest its bleeding. Felt the blood trickling into the hollow there as into a tiny cup. Rocco put his feet together and a glove on both of Kid Class's shoulders, to shove him sullenly away. And must have looked strong doing it, for he heard the crowd murmur a little. He was in Solly's corner at the bell and moved back to his own corner with his head held high, to control the bleeding. When his handler stopped it again, he knew, at last, that his own pride was double-crossing him. And felt glad for that much. Let them worry out there in the rows. He'd been shortchanged since Graduation Day; let them be on the short end tonight. He had the hundred—he'd get a job in a garage and forget every one of them.

It wasn't until the tenth and final round that Rocco realized he wanted to kayo the boy—because it wasn't until then that he realized he could. Why not do the thing up the right way? He felt his tiredness fall from him like an old cloak at the notion. This was his fight, his round. He'd end like he'd started, as a fighting man. And saw Solly Kid Class shuffling his shoulders forward uneasily. The boy would be a full-sized heavy in another six months. He bulled him into the ropes and felt the boy fade sidewise. Rocco caught him off balance with his left, hook-fashion, into the short ribs. The boy chopped back with his left uncertainly, as though he might have jammed the knuckles, and held. In a half-rolling clinch along the ropes, he saw Solly's mouthpiece projecting, slipping halfway in and halfway out, and then swallowed in again with a single tortured twist of the lips. He got an arm loose and banged the boy back of the ear with an overhand right that must have looked funny because the crowd laughed a little. Solly smeared his glove across his nose, came halfway in and changed his mind, left himself wide and was almost steady until Rocco feinted him into a knot and brought the right looping from the floor with even his toes behind it.

Solly stepped in to let it breeze past, and hooked his right hard to the button. Then the left. Rocco's mouthpiece went spinning in an arc into the lights. Then the right.

Rocco spun halfway around and stood looking sheepishly out at the rows. Kid Class saw only his man's back; Rocco was out on his feet. He walked slowly along the ropes, tapping them idly with his glove and smiling vacantly down at the news-papermen, who smiled back. Solly looked at Ryan. Ryan nodded toward Rocco. Kid Class came up fast behind his man and threw the left under the armpit flush onto the point of the chin. Rocco went forward on the ropes and hung there, his chin catching the second strand, and hung on and on, like a man decapitated.

He came to in the locker room under the stands, watching the steam swimming about the pipes directly overhead. Uncle Mike was somewhere near, telling him he had done fine, and then he was alone. They were all gone then, all the six-bit hecklers and the iron-throated boys in the sixty-cent seats. He rose heavily and dressed slowly, feeling a long relief that he'd come to the end. He'd done it the hard way, but he'd done it. Let them all go.

He was fixing his tie, taking more time with it than it required, when she knocked. He called to her to come in. She had never seen him fight, but he knew she must have listened on the radio or she wouldn't be down now.

She tested the adhesive over his right eye timidly, fearing to hurt him with her touch, but wanting to be sure it wasn't loose.

"I'm okay," he assured her easily. "We'll celebrate a little 'n forget the whole business." It wasn't until he kissed her that her eyes avoided him; it wasn't till then that he saw she was trying not to cry. He patted her shoulder.

"There's nothin' wrong, Lil'—a couple days' rest 'n I'll be in the pink again."

Then saw it wasn't that after all.

"You told me you'd win," the girl told him. "I got eight to one and put the whole damn bank roll on you. I wanted to surprise you, 'n now we ain't got a cryin' dime."

Rocco didn't blow up. He just felt a little sick. Sicker than he had ever felt in his life. He walked away from the girl and sat on the rubbing table, studying the floor. She had sense enough not to bother him until he'd realized what the score was. Then he looked up, studying her from foot to head. His eyes didn't rest on her face: they went back to her feet. To the scarred toes of the only decent shoes; and a shadow passed over his heart. "You got good odds, honey," he told her thoughtfully. "You done just right. We made 'em sweat all night for their money." Then he looked up and grinned. A wide, white grin.

That was all she needed to know it was okay after all. She went to him so he could tell her how okay it really was.

That was like Young Rocco, from Graduation Day. He always did it the hard way; but he did it.

Miss Donahue would have been proud.

el presidente de méjico

Portillo, a bridegroom of six weeks who looked like a youthful Wallace Beery, kept us informed of as much of the life of the town as he could see from the run-around; he had lived in the place all his life.

"There go pretty girl," he would observe, "walkin' with one ugly man."

All winter we had been waiting for court to convene. It opened any time in spring and closed as soon as the circuit judge disposed of cases accumulated during the winter; then he moved on to the next wide place in the road, usually reaching El Paso in time for the fall hunting.

Portillo didn't have to stand trial because there was no charge against him. The sheriff had simply picked him up to ask him the whereabouts of a certain still. Portillo didn't know. So the sheriff kept him in the run-around in the hope that he might remember. He kept him out of the cell block itself, as much as possible, because of Jesse Gleason.

Jesse was a wiry little man, about thirty, who had once killed a Mex over a game of dominoes, on the American side, and had gotten over the river in time to avoid arrest. He had lived in and around Juarez then, with a Mexican woman, until he had come another cropper and had gotten back across the river only half an hour in front of the Mexican authorities. He had surrendered himself to the local sheriff with the explanation that his conscience had at last brought him back. Everybody had liked good old Jesse for that and the sheriff had shaken his hand and called him "Hair-Trigger."

Yet the affair in Juarez had been simpler than any difficulty of conscience could be: he had killed the Mexican woman over a game of checkers. Here in Cactus County, however, he had more relatives than the sheriff, and was confident of beating the rap.

"There's more bad Mexicans in West Texas than good horses," good old Jesse was fond of saying.

The law apparently bore him out, for shooting a Mex was still safer than stealing a horse. There were second-offender horse thieves doing twenty to life at Huntsville, but nobody got that for shooting two Mexicans. Jesse himself had said that Crying Tom, whip boss of the Huntsville pea farm, was tougher on horse thieves than anyone, having once lost a pair of army mules out of his own corral. The whole thing was a legal hangover from a time when stealing a horse meant leaving its rider helpless in the desert.

Jesse was the bad-man of the tank, and everyone soothed him. "I'd trust my own sister with a man like that," his cell mate Wolfe would vouch. And Portillo, watching for a sight of his wife from the window, would agree absent-mindedly. "I trost sister too." Portillo wasn't looking for trouble. He was fair stuck on his own girl.

Jesse never exercised, but possessed a wiry prairie strength that five months on two thin meals a day hadn't modified. He could make the overgrown Wolfe howl with no more than the pressure of two fingers on the shoulder.

Wolfe was voluble and timorous, chattering all day and after the light was out, in a kind of snot-nosed New Jersey singsong. Until Jesse said, "Naow shet up!" Wolfe wouldn't so much as finish what he'd started to say.

There were days when Jesse said nothing, all day long, save this good-night admonishment to Wolfe. While Wolfe sat cross-legged in one corner of the cell like a tailor, Jesse squatted on his haunches like an Indian in the other. Both pitied the other's posture and spent hours trying to straighten each other out. Once, when Jesse managed to get his legs crossed beneath him, he was unable to disentangle himself and regained his feet only with difficulty. He was white with rage by then and made Wolfe squat "like a white man" for hours after. For Wolfe wished, more than anything in the world, to be a "white man," and suffered the agonies of the damned trying to achieve purity.

We all suspected, without saying so, that Jesse Gleason was insane.

Although he would have friends on the jury and already had a job waiting for him, we said we felt sorry for him because he had been arrested in the fall of the year. But we told the friendless, penniless, luckless, witless Wolfe he was altogether too lucky for one man, for he hadn't been picked up till spring. We pretended that any man who timed himself that closely to trial time must be a pretty slick customer. "Lucky as a dawg with two joints," was the way Jesse put it, "gittin' out of all thet jawbone time."

It must have been Wolfe's adulation for Jesse that made Jesse tolerate him. For when Jesse heckled the boy it was often good-naturedly. "Hey, Buckethead," he would ask seriously, "are all them Jews as crazy as you?" Wolfe was the only Jew Jesse had ever known, and he was quietly amused by Wolfe's peculiarities. "You got good sense though," he would assure Wolfe. "The only trouble is that, day by day, ever'thin' you do 'n say gets screwier 'n screwier."

Wolfe told us he had run off from a Passaic high school and insisted that, had he stayed only a week longer, he would have earned a letter in track. Although how anyone who had to breathe with his jaw hanging halfway to his navel could have run fifty yards was hard to understand. Yet he knew cowboy songs that Jesse had never heard, and could tell the circumstances of every Western outlaw's death from the Quantrells' to Billy the Kid's.

He was in for breaking into a hut somewhere along the river and stealing a rifle. He'd been wearing a CCC uniform at the time, but had since traded it off, piece by piece with the exception of the belt, to Jesse for corn bread. Thus Jesse wore oversized khaki trousers and CCC shoes, while Wolfe wore undersized county overalls and shoes so small he'd had to cut out the sides; and he still looked hungry enough to trade off his underwear to boot. His hunger would increase as the hours wore on toward night, till he looked most wondrously sad; toward evening he would sing in his adenoidal tenor:

> Billy was a bad man
> And carried a big gun
> He was always after greasers
> And kept 'em on the run.
>
> He shot one every morning
> For to make his morning meal
> And let a greaser sass him
> He was shore to feel his steel.

Jesse would never appear to be paying him any attention; but nevertheless he never ordered Wolfe to stop singing that particular song.

Every morning the sheriff came up with the breakfast tray. Jesse distributed the oatmeal and black coffee, calling the rightful owner of each as if a name were engraved on each tin plate. Alternately, either Portillo or Wolfe came up with a short piece of corn bread.

"My little ol' half-piece o' corn bread got cut wrong," Wolfe would complain as though getting ready to cry, but without daring to look accusingly at the piece and a half on Jesse's plate. He would whine until Jesse said, "Naow shet up!" Wolfe tried sulking, leaving a hunk of the stuff on the spoon holder above

his blanket every day, as though too disappointed to bother
with it. But by evening, after dark, he would put his head
under his blanket and eat his undersized hunk all to himself:
we heard his jaws moving softly in the dark, and wondered
why he was always so secretive in such small things.

One afternoon, just after the courthouse chimes had tolled,
Jesse reached up for the hoarded corn bread, bit it in two, and
tossed the short half over to me. Wolfe leaped up wailing,
thought better of it, and returned miserably to his blanket.

Late that night I wakened and heard him crying; he was
mourning for corn bread, in his father's tongue, or for the letter
in track he would have gotten in another week. It was hard to
tell. There were still crumbs in my teeth that held the fine
salty tang that corn bread takes after standing a day and I
determined that, the next evening, I'd get his corn bread before
Jesse; then Jesse would have to take the short half. As though
dreaming of the same thing, Jesse said aloud in sleep, "Naow
shet up!" And the wretched mourning ceased.

Wolfe never hoarded his corn bread again, however, and
that convinced me that, as the others had suspected, he was a
slippery devil all right.

After breakfast he always washed Jesse's plate, cup, and
spoon, as a tribute to the fact that Jesse had once taken second
prize in a local rodeo. But everyone else cleaned their own, and
when the sheriff came up the utensils were always clean and
lined up in front of Jesse's blanket as though Jesse himself had
washed every piece of tin in the tank.

"I turned yer spoon toward the wall 'stead of 'way from it
when I hung it this mornin', Judge," he would advise Jesse.
"Was that all right?"

Jesse would deliberate, observing the spoon in the iron
holder above his head as though it were the first time he had
observed it hanging in precisely that position.

"There's always the right way to do a thing, Melonhead,"
he would say at last, affecting extreme patience. "An' then

there's the wrong way. This time you picked out the wrong
way. Now hang it like other people do."

Thus it was largely for Wolfe's benefit that Jesse added a
rule or two to the regular rules of the kangaroo court. These
were penciled, in Jesse's labored hand, on the wall below the
unshaded night bulb:

These are the rules of the kangaroo court. Any man found gilty
of braking into this jailhouse without consent of the inmates will
be fined two dollars or elts spend forty days on the floor at the
rate of five cents per day, or elts take fifty licks from a belt with
a belt bukle on it. Every man entering this tank must keep clean
and properly dressed. Each day of the week is washday but not
Sunday. Every man must wash his face and hands before handling
food. Any man found gilty of spitting in ash tub or through
window will be given twenty licks. Each and every man using
toilet must flush with buket immediately afters. Man found gilty
of vilation gets twenty-five licks from the belt-bukle belt. Throw
all paper in the coal tub. Don't draw pictures on your wall, somebody's sister might come visitin. When using dishrag keep it clean.
Any man caught stealing from inmate of this tank gets 500 belt-
bukle licks. Every man upon entering this tank with a ver'al
disease, lice, buboes, crabs, or the yellow glanders must report
same immediately. Any man found vilatin any of these rules will
be punished according to the justice of the court. Anythin not
covered here will be decided by the justice of this court. The
judge of the court can search everywhere. He can search anybody.
The judge could be treasurer too if he wanted. He is Judge
Jesse Gleason.

And above the bowl some wag of another day had scratched
a simpler legend:

A flush here is better than a full house.

Before taking the breakfast tray back downstairs the sheriff
always appointed either Portillo or Wolfe trusty for the day.

This meant being allowed in the run-around until his return
in the evening, and Wolfe vied slyly with Portillo for that
honor. A trusty went through the motions of sweeping for an
hour, emptied the ash tub, and then looked out of the small
unbarred window until dark.

Wolfe wanted only the distinction involved, so as the day
waned his enjoyment decreased as his hunger increased; he
was always happy to hear the sheriff's military footstep on the
stair when it was time for him to come back in the tank with
us. To Portillo, however, the job was both a means of staying
out of Jesse's way and a chance to wave at his wife on her way
home from the Iglesia Metodista after vespers.

He seemed to suffer more from his separation from her than
from hunger. It was for her sake he avoided Jesse: when Jesse
shaved, Portillo's eyes never left Jesse's razor hand. He was
usually up before any of us, his swart, high-cheekboned face
washed, his Indian hair combed back to a black gloss, and his
bridgeless nose pressed boyishly to the cold blue bars, waiting
for the sheriff to let him into the run-around. He would take
his breakfast out there, but it would stand until his wife had
passed and waved. Then he would eat with relish.

She would stand in the middle of the rutted road, a slight
girl in a bright Sears, Roebuck printed frock, pointing proudly
to her belly. He would cup his hands, the broom beneath his
armpit, and call down to her that he and the baby would be
out the same day. When she left he would feel so happy that he
looked drunken. He would squeeze himself with both hands,
wave his arms aimlessly, and would go through a little love
dance, pretending the broom was his bride.

Once he paused in this routine, turned slowly, and looked
at me searchingly through the bars, as though seeing someone
he had never seen before. He put one hand on the back of my
neck with a look so direct, and so questioning, that I laughed.
Immediately he broke into a wide white grin, as though he,

too, thought it funny to have a question for which there seemed to be no words in either Spanish or English. "I weel leeft you," he told me, like promising an award.

And sure enough, the first thing he did upon being let back in the cell block that evening was to walk up to me and, without warning as it was without apparent reason, "leefted" me.

"See, I leeft you."

And up I'd go by the elbows. Although I never divined what significance this odd ritual held for Portillo, he repeated it often; and always it seemed to him to be the same good joke.

"I'll bet your boy be *Presidente de Méjico* someday," I assured him. He looked at me as though startled, repeated the phrase to himself, then seemed to sadden and turned away.

"*El Presidente de Méjico,*" I heard him telling himself wistfully. "*Pequeño presidente infeliz.*" And stood looking out at the rutted place where his wife had stood that morning, rolling his head in a deep and Indian mood.

Although he never spoke to Jesse and Jesse never spoke to him, Portillo talked easily to Wolfe. Wolfe would lean through the bars, joking about the still which, we all knew, the sheriff claimed Portillo operated and of which Portillo had consistently denied all knowledge.

"I bet when your kid is born you'll put him to work out there in the bear grass before you name him," Wolfe ventured.

"No," Portillo answered seriously, "I name first."

What troubled me was why Jesse kept using Wolfe to pump the Mex about that still.

But there was the morning when Wolfe and Portillo were both, inexplicably, turned out into the run-around as trusties together. They took turns sweeping, though there wasn't enough work to keep one man busy. And then, from somewhere, Wolfe provided a bottle of tequila. He and Portillo finished the bottle between them, passing it back and forth as though no one else in the cell block existed. By noon Wolfe was sick and Portillo was huddled on his heels in a corner, singing loudly to the wall.

Una noche serena y oscura
Cuando en silencio juramos los dos
Cuando en silencio me detesto mano
De testigos pucemos adiós
Las estrellas, el sol y la luna——

He broke off and consulted himself seriously. *"El Presidente de Méjico,"* he told himself. And sat laughing softly at the idea awhile.

Toward evening I heard Jesse laughing softly too. For several days thereafter I observed that Jesse split his corn bread with Wolfe, for some reason.

Portillo was released suddenly two days later, on a morning when the mountain rains came slantwise across the courthouse wall, and the courthouse chimes tolled evenly, as though tolling some long sea hours.

The night bulb, that usually faded each morning at six, burned that morning until almost nine. We knew it was nine by the courthouse chimes, a minute after the bulb dimmed slowly, leaving the cells still shadowed with night. By standing atop the bowl at the end of the cell block we could see the ever-lasting mountain mist crossing a line of Texas-Pacific boxcars, shrouding them to the roofs: we could see the car roofs being shunted across the arroyo for the noon run to El Paso.

After breakfast I crawled back into my blanket and considered how cold it would be riding one of those T-P boxcars into El Paso on the noon run. There'd be ice along the spine of the cars. I dozed off with my arms clasped under my knees and dreamed I was hunched up in a reefer. I wakened shivering, yet realizing I'd rather be riding than be where I was another hour. I was that dead sick for home.

"There goes the sheriff," Wolfe announced from the run-around. And I heard the muffled roar of the big car wheeling around the courthouse square and off toward the arroyo road. I fancied it swaying from side to side down a gravel road, its headlights cutting the fog like a train's through a tunnel. When it got off the gravel it would take the sand roads softly, and dust would follow into the mist. And there would be the smoky smell, through the fog and dust, that March brings to the chaparral and the long brown bear grass. The car thundered distantly across the arroyo and I was sick for the traffic of home.

Wolfe was making scratches on the wall with his fingernail again. He preferred such a tool because, he explained, a knife wouldn't be sanitary. He spoke as though his nose were clogged, and he was putting the final flourishes on a legend begun the day before, with his tongue caught between his teeth:

Me and Frank stayed overnight in this cell once—JESSE J.

He had scratched up a whole wall with similar myths.

Pretty Boy Floyd escaped from this cell.

And:

I got to be a copper-hater here myself—"Fox" WOLFE.

Of this outlawry of the West, almost to a man, all had effected escapes. Yet I never saw him use but the one fingernail. And never saw him blow his nose.

All that March afternoon the slant rain never ceased. We gathered together uneasily as dark came on, to read the rules of the kangaroo court to each other, like men reading Genesis, on a raft at sea, with a great wind rising. A couple minutes after the night bulb came on we heard heavy boots climbing with difficulty, as though burdened, and then the tank door being opened.

It always took the sheriff longer to open the tank door than the outer doors because the tank door was opened by an air brake locked in a box on the outer wall and the key to the box, smaller than his other keys, usually eluded him for a minute.

We listened while we knew he was fumbling for it; and sensed he was not alone, as the door opened slowly.

There was the sheriff and the sheriff's grown son and between them Portillo, bent double, his face shadowed by his cheap straw sombrero and his toenails scraping the concrete as he was half dragged and half carried in.

The hat was the color of sotol cactus, and beneath it his face had been so drained of blood that it was ageless. He no longer looked like Wallace Beery; his face seemed smaller now, and held no expression at all. It looked like a plastic face; and he sagged in his middle. Behind the parade came the local doc, carrying the sheriff's bear gun. He handed it back to the sheriff as Jesse bundled a blanket through the bars.

Portillo's mouth gaped when he was stretched out upon the blanket. He placed his hands across his stomach, still clutching the gray sombrero, and said, "Oooo—*pobre mujer*—oooo—poor belly."

"Shouldn't run when the law hollers, boy," the sheriff advised him, looking down at the poor drained face; the fingers began searching feebly for the wound.

"When ah seen him vomitin' ah knowed ah had him," the sheriff explained earnestly to Jesse.

Jesse's interest was professional. "That's how ah got mah'n," he reminisced, "only a little higher 'n he were comin' *to'd* me."

I had never seen a man dying of such a simple thing as a gunshot wound through the stomach. His face was grayer than I had ever seen a living face and the eyes were dilating with shock. They stared, fixedly and without understanding, at the monstrous and ragged navel of his wound.

"Shouldn't have turned rabbit, boy," the sheriff repeated. The doc leaned over and swabbed the belly with cotton batting.

"He jumped out of the car comin' back across the arroyo," the sheriff was explaining as though he were already in court. "I hollered, but he just bent over 'n stahted zigzaggin'. They all try that. Zigged when he should of zagged."

Portillo's shirt was the color of the cactus-colored sombrero: the dead gray of his fumbling fingers, the gray of the cells we called home; the color of the concrete upon which he lay, and the color of the land upon which his eyes were fixed. His toes, still damp from the bear-grass rain, twitched occasionally and they too were gray.

"We'll have to op'rate, Poncho. Say 'Okay.' Say '*Sí.*'"

Portillo didn't answer. His fingers found the sombrero's rim and twisted it weakly, the dilated pupils never wavering from his stomach, still trying to understand something through the curtain of shock and horror and the nightmare grip of his weakness.

"Should've brought him to the hospital 'stead of up here," Jesse complained to no one in particular.

"Tell us we kin op'rate, Poncho," the doctor asked. "Ah got to sew you."

The sheriff inclined one ear downward in the hope of catching a whispered consent. The fingers forgot the sombrero and wandered, aimlessly as a madman's, about the wound's gray edge, tracing the torn tissue; the doctor laid the fingers back, and the sheriff confided in Jesse.

"First shot creased his laig. Second caught him four-squwar."

Outside the rain ceased a minute, as though listening with us for the whisper of consent. The doc looked up inquiringly at the sheriff and the sheriff looked down at the kneeling doc, his face a mask of impassivity. The odor of iodine began filling the tank.

"You tell yes, Poncho," the sheriff suggested softly. "You tell *sí* . . ."

"Ooo—*pobre mujer*. Ooo—poor belly."

"His wife's downstairs with Martha," the sheriff's son offered. "Maybe she'll say yes for him."

The doc rose heavily.

" 'Cordin' to *mah* understandin', so long as he's still concious, he got to say it hisself. Elts ah'm liable. Ah give him first aid 'n that's all ah kin do within the law.'"

I remember Wolfe staring down like an idiot trying to remember something important. He watched the seeking fingers falter, until his own eyes faltered. While outside the rain began again and I heard its whispered consent at last.

"Sí, los pobres, sí."

But no one heeded the rain. For the rain came every day at any hour, and forever whispered whatever one wished to hear.

The last I saw of "Fox" Wolfe was in a crowded courtroom about ten o'clock of a windy April night. He seemed to have had the notion that, whatever the jury decided, he and Jesse would, for better or for worse, somehow remain together. But Jesse had been free for hours, and Wolfe had just been sentenced to four years on the pea farm at Huntsville and the sheriff had one hand on the back of his CCC belt and with the other was shoving him past the jury box. He would wait a couple weeks for the wagon to Huntsville and he wanted to cry, I believe, at the prospect of going hungry another two weeks, another four years, another forever. Yet, somehow, he was managing to look Jewish and stubborn, as though assuring himself that he wasn't sorry, even now, about not waiting that extra week to get his letter.

When I got a floater out of the state I planned to ride as far as El Paso. But at the last moment, with the train in sight, I decided to go east instead just to change my luck. I leaned against a water tank in the dark, feeling that getting out of Texas in any direction was a job and that I had my work cut out for me, when I spotted Jesse Gleason leading a little girl by one hand and carrying a full grocery basket in the other. He was still wearing Wolfe's CCC uniform, tucked, at the middle of the calf, into a spanty-new pair of black Spanish boots.

The boots were sharply pointed, high-heeled, and spurred like a fighting cock. I started to call out, then saw he was now a respectable citizen and remembered in time that I was still a bum.

Each of the boots bore a red star in a white circle toward the top. I stood in semidarkness and saw the spurs catch light from the big Western arc lamp at the corner. Under the lamp he put the basket down to shake hands with a well-dressed youth in a college-cut topcoat and he wasn't fifty yards from me then. He'd gotten a barbershop haircut, leaving long Spanish sideburns, and he swept the sombrero off his head and began twirling it, in an off-center spin, about his middle finger. It wasn't till he stopped twirling it that I could tell for sure. Then I could tell all right. It was Portillo's sombrero.

There are still more bad Mexicans than there are good horses in West Texas, the argument runs.

kingdom city to cairo

One wet December forenoon fifteen years ago I was leaning against a signpost that read WELCOME TO KINGDOM CITY, waiting for a lift. A whitish fog lay on the highway and overhead the big wet sky of Missouri moved, unseen, across the unplanted land. A Ford truck with one cracked headlight glowing dimly limped past, followed now and then by salesmen trying to make time into Cairo. Then a Chevvie coupé went by fast, screeched abruptly to a stop twenty yards up the road, and slammed into reverse. "He makes his decisions fast," I thought as I scrambled into the seat, and he had the speedometer back to sixty before I got the door closed behind me.

A scratchy, big-nosed man with a hospital complexion, in a potato-colored collar and a dark clerical suit; he held the wheel as though unaware of the fog and looked as full of starch as his collar.

"I'm not a minister any more," he explained. "I'm getting into a new racket. I was ordained by the Seventh-Day Adventists but they threw me out before the week was up. You see, I have a weakness. What time is it now?" He sized me up in chickenlike jerks of his neck; the knuckles on the wheel were bony, the fingers yellowed by nicotine. "What time *is* it?" he demanded impatiently, ignoring a sign that read: SCHOOL —SLOW.

"Do you have Standard Time? New York Time? Postal

Telegraph Synchronous Time or just plain good old Daylight Saving? Are you from Babylon, brother? I have to be in the post office at Sodom before dark. What time *is* it, brother?"

I surmised that it must be almost noon and nodded suggestively to a yellow-and-black warning: DANGER—CURVE AHEAD. He smiled smugly, as though he had planted the sign there himself just for a prank on others, and swung around the rear of a truck on the sheerest assumption that nothing might be coming from the other direction, swerving back to the right side of the road directly below the peak of the grade. His shadow-rimmed eyes fixed on me. I grinned weakly, and he patted my shoulder paternally.

I didn't like his shoulder-patting.

"You know why I stopped when you flagged me? I need advice is why. Maybe everything'll be all right now after all. You see, I have a weakness—you don't mind listening?"

"Just don't forget the wheel, Reverend. That's all I ask."

"Reverend. Yes, Reverend. That's just it. I'm *not* a Reverend. When my flock in Kingdom City found out I was running the tourists' concession in Hotel Ulysses they told me I'd either have to give it up or get out of their pulpit. That concession got a bad name hereabouts, but it's a little gold mine. I can't figure out what to do. If I didn't have such a *weakness.* Don't you think our meeting *means* something?"

"It probably means we'll end up with our little toes turned up in a ditch if you don't hold onto that wheel while you're preaching."

"No offense," he grinned, "no offense. I'm just a Seventh-Day Adventist off on a six-day binge. But you can't buy a snort in Kingdom City for love or money. Do you drink, brother? Smoke? Chew? Swear? You *should,* you know. I can quote you chapter and verse for anything you want to do, including arson, rape, incest, gluttony, breach of promise, or tapping a gas main. It's all right there in the good book and no fee for the service—now isn't *that* wonderful?"

"I don't know. The way you drive is, though."

He patted my shoulder again.

"The wheel, Reverend, the wheel."

"I could be like a father to you."

"I don't miss the old man that much."

"I'll be a brother to you."

"Okay. You be a brother: brother that wheel awhile."

He put his eyes on the road once more and we drove on in an uneasy silence, while I brooded over my peculiar luck in meeting the wrong people. The fog lifted as high as the telephone wires. This was Illinois country now, rutted and seedless and tough as its own scrub oak, laced only by Sears, Roebuck fences and U.S. 66.

"Don't worry about my driving, brother," he assured me. "I always drive like this. I believe in fate is why: when it's my time to go I'll go."

"That's all right," I reminded him, "but I might not want to come along right yet."

"Look at that life line." He showed me his palm. "I'll live to be a hundred and eight."

"You won't live twenty minutes if you don't put that life line back on the wheel." I looked at the long Illinois fields and thought nostalgically of coffee.

"I just had an operation," he said, as though explaining his recklessness. "Can't seem to go anywhere slow any more. Always in *such* a hurry. Thyroid trouble. I've only got one kidney. I have a weakness, but I can't stop now. Oh my, what I've been through. What time *is* it?"

For some reason he smiled quite gaily and added flippantly: "Aren't things getting *terrible*? Isn't everything just *awful*? Aren't things bad enough without everybody making them worse by *talking* about them? And aren't they getting worse all the *time?*"

I agreed that they were. "Your driving isn't getting any better either," I felt compelled to add.

He slowed a little at last, seemed to collect his thoughts, and managed finally to give his hard-luck story without watching me instead of the road.

"It's like this. I'm in *love*. But that's only *part* of it. I'm married and so is she, but not to each other. That's why I have to run a rat race to the post office in Cairo like this. That's where she writes me. I'm always afraid her husband is going to pick up one of her letters there. It wouldn't be hard for him to do. He's my brother. We have the same mailbox there. I always have to beat him there on account he's deputy sheriff." He paused to catch his breath. "What do *you* think?"

"In that case you better step on the gas."

He got that idiotically happy grin on him again, as if the whole affair was the funniest thing ever. "That ain't *all*. I bought this concession off a Jew from Chicago, a disbarred attorney. Sunk my last dime in it. Now they want me to give it up. I don't give a holy damn for the pulpit, but it'll mean not seeing *her*. I'll be living in Cairo and she'll be in Kingdom City. As long as I had the pulpit we could cover up—I had business there. But now I don't, and the brother'll catch on as sure as hell's on fire if I start chasing back into Missouri twice a week.

"Of course she could leave him and come to Cairo. That'd be just fine and dandy, like sugar candy. Just about the time my wife'd be putting a hole through the girl friend's head the brother'd arrive with a posse looking for me. A nice kettle of fish, I will say. But it does me good to talk to someone about it, someone I won't see again, who won't see me, that I don't know from Adam and who don't know me."

"If I ever get out of this car I guaran*tee* you won't see me again," I decided to myself.

"Leaving my flock is the least part. They're just a bunch of tarts and rumpots anyhow. Rams and ewes, brother, rams and ewes. I'm no better and no worse—but my ewe is the

sweetest ewe of all. If I thought I had to give her up I'd run
this car into the ditch around the next curve. Only why should
the blind lead the blind? Beside, I got a good thing in this
concession—— You got a place to stay tonight, brother?"

I'd been nodding, and shook my head, no, I hadn't. I
hadn't slept in a bed in four nights.

"You can stay at the hotel if you want. Don't thank me.
No trouble at all."

It wouldn't have been much trouble. But I was too tired
to care where I slept. I dozed while he chattered on.

"The slut is bleeding me white. She knows I can't give
her up. I should've had that draft sent to Alton. Got to be
back for love meeting in the tent by ten." He nudged me.
"There's a half pint in the side pocket. If you fall asleep I'm
likely to do the same thing. Help yourself. Take a slug 'n think
real hard 'n tell me what I should do. Take a slug and then
say the first thing that comes into your head. It'll be a sign
for me, a pillar of cloud. Go ahead, brother, in the side
pocket."

I drank and put the bottle back without passing it to him.
I figured we were just staying alive by luck anyhow, so why
press one's luck? He watched me drinking, waited a long
moment, and then said, "Well, brother?"

"Brush the ewe off, Deacon," I told him confidently, "before you get the brush yourself. Even if she don't brush you,
sooner or later your brother will. Quit while you're still even.
Strikes me you must make love like you drive. Step on the
brake before you smash up."

Without acknowledging this opinion, he said abruptly,
"Do you have a good home, brother? What are you chasing
yourself around Little Egypt for? A good home, stay in it. Or
is your life a shambles too?"

"My life's all right," I told him curtly. "What'll this hotel
deal cost me? I don't have much money."

"Not a crying dime!" he cried happily, almost jumping

out of the seat. "Not a Confederate penny! Not a Mexican nickel. Stay as long as you like, just like Adam in the garden." His voice leered slightly. "We may even find a loose Eve or two wandering around the concession."

I didn't say a word. We were coming into the outskirts of Cairo.

The hotel was down by the levee. You could see Kentucky from the front windows. Upstairs, I was told, was the bedroom in which Grant had slept before Fort Defiance. I remember the boarded windows and the broken panes by the river, and the abandoned feed stores facing the moving Ohio. Long freights passed in the woods in Kentucky. Their shadows, as any army's shadows, moved south on the moving waters. I remember their engine boilers lighting fragments, of floodtime in old December, strewn on Kentucky's shore.

And thought of the big rivers of the Republic, running the unplanted land and the littered shores of Kentucky. Saw, as always in those years, the big wet sky of the Republic over the big wet land. On that long-ago evening, from the musty lobby of that decaying Civil War hotel, I saw the cottonwoods crowd for warmth behind an abandoned filling station: a thousand nameless weeds thronged the prairie water front. They say, in summer, these grew rankly by day and stank by night.

The Hotel Ulysses squatted like a blind red ox, squat as Grant himself, staring blindly toward Vicksburg at midnight. At the barricades built against floodtime, above the blockaded river. Above an endless army's shadows, moving south through the woods through Kentucky.

I believed in the bedroom where Grant had slept, but doubted the storeroom in the basement which the disbarred attorney had decided had been a prison. He had charged tourists fifteen cents to see the dungeon where the Rebs had been kept. The Reverend had knocked a few more bricks out of the wall and raised the ante to a quarter. When I assured him that it looked moldy enough to charge a half dollar he grew a little prim and explained that that wouldn't be right as some of his own people, on his mother's side, had been Rebs. He was quite frank about it all, however, and seemed to enjoy taking me up and downstairs, not even omitting the rope fire escape with which Grant's room was still provided.

He had a colored bellhop who ran the elevator and conducted the tours. The boy got a nickel out of every quarter which the tourists invested in the place; the hotel got a dime and the Reverend got a dime.

What the Reverend omitted in his description was that he had two country girls, sisters, rooming together on the third floor, who were available to tired tourists. Their room was across the hall from the one in which Grant had slept; when I glanced in at Grant's bed it looked as rumpled as though the general had just risen from it after a bad night with the bottle.

"This may not be Gomorrah," the Reverend told me slyly, "but we give them hell here all the same."

He said something to the desk clerk, nodding in my direction, and then came over to tell me that any time I wanted to hit the hay just to go on up to room 39. I trudged up to the third floor, hunted down the uncarpeted hall awhile, and then pushed into room 39.

There was a woman, fully clothed, on the bed, and a man shaving at the dresser mirror. The women looked at me leisurely over the cover of a movie magazine while I stood trying to apologize. "It's all right," the women said, "try another door." Just like that. I backed out feeling confused.

And saw then, on either side of the hall, that none of the doors had locks. Some stood open and some a little ajar; not one was fully closed. Some hotel, I thought. Some concession. I hesitated in front of a room from which no light showed, poked my head in, and asked politely. "Anyone in here?"

There was no answer. Nor was there any light, save a dry kerosene lamp. I lit matches and discerned a bed, a chair, and a mirror. That was all I needed. I backed the chair against the doorknob and threw myself across the bed.

I was in the very depths of sleep, dreaming that I wanted to waken; every time I nearly attained wakefulness I'd slip back into the abyss of sleep. It was like being drowned in some gigantic aquarium, for I could feel, like one awake, the whole weight of sleep, like the weight of deep waters upon me. Then something woke me sharply and I was sitting on the edge of the bed and the whole room was moving. The walls, and the floor, as though carpeted, stirred restlessly. Down from the mirror, across the floor, along my arms a living carpet moved. Then they began biting.

A civilization of bedbugs had come out of the walls, from between the wallpaper, from the bedposts, from the mattress and the ceiling. I brushed them off my arms in a panic of disgust and they surged back up my legs. I yanked the chair away from the door and fled down the stairs half covered with a dark and rippling sheet.

No one was at the desk as I ran past: only a small night bulb, which, it seemed to me, was shaded by them.

All that night I walked the darkened, rutted roads of southern Illinois, too sick with horror and fatigue to find the highway. I crushed them between my palms as I walked, I stopped and burned them until I ran out of matches; stood, shivering in the December chill, crushing them between my palms. And with every step I took they bit, as though resenting movement. They bit my back, hips, and neck, and all I knew to do was to keep moving, in a kind of desperate hope of shaking them off.

In the whitish fog of morning I came on a railroad spur where a boxcar, its floor covered with straw, stood waiting to be switched. I crawled in and found, in one corner, a sleeping hobo. I wakened him and he gave me matches. By the time the train began moving I'd gotten rid of them, although I'd had to throw away my shirt out of simple revulsion, in spite of the cold.

Late that night, going through Joplin, Missouri, I stole a shirt off a clothesline at a water stop, and three days later, in New Orleans, I found a Salvation Army Home with a shower.

Tonight, a decade and a half after, I'm still wondering whether the Reverend's weakness was women, whisky, his single kidney, or practical joking.

that's the way it's always been

We used to stand reveille in Wales with the smoke from the mess hall blowing into the rain. In the east the sky would be torn with light, like a sky going pleasantly insane. With a particular sort of savagery in the way the orderly-room wires cut blindly across it.

The days, like the sky, passed in a pleasant decadence; they were conducted for us by mildly demented quacks and a few specially selected cretins. One day would be about the same as the next: chow, inspection, and then, like a call to arms, all men not on detail would be summoned to a stoveless, chairless Nissen hut on a hill to listen to The Man without Any Brains beat his gums till noon. The rank and file preferred detail to listening to The Man. He had no back to his head and the tip of his little sniffing nose was as fiery as his hair.

He would begin by assuring us that the Germans were halfway to the channel ports, that some of us wouldn't be seeing another Christmas—but that he, The Man without Any Brains, would see us through.

"If that man had a hummingbird's brains he'd fly backwards," one hillbilly used to say of him. "If what he got is brains I'll take horse manure."

This Kansas abortionist, who wore silver leaves on his padded shoulders, would have wept had the war ended leaving him only leaves instead of the eagles for which he lived. "I get frightened sometimes," he confided to one of the officers, "that the war might end before we really get in the thick of it." There's your communication-zone hero for you—the only thing he fears on earth is being home in bed with his wife instead of advancing contentedly against German mortar fire.

Not that he had courage. It was just that he needed a florid screen of ribbons and citations and decorations behind which to conceal the whimpering little embryo that was, in reality, all that there was to Colonel Bull. He was a washout and he sensed it, but he couldn't face it. He had to face panzers, no matter how much he feared them, in order to appear to himself as a whole man. And there wasn't enough fire power in the whole European theater to make a man of that strutting stage prop.

"If the enlisted men get to hating one of my numcums then I know I have one numcum who's doing his job all the way," he was fond of saying. We'd have to crowd into the unheated Nissen hut to listen to stuff like that. He was as phony as a three-dollar bill and as vain as a perfumed matinee idol.

He'd wind up advising us that, under any circumstances, in garrison or field, he was sure we'd always live up to the proud tradition of combat medics. We would always remember that the wounded came first. As though we planned secretly, each night in barracks, to abandon the litters and finish off the cripples at the first whine of an .88 overhead. It'll go hard with the man who fails to remember *that,* he'd remind us with a smile as reassuring as that of a half-crushed snake.

After the wounded the enlisted men rated next, said Colonel Bull. If there were a shortage of chow, what there was would go to the men. He would tell us this brazenly, although the chow was already short because his officers were using the enlisted men's mess to entertain their Welsh girl friends. Our breakfast had been reduced to tea and Pep because the eggs and oranges were consumed nightly by the officers' happy little consorts. They never used their own rations to bargain for the girls' favors; it was cheaper to use ours.

When the enlisted men bitched about the monotony of Pep and tea for breakfast, the mess sergeant defended himself by reporting that his supplies were being raided. He didn't say by whom. But everyone knew that only enlisted men could do such a thing. With the result that we got an extra night detail of guarding the mess hall from other enlisted men, while the officers rioted within, still frying our eggs and scattering orange peelings over the floor for us to police up in the morning.

Well, we'd brought it on ourselves, the chaplain assured us. "That's the way it's always been," he said, "so I guess that's how it's going to be. At least, it doesn't look like anyone's going to change it." We quit bitching about breakfast, and the guard detail was held, like the Damascene sword, in abeyance.

The most comical aspect of the colonel's attitude was that he sincerely felt we had confidence in him and his staff. In the presence of the officers he'd assure us that, when we went into mined areas, it would always be the officers who would take the main chance: it would be their sacred trust never to expose an enlisted man to land mines unnecessarily, since the latter were the backbone of the whole hospital. While to a man we knew that not an officer there would risk the skin of his little finger for the colonel if there were still an EM available to risk his behind instead. Most of them would have sent out their mothers with detectors before putting a foot on mined earth themselves. They were all heroes on the bar front—but in the zone, no.

After the enlisted men came the nurses, who were officers first and women only incidentally, we were told. Yet we always had the impression that the officers prized them more for their femininity than for their bars. And when it came down to it, they turned out to be better men than the officers. They worked at their jobs, and off duty had more innate common decency than all the male brass combined. They earned their pay and they maintained discipline among themselves; and sometimes, when no officer was looking, they shortened their work by doing things their own way rather than according to the colonel's book: the way it always had been, that no one was going to change.

But your average second lieutenant is a loose fish, and a disciplinarian to boot. He'll check you for a loose button on your field jacket, go off and get himself so drunk that he's sick in the taxi coming home—but be damned certain that the first thing he'll do, as soon as he's borrowed taxi fare and his head has stopped aching, will be to check you on that loose button. He'll show you he's one who remembers from one day to the next and no nonsense about it—though the borrowed taxi fare is already forgotten and he's off for the hair of the dog that bit him. Discipline is what he believes in, the stuffed hyena—discipline for you and the little girls for him, you'll find out soon enough.

Last of all, the hero who must go down with the ship, the one who'll stand like Jackson at Antietam or wherever it was, even though a Mark IV is bearing down on him, the one for whom no sacrifice is too great and no enlisted man's trouble too small to minister, was Colonel Bull himself: the selfsame hero who must be served first, though he's the last to get up in the morning, at a table by himself with his plate warmed to just the right temperature. No, it didn't do any good, his telling us where he was going to be when the going got tough and the guns got hot. He'd sent our best nurse back to the States properly knocked up to await a dishonorable discharge, because of his personal carelessness, and another had transferred out to avoid his pursuit. We knew where he'd be all right, the little remaindered lush. He'd be after the nurses when they were off duty and nursing a fifth of Old Quaker when they weren't.

He'd show us how cool he could be all right, if there was enough ice left for the highballs.

This pint-size poseur would have liked to live on a platform. But in barracks the hillbillies spoke of him as children might of the first clown they'd ever seen—laughter tinged by fear. He made them mad, but he was ridiculous to them, too.

Particularly when he'd deliver a threatening epilogue on security, and how some of the enlisted personnel were endangering their own lives as well as those of their buddies by talking too freely in town.

The truth was that our most accurate rumors came from town, for we were always preceded there by officers who consorted with everything in skirts and sometimes flitted from sex to sex, like so many butterflies. It was all one, the "numcums" could be depended upon to get them back to garrison.

The civilians always knew: they told us our sailing date, when the ambulances would leave, when the advance party would land, and the kind of ration we'd carry. They knew everything, even the name of the boat, and not an enlisted man had had a pass in three days to hand out anything like *that.*

Everything was known in town and everything in garrison was hushed. After the officers had left the horse out, we were blamed because the barn doors were open. Even in barracks troop movements were not to be discussed, lest there be a fifth-columnist under the stove. While the officers' boastful confidences to their civilian friends were being openly mulled over in the Welsh streets.

The officers drank up their own liquor ration, then they consumed the nurses'. When that was done away with, the chaplain slipped them half our cigarettes to trade off in town for Irish whisky. And all the while keeping a sharp eye out for excesses on the part of the enlisted men.

Precious little danger of excesses there was on our part. We couldn't get to town often enough for that. It was all we could do to get our cigarettes, candy, and soap out of the chaplain before he sold them. We only paid a half dollar a carton for cigarettes, and he could get ten and twenty times that amount from the civilians.

You could hardly blame the chaplain. He was out for all he could get. The colonel had set the example. And all the other marked-down med-school Don Juans had followed suit.

"You ought to have seen them at chow," the mess sergeant would chortle. "My old man's sow got better manners." The nurses breakfasted once with The Man and his staff, and thereafter refused flatly to come into the mess until the officers had left. All the while we were in Wales they ate after the officers, preferring to subsist on what was left rather than to tolerate the overweening vanity, inbred bad manners, and unrestrained swinishness of these cavaliers. The colonel first, the officers next according to rank, then the nurses, the enlisted men, and finally, God help them, the wounded. That's how it *really* went in the hut-two-five.

"We may outnumber them," the mess sergeant mourned, "but they sure as hell outweigh us."

It wasn't an outfit. It was just a couple hundred oddly assorted Tennesseans, Texans, and Chicagoans who wanted to go back to their respective hills, ranches, and streets. When we reached the Rhine the Germans were using hazardous fire, over our heads, toward an artillery emplacement to our rear. In his haste to get those eagles, The Man had brought us forty miles ahead of our clearing station: they were looking for us to their rear. We were supposed to be ten miles behind them, to evacuate their wounded. Instead we were raising ward tents, ankle-deep in Kraut mutuel tickets, on a bombed-out race track in the woods above Düsseldorf. We put up the whole circus at night, under fire, including a tent to be used as an officers' club —and that one was up before we could erect our own squad tents.

The day we went into operation The Man summoned us,

and we listened, standing at ease, while he outlined the history of mankind from the Peloponnesian Wars to the Lindbergh kidnaping, which was the last time he'd read a newspaper. We stayed there two weeks, while the 94th Division casualties were being bumped blindly about, over rutted roads, fifty miles to our rear, looking for us. The only ones who knew where we were were the Krauts, and they were too busy to give a damn *what* we were doing there.

We finally got two patients: a Kraut kid who came running up with his hand blown off, from fooling around with a booby trap in the woods—and The Man.

He had had a slit trench dug in his tent, had had his cot and himself lowered gently into it, and had slept there, safe from concussion, according to the book. But he caught a heavy cold, and for hours we lived in a trembling hope that it might develop into pneumonia. There wasn't an enlisted man in the outfit who wouldn't have passed up chow for a chance to throw a shovel of dirt across that phony phiz.

"I'll contribute my mattress cover any time," we assured each other. And more than one really meant that all the way down.

The only officer we had who worked at his job was an Assyrian with a face like a side of mutton. He undertook everything in the hope of someday becoming a first lieutenant. Even the First Soldier ordered him around. Morning till night he directed athletics, ran errands for special service, gave us talks on sex hygiene, military courtesy, and orientation—he was into everything, knew nothing, and we always liked to hear him for his phenomenal knack of saying exactly the opposite of what he intended. And when he gave us "caliskonectics," as he called them, that was the best.

"Let your arms hang loozly 'n your legs parell your stumick," he would order. For some reason he called the stomach muscles "stahara," with a great rolling of the *r*. Then he'd have us growl at each other while we rolled the muscles of the "staharrrrrra." It was so absolutely idiotic, and he was such an absolute idiot, that we'd growl and froth and snarl like so many hyenas, just to hear him keep on. "Kwigly, men, kwigly —throw the right simontaneously." But simultaneously with what we never knew.

The other officers were out looting. A captain returned with two German dental chairs and detailed four enlisted men to disassemble and box them for shipment. Swiney, who had been a bellhop before getting his commission, came up with two great Danes, immediately chained them to the enlisted men's mess, and set them to work on the EM rations. They hadn't eaten in days. We didn't say a word. There weren't any more regulations covering great Danes than there were to cover officers; we'd learned that long ago.

Then Di Forti, the mess officer, announced that champagne and cognac would be available to the men after evening chow for fifty marks a bottle, which was cheap. Money was easy and five bucks wouldn't break anybody. Nevertheless, we learned from the mess sergeant, who was getting fed up, that it had been requisitioned with the understanding that its distribution among the men was to be without cost. Di Forti was chiseling the mess sergeant out of his cut. To make it stick, he broke him the following week, and he didn't get his stripes back till he stopped wondering publicly how Di Forti was able to send home a check for twice his officer's pay every month.

But the chaplain was the busiest of all. His name was Ingle, and he had a furtive, lopsided face, more like that of an Aberdeen rabbit than that of a man. He was an officer first and a chaplain only as an afterthought. His assistant conducted services for him, for Chappie was either in bed, Sunday mornings, nursing a hang-over, or was hanging over a nurse in bed.

Sometimes the colonel dispatched him for loot on Sundays, and it upset Ingle to have to drive the jeep himself then, for his assistant would be conducting services for the faithful. So

he was given a second assistant as a driver, and toward evening would return with a jeepload of Leicas, binoculars,
Mausers, engraved swords—and even one of those global maps
which revolve on a pedestal, from a schoolroom. The officers
hand-picked the load according to rank and seniority, with the
colonel first and the Aberdeen rabbit anxiously bringing up the
rear. Then followed the First Soldier and the first three grades
of "numcums." By the time it got down to the Pfcs and buck
privates there were usually a couple broken swords, a box
camera or two—often made in the States—and a beat-out
Mauser remaining. We could help ourselves then, but were
warned not to be greedy about it, to act like soldiers and not
like a bunch of damned niggers.

That was the colonel's phrase. "Act like white men just for
once," he'd plead. After he'd sent home five Leicas, four
Lugers, two sets of binoculars, a set of Russian furs, and at least
a quart of a perfume called Cuir de Russie.

Chappie didn't care for souvenirs for themselves. He took
them in order to sell them. And he always had a few Kraut ash
trays, iron crosses, and SS belt buckles which were available to
the men—through his assistant—at reasonable rates.

On V-E day Pfc Hendy got a letter from home: his brother
had been killed at Okinawa. We heard him crying six tents
away. One of those surly, closemouthed kids who takes orders
well but never makes friends. If you made a friendly remark to
him he'd look at you suspiciously, and if you repeated it he'd
offer to climb all over you for a nickel. That's how he was. He
could take care of himself, he said.

But he couldn't that morning. No one knew what to do with
him. When the men in his own tent tried to console him he
wandered away from them, trying blindly to be somewhere
alone, and sat down at last, in the rain, against a half-empty
lister bag with the letter crumpled in his hand and getting
splotched from the rain. He sat there with his mouth open,

bareheaded, looking oddly thin and small, his face wet with rain and anguish. He didn't even know where he was, it looked like. Heartbreak is harder to look on than death sometimes.

Somebody went and told Ingle, and Ingle sent both his assistants. They stood in the rain looking down at Hendy, a T/5 and a Pfc. When he had cried himself out they supported him back to his cot, somebody gave him a drink, and the next day he was as closemouthed and surly as ever. Ingle never even asked what had happened to him.

Still, that's the sort of man you were expected to salute, to wait on, to respect, and even to confide in.

They couldn't get interested in the war, our officers. They didn't know what it was all about and they didn't want to learn. All they were aware of was rank, whisky, women, grub, and gossip. All their waking hours were devoted to these ends, distracted only occasionally by an enlisted man who had been caught fraternizing.

For it wasn't only forbidden us to fraternize with the Germans; Poles, Russians, Netherlanders, Belgians, French, and Yugoslavs were equally *verboten*. We couldn't fraternize with any of these, we were informed, for the simple reason that if they were Germans they'd tell us they were something else, and we, lacking the officers' astuteness, just couldn't tell the difference. Even association with our own nurses was frowned on by The Man. He was as jealous of them as a ram of a flock of ewes. What he couldn't have himself he didn't want anyone else to have. Like a dog, what he couldn't eat himself he defiled.

Risen from his sick bed, he crept about the outskirts of the hospital area for a few minutes each evening with a pale and walleyed look. What he was looking for there no one knew. He slept with a bottle, rose with it, and wandered about in the dusk, aimlessly. Perhaps he felt that, in the dimness, he might not be taken for an officer and some enlisted man would fail to salute him. He needed the assurance of the salute desperately.

It made him feel that, after all, he wasn't such a big stuffed bum as some people seemed to think. But we all knew that creepy shuffle and he never failed to get a proper salute.

For two weeks we hadn't tasted fresh meat. That would have been all right, but for The Man giving a little party for a few nurses and officers at his quarters and ordering us to build a barbecue pit one Saturday afternoon because it had to be ready for the party on Sunday. We had dehydrated potatoes, cold Argentine corned beef right out of the can, and oatmeal pudding with cocoa spilled over it while they were frying steaks. Yes, and we policed up the empty whisky bottles the morning after, too, and the cigarette butts as well.

The same day I received a letter from my wife saying, "Finish the job so that you can get back home. We are proud of what you are doing."

She was proud of what we were doing.

I got checked one morning for going to chow in shorts. The Man checked me personally: "You'll either wear pants in the mess hall or you won't eat here." Well, a rule is a rule. But the same afternoon he came to dinner himself in shorts. "That's my privilege," he explained.

"It's the way it's always been," the Aberdeen rabbit said sagely, "so I guess that's how it's got to be, fellows. At least, I don't see any chance of changing it right now."

One day we discovered, through secret channels, that we had $152 in the company fund. So we figured we could have a company party. The First Soldier asked the colonel and he gave permission for us to draw fifty cases of beer. Saturday was going to be a big day for us. Free beer and a couple boxing bouts and lots of fun.

On Saturday The Man came with us to pick up the beer and we were saying that maybe he wasn't such a bad egg after all. But when we were ready to pick it up he decided fifty cases was too many and would only pay for thirty. When we got back to camp he took five cases for himself. Nobody protested, and nobody bitched. He told the mess sergeant to ice up the remaining beer for us, with as grand a gesture as though it were a personal gift.

Not a man attended the party. Some went to the movies, some wandered off, and some just sulked, saying they didn't feel well or had taken the pledge or something.

The next morning The Man called his "numcums" together and told them we'd all pay for ignoring the party, after all the trouble he'd gone to for us. We would get up half an hour earlier, work half an hour later, and, if necessary, do eight hours of close-order drill a day. Also, our tents weren't in good shape, and unless they were spick-and-span right off, inspections would be held twice a day. Then he pulled out the Articles of War, read the paragraphs dealing with mutiny and sedition, and ordered everyone back to work as though nothing had happened. "Go back to your tents and forget it," he told them, abruptly forgiving them all.

The chaplain, however, stood us in good stead. "That's the way it's always been," he said, "so that's how it got to be. At least, I don't see much chance of making any changes right now, fellows. You understand."

We understood all right.

the children

Two weeks before Thanksgiving the third-floor guard hung a bright wall motto above the piano in the playroom:

I GROW OLD
LEARNING SOMETHING
NEW EACH DAY

States Kaszuba stood studying the motto while fingering a five-and-dime toothbrush hanging by a string about his throat. About him stood nine other youths, in varying attitudes of spiritlessness, each in the same gray clothes. They were waiting for a rehearsal of their Thanksgiving Day play, to be offered, ultimately, to the ladies of the Polonia Women's Federation. Until the arrival of that group's representatives, the boys had a few moments in which to scoff at the new motto. Kaszuba alone refused to scoff; in fact, he began reproaching the scoffers.

"It says just right," he told them. "Every day you could learn up somp'n new, if you just stay on yer toes. Look at me. Here fer larceny of a V-8. But if I'd learned up somp'n new, I wouldn't be here fer no t'eft a-tall. I'd be here fer tamperin' is all. It'd be a missed-meaner is all. Like when you strong-arm-rob a guy'n it's just m'licious mischief."

"Yeh," the boy called Silly Louie offered. "Like when it's a dame 'n then she says you sex-utory-raped her."

Three overdressed women bustled in behind the guard, and the talk stopped dead. One of the women twirled the piano stool downward and ran her fingers down the keyboard. States had seen her play at a dance: he had watched the dancing through an alley window. He watched her pull the stool up in an effort to circumvent her bosom, till he couldn't see the stool for the spread of the hips. The stubby hands poised dramatically above the keys and she glanced sidewise without turning her head, like a hen, to see that no one was slouching. Each boy laid his hand on the shoulder of the boy ahead.

"All right, boys! Indian braves!"

The two other women and the guard applauded lackadaisically, the piano began with a bang, and States led his tribe, loping indifferently, onto the uncarpeted stage; the planks bent under their feet as they circled it. Then they faced an imaginary foe in attitudes of Comanches drawing Comanche bows, and sang halfheartedly:

"Ten little Indian braves are we
None but da birds so free as we!"

"Some song," States murmured sullenly to Silly Louie. What were the crows always coming around to rub things in for? His tribe loped, in a heavy-footed war dance, slapping their mouths with their palms.

"Ay-yee!   Ay-yee!   Ay-yee!"

"Some Indians," he added from the corner of his mouth, nodding toward the three Negroes at the end of the line. And wondered vaguely why they couldn't be paratroopers for a change. The pianiste waved absently, and the braves become squaws:

"Ten little Indian squaws at home!
Grind the wheat! Grind the corn!"

She brought the pedal down hard on "corn." Bent over an imaginary urn, grinding imaginary corn, States eyed the wall motto furtively. If you wanted to use phony dice, slip them to a sucker and let the sucker make the passes. Ride with him for a half a dozen passes, then grab your hat and let the sucker try talking his own way out. Let the suckers take the beatings. That's what suckers were for.

"All right, boys! Papooses now!"

"It makes them ferget their little troubles," the guard explained to the ladies.

The boys bowed their heads to their knees and murmured:

> "Sleep, little Indian, safe from harm
> Daddy's a-hunting the wild fawn."

"Daddy's a-huntin' a wild skirt is all," States offered under his breath. Silly Louie's hands flew to his mouth; when Louie started giggling he couldn't stop. The piano paused and the guard's earnest voice dropped discreetly; then everything stopped but the papooses' persistent murmuring. They rose heavily, one by one, and began a disordered out-of-tune clomping, toothbrushes bobbing, and went on clomping bravely, to minimize Louie's irrepressible tittering.

"Stop! Hiawatha! Stop! Come here!" The pianiste was plainly outraged.

Silly Louie came to the edge of the stage, his hands holding his stomach. He turned his head away and regained his self-control only with an effort.

"What were you laughing at this time, Louis?"

"I tawt of somp'n *funny.*"

" 'Thought,' Louis, not 'tawt.' "

"Yes'm. I tawt of somp'n real funny."

"Well, go back to your place and pay more attention to the play and less to Kaszuba. Or you can't be Hiawatha on Thanksgiving." Then, to reproach them both with a single blow: "I thought *you* could be depended upon, Louis."

"It helps them ferget their little troubles," the guard repeated vaguely. "They're all lookin' forwards to T'anksgivin'."
He was an aging Norwegian, with a heavy head and a paunch, who had been a truant officer until his legs had gone bad. Between illness and poverty, he felt, somehow, that the children had tricked him. During waking hours he controlled an impulse to strike out blindly at the sight of them: as though, by punishing one or two, he might get a bit of his own back. Although he never acknowledged this impulse to himself, he dreamed persistently of triumphs over the children.

In such dreams he was often a distinguished jurist who sat sentencing children to incredible punishments: one night he sentenced an eight-year-old girl to hard labor for life for thumbing her nose at him. He announced her sentence with a rollicking disregard of her offense, then cursed her obscenely while, in the back rows, men and women applauded: they loved him for expressing the hatred and fear that they, secretly, had long shared toward the children.

"We let them keep their little toothbrushes when they leave for St. Charles," he said aloud to the ladies. Then he spied States sneering at the pianiste and called out sternly:

"Watch each other, boys! Not too close together!"

After the rehearsal the ladies signed the guest book in the chapel, under a motto that read:

UNLESS ONE TRIES
ONE CANNOT SUCCEED

and the pianiste herself observed, looking at the holy pictures on the walls, that she "just couldn't see how *any* child could do anything *bad* after being in *here*." The aging guard said he didn't understand it either and hoped they'd all quit doing bad things pretty soon.

After dark the boys lay in the dormitory and spoke in whispers. For it was Wednesday night and there were no lights on

Wednesday and no speaking was permitted when there were no lights.

The cots in the dormitory were numbered in bright, bald tin, and the pillows lay, alternately, at the foot and at the head of each cot. Thus each boy slept facing his neighbor's feet, the even-numbered ones with their feet to the wall and the odd-numbered ones with their feet to the aisle.

"I'd like t' be a paratrooper 'n just fly around," Silly Louie was saying dreamily to himself.

"If you ever catch more'n one finger," States cautioned him hoarsely, "play ball with the cops—'cause if you just cop a plea fer the one you got caught in, when you done yer stretch they'll show up with dew process, 'n that's when they make you stand sep'rate trial fer the ones you didn't get caught on. You oughta cop a plea fer all of 'em in the first place. It don't take no more time 'n you get 'em all settled fer keeps. Now it don't make no diff'rence," States went on gravely, "whether your rod is loaded or not—you'll do time fer havin' crim'nal *in*tent all the same. The only diff is, if your rod is loaded you get a chance t' do it in the pen 'stead of the workie, 'n that's where you get all the breaks. Down there you do it on yer ear 'n no trouble a-tall. You gotta watch out fer yourself these days."

"I wouldn't want t' carry no rod though," Silly Louie confessed. "I want t' be a paratrooper 'n just fly around."

States dismissed Louie's flighty ambitions. "Awright then, so you're a strong-arm merchant instead. You go in fer raw-jaw 'n mayhem, Louie—like Commandos. Then you know what you do if you catch a finger?"

Silly Louie didn't know that either. Silly Louie didn't know anything.

"Well then I'll tell you. You plead D. & D. That's drunk 'n disorderly. Say you're drunk 'n fightin'. It's like malicious mischief too, sort of. Catch on? Get it, you?"

Poor Louie did not answer. He had dropped off to sleep.

States continued his conversation with himself, reviewing all the angles in his mind, brushing up on his law, planning for his postwar future. He heard the passing of the Ogden Avenue cars and the coughing of a city dredge down Roosevelt Road. Heard the endless crying of a freight train going somewhere all night long. And all the sounds of night seemed like sounds going always away from home, all night.

"Always use a blue-steel," he warned himself hurriedly, thinking and planning fast now to keep down the fear of the night and the streets rising in him. "They can see the nickel-plate kind in the dark. Them .38 Policemen's Specials is the best; but with the nickel-plate kind—that's how you wind up with your little toes curled up in a ditch when they see it in the dark."

He felt himself growing sleepy, and, with his last waking thoughts, promised himself happier times: "When I get t' St. Charles," he assured himself, "I'm gonna learn up somp'n new every day awright. When I come out I'll be like a Commando all on my own. I'll be my own army 'n then they all better look out."

Silly Louie tittered softly in his sleep, as though he were dreaming that States had to be Hiawatha, instead of himself, on Thanksgiving Day.

million-dollar brainstorm

A roaring was still in his ears, and the ceiling was circling slowly above his eyes; he became aware of familiar fingers prodding him passionlessly back toward consciousness. As the ceiling came to a slow halt, he saw that steam, circling about the pipes overhead, had caused him to think it was the ceiling that had been moving.

"I won't get in no ring again, Myer," he assured the familiar fingers. "All I wanna do is stay home 'n play wid Kingfish." And fell into a snoring sleep, to dream of Kingfish, his muscle-bound cat.

The fingers covered the oversized fighter to the forehead with the sheet, as though covering him for keeps. They scribbled a note and pinned it, like a lily, to the sleeper's breast:

TINY:

I put a half-C in your wallet. In case I don't run into you the next couple days I want you should remember, you can't drink no more. A couple shots with you is like a quart on somebody else whose jaw ain't been hit so much. Go four rounds every day. I'm telling the papers it's a big comeback if they'll only listen. No joints. No women. And forget about that damned cat.

                                                                    MYER

"Yeah?" Tiny Zion snickered to himself, reading the note laboriously an hour later. "Whobody said I got no nice cat? I got a *nice* cat." He thought of Kingfish's lion-colored eyes and deep fur with physical pleasure. "I'm gonna pet him t'night," he promised himself.

He dressed dopily among the abandoned lockers and left carrying a scarred black bag: one he had carried to his first pro fight one late fall night when he'd been a Golden Gloves title-holder and all over the West Side his relatives were calling him champ.

"You're too big to be any kind of champ," some rum-dum had told him, on that half-forgotten night. Tiny grinned complacently now at the memory. He'd showed that rum-dum he wasn't too big that night. "I hit him so fast he was layin' there wrigglin' like a pig before he got through talkin'. ' 'N I'm still growin', too!' " he had told the rum-dum.

Some rum-dum. Some champ.

Now the bleachers about the darkened ring were littered with peanut shells and programs as he passed. Like on the afternoon he'd bet the purse of his first fight on the White Sox and they'd lost, 11-0, and the crowd had begun going home in disgust before the seventh inning was over, and by the time two were out in the eighth he'd been practically the only one left in the grandstand, with a chill wind blowing, still hoping for a miracle. He'd been hoping for miracles ever since, it seemed.

How the late fall wind had come off Shields Avenue that long-ago afternoon, blowing paper cups and score cards across the diamond while thirty-two Comiskey ushers, each with a great "C" worked in gold braid across his breast, had marched out stiffly and stood in a phalanx about the littered infield, guarding the spiked sand and the unmarked score cards with their arms locked before them, protecting the empty diamond, pretending that the park wasn't really abandoned at all.

That afternoon there hadn't been even one small boy asking Ted Lyons to sign a smudged autograph book; yet the ushers had remained, arms locked before them haughtily, as if the Sox had just taken a double-header from Boston.

"Poor old Sox," Tiny reflected sadly. "Poor old pugs. Poor old people. They certainly have a time."

Had he only been a weak sort of kid, he reflected vaguely now on the half-empty car, a kid with a brace on one leg or cockeyes or the shakes, and had had to read books all day to kill the time, maybe he would have turned out to be a lawyer, the way the old lady had always wanted. A motory public anyhow. The old man had stayed out of the doghouse, but here was his kid Hymie still living off the old lady half the time. He hung his hands loosely before his eyes, squinting at the long index finger that hadn't been set right after he'd broken it against Newboy Miller; above either wrist the hairs were bent like small reddish grasses, where the crossed laces had lain. He had always liked to wear them too tight.

"A motory public," he planned vaguely. "I could still get to be one, I bet. If I could just get hold of a seal I'd motorize the whole damned public. All I need is a million-dollar idea." He shoved his hands up past his ears, pushing up an imaginary head guard to rid himself of the constant faint ringing in his ears, for which he'd been to half a dozen doctors. "It's just the blood circulating, Tiny," the kindest one had told him. Because the ringing grew steadier, he crossed the street to Manny Doonick's Playhouse, slipping on a pair of sunglasses as he entered to conceal his discolored eye.

Doonick's shack was lined with photos of fighters, mostly Jewish. Tiny leaned across the bar at a photo of Bat Levinsky, who'd fought Carpentier as though he'd trained three weeks in a wet paper bag. But the second Levinsky's picture wasn't there. Manny Doonick was still mad at him for sitting down on the ropes against Louis.

"I wouldn'ta done like *he* done, Manny," Tiny assured little Manny now. And Manny nodded kindly, assuringly. "I know *you* wouldn't, Tiny."

"My mother should find me in bed wid a whore first," Tiny vowed fiercely. "Before I'd get counted out settin' on the ropes she should find me dead like that 'n call all the neighbors in."

"Take it easy, Tiny," Manny asked. "We know *you* wouldn't."

His eyes strayed uneasily toward a picture set aside from the others and shrouded by the juke's shadow as well as by dust and time: a rabbi's son from Dubuque who came up the hard way and beat the best. It read simply: In Memoriam, Miltie Aron.

The farther wall held a longer line of photos: the great Jewish lightweights: Leonard, White, Tendler, and Sailor Freedman; Louis Kid Kaplan, Al Singer, Sid Terris, Ross, Dublinsky, and the skinny, round-shouldered, cave-chested, careless kid who had talked himself out of a title: Davey Day.

"We make good little men," Tiny thought happily, as though he weighed 132 stripped instead of 228. His eyes avoided a parallel line of certain big stuffed bums labeled Great Jewish Heavies.

He thought, rather, of the lightweights and welters, all the unbeatable West Side wonders who were all going to retire undefeated. All the fastest, sharpest Twelfth Street wonders who had never been knocked down and had never lost and could never be beaten at all; the ones who were the toughest of Chicago's toughest, who were smarter than everyone and would never be beaten at all.

Tiny snickered to himself mockingly. They were all beat now, one way or another. One running a ferris wheel at corner carnivals in summer and boozing all winter, one hung up on a morphine kick, another carrying buckets at the Marigold on Monday nights, and another walking around with a load of ties, under which he concealed defective contraceptives at cut-rate prices. "Some clowns," Tiny thought of them with disdain, fingering his discolored eye. "But all a guy like me needs is a million-dollar idea."

He placed the scarred bag beside a cuspidor and one foot on the rail and someone called to him from a booth: a middle-aged barfly, blonde and blowzy. He took his beer over to her table and sat across from her, keeping his cap on to conceal his bald spot.

"I seen you fight lots of times," she explained. "Call me Sara. My husband's still overseas 'n I hope they keep him there. You wanna go drink dime beers all night? I know a place where they sell it in glasses."

By the time the bottle arrived he was confiding anxiously in her.

"Sara, I seen my best days. I'll never climb in no ring again. There ain't that much money in Chicago, to make me. T'night was my croosical fight 'n I losed. I knocked him down twicet before the customers got their coats off. He got up 'n run like a t'ief. I got exawsted chasin' him, sort of dizzy-like. Then I sort of fainted. So they say I losed."

"You wanna drink dime beers all night? I know a place."

" 'N now I'll never fight again," he concluded dramatically.

He held up his right fist, in the booth's half-light, like a club for her to admire. She feigned fear instead, covering her face with her fingers and squeaking coyly; he took her hand to reassure her and found he could envelope her entire fist in his own. That pleased them both, and while being pleased she ordered again and took off his sunglasses, folding them resolutely into her palm. But he wouldn't let her remove his cap.

"It makes me unconscious, 'cause I got no hair," he explained. He reached for the bottle and drank directly from it.

"Just washin' down the pretzels," he explained solemnly, flecking salt and saliva off his lips, and started speaking of a fight he had had in Des Moines. Then broke off and buried his head on his arms on the shadowed table. She took off the cap and patted his skull sympathetically, while he wept hoarsely. She moved over beside him, put one arm about him; but he would not look up. And touched the bulge of the wallet at his hip with her index finger, lightly. The finger rested one moment, lightly, on the pocket's broken button; rested lightly on the wallet's edge. Her arm straightened from the elbow, but did not bend; her wrist did not bend; her fingers were rigid on the leather. Then she raised her whole body, slowly, bringing up the arm like a locked lever. Slipped the wallet beneath her as though straightening her dress, seated herself upon it while stroking the mangy fringe of his skull tenderly.

"I know a *good* place, hon," she assured him.

He leaned his bald spot against her breast and she slipped her hand into his. He rose heavily with her, walking with docility to the door, where she returned the scarred wallet deftly to his hip and the scarred bag to his hand. He reeled off with the lake wind urging him south, thinking she was shoving him playfully.

"Somebody's gonna get it for this," he singsonged amiably, threatening her playfully. "*Some*-body's gonna *get* it."

When he realized it was only the wind, he let it kid him along down Wabash; then began feeling vaguely afraid of the wind's urging: of the open street and lightless places.

He felt for the wallet at his hip, touched its edge, and rolled on, laughing low and confidently. "I give her the slip real neat," he congratulated himself. "I knew she was out to clip me as soon as she called me over. That's why I ducked. No women, Myer says. The hell with Myer. I got million-dollar ideas. Me'n Kingfish, we'll make a million."

It was not until he boarded a Twenty-second Street trolley west that the first dim sense of loss came upon him. He held the conductor's shoulder with one hand and proffered the empty wallet with the other. And felt himself shoved from behind; angry voices near at hand seemed suddenly going far away. He tried to climb back on, but the car door slammed and caught his coat; he ran frantically, as the car gathered speed, trying to catch up with his tearing coat to keep from being dragged, the scarred bag signaling frantically overhead till the sleeve ripped to the shoulder and he fell headlong, while the severed sleeve, still caught in the door, waved him a wild good-by in the wind. He had a vague idea he had lost an arm and collapsed pitifully on the curb beneath the Federal Street viaduct, clasping his shoulder. When he found his own arm still in place he pondered dismally, "Who the hell's arm *was* that?"

He sat with his head in his hands while the gutter giggled at his feet like any blowzy blonde. With both hands braced against the fireplug he got sick; then continued on toward the vast West Side waving the bag aimlessly over his head, through streets that seemed forever narrowing, boasting to the darkness of his accomplishment in getting sick across a fireplug.

"Popped my cookies!" he congratulated himself, awe-struck by his deed. "Flashed the old hash all over Twenny-second." He was inordinately impressed by that feat. "I didn't know I had it in me!" And was immediately overcome by his own wit. " 'I didn't know I had it in me.' Wow! I think things nobody ever thinked before. We'll make a million. Me'n Kingfish."

Once a woman's face, pallid with luminous eyes, appeared near to him and then faded quietly away. He extended the empty wallet toward the place where she had been.

"Save my life, lady," he begged. "Save my life. Eight cents carfare save my life."

Toward morning some dim and wavering figure handed him a punched-out transfer and he rode four blocks further west, in a car crowded with Negroes, before the conductor tapped his shoulder for a fare. This time he disembarked with dignity; and with equal dignity boarded the next one, on which he lasted two blocks. By this slow yet certain process he progressed toward Horwitz's Restaurant and Bar. Where he arrived at last, like a reeling transport after rough seas, safe into port exactly on the stroke of noon.

The bar was lined, and the tables were filled with Horwitz's happy little clothiers, lawyers, and doctors: they sat in respectable rows and drank iced tea with lemon, amongst the silver and the strains of Winsburg's three-piece violin ensemble.

Tiny came in jarring the tables, hawking into a dirty rag, and leering into the little white faces of the frightened diners; he knew most of them by name.

"Eight cents, Solly, save my life." He drooled into Solly's linen, fumbled with Solly's martini, and grasped Solly firmly by both lapels. "Buy the big Jew a beer, Solly. Buy the big Hebe a beer."

Horror sat on Horwitz's head for a single moment; then he shepherded Tiny into the back, where he spoon-fed him black coffee personally; but there was no use urging him to leave. Tiny was too happy where he was. He laughed and slapped his thigh at the recollection of last night's fight. "Ahhh, Harry, he's only a slugger, all he can do is slug." He rolled his great head happily, thinking of the slob they'd put in the ring there with him. What a laugh, putting him in there with a bum like that. Then he rubbed the back of his neck and changed the subject.

"Gimme a sweet roll, Harry," he begged. When Harry gave it to him he was weeping piteously into the coffee; took one moist look at the dry roll and brushed it, plate and all, onto the floor.

"No peanuts on top," he demanded angrily, and before Horwitz could stop him he was on his feet, ambling between the tables again and extending his empty wallet for all to see.

"Save my life, boys. Eight cents carfare save my life. Buy the big Jew a beer."

Horwitz phoned for Myer Salk. "And if you ain't here in ten minutes I sue."

He was still begging around, stealing caraway seeds off rolls, when Myer arrived, freshly shaven and picking his teeth. He winked at Horwitz and took Tiny's arm; but it took the two of them and a waiter to get him into Myer's Chevvie. Tiny nodded all the way to his mother's, looking up only occasionally to watch the bright sheen of the afternoon pavement.

"Save my life, Myer," he mumbled. "Eight cents carfare save my life."

Leaning forward from the rear seat, he blew his bad breath down Myer's neck and extended the wallet that Myer, too, might see its emptiness. Myer saw.

"As if I didn't know."

His life was an empty wallet. And he was sleeping when they reached the aging staircase that led to the dingy Kostner Street parlor called home. Myer began feeling sorry for Mama Zion as soon as he heard her padding down the uncarpeted stairs. She had fallen once, and took them now with care. Holding onto the banister with one arm, with the West Side sun filtering in from a single dusty window, she waited, always, for the worst. She had always expected the worst and had never been disappointed. Myer lugged his burden onto the red plush couch and Tiny sat down with a great plunge, jumped halfway up and plunged down again, grinning from ear to ear. "I *like* to set on plush, Myer. Look at me, I'm settin'." He bounced to his heart's satisfaction, while his mother and his manager looked gravely on. Then relaxed to let his mother take off his shoes. "Don't tickle," he warned her.

Myer watched her hauling on the oversized shoe, wiping her eyes and tugging blindly at the laces. While Tiny dangled the wallet like a toy before her eyes. Myer felt like leaving.

"How's your head feel, Hymie?" Myer asked.

Tiny rubbed the back of his skull reflectively, then grinned triumphantly. "It don't hurt no more, Myer."

"How's your jaw?"

Tiny waited a moment, to find out. Till all the hollows in his broken face filled with a coy pride.

"It hu-urts, Myer."

He was blushing.

"Don't let it hurt Monday night."

"What's Monday, Myer?"

"That's your big comeback night."

Myer was looking closer at his boy. There was a new thickness in his voice that Myer had not heard before.

"You got a piece of dirt in your eye, Hymie," he said, and with swift fingers peeled back the lid. Hymie's eyes rolled up fluttering. When the hand was removed they descended too slowly.

"Oh boy, Myer, my big comeback night. I'll be in there pitchin' too, I bet."

"It's a setup," Myer confided. "We'll murder him. You'll be my comeback kid." He brought forth a package of gum from his vest, offered the kneeling mother a stick, regarding her thoughtfully. She shook her head blindly. Myer tore the wrapper off with unnecessary energy, took a stick himself, and shoved the other four between Tiny's teeth.

"Chew, Hymie."

Hymie chewed, happiness dawning hugely on him, like a sunrise. His face always reminded Myer of a battered baseball mitt; now it began taking on a dull gleam as he chewed.

"It don't—hurt—when—I—chew, Myer." He rose heavily, shambled over to the ancient vic, and fumbled helplessly a moment with it. "Turn it on, Myer. I ferget how."

"A lawyer would have made me happy," the old woman mourned softly. "A motory public even."

Myer started the record disk turning and reached for a record, but Tiny's hand stayed him. "No music, Myer. No music." He stole softly to the sofa where his great scarred tom slept and scooped him up softly, sofa and all. The cat stirred sleepily, till Tiny placed him firmly on the whirling disk and held him there.

Myer backed toward the door. "What you doing, Hymie?" he asked politely.

"I'm makin' a record, Myer. It'll be a new idea." The cat was struggling frantically to escape, but Tiny was determined. "It'll be like 'His Master's Voice,' only with a cat instead. You get it? It'll sell a million, Myer." He frowned with displeasure at Kingfish for wanting to get off too soon.

"Say somethin', King," he coaxed sweetly, "say somethin' funny, 'n let the people laugh."

"The cat'll get sick, Hymie," Myer warned him. And closed the door softly behind him. Going down the staircase, he heard the old woman begin wailing and the wail was lost in a long cat-scream and Hymie scolding the two of them in Yiddish. Myer paused a moment to listen. "She won't be able to handle him no more," he realized thoughtfully. "Can't nobody handle him no more. I seen it in his eyes."

Then, as he came out onto the open street, in a realization tinged with relief: "It ain't none of Myer Salk's business no more," he concluded. Two stories above him a window opened and Kingfish came hurtling toward the sidewalk with the voice of Tiny Zion bellowing in disappointed rage overhead.

"You ain't smart enough to be *my* cat! Your brains is scrambled! I don't want no cat the people are all laughin' at! Don't come back to my nice house no more!"

Kingfish scooted down the alley as though he understood every word, and Myer Salk climbed into his Chevvie.

"He'll be throwin' the old lady out the winda next," he surmised as he switched on the ignition. "Or jumpin' outa it hisself."

pero venceremos

"I been in more ballroom brawls," O'Connor assured me, "I been in more ballroom brawls."

But no one pays O'Connor attention any more. O'Connor is O'Connor and we've heard it all before. There's bock beer and a bingo game that you almost beat and a juke box that still plays "Lili Marlene" and we all have our own troubles anyhow.

"At Sierra La Valls, a place we called The Pimple, we attacked with the Mac-Paps and the English. There was a Moor in front 'n one behind 'n I fixed him in front through the groin the same second the steel of him behind come through me here." O'Connor tapped his left shoulder.

"It's the other shoulder, Denny," I reminded him, "and it healed up long since."

He gave me the glance as though I hadn't heard it all a hundred detailed times in the decade since his return from Spain. I could have given him back the story word for word.

"When I got him in front through the groin the steel of him behind come through me here—I didn't *feel* it, I *seen* it 'n come around fast with the butt before he could loosen 'er. Caught him square with the flat of it 'n he went out cold 'n I finished him where he lay with his bayonet still in my back. It tore me up pretty bad, turnin' so fast on him that way, but I didn't faint till I seen he was done for keeps. Them was Black Arrows 'n Falangistas 'n you can't give that kind a chance. *We* had to be sparin' with cartridges, but they could use an anti-tank shell on anythin' that moved. They had more anti-tank shells than we had cartridges, they had more planes than we had machine guns. They could lay down an enfilading fire like pushin' on a button—'n keep 'er right there too, like they'd went off somewhere 'n forgot to turn somethin' off. They could land shells in the heart of a trench, movin' down the middle of 'er foot by foot 'n never miss the middle. Like a champ horseshoe pitcher in East St. Louis I used to know who'd never miss a ringer."

He picked up a half dollar and a dime lying beside his glass. "See that?" Holding up the half. "This is overhead shrapnel, this here's a hunk no bigger 'n a half dollar." He put the coin down. "You know what a hunk that size will do to a man? It'll cut him in half. *Sever* him. It'll slice off his neck or maybe both legs, just a hunk that big. Now this"—exchanging the half for the dime—"this'll slice off a hand like slicin' through cheese—a piece just this tiny." He brought his knees up to his chin in the booth, yanked up his trouser leg to the knee, and slipped off his shoe and sock.

"Here, I'll show you somethin'."

I'd first seen that leg after Sierra La Valls. It was marked four times from shrapnel between the ankle and the knee; the heel wore a crusted wound, like a sea shell's crusted mouth, and was crossed twice by thin white scars, as a hot-cross bun is crossed with sugar. After ten years it was still open and the edges were hard as cement. Within, like O'Connor, it was decaying.

"See that? That's rot. I used to think it'd stop but I don't think so no more. Some one of these days they'll be takin' 'er off me—'n you know how much shrapnel they took out of that job?" He touched fingertip to thumb to indicate a pellet the size of a grape seed.

"That much did *that*. Now you know."

He yanked down the trouser, looking pleased with himself, and slipped the shoe and sock back on with an air of finality. A second world war had come and gone and Denny hadn't yet spoken of anything else but overhead shrapnel on the Ebro and a man's need for taking care of himself, of being alert for physical disaster that might come any hour of the day or night in any of a thousand guises. He was still frightened of the hand-to-hand stuff. It wouldn't be so bad if he'd invent a little sometimes as he went along. But it's always the same thread-bare routine.

"I was raised in East St. Louis," he went on, "a couple blocks south of the Valley. I been in more brawls on land 'n sea than you got fingers 'n toes 'n I'm a good union man to boot. You got to be in East St. Louis. That's where I learned to hold my fire."

I was wishing he'd hold his fire long enough for me to put a nickel in the juke. I knew he hadn't belonged to a union since Pearl Harbor. Abruptly, as though suddenly afraid of losing my attention, he sloshed his beer across the floor, shoved the glass into his pocket and, covering it with his hand, broke it neatly on the corner of the table and withdrew it jagged and cracked. He emptied the fragments on the floor and held up the bottom half.

"No one can touch you when you're fixed up with somethin' like this," he assured me as though we were being threatened from the next booth. "Even if a guy got the difference on him he don't want to get too close to no man with broken glass in his hand. So just work up close to him 'n ask would he like one of his lamps trimmed." He described a circle in mid-air with a screwlike movement of the glass and reassured me that the fellow would put the difference back on his hip where it belonged.

But his heart wasn't in it after all. He put the glass down, looking tired, and apologized indistinctly. "I'm just a poor boy doin' the best he can. Maybe I just wasn't raised right."

"Maybe it was that war, Denny. A lot of the boys got hurt in the big one too, you know." Anything to get his mind off Spain.

"Oh, *that* one," he said. "I guess it was bigger all right. But ours was tougher." He always referred to the great war as "theirs" and to the war in Spain as "ours." "Not one guy in ten even got shot at in the big one," he added. "We had the hand-to-hand stuff." He had something there, I had to admit that.

"At Sierra La Valls," he started in again, "two of them jumped me. It wasn't yet mornin' 'n still foggy, one in front 'n one behind, I was comin' back from a all-night scout, I got the one in front through the groin 'n drew it out clean the same second the steel of him behind come through my shoulder. I didn't *feel* it, I just *seen* it 'n come 'round fast with the butt. Laid one out cold 'n got the other where it counts. Finished him where he lay, him I'd cold-caulked, 'n his own steel stickin' out of my back when I done it."

I rose indifferently, shoved a nickel in the juke, turned the volume on "loud," and returned to the table till the piece was almost finished: a Dorsey recording called "As Long As You Live You'll Be Dead If You Die." Then I bought a quarter's worth of sixes at the twenty-six board. I made it last, shaking slowly. On the last roll I needed but one six and it came all fives and deuces and I saw him coming again, limping a little, like he does on flat surfaces. So I bought another quarter's worth in a hurry and offered him the box. He didn't want it, of course. He'd just watch. That's all he'd been doing for a decade: watching. He wasn't interested in dice any more than in beer. Or in women, or swing, or the opening game at Comiskey Park, or Woodcock's chances against Louis, or any of the good American things he's been raised on and lived by.

He had gone to sea at eighteen and had helped chase Sandino, one afternoon in Nicaragua, and now he wished to tell

me more about Sierra La Valls. That was pretty little to grant
a man, but I took sixes again and thought of him at forty. He'd
only have one foot by then, if he was still around. In a way he
wasn't much here any more at thirty-five. He too lay among
the dead at Sierra La Valls. He'd keep on talking awhile,
though, to whoever would listen, about that foggy morning at
The Pimple. Then curtains. Game called, darkness.

"At Fuente de Ebro———" he began.

"Maybe you'd better forget Fuente de Ebro," I advised him
directly. "After all, that's a hundred years ago."

He looked at me a long moment, as though trying to understand what I'd said. He was trying so hard that he was biting
his lip. Then seemed suddenly to understand at last.

"Why, no," he told me, a little dreamily, "it ain't that long
ago at all. It's just like yesterday."

He rose slowly, his last nickel in his palm, and leaned as
though resting against the juke while it began, for the last time,
"As Long As You Live You'll Be Dead If You Die." When it
was finished he returned slowly and asked me, "Did I say *yesterday?*" And shook his head like a man recalling an endless
dream. "It wasn't even yesterday, the way it feels."

"How does it feel, Denny?"

"It feels more—like tomorrow."

I hadn't thought of it just that way before.

no man's laughter

Nineteen whorls on the index finger. A spiral on the thumb. No regular address. Pick up for investigation.

That was Gino Bomagino to the auto-theft detail.

He gave the detail trouble before he was twelve, when he was hauled out of a stolen truck he had crashed into a parked Pontiac on Mother Cabrini Street. He was wearing a pair of women's high-heeled pumps, no stockings, and a pair of man-sized overalls that fitted him like an awning. If it hadn't been for the pumps, he assured the detail, they'd never have gotten him: he couldn't run in them. And admitted, when pressed, that he'd picked the pumps out of a Goose Island dump and stolen the overalls. That he had quit school "because the kids pointed on me." His small chin jutted, warning the officers they'd better not point either; while his hair, which was red, hung angrily before his eyes.

"I'm one hood don't like gettin' caught," he explained solemnly. "I don't like hangin' around the house neither, 'cause Nicky 'n Carlo 'n Steve sleep on top." It developed that he meant on top of the bed, because they were older, while he slept underneath. His terrier's face lit up. "I wanted t' take a ride somewheres. I can drive like hell."

And paled with rage when the officers snickered. They

turned him over to Juvenile Detention, and somehow or other he grew up.

By the time that happened they wished they had mugged and printed him, six years before, at Juvenile.

For he certainly could drive like hell.

Within those six brief years the redheaded fledgling found wings. The more time he had to get anywhere, the sooner he arrived. When Jeanie, who loved him, asked what the hurry was, he would reply, "The faster I go the safer I feel. I feel like I'm gettin' somewheres. The brothers used to eat before me at home, because they was bigger, and at Joov'nile it was worse, always gettin' shoved back to the tail of the line: when I got out it seemed like everybody in the world was all tryin' to push me off the curb. When I get behind a wheel, though, that's when I pass 'em all up. That's when I got the world beat. When the cops start chasin', that's even better. 'Cause after I get away I feel like nobody'll ever catch me 'n ain't nobody caught me yet."

"When they do it'll be too late," Jeanie warned him.

"Too late for what?"

"Too late to start sleepin' nights 'n goin' to work days, Gino. That's the only *safe* way."

"I don't play nothin' safe," he told her. Then turned it off into a joke and made her forget her fear. Because sometimes Jeanie liked to drive fast too.

There was the afternoon that the squad spotted him wheeling idly back and forth around the northwest entrance to Humboldt Park, and forced him to the curb. Gino waited for them, grinning. Then slammed into reverse and wheeled into the scrub bounding the park, zigzagging between trees and crushing bushes, onto the winding park boulevard. They didn't come that close again for a year.

Then, in the early-morning dark, a gray sedan passed a streetcar on the wrong side at Polk and Halsted. There were three men in the auto, which resembled one used earlier in the evening in two tavern robberies. The squad car followed it, firing, for a mile eastward on DeKoven Street. Just east of Clinton the driver ran up over the curb, swerved around in a hairpin turn on two wheels, and headed back west, narrowly missing the squad car. By the time the officers had turned their car the other was out of sight.

In the same week police spotted him in the Loop going north on La Salle. The bridge was up at Wacker, but Gino didn't falter. He wheeled the car down through the streetcar tunnel, bumping over the wooden ties, and showed up, for one moment before vanishing again, on Hubbard Street across the river.

"I'm a guy like this," Gino explained to Jeanie; "I like anythin' against odds. I don't like nothin' safe. I'm a guy like this too: I don't like gettin' caught. But mostly I'm a guy like this: I don't like gettin' laughed at."

He lived as he drove, as he gambled and as he loved: for keeps. Taking no man's laughter. And letting the small stakes go.

The next time the detail spotted him he was brandishing a .38 blue-steel in a back-room bookie on West Chicago Avenue. He had fifteen men flat on their faces on the floor and his hair seemed bristling under his cap. They took him from behind, struggling until he was crying, weakly and desperately. "Who are all these guys makin' half a grand a week 'n me not makin' a cryin' dime?" he demanded to know in the wagon.

He refused a lawyer that time. His defense was farfetched, but brief. He decided to stand or fall by it, and he fell: "Some guy run past me just as I come in to make a little bet 'n stuck that gun in my hand. So I just thought I'd see how everybody'd look layin' down. That's all."

He got six months in the workie for that one, and came out mean: a closemouthed fighting cock with a bitter grin and a trick of keeping his fists doubled at his sides. As though any passing stranger might prove a citizen-dress man straight from the Gun Bureau.

Nineteen whorls on the index finger. A spiral on the thumb. No regular address. Pick up for investigation.

When the mailman dropped his neighbors' greetings into Jeanie's mailbox, Gino threw the notice away. They had to come and get him.

Jeanie was worried then, but Gino had it down for the biggest laugh in the books. He kidded his way through his physical, until he saw they really meant it. Then he told the doc: "I got bad teeth."

"That's all right," he was assured. "We don't want you to bite them Japs."

Then he saw the police record attached. There were no federal offenses.

"You wouldn't steal anything in the Army?" he flattered Gino.

Gino pointed to the steam radiator in the corner of the office. "You see that raditor there?" he asked.

"Yes."

"You step out for five minutes and I'll take it home under my coat."

And the doc thought he was being kidded.

Two days later Gino was handed a carbine and asked whether he'd had any experience with guns.

"No," Gino answered, playing safe, "I been afraid of them things all my life."

But he did admit to a knowledge of things which make automobiles run fast.

"Then maybe you can learn what makes airplanes fly," he was told. And he learned his stick so fast it was shocking. Though he didn't get along even with his own uniform at first, later he took a sneaking pride in it. He was never able to bring himself to salute as though he meant it; he made each salute smack faintly of nose-thumbing. And remained forever on the defensive, forever bristling at fancied insults and always turning a casual ribbing into an open challenge, to be settled openly and without compromise. A stretch in the stockade only set him brooding on his wrongs, and served to convince him that, even here, he must remain forever on the outside of everything except the nearest brig.

He had belonged to nothing save to the car he happened to be wheeling, and Jeanie; in similar fashion he attached himself to the first plane to which he was assigned—and named the plane to himself, secretly, *Jeanie*. He learned to stay out of trouble by spending his days over the engine and his nights over the stick, avoiding his messmates as sedulously as they had learned, early, to avoid him. They had him down for a humorless runt too mean to fool with. Once he became so lonely that he started a letter to Jeanie; but the effort blunted the edge of his loneliness, and the letter was never finished.

"You're the best damned mechanic in this outfit," his pilot conceded reluctantly, as a simple statement of fact. "If you can fly like you can fix, you'll have your rating in a month."

Gino grunted. The fellow talked as though he were saying something that no one else knew. Wasn't he Gino? The best wheelman on the Near Northwest Side?

"You're mad at the whole world," the pilot went on, "and maybe you got good reason. But if you forget your grudge you'll fly that much sooner. And that much better."

Gino looked him up and down. "When I'm ready to fly I'll fly," he assured his man. "When I'm ready I'll take the stick. The hell with the rating. The hell with you." It was the longest speech any man on the field had heard him make. They joked of it in barracks for a week.

Gino may have softened with time. But before the softening process had set in, he had a letter from Jeanie:

G<small>INO</small>,

I know you won't blame me for what I got to say, but it's time for me to start playing it safe even if you don't want to. You know the old saying: "Absence makes the heart grow fonder, for somebody else." Well, I got married at St. John's Sunday morning. You don't know the fellow but I bet you'd like him. He got picked up once for driving a horse and wagon without lights. Stay as sweet as you are.

"I bet I'd like him too." Gino reflected moodily, and tore up the note with deliberation.

"Sometimes a soldier sort of finds hisself up there," the pilot philosophized vaguely to his bombardier, without mentioning any particular soldier you might name. "Sometimes if a soldier with something twisted up inside him gets off the earth alone with it, he untwists a little."

Gino was on a night-scouting detail over the Aleutians, the week after the fall of Bizerte, when, in his own fashion, he untwisted himself. Returning to his base in a single-seater, flame in the sky told him he was riding into more than a sunrise. He flew directly into it to conceal himself—and saw the great low-lying cruiser with the rising sun on the stern slipping back out to sea, leaving a long line of installations in flames. Gino swung out to sea after it, liking the feeling of being, just this one time, the hunter instead of the hunted.

There wasn't anything he could do, with the crate he was wheeling up there, except to keep the cruiser's movements relayed back to his base long enough to bring up a couple of the big boys. He hung on just out of range, between the sunrise and the sea, pretending that he was cutting the cruiser off to the curb, as life and the auto-theft detail had so often cut him off.

The cruiser's anti-aircraft battery got its data together as soon as he appeared off-stern, before the pounding of feet on the iron ladders had ceased. It pleased Gino, hopping from

cloud to cloud, to know that the great guns being manned
below were being manned for no one more important than a
petty-larceny punk from West Chicago Avenue. Across the
bottomless Alaskan sky he flittered, leapfrogging the clouds
parallel with the cruiser's course, into the ice-green sky ahead
or streaming back into the blaze of the morning sun. He kept
the gun crews in their places like groups of statuary, cursing
the Yankee who didn't have sense enough to understand that
he couldn't keep hanging in the sky all day like a kite.

And all that ice-green forenoon the kite hung on, calling for
help that never came. And wheeled on into the green Alaskan
dusk. When fog came settling down over the sea and the
cruiser was only a dim gray blur in the endless grayness, he
called on his reserve tank and came down on her tail, following
her by the wake of the waves, and would not let go and go
home.

The stakes were too big for Gino to quit. He had played
every game for keeps, and this was the biggest game of all. He
believed in his luck, he believed in his wheel and his stick; and
what no other man had yet believed in: himself.

Like waking from a dream, the fluttering needle told him he
wouldn't be going home. And fancied he heard light mockery
then from the decks below: high, taunting laughter; and the
guns pointing like a jeer. Like that first time, so endlessly long
ago, when the bigger boys had "pointed on him." And came in
low with ack-ack taunting him on, to drive the single-seater
through the cruiser's wall like a locomotive through a barn.

Then, crippled and trapped forever, in a fever of swimming
pain, he felt, with a single leaping flame of joy, the first great
explosion on the deck above. And felt himself wheeling easily
through the brush of a land at once strange and familiar, zigzagging numbly down an ever-narrowing way, with the roar of
the El overhead and his last swift pursuer hard upon him. And
realized, in one last blind swing of that last pursuit, that he was

coasting gently downhill at last, toward a land where he'd be unpursued forever.

"They must of made him mad," the pilot observed thoughtfully to the bombardier, watching the great cruiser floundering in her own flames below. "He must of thought some monkey on the deck was laughin' at that crate he was wheeling."

katz

This is no laughing matter . . .
Popular Song

At nine o'clock of a midsummer evening a young man named
Katz stood on the corner of North Clark and West Erie streets
in Chicago. He had sixty-five dollars in a wallet on his hip,
four shots of Old Fitz under his belt, and no one but himself to
believe in.

He had no need of any other, having sixty-five dollars. The
delightful, varying ways he could distribute this sum, in all the
devious city ways, crowded his mind. There was no room, in
his anticipation, for anything but the city's changeful colors
and the fastest means of spending sixty-five fish.

He had no friend, though he had lived in the city all his life.
Yet he knew every shadowed corner of North Clark Street,
every poolroom with darkened windows and a fake padlock on
the door. All the curtained parlors and the right way to ring:
one long and two short and ask for Marie.

He decidedly firmly against Marie. She had a way of never
letting him go until he was broke. He wouldn't ring there until
he was already badly bent. He was tempted by the poolroom
with the fake padlock, for he held a good stick of rotation and
had once lived on it for almost two weeks. But that took too
long, the endless waiting for the other fellow to finish his hand.
And he didn't want to drink any more: that could well spoil a

man's evening. It was depressing to wake up on a plank in the Chicago Avenue Station and have to wash up with a bunch of underfed derelicts from God-Knows-What-Alley. And, on top of that, to have to wait half the morning for some Dago judge to come around to tell Katz he could go home.

So it was Sheeny McCoy's. McCoy was a sport. So long as you didn't call him Sheeny. All the boys were sports. None of the boys were sheenies. But he'd have to play tight from the pocket. The Sheeny ran a tight game.

Up two flights, the long moment of being surveyed through a peephole and the hard-faced welcome. The bitter, unemphatic invitation:

"Seat open at the corner table."

That was the sort of sullen welcome Katz appreciated. It showed that the Real Sports believed in Katz's bank roll. It showed that, so long as he had money, he had value and a place. It was something for Katz to belong to.

Katz didn't want to be judged, this night or any city night, by anything but his bank roll. He didn't want to be welcomed anywhere save for what his hip pocket was holding. All other welcomes were false, all other faiths unreal.

At twenty minutes of ten Katz had eighty dollars on the hip and twenty-two singles before him. At ten minutes of he had ninety in the wallet and forty before him. It came so fast he became confused and had to depend, silently, on the dealer's alertness. The dealer was a sport too. Every time Katz won he tossed a half dollar back across the green baize of the table; the dealer rang it against the shaded bulb above him to show it was his and not the house's, and said "Thank you" to Katz. That let them all know that Katz was a Real Sport too.

At five after ten he had nothing in the wallet but his photostated discharge. Eight quarters, the last of the bank roll, were stacked pathetically before him, a remnant of his brief power. Katz blew, holding the quarters tightly, and feigning indifference.

"Tell 'em where you got it, 'n how easy it was," McCoy encouraged him at the door, offering him a dollar.

Katz declined the bill. "I'll be back," he said tersely. Nothing like keeping up a front. He wasn't any Chicago Avenue bum, from God-Knows-What-Alley, to be taking a handout. Not yet.

But the good feel of the liquor was gone, with the good feel of the money. And the old luck feeling was slipping fast.

On the corner he shifted uneasily, one foot to the other, replaying that last big hand in his mind for one last time. He let himself win it; then put it out of mind forever.

Nobody was through in Chicago. Any Saturday night. Not with change in his pants and a little heart under his ribs. Katz believed in the city. Katz believed in himself. Katz believed in lucky bucks, fast money, and good women.

Sure it was a lucky buck. He could feel the luck-stuff by rubbing the quarters against each other in his pocket. Which was the luckiest? He chose the smoothest, turned swiftly into the nearest bar, and laid it face down on the twenty-six board to keep the luck-stuff working. He rolled thirty-four before the girl behind the board realized she was beaten.

So he bought her a shot of Old Fitz and ordered the other seven shots lined up in a row before him on the bar. When they were all set up he started at the left, for luck; and downed them like a single drink.

The luck feeling was returning. All he had to have now was a game. Any game. On seven quarters? He laughed confidently to himself, feeling the liquor; as though the joke somehow was going to be on someone else just this once.

He returned to McCoy's steadily, in the manner of a man who has just replenished his purse.

"Your seat's took," McCoy told him suspiciously.

"It's open," Katz contradicted him flatly. "I told you I'd be back. It ain't ten minutes."

McCoy motioned, behind Katz's head, and the shill called

High-School got up to make room for the live one. As he sat down Katz's eyes avoided the warning above the dealer's head:

PLAYERS MUST START WITH FIVE DOLLARS

"How you playin'?" the dealer asked as though he couldn't place Katz.

"Pocket," Katz answered, tossing the seven quarters negligently on the cloth. If McCoy asked him to show folding money he'd tell them a thing or two. He bet one of the quarters blind.

Three hands checked. When it came around again Katz looked, saw nothing remarkable, and bet a half as though he had them. The remaining hand saw him. Katz bet a dollar he didn't have, fumbling in the coat laid over the back of his chair, coming up with his palm half closed on nothing. The hand checked and Katz shoved the empty hand down his pants pocket as he took the pot: three-fifty to the good.

High-School took the place of the player beside him.

Katz hid in the weeds for five hands running, feeling the shill's nearness shadowing the luck-feeling. Then came up with a pair against High-School that brought him four singles and some change. He bet the four back blind on the next hand, caught the case ace, and was back in business with nine singles. High-School sat back looking sullen. Did they call him High-School just because he'd never gone near one, Katz wondered idly. And raised the next pot to the limit.

Found himself with nothing and bet with confidence. McCoy, with a jack showing, called. McCoy bought a second jack. Katz, on a loose call, saw him, every card, all the way to the last closed card. The singles dwindled. The last one was a trey. He glanced at his concealed cards and saw its mate; a pair of treys against a pair of jacks. If he played them strong they could be—just possibly—good. Let the luck-stuff hold now. McCoy hesitated, checked, and Katz bet the limit without faltering. McCoy put his great paw on his money as though to guard it, then laid it over his cards to guard them too. Then waited, peering down into his folded hand. Katz waited. The dealer waited. High-School waited. McCoy glanced, furtively, through the drifting cigar smoke at Katz. To Katz the big man seemed to be crouching. But behind McCoy's eyes he sensed McCoy's slow mind working, like a heavy door being opened slowly by an unseen hand. With the swiftest flash of insight he had ever felt, Katz heard himself drawling slowly, as one good-time sport to another, in a take-it-or-leave-it-I'm-no-chiseler tone, "I got threes, McCoy."

McCoy tossed over his cards. "Threes beat a pair," he said, satisfied and grateful. Then pointed steadily at Katz's cards. The dealer turned them up. Two lonely treys.

"What I thought," McCoy said. "A Jew trick. It don't go." His hand covered the pot.

"I told you straight," Katz said steadily. "You dropped cold."

"Back off," McCoy told him. "A Jew trick."

And didn't sound grateful at all.

"I'll back off," Katz conceded good-naturedly. He'd be glad to get out of the joint with the pot. He shouldn't have tried anything at McCoy's. He should have gone to Marie. He could still go there all night on the change in the pot.

There wasn't any pot. It was McCoy's house and McCoy's game and McCoy's dealer.

"I told you back off."

"I'll take the pot first. I win it."

High-School hit him from the right side and the dealer hit him, as he spun, from the other. With his hands strapped behind him, McCoy came at him heavily, lifting him by the crotch.

Katz lit on the bottom step with one leg bent beneath him. McCoy stood on the top step looking down. His cap lay at McCoy's feet. McCoy kicked it down to him, with contempt in the kick, as toward anything belonging to any Katz. He unbent the leg, still sitting, tested it, and rubbed his cap across his mouth. The cap came back bloody. He licked his lip, looking up at the big man, and swallowed a slow trickle of blood.

"You'll make me mad at you, Sheeny."

"Some Jew trick," McCoy mocked. " 'I got threes, McCoy.' "

"Come on down here, Sheeny. I'll show you another Jew trick." Katz rose heavily. "You'll wind up spittin'." He wiped his stained fingers across his mouth, put one hand on the doorknob to be sure it wasn't locked, and added, "Get back up in yer sheeny joint 'r I'll come up after you." And left fast.

But behind him, from the half-open door, heard big McCoy chortling, "Tell 'em where you got it, Katz, 'n how easy it was."

design for departure

And it is one with them when evening falls,
And one with them the cold return of day.
Dowson

Although Sharkey was the little girl's father, the Widow was nobody's mother at all. She was a widow only in her own half-fevered fancy.

"I got neither chick nor child," the big woman would mourn, "a poor homeless wanderin' widda wid nowheres to lay me head." She would sniffle reminiscently.

She was neither widow nor mother: she only yearned for the dignity of a woman who had once belonged, somewhere, to somebody. She had belonged to no one, for she had never wanted chick nor child. Her idea of home had been any side-alley entrance and a pint of tinted gin. All she had ever striven for was small change left lying by strangers on North Clark Street bars; and any man's bottle at all.

"I'm not beholden to no man," she would inform the little girl, as though the child were accusing her of panhandling; yet in all her fifty-odd years she had never earned her own way for a day. She had traded her younger hours for barrel whisky, and now the later hours swung her, like a heavy pendulum, between two drunken moods: pity for herself, because no other's pity was offered; and a dull rage at the ruin that men and time had made of her in return for the change on the bars.

A big, ungainly woman, half an inch over six feet, with a jutting jaw and a rump like a camel's hump; she stuck out so far behind that her back appeared to have been broken. As broad in the beam as any two women, she slopped about the little basement flat shoeless, her stockings half down and dragging.

Old Sharkey always pretended he couldn't remember where, on God's green earth, he had ever found such a being. But the 700 block on North Clark was never more than half a block west, wherever Sharkey lived, and he was given to vaguely lofty impulses. When the woman followed him into the basement one night, Sharkey apologized to his daughter: "I brought home a good lovin' mom to make a good home for my poor dear sweet little orphant kid," he explained, looking absently around for the beer bucket.

"She's *twicet* as dear 'n sweet as what you say," the Widow let him know right off. And began shouting Sharkey down with protestations of love for the child and for her pitiful motherless state, while the little girl trembled in a corner like a dog in winter. After all, it was a place to stay.

Mary trembled even in sleep. The sound of the two big people roaring home drunk was enough to start her screaming in her twelve-year-old dreams. Sometimes she screamed in sleep without waking at all: as though the fear she felt in her dream was less than the fear she would know upon waking. She had a small, ragged birthmark under her right eye and always hoped, upon waking, somehow to find it gone.

A month's empties lay under the sink and across the carpetless floor. Kleenex, fifty-cent horse tickets, and cigarette snipes had been stamped and trampled into the floor's ancient cracks.

There was no time to sweep. For the Widow had to decide, once and for all, which one of them pitied the pitiful orphant most. She belabored the point by the tinted pint. When Sharkey wasn't yet drunk enough to argue back, she harassed him with dire predictions of the child's immediate future.

"What do you think will become of the helpless orphant child?" she demanded to know one night. Though she never mentioned the child's birthmark.

"I think she'll go to hell on a handcar if you keep on hangin' around where you ain't even wanted," Sharkey answered easily. "I think she'll wind up dead-pickin' like you." Being called a dead-picker hurt the Widow where she had lived.

"You been callin' me dirty names all night," she bawled. "You've called me everythin' but a white woman. Now I'll tell *you* somethin': you curse at me just once more 'n I'll be all over you like a mess of ants."

"You mean you'll be in hell with your back broke, sister. You're a piece of trade. Go on out to the dog pond 'n let 'em smother you."

The Widow hesitated, torn by the desire to prove by her fists that she wasn't a dead-picker, and pulled the other way by her outraged pride. Unable to make up her mind, she wept.

"Here I am, a widdad victim of circumstances, a wanderer widout no home, mindin' my own business. Just settin' in a little corner wid a bottle like a lady—'n you call me *that*."

She rushed to the single faucet and began splashing water about, preparing to leave him forever. "I'll prob'ly shoot myself," she warned him.

"I'll loan you the gun." It was one way of getting her to wash her face.

When all of it was washed she started losing her nerve, for she was deathly afraid of being alone on the streets again. She fastened her garters slowly, wishing she hadn't talked so much; hoping Sharkey would ask her, just once, to stay.

"You want to jump off the roof?" he asked. "I'll get a ladder."

Mary felt a strange tug at her heart for the big homeless creature, so forlorn and afraid, while watching her tie a toothbrush about her neck like a locket. It was real ladylike to carry one's toothbrush that way, the Widow believed. It showed some people who one really was. When it was securely fastened, and there was nothing left to do but leave, Sharkey began sweeping up, making wide, deliberate sweeps.

The Widow started laughing till her tongue was lolling like a cat's.

"What in hell you think *you're* doin'?" she asked at last.

"Sweepin' out the bad rubbish."

"I s'pose I don't even know how to keep house fer such a duke like you?" she asked. Sharkey did not reply.

"I can fight like a damned man," she warned him. "You better gimme that damned broom."

No answer.

"I give you myself com-pletely," she reminded him. "Now yer thrunin' me out in the street. You wouldn't care if I slept in the station house or where. My life is rur-int. You rur-int it."

"On the street is where you was born," Sharkey answered without pausing in his house-cleaning. "In the station house was where I first seen you. Nice to have knowed you. Don't slam the door."

"It wasn't in no station house," she contradicted him.

"Could just as well have been. You been arrested enough."

"I never been arrested," she repudiated him flatly. "Maybe I got picked up a time 'r two now'n then. But I never got *arrested.*"

"Just because they seen you so much before they never bothered to book you even, that don't mean you wasn't arrested."

"If I wasn't booked I wasn't arrested," she persisted, fancying that Sharkey was pointing accusingly at her with the handle of the broom. Weaving on his thin old legs, he had succeeded in making a dune, of bottles and butts, against a leg of the dresser.

"I s'pose I don't keep everythin' spanty-clean like yer *legal* old lady never used to neither?" This was intended as sarcasm, but went unheeded. "Now gimme that damned broom." She lunged for it, stumbled, and skidded flat on her face. Mary heard the broom handle snap.

The Widow rolled over on her back, rolling the whites of

her eyes up to the light. She crossed her hands over her breast and said, "Now I'm dead 'n you kilt me, you duncey Irish stewbum."

And remained, playing dead, looking straight up into the little unshaded night bulb.

Mary waited for her old man to laugh: it always eased her a little when Sharkey laughed. But her old man had folded up on the edge of the bed with his head in his hands and the broken broom handle across his knees. His cap started slipping forward off his head; she caught it and stood caressing it beside him. She watched his troubled breathing, and felt troubled by it; then watched the Widow trying not to breathe at all.

The girl's single braid caught an auburn gleam from the light overhead. Stood hoping it was true, truly true, that the Widow was really dead.

Then there was no sound in the room at all, and then this was what death was like: no noise, no fighting, no shouting, no arguing; no cursing and no blows. She felt herself growing quiet within; felt, for the first time she could recall, a little less taut with fear. She came up close to the Widow. Now the woman's eyes were closed as in death and there was no sign of breath at all. The color had left her face and her hands lay lifelessly at her sides. Mary bent over and touched the woman's cheek, curiously and tentatively.

"Tell that idiot-lookin' bastard he kilt me," she whispered hoarsely out of the corner of her mouth without flicking an eyelid.

The little girl tiptoed quietly into her cubbyhole behind the curtain. She wanted to cry because the Widow wasn't dead after all. She curled her knees up to her chin on her cot and pretended that she was dead instead. And found that she liked playing dead.

After that, whenever she became afraid, she pretended she was dead and lay on her back with her hands crossed, looking straight up into an imagined vigil light. Sometimes, in school, when she didn't know her lesson, she bowed her head in her hands and pretended that she had died right there at her desk.

She thought of death as a warm and windless place, like thinking of a room with a key all her own. A cornerless room, that was quiet all night long. Where not even the night wind might wander in. Where she would hear foghorns far out on the lake and no other sounds at all.

Even when hungry she would loiter in the schoolyard, making herself too late to eat with the pair of them. Or, if they were sitting at the table with bread and beer before them, she'd pretend she wasn't hungry until they'd finished. She made a lie of each new day and a lie of each troubled night.

In every classroom she sat in the very last seat in the very last row. The taunts of smaller children, who knew how to spell words she had never, somehow, even heard of, troubled her only faintly. Sometimes a teacher smiled pityingly and patted her small dark head. That would make the little girl tremble with shame.

The night wind wandered past each night. The years closed in like a fog bank. Till the wind felt like someone crying, and the fog felt like a wall. While overhead, in the city nights, above the endless maze of telephone wires, an ancestral moon looked calmly down, like the great moon of forever.

The girl grew up between Sharkey's irresponsible laughter and the Widow's brainless bawl. She learned a secret passion for darkness and aloneness.

One day Mary had taken a nervous, secret taste of the tinted gin and it had spilled down her dress. In the close little classroom there was the faintly sweet odor of the stuff. The teacher bent over a couple of the tougher boys, trying to find the culprit without success. But at recess the children discovered her. They formed a mocking circle: "Mary's drunk! Mary's drunk!"

She didn't go back to the room after recess. And the deep, the abiding sense of shame she felt on that forenoon never left her the rest of her days.

Each morning thereafter she hid her books under a porch and returned to the basement, after a day's aimless wandering, as though returning from school.

She returned with enormous lies: how she was sitting in the first seat in the first row now and all the children liked her and the teacher always called on her when no one else knew the right answer.

When she perceived that neither of them cared whether she went to school or not, she continued to live out the lie. She liked to feel she was tricking them anyhow.

Someday, she hoped, she would make up a lie so great that somehow it would kill the Widow. Just how this would happen she wasn't sure. But she remembered the Widow lying dead, looking blindly up at the unshaded night bulb.

"I'll tell her my real ma ain't dead after all," she planned. "I'll tell her my real ma's comin' to have her arrested."

She stole the Widow's face powder and tried not coming home at all. When she stayed away for a week, the year she was fifteen, the Widow reproached Sharkey for not worrying.

"If it was my own dear motherless kid," the Widow asserted, "if that was my own dear sweet little honey-kid, she wouldn't be wanderin' around unpertected t'night."

"She's prob'ly takin' better care of herself t'night than you are," Sharkey reasoned affably.

"Well, I may get drunk," the Widow admitted, "but I don't stagger. Sometimes I fall down. But I don't stagger."

Then she saw that her compact was gone. She snickered, and was secretly glad. "Powderin' that birt' scar won't hide it now," she assured herself vindictively.

Mary lived in a room of her own at last, in one of those great city caverns which are halfway between a rooming house and a cheap hotel. Every door has a number; and no one knows anyone else and nobody keeps the hallway clean because nobody rents the hall.

The beds are rented by week or by night. They are rented along with the air and the hours. There is just so much warmth, just so much air, just so much freedom in going to and fro: Kindly Do Not Leave Door Ajar. With the house rules tacked to the back of each door: No Extra Person in Any Room Over Six Hours, and rent day always arrives on time. One clean towel each morning and the housekeeper keeps the key in case of funny business: All Rooms Are Responsible for the Disorderly Conduct of Their Visiting Friends.

It is in such places that one feels life more deeply than is possible in the unrented places, where one keeps one's own key. For when life goes by in rented moments, in measured inches, then each dawn bears a dollar sign and yesterday's dollar cannot buy it back. Then each hour must be purchased with the sweat of fear and every meal must be eaten with privation, like a false friend, sitting on the other side of the table counting each forkful; then it is that the simplest things become infinitely precious and nothing—not a grain of salt—is taken for granted.

Life binds one's arms in such places, then jostles, shoving capriciously this way and that just to show there really isn't enough room for everyone after all. Whenever Mary felt that her back was up against her own rented wall she sought the sanctuary of sleep.

Thus she lived in a twilit land between sleep and waking. And in sleep saw the terrible maze of the city's million streets. Saw a million friendless faces, all going one way down a single avenue, each alone. Saw herself among them, touching strangers' faces curiously, touching many hands; yet always untouched by any man's hand and befriended by no woman.

Waking, she walked the same gray streets, untouched and unbefriended. For some seemed to smile with the Widow's furtive smirk; and some eyed her absently, with Sharkey's blurred, unseeing stare.

And when she was tired she made up a lie, all to herself, about a doorless room which she'd never have to leave at all.

A little windless windowless room in which she lay quietly and white, half awake and strangely dreaming, safe from human voices.

The strangest thing about this imagined room was that, although she had never seen it, yet it was more familiar to her than any room which she might rent. Always half lit with a dull gray gleam, as though a fog were rising from somewhere below: the pavement-colored light was to her the very color of sleep.

Each morning she took the Racine Avenue car, got off in front of the stockyards, and went mechanically to her bacon-wrapping job. Her fingers learned to work without her mind's attention. But her mind, once freed, wandered to no green hills or wooded places: it returned always to the doorless room lit by the fog-colored gleam.

And returned to sleep each night curled up like an infant, her knees to her chin.

This sweet and dreamlike way of life was interrupted, when she was nineteen, by a man. He came into the room simply to find out what went on in there; and stayed to break through the wall of pavement-colored light she had built between herself and the sun.

He was deaf as a stone and prodigiously strong. When he swept the halls he paid attention to no one trying to squeeze through the space between the wall and his broom: he swept the dirt sullenly, with deliberation, over any shoes that passed. If anyone paused to reprove him he would lean the broom deliberately against the wall and begin working the over-developed muscles of his right arm with his eyes pretending to see no one near.

"Back off. Get lost. We don't want your kind in here." His voice would have the unemphatic corner-of-the-mouth monotone employed by the institutionalized; but his eyes would be amber flares.

All he knew he had learned in institutions: as a child he had learned to read lips in one. So that he could tell, by the juke's vibrations, what song the juke was playing. Later on, in another, he had learned something of the extortion racket. Now, when the juke had finished, he leaned against the wall and wrote with the stub of a pencil, wetting it with his lips as he wrote and slipping it under Mary's door when it was finally done:

> Dear Miss? Althou I dont even know you cannt we be pals
> CHRISTY

The note frightened her. She pretended not to hear when he knocked.

He knocked each night for several nights. Then got into the room with the housekeeper's key while she was at work. He closed the door quietly behind him and investigated the clothes closet. He touched her brush and comb and shook face powder into the palm of his hand. Then he opened the dresser drawer and fumbled in her underclothing. He sat on the bed's edge with her extra slip lying limply across his knees, touching it almost reverently at first. Then, without taking his eyes off the slip, he drew a bottle off his hip, drank blindly, and blindly replaced the bottle.

When Mary returned that night a familiar faint sweet odor hung in the room. And he was waiting for her, on the bed's edge.

He closed the door behind her, while she stood, a frowsy flowered hat held helplessly in her hand. No one knew better than herself that she could not fight. She could only whimper a little, and crush the hat.

"I guess you're real glad to find comp'ny waitin' fer once," he said. His voice was as flat as the look in his eyes and he eyed her sidewise, like a rooster. She had powdered the birth scar heavily; that side of her face had a curiously dead aspect. Her hair was still braided about her head, and she wore heavy-ribbed cotton stockings and low battered shoes.

246 the neon wilderness

"I like yer style, Mary," he assured her, eyeing her from head to toe appraisingly. "You look like somethin' that started out to be a bobby-soxer 'n decided to go to a funeral instead. Why all the gloom? Don't you like no good times?"

She put her hat on the dresser and sat by the window, looking out at the night-fuming neon all the way down Congress to the El. When he came to her she struggled a little and pleaded awhile. Yet knew she was beaten beforehand as surely as though the Widow were waiting on the other side of the door with one ear pressed to the unpainted wood. " 'N I tawt all the angels was in heaven," Christy whispered.

All night the gas beneath the old-fashioned radiator whimpered while the southbound El thundered its disdain overhead, plunging down the neon wilderness. She missed work in the morning.

"No woman of mine toils," deaf Christiano boasted, " 'neider does she spin." But when she went for her check in the afternoon, he went along. "It's okay," he reassured her. "I'll stick to you t'ru t'ick 'n t'in." And saw she was actually pleased at such a prospect.

For it was so: he pleased her. Her crying need of loving, and of being loved, had found an outlet at last: he was overwhelmed by the vigor of her devotion. When she learned that his perfunctory strolls with a broom had nothing to do with his means of a livelihood, except to provide a front for it, it made small difference to her: Christy was Christy, and she wanted nothing about him changed.

Christiano had first practiced extortion on men—employing a policeman's badge provided by Ryan of the Jungle Club. Christy now returned the badge—he had an older and less risky game to play now. Christiano and Ryan were going into the badger game.

All Mary had to do was sit in the back booth of the Jungle Club, just like sitting in the last row in school. And watch Ryan in the long bar mirror. She learned to brush off a man when

Ryan went to the damper and rang up No SALE. That meant
the sucker was a waste of time, a bad risk, or somebody's friend.
But when Ryan rang up CASH, that was the green light. That
meant work fast and give the sucker boots and shoes. Ryan
could tell. Sometimes a man looked like a regular duke and
didn't have a dime, and sometimes one dressed like a trucker
on his lunch hour would turn out to be a live one. Ryan could
tell all right.

She would give the sucker the room number: he would be
up the stairs two minutes after. And Christy would be up five
minutes after that.

Sometimes she sensed him listening at the door: though the
room would be still, and deaf as he was, he never timed himself
wrong. He sensed things better than most men with good hearing. For Christy could tell too.

It didn't always work. Sometimes they had to move, fast, and
lie low in another hotel a few days or a week. And when it
worked, and she suffered consequent small qualms, he would
assure her that the fellow had just been some cheap crook of
one sort or another, that all they'd done was to take something
he'd taken off someone else. All the men they trapped, he
assured her, had had it coming to them for a long time because
of the way they treated decent people.

"Still, it seems it just ain't me, I just can't think it's me doin'
this," she would complain uselessly. "I just can't think I'm no
better, after all, than some people." He took that to mean himself, and struck her contemptuously, with the back of his hand.
She didn't bother to explain that she had meant the Widow.
She didn't mind his striking her now and then: what were a
few blows, so long as he kept on loving her? And never, never
left her? But to herself she had to admit: "I'm even *worse* 'n
her."

Christiano was not a vicious man; he was only a callous one.
And kinder than most, as such men go. She often found him
boyish and strangely innocent. And he never exposed her to

needless risk or humiliation. He spared her as much as he could, was frequently considerate in small ways, and not only demanded fidelity, but gave it in return. He was never too late, coming up the stairs, to risk that. When she was tired, or ill, he tended her; and at all times protected her.

He knew how to use the needle. He had been on the junk, off and on, in prison and out, without ever succumbing to it as a habit. When Mary was unable to sleep, he showed her how to sleep the fast way; when she needed a lift, he gave her a lift—the fast way. She couldn't imagine anyone wiser or better than this flat-faced, dead-pan coneroo who spoke without moving his lips, who lived without changing his expression; and who loved her with a violence camouflaged by outward indifference.

She regarded every room they moved into as the last. She never seemed able to understand that they might have to move out within the hour. She would make the bed up neatly and sweep up even the remotest dust. Once, when they had been three days in the same place, she bought curtains. But they were never hung, because she wasn't tall enough, even standing on a chair, to reach the curtain rod. And Christy was too lazy to climb onto a chair. He could sit all night in a cold sweat through a stud session, but he didn't have time to put up a curtain.

The curtains, like everything else that lends decency to any room, were forgotten. They lay, like her memories, gathering rented dust.

She let the curtains go. She let everything go. He bought her clothes; but she took little pleasure in clothes. "I don't even care to do the things I like to do no more," she once told him in a moment of melancholy. Her sole pleasure was in him, and when he was with her she had no need of anything else, not even of the needle.

She would sit all evening watching him getting drunk on someone else's money.

"You still like me?" she would ask hopefully.

"Sort of. In a way. I guess so," he would acknowledge.

"Why?"

"I dunno. You make me feel like I'm takin' care of you sort of. You still like me?"

"Uh-huh. Sort of."

"Why?"

"You make me feel like a woman."

She sounded more certain than he.

Once he left her asleep in the early forenoon and returned at midnight to find her still asleep. When he wakened, at noon, she was still sleeping. She hadn't even stirred. He grunted. Some dame. All she does is sleep.

After that he sometimes watched her curiously as she slept, knees to her chin and her head cupped in her hands. As an infant that seeks with all its instincts to return to the nothingness out of which it has come into the roistering light. At such moments she looked oddly shrunken to him and the birthmark grew deeper in hue.

"You need somethin' to liven you up, sister, 'r you'll be goin' to sleep on me for keeps," he told her.

The sailor was long on money and short on leave. Ryan cautioned Christy because the sucker was a sailor and it was going too fast. He punched out No Sale, to indicate that the sailor was putting it on a little, he wasn't that drunk.

But it had already gone too far. The sailor wakened, upstairs, hours before he was supposed to waken, to find eighty American dollars gone out of his wallet. He leaned out of the window, put two fingers across his teeth, and whistled for the law.

Ryan got Mary out of sight and dispatched a grapevine alarm to Christy, playing stud on a pool table two blocks south, to stay away until he was sent for. The warning arrived a few minutes late and, from behind a drawn shade three stories up across the street, Mary saw him walk into the officers' arms.

From the window she saw them taking him: the one human being who had been kind to her, with the noon sun glinting on his wrists and his wrists behind his back. And the faces of strangers, metallic and pale, gawking glassily from the hot-dog counters, the tattoo parlor, the barbershops, the Peekholes of Paris, and the Penny Arcade.

And heard a long and rising warning wail as the paddy wagon pulled away south down State, like the whole city's voice warning everyone against Deaf Christiano.

This she saw, and heard. And half an hour later, having a couple shots on Ryan, she asked him resentfully, "What they have to put manacles on Christy for, Ryan?"

"Manacles?" Ryan paused in scooping off a beer. "You been seein' things, Mary. He went along as nice as could be. What you think they got him for—murder? Don't worry. The fix is in."

She drank without spilling a drop.

"I seen the sun sort of shiny on 'em," she protested. " 'N that damned siren. I'm still hearin' it."

"You got a little fever, I think," Ryan told her. "They ain't got sirens on them old jalopies. All they got is bells."

"I *seen* the damn manacles."

"Then you seen a damn lie." And he went on his business about the bar. He didn't have time to argue with hopped-up dames. "You better go upstairs 'n read your catechism," he advised her later. He had a worn catechism he often loaned her and which she read avidly. He kept it behind the damper and handed it to her now. " 'N lay off the happy-gas," was his final order.

But that night she took a twister with a medicine dropper and an improvised sewing-machine needle Christy had called his "Tomcat." And dreamed she was back in the Huron Street basement with the one door padlocked—for some reason—from the inside. She was locked in with the Widow, and Sharkey had long been dead. "You come back to give back my com-

pact," the Widow was telling her. "Nobody can get out of the
bughouse until you give it back." And there in the corner sat
old Sharkey sleeping off a drunk, his head bowed between his
hands, his hands crossed to support his chin, and a broken
broom handle across his knees. She saw his cap sliding forward
off his head and wanted to catch it; but could not, for, just in
time, she saw the light glint across his wrists: he too was mana-
cled. "They handcuff everyone who dies now," Ryan told her,
handing her a worn catechism with a great sewing-machine
needle, instead of a crucifix, engraved on its cover. A low wail
began in the hall, rising near at hand and coming nearer until
it was drowned in the curving screech of an oncoming El and
she wakened as it slowed down to the station above her bed.

When she took a chance on visiting Christy, in the Central
Police lockup, she found him lolling comfortably, smoking a
cigar and laughing with the thief with whom he was confined.

"Don't worry about a thing," he assured her, "the fix is in."

Although the sailor was back at his base, and Ryan had told
her the police weren't interested in her, she trembled in fright
every time one passed her in the long gray corridor. When she
regained the street the fear followed her, unreasonably, all the
way down State and back into Ryan's upstairs and into the
bed. She was frantic for a charge. But the money was running
low, and she was helpless, without Christy, to get any. She
bummed two dollars off the housekeeper for veronal, and spent
the evening dipping cigarettes into it and chain-smoking them.
Abruptly at midnight she dressed, put up her hair, went down
to the bar, and said to Ryan, "The fix is in." Then turned,
went back upstairs, undressed, and went to sleep dreaming she
was still talking to Ryan.

Three days later Christy got a three-year jacket and was on
his way.

She drifted without effort into the fluorescent jungle of the
fourth-rate cabarets.

This was the true jungle, the neon wilderness. Sometimes

the dull red lights, off and on, off and on, made the spilled beer along the floor appear like darkly flowing blood. Sometimes the big juke sang.

And always voices, half subdued, merged with the mechanical voice of the juke, till the human voices sounded mechanical, and the juke sang in half-human tones. Sometimes the people sang as though they were being turned on and off, on and off, by a giant lever; some secret lever which Ryan held somewhere beneath the bar. Sometimes the juke sang personally, to her alone, for no one else to hear. Sometimes an M.C. sang, sweetly and sadly and low, just for Mary to hear:

> "It's a Barnum and Bailey world
> Just as phony as it can be . . ."

The poor people, Mary thought, the poor people, they certainly have a time.

Even the poor old juke. But at least it paid its own way.

While half a mile across the Loop, over the hump of the Clark Street bridge, in a shadowed corner of another all-night honky-tonk, the Widow drank on with old Sharkey.

They were divided from Mary by the Clark Street bridge and five years of forgetfulness. Now they lived on separate planets, a million light-years apart.

"Maybe I been picked up now 'n then," the Widow was confessing. "But I never been *arrested*. Maybe I do drink too much. But nobody can say I *stagger*."

Her record was still clean.

Toward the end of Christy's second year Mary became ill. She spent a week taking the fever treatment at Twenty-sixth and Wabash, and was sorry when the week was up. After the first hour it had been like resting in a swimming pool in summer. At first her heart had beat a little faster, and then had steadied. She lay in a warm and circulating mist, feeling the green and living water moving beneath, beside and across her body, with a nurse always near at hand. At the end of each day she was given a sponge bath and sent to bed.

She could not sleep: something sat in a chair outside of her door, all night long, breathing heavily, like an aging animal. She would lie there, listening, and picking lint out of her pillow: she knew that, when she had all the lint neatly plucked, they would come in and tell her to put on her clothes and Christy would be waiting for her at last.

But when the week was over, it was all over. It had come to nothing more than a week of hot baths. Perhaps she hadn't gone soon enough. Perhaps she should have gone somewhere else. Perhaps she should have been more careful. And perhaps it was partly because she didn't give a damn whether the cure took or not.

Riding the State Street car north toward the Loop, she stuffed all the hospital literature under the seat and got off in front of the Jungle Club. Ryan had stuck a letter from Christy behind the damper for her, and she read it sitting at the bar over a double shot of barrel whisky. She couldn't make much out of the letter, except that he was coming up for parole and would make it if nothing went wrong. It was the first word from him in months, and it didn't make her as happy as she had once thought it might. She put it in her purse and went upstairs to her old room to wait.

What she was waiting for she didn't know. Death or Christiano. The loony bin or a miracle, she didn't know which. She was waiting to find out. It no longer made much difference. It never really had.

Streetcars ground regularly to a stop all day below her bed; paused there till the traffic lights winked green and started up again with an unfinished scream; each time she cringed inwardly. When the traffic stilled she heard half-murmured echoes and rumors of sounds all through the great gray frame hotel; even to tiny rustlings in the walls, where a civilization of roaches bred.

And strange walkers, out-of-step shufflers to nowhere, passed and repassed on the pavement below: beneath her bed she heard the muted laughter of the men she had known in the past months since Christy had left. All like the men the Widow had lived on: they laughed and stood closely together and nodded significantly toward the staircase leading to her room, and she knew even now they were talking about her.

She had seen them saunter to the bar in pairs and speak there in whispers, that she might not hear what they were saying about her: they would play the juke just to keep her from hearing. They were afraid to speak up because they knew in their hearts it was all lies, a lot of big lies. She would pretend to be unaware of them; but she knew, she knew all the time. Mary knew.

She would lie listening to all the juke tunes she used to know; and it seemed to her that the times with Christy had been a wonderfully happy time. Memory sifted out the shame and the fear and the uncleanness: it left her a gay, bright time, full of laughter and happy evenings with many friends. All night long these people—the happiest in the world—had sat together, trusting and loving each other without bitterness for the dawn or sick dread for the night.

Now it was gone: the happy time was gone, never to return. The time that never had been, and the friends that never were, were gone with the mornings that had been so gray and the nights that had been so long.

Yet, even now, she felt light and unworried, and everything was going to turn out all right after all. She rose and moved with pretentious elegance across the room; like a famed dancer in the silence that precedes thunderous applause. In the chill and darkened room, with the shadow of traffic moving menacingly across the windows, she danced.

Till of a sudden the big juke stopped, and she knew they were at it again with their lies. Knew that they were planning, one by one, to come by her door and listen secretly to see what

she was up to now. And returned to the bed like a child caught
in an obscenity; felt tired and old and cold and ill, and needed
the needle like never before.

Once one of the nerviest ones had stopped right outside and
said loudly and clearly, "That one's just another piece of
trade," with just the same voice with which Sharkey had once
called the Widow that. A voice as suddenly familiar as the
night's last local or as the red-and-yellow neon that flickered on
forever. The ceaseless, night-fuming neon, that moved like
living flame, all night, up and down the fire escape.

Like the cars, like the lights, like the all-night rain, like the
solitary walkers and the Jackson Park Express: they came on
all night forever. South down State and west to Wabash, east
down Harrison and northward toward the Loop, the cars and
the colors, in an endless and shrieking maze. Cables struck pale
green lightning across the room: she would waken and the
whole room would be blazing with ice-green flame.

Against the wall at the head of the bed a blood-red shadow
passed and repassed, without cessation from dusk to dawn; at
four, when the juke stopped so abruptly below, it stopped
abruptly too, and she would waken, no matter how deeply she
had been dreaming. And would wonder when everyone would
find out who, after all, she *really* was.

For Mary alone, in a dream, had found out who she'd been
all along. It was a secret all her own, like her single dress. Like
a single phrase from Ryan's catechism that recurred again and
again to her brain. Like her one shabby memory; and her
single dread.

The memory was one of waking at night to find the room
in an ice-green blaze, and Jesus Christ, with Deaf Christiano's
face, impaled there on a blood-red cross. Thus she knew what
she had so long suspected: that she was, in truth, the Virgin
Mary.

When it was too late the Widow would learn of it, and the
others too, and that would serve them all right when they were

all left out. She fancied that Christy had really known secretly all the time; but had been too ashamed, somehow, to say.

"He was better to me than anyone," she reflected. "He was a real man. He never acted like I wasn't no real woman."

On the dresser stood a half-empty bottle labeled Mlle. Mitzi's Golden Blond-Bak. Once she put her little finger in it for a cork and shook it, wondering if there were enough left in it for just one more bleach. She had glanced at her hair in the tilted dresser mirror: it was done into a platinum pompadour. But at the roots in the forehead it was strangely black. Innumerable bleachings had seared the natural auburn of it to a whitish gold; but at the roots it was turning black. She'd tried to henna the stuff when she'd first noticed that, and that was cheaper than Mlle. M's, but it only made the platinum pompadour look streakish and freaky, and a girl had to be one or the other, a platinum blondie or a cute redhead, the way the traffic was carrying on these days.

In the months since he'd been gone she'd been in a thousand corners with a thousand men and had feared them all, each one, each time. Now she saw the hair, always bright, coming out dull black like the catechism's single phrase had warned her: *The cerements of the grave.* What it meant she no longer knew; but the phrase recurred even in sleep. She would remember, just in time to calm a rising panic, that Mary's hair, too, had been black; this conviction made her feel that nothing in her past had really happened at all. She forgot the bottle and studied herself solemnly in the tilted mirror, her fingers resting tentatively in the shadowed hollow of her throat and her peaked face, in the unbalanced air, as grave as a child's.

"I still look like the churchgoin' kind in the eyes," she had concluded, although she had never seen the inside of a church. But her mouth looked tough. Her lips had taken on the pallor of the stepped-up gin. She needed a drink and the room smelled of Flit and there was no church in Chicago for that kind of mouth.

Nor any church on earth, with a cross or without it, to return the bright auburn sheen to the hair.

Veronal. Allonal. Luminal. Veronal.

She always returned to veronal, for sleep. She'd started on benzedrine, for a lift, when she could no longer afford the needle and she'd tried them all and always returned to veronal. For sleep.

"I'd like to be as high as Pikes Peak once more," she wished. "I'd like to be high as the moon 'n full to the scuppers. I'd like a verification shot in a paid-up room all my own." She couldn't extend Ryan's credit too long, she knew, although he had assured her she could stay in the room until Christy returned. "I'd like to be so high I'd never come down," she wished. "I'd like to be so full I'd never come to."

But that much, even if she knew where to get it, would cost more than she'd made in a month. Five dollars would do it. Five dollars and Christy would do it. He'd do it for her. He knew just where to go.

Along the pavement-colored hall doors stood half open on either side, all the way down; each one was numbered in bright bald tin, each one stood just so much ajar in the gas-lit corridor. Just enough to reveal half-dressed men and women waiting for rain or about to make love or already through loving and about to get drunk; or already half drunk and beginning to argue about how soon it was going to rain or whose turn it was to run down for whisky or whether it was time to make love again or forget it for once and just wait for rain.

For the hall, like their lives, was equally gray by daylight or dusk. And daylight here was as gray as the sidewalks of Harrison Street; as endless as South State. Forever crowded with men and women: yet each wandering alone, all night, unwept by any and less than lost. Lost even to themselves. And there were no mourners in the world for half-forgotten strays. Lost, by the long rain alone remembered. As she, alone, remembered the long rain.

A rain that wandered, all night long, through narrowing streets; looking, like everyone else in the world, for a place to get in.

Luminal. Veronal. Allonal. Veronal.

She was afraid to return to the clinic uncured because Ryan had told her no one bothered with the uncured there: she'd had her chance; they'd give her the black bottle for sure now. Her fear of these unseen enemies was such that she had come to imagine that all her movements, even the smallest, were clearly heard all over the old hotel; and so crept, tiptoe and shoeless, all day about the room, laying objects down quietly so that whoever kept listening at the door would not be able to tell what she was up to inside at all. Perhaps, in time, she hoped vaguely, they would forget her altogether; then the room would be hers for keeps and no one would bother her ever again.

She paused, regularly as the cars below, to listen at wall or window or door: for steps on the staircase. For cries from below.

For some half-forgotten voice to call her by her own half-forgotten name.

Once the housekeeper stood in the doorway and asked, "Well, Mrs. Badger?"

Mary knew what she meant all right. Mary owed her two dollars.

"My name ain't 'Mrs. Badger,' " she had answered evasively. That name had followed her, mockingly, ever since Christy had gone, along a dozen bars and out of the curtained corners.

"What is it t'day?"

"It's Mary, same as always."

"Humph." The housekeeper had ventured a step further into the room. "Had me a yella alley cat name of Mary once."

She was a big woman and was surprised when Mary had struck her. She had struck her on the chest, without strength, and the woman had looked down with a hurt expression. She had backed out slowly, and when her hand had touched the knob behind her had said with determination, "I'll have you put where there ain't no rent."

So there had been no time to tell her that no one should talk to Mary that way. And that night there returned, to sit in a chair by the door, something that breathed and waited, like an aging animal.

But all of them being made so easily afraid of her like that had made her a little sad. She had leaned her head against the bedpost, feeling the heat of the day trapped in the brass, and faintly, from somewhere far below, had come the brassy "pshdang! pshdang!" of the slot machine. It sounded like Christy playing it. Twice. She had listened alertly for the return, sharing his anticipation.

And had felt strangely relieved when she heard no return.

Sometimes Mary thought that everyone, even the housekeeper and the Widow, were Virgin Marys. That every man, even the worst, was Christ.

Sitting alone by the Harrison Street window one night, she heard the drunken men coming out of the taverns: the last floor show was over, the final gay party was done. The buzzer began, first occasionally and then faster, until it was one continuous cry; and an air of haste and the odor of Lifebuoy spread through the rooms into her own room.

Someone knocked lightly, and yet not like the housekeeper would have knocked at all. She stood stock-still, her sallow face cocked like a curious puppy's. Listened to the knocker's breath, ear pressed to the unpainted wood, thinking this was a small boy's breathing or a young girl's—some child whose voice she had never heard and whose hand she must never, now, touch—but who would call her by some friendly careless name the moment she opened the door.

Her hand took the knob, then drew back. For what if it

were neither a boy nor a young girl? Nor the housekeeper nor even some drunken woman? Nor any man nor any woman at all? But only someone precisely like herself, in a faded and flowered kimono and run-down red cork heels; who liked raw gin and dipped cigarettes in veronal and was so strangely fond of the odor of ether. Who had worked two years in a common whorehouse, always liking the men who looked like murderers best—and had once learned the Embassy Stomp all by herself.

She did a soft little mock stomp away from the door, smiling a little to herself with pleasure at her grace; till she saw the knob being turned, furtively; as though they were all planning, secretly, to force the door. She put her lips to the crack of the door and said earnestly, "Only Jesus can come in this room."

There, she'd said it. She'd told them all, at last. And heard faint laughter, far down the hall. The door opened slowly. It was Christy, in a dark red turtle-neck sweater.

"I didn't expect no comp'ny," Mary said defensively, he looked like such a stranger. And she was suddenly aware of the littered snipes on the floor, of the disheveled bed and her own disheveled aspect. She brushed her hair back nervously and held her kimono tightly about her.

"You got to take better care of yourself than this," he told her, looking around. "You got to clean up a little 'n get back on your feet. You'll be blowin' your roof you keep on like this."

Suddenly she felt happy for the natural way he spoke, like a natural friend. Why, this was *real* company. She shoved the chair toward him and said, before she knew what she was saying, "Will you have a bite? Coffee and a roll? Will you?"

"If you got any, sure," he grinned. "Only, you ain't got any. Here." And he laid a ten-dollar bill on the dresser, beside Mlle. Mitzi's. It's his release money, she thought.

Not even a cup of coffee. She sat on the edge of the bed,

hugging the warmth of the brass bedpost while the rest of the room grew cold with evening, and studied him; they watched each other in the gathering dusk. And the endless rain began, and ceased, and began again. She opened the window, to let in a little air, and the rain played along the sill. It brought a coolness into the room and she shivered as the damp crept in. He pushed his chair over to the radiator and pointed, that she should sit in it. He was going to light the radiator.

She watched him without taking her eyes off his scarred and sullen face. He looked younger and thinner now, she saw.

It was lit by thrusting a flaming scrap of paper far beneath; no match would reach, and she had never known how to light it on damp evenings. Now it made a whispering sound, as of many voices whispering a single warning. One voice, yet many voices. It said many things. Yet forever the same thing. And forever new meanings, like patterns woven by human hands. It said strange new things which she'd never heard before nor ever thought of—and yet they were all old, familiar, oft-told things. For they were all of Christiano and how every man was Christ.

"You shouldn't ought to be here," she told him bravely, feeling, somehow, that he would never leave her by herself again. "I been sick. Real sick. I ain't no good no more. I'm a piece of trade." And kissed his sleeve.

She saw him reading her lips, his own moving with them. Then he coughed. In the gloom she saw him, looking slighter and more boyish, with his head half turned, than she had ever seen him. When he moved it was as the dusk moved: soundlessly, within a soundless dream. The blood-red sign came on below, as he paused by the tilted mirror.

"How sick?" he asked, as though he really knew all along, as though he'd been told below.

"Real sick." And pointed to her head, making circles with her finger about the temple. Smiling weakly at her confession, she was at once ashamed and yet a little proud that she was still well enough to know how ill she really was.

"If you want I'll get you a croaker," he offered, without looking at her. And meaning only any convenient doctor.

Suddenly she felt sly, as though realizing that she shared, with him alone, an unspoken understanding: he had spent the first half of his life in institutions; now life was preparing her to spend the remainder of hers in them. He had salvaged the ruins of his life out of those places; now he would help her, because he loved her a little, to keep what remained of hers out of them. She pointed to the bill he had laid on the dresser.

"You can bring me the kind of croaker that'll do me some good for that," she suggested. "That's the only kind of doc can do me any good now. A *real* croaker."

"You mean the whole ten bucks' worth?"

She nodded. "Put the fix in for *me* now, Christy," she begged.

And knew he was gone by the quiet closing of the shadowed door, while the rain tapped derisively; small mockeries, for her and Christ alone. A child coughed, in an upstairs room; then whimpered as though it, too, had been left alone.

Below, above, beside her bed, she heard the traffic's iron cry. The rushing of city waters, beneath the city streets. And down the stair well a door slammed faintly.

Then, like a bearer of peace, she heard Deaf Christiano's shuffling ascent up the Golgotha of the stairs.

And down the uncarpeted hall.

"The fix is in," she thought dreamily. "I'm Mary. 'N Jesus Christ hisself is puttin' in the fix."

the heroes

Corporal Hardheart wasn't much of an Indian, even to look at. He didn't like to hike, he hated living in tents, he was afraid of horses, and he was blind as a bat in the woods after dark. I'd spent one night on bivouac with him back in the States, and the little joker had gotten lost three times before morning. He couldn't even start a fire with matches, far less with flint. But he liked firewater fine; that's why we sometimes called him Chief Boozeheart.

He was mostly Mex, with a touch of Osage in the eyes, but liked to pretend he was full-blooded. He had the deadpan Indian look when he wanted to put it on, and he loved putting it on. Standing with arms folded across his mess kit at the head of the chow line, wearing a fatigue cap as jauntily as a crow feather, he'd maintain a stolid silence until he saw there was nothing but warmed-over C-ration or cold Argentine corned beef again.

"There are better ways to die than to starve, Paleface," he'd announce solemnly to Mess Sergeant Infantino, who was twice as dark as himself. "White man kills the red man's buffalo. Red man must have buffalo: the meat to eat and the hide to keep him warm." He'd go on in that vein until the mess officer came in to see what was holding up chow. "I have spoken," Chief would conclude with dignity then—and grab a double portion of everything, whooping and hollering like a fool; then dash off to Special Service to find out when they were going to start showing movies.

Chief had gotten his education at movies. He hadn't missed anything with Yellow-Hand, Geronimo, or Sitting Bull in it for fifteen years and knew most of their lines by heart. The most moving sequence he'd ever witnessed was from *Western Union*, wherein Yellow-Hand plants an arrow directly between the shoulder blades of a telegraph lineman. Chief liked to lie back on his cot, with a half-empty cognac bottle in his hand, and reflect nostalgically on Yellow-Hand's accuracy.

"The beauty part was," he'd explain, "where he come down head over heels 'n that arrer stickin' out so far in front you could've tied a ribbon on it." Outside of the mess line he didn't talk much like an M-G-M Indian. But he knew how to corral cognac.

My cot was next to his, and we started buddying up, though not because of the proximity of the cots. He didn't want any Paleface buddy, he said: he was a lone wolf, being both the only Indian and the only volunteer, Regular Army, in the outfit. But I pleased him, accidentally, one morning in southern Germany, when he had to get out the guard, by reciting for him:

> "By the shores of Gitche Gumee,
> By the shining Big-Sea-Water,
> Stood the wigwam of Chief Hardheart,
> Sergeant of the Guard, Chief Hardheart.
> Ewa-yea! my little owlet!"

"Say some more, Lineman," he asked. But that was all I could remember or invent. I'd hooked an oversized German pocketknife in my belt, the way I'd seen infantry linemen do, and it had reminded Chief of the lineman of *Western Union*.

That was the basis of our friendship; it was that sort of friendship. He was constantly suggesting that I climb up something: if no telephone pole were handy he'd jerk his thumb toward the flagpole in front of the receiving tent.

"You ought to learn to shinny up that thing like a *real* lineman," he'd insist. "Then you'd be the real thing and could get transferred to the infantry."

"Maybe you could learn to fly and get transferred to the paratroops," I'd tell him. He didn't want any part of that, of course. He didn't want to fly any more than he wanted to climb. In fact, it was all he could do to climb into his cot half the time. It always seemed four or five feet high to him when he got stiff, for some reason.

And I would have to admit that Custer had been more of a terrorist than a soldier. "He'd of been court-martialed if he'd lived to go back to Washington," I'd concede.

"It's a lead-pipe cinch he *should* have been," Chief would assert, and would add seriously, "Custer never should have gone West that time in the first place."

"Why not?"

"Because who'd want to leave Olivia De Havilland to all those Washington wolves?" And he'd whoop and holler his bucktoothed laughter. He was like that all the time: when he was most serious he was joking and when he was joking he was most in earnest.

One night we put on our medic armbands, for protection against snipers, to hunt for cognac. The armband was the best protection a medic had. It said in the book. Some protection. Chief shoved his .45 into his raincoat pocket and handed me a British .22. Some Indian.

"White man is soft," he assured me, loading the .45 with the barrel pointed at my toes. "Paleface need red man for guide. Red man protect Paleface from evil forest spirits."

"You got most of the evil spirits in Germany inside you already," I told him. It was after two in the morning and he already smelled so I was afraid the odor might waken the guards. The guards could sleep through gunfire, but would sit bolt upright at the faintest hint of schnapps in the wind. In front of the receiving tent Witzel, a little Pennsylvania weasel, private of the guard, was sleeping one off. His rifle had been jabbed, barrel down, into the mud a dozen yards away and he was sleeping hunched up against the flap of the tent. Holding down that flap was the first work I'd ever seen him do.

He had turned me in once, at Camp Twenty Grand, when I was cooking up K-rations in my tent instead of remaining on duty guarding the officers' latrine in the rain. The enlisted men had developed an outrageous habit there of using it, instead of their own, during the night; although their own was a perfectly good one only half a mile out in the woods, which were mined. I'd wanted to even up on Witzel for the week of detail he'd gotten me that time, so I grabbed the rifle and shoved it under my coat, intending to drop it down the first convenient sump, but Chief had an even better idea.

"We'll get schnapps out of some Kraut farmer for it," he decided. "Then in the morning we'll turn the Kraut in for possession of firearms 'n we'll both be heroes." We got out of bounds talking like that, and it was so dark all I could see was the fall and rise of the Chief's hunched shoulders in front of me.

"Red man has eyes in the dark. He speaks the tongue of the forest creatures," he told me.

"You walk into a couple combat MPs you won't need your damn eyes," I told him. "They'll show you the way." And he dropped the Hollywood Indian line for a while. Funny, recalling it now, that we worried about Special Guards and Hospital Guards and MPs and officers and noncoms—everything but Krauts.

Once a plane came over and we paused long enough to be able to tell, by the break in the motor, that it was German. But there were so many more immediate dangers, from our own buddies, that the Kraut stuff always seemed sort of remote, so long as you didn't see anything but the distant flare of guns or the hum of a motor in the darkness overhead. Our war was with the second lieutenants, the MPs, and the cooks.

Whenever I'd get hungry I'd think of the breakfast they'd be planning, about this hour, to poison us with, and I wouldn't feel hungry for a while. Our cooks could have messed up the Lord's Supper.

I'll never know whether my little owlet found the house by accident or design—but they'd left a tiny kerosene lamp burning and we caught its glint through a rent in the black-out curtain and shoved in. They tumbled back against the wall like frightened rabbits and there wasn't a man among them.

A grandmother, a middle-aged daughter, a couple middle-aged *hausfraus,* a girl of seventeen, and half a dozen Kraut sprouts between five and twelve. They just huddled up, the women in front of the sprouts, waiting for us to mow them down. Chief turned off the lamp and played his flashlight along their faces, lingering a moment on the seventeen-year-old's. *"Foy-yer verboten!"* he scolded, as though by shouting he could make himself better understood, and the grand-mother began throwing water into the stove.

"Nein," I said, *"licht verboten,"* and pointed at the dark-ened lamp. So it was all right to keep their stove burning and there I was with another man's rifle, holding half a dozen helpless women at bay while Chief began prowling around for firewater. He turned out a couple drawers, threw some papers on the floor, then retrieved one and returned to me with it. It bore a swastika in one corner and looked like some sort of diploma. All I could make out of it, by flashlight, was that it certified some *fräulein* to belong to the local Kampfire girls.

We wouldn't have known that we had a good thing, but the seventeen-year-old came forward, her face rigid with genuine fright.

"Mine," she acknowledged heroically, and added, *"me nichts Nazi."* She tried to convince us then that she wasn't an international spy because she belonged to the Kampfire girls, but we weren't having any. We knew better.

"You Mata Hari," Chief told her with dead-pan conviction. He'd seen that one too.

"Nein. Harry *gefangene,"* she asserted. Harry must have been her boy friend, for she crossed her wrists to indicate a prisoner of war. I wavered when she went down on her knees then, to beg the damning indictment back, but Chief was adamant.

"Paleface squaw must not fear her red brother," he told her, and Muni himself couldn't have looked more immovable when he said it.

"Trinken," I told her, to shorten her anguish, *"wir wollen schnaps."*

Without further pleading the girl rose and left the house quietly, wearing a sort of shawl to protect her from the rain. We weren't too sure where she'd gone, what she'd gone after, or what she'd come back with. They weren't supposed to be out after dark any more than we. But we sat down to wait, well clear of the windows.

She must have crawled along hedgerows to get wherever she had gone, because she brought it back in about twenty minutes. It was almost a full bottle, too. Chief passed it around: everybody had to drink, even the little ones had to have their lips wetted with it. It wasn't until that had been accomplished that Chief returned the diploma to the girl and there was still enough left in the bottle for one good snort apiece. Then the party was over and I made the girl kiss Chief good-by and he made me kiss the grandmother.

The *hausfraus* shook their heads disapprovingly at this crazy stuff, really offended that we weren't going to take them seriously after such a promising beginning.

It had stopped raining, and a sweet wet light was blowing

hard through the trees and we didn't have to stand reveille. But we did have to be on litter duty at seven, so we ditched the rifle and at chow I told Witzel where he could find it if he still wanted it. He didn't seem to get mad, although he was usually an explosive little rat. And when we got into the mess hall Sergeant Infantino remarked that Germany had capitulated sometime in the night and I thought that's fine, maybe the war'll be over one of these days.

It didn't feel like it was over. Witzel turned us both in for stealing his rifle and Chief lost his stripes the same afternoon. They couldn't break me down to anything but a yardbird, which I was most of the time anyhow, and Chief came out to watch me haul buckets of dirt out of one hole in order to fill in another. After a while he took off his shirt and got a bucket of his own. Then I'd empty the dirt into his bucket and he'd cart it back to the hole I'd dug it out of, and I'd dig it out and carry it back to his bucket. This simplified the detail, as we could alternate in resting while the other hauled, and half a dozen Kraut PWs came up to watch us with solemn envy. They envied anybody who was working at any methodical task, and wanted to help us at first. But we wouldn't let them because they'd just lost the war, and after a while their solemn envy turned to solemn wonder, because they couldn't figure out what we were trying to build. Just stood watching the crazy Americans working up a sweat hauling dirt from one hole to another until their wonder became annoyance and they muttered gutturally, looking around for someone with bars on, as though they'd like to turn us in too. There was quite a hard feeling rising, especially when we began barking orders at each other and their heads would turn from one to the other and they couldn't tell who was the superior. They didn't see anything funny in it and the colonel didn't either.

He felt the Chief had mocked the assignment I'd been given, so he took me off and Chief had to carry a full field pack up and down in front of the orderly room from reveille to retreat the next day. It was a lucky thing that he'd filled it with empty cardboard ration boxes, to make it look like he had his equipment in it, because everything he owned was concealed in my duffel bag; so there wasn't anything to the detail except walking up and down.

By night he was so drunk, from the cognac that sympathetic buddies had given him to sustain him in his long ordeal, that he became convinced he really was a paratrooper and wanted to jump off the bulletin board, pack and all. Only he couldn't climb that high, and I refused to boost him. So he ordered me to recite *Hiawatha* over the public-address system, and when I refused he threatened to have me transferred to the infantry first thing in the morning, and I told him that Custer could have licked Sitting Bull in a man-to-man fight, and he started getting sick. He wanted to heave and he couldn't, so I put a finger down his throat to help him and he damned near bit it off. I think I hit him eight or ten times before he let loose, and there was quite a row and I thought we were in for it again.

But it was all right because the colonel wasn't around, he was sleeping off a drunk in the nurses' quarters and it looked like he'd stay that way three or four days anyhow. He usually did, and put it down on the schedule as classes in orientation. But everybody liked him better oriented that way anyhow, as that was the only time he talked like he might be related to the human race.

Chief sobered up and behaved himself nobly for a week, but we weren't on friendly terms any more as his face was still swollen and my finger still bandaged, and after a week I guess he had enough of good conduct, because he went off to look for the house where we'd corralled the cognac by himself.

He went off sober, while it was still light, and took the same path we'd stumbled along in the dark, but he would have been better off to have left drunk and by darkness. A hundred yards from the house he stepped on a Teller mine and we didn't get to him for almost an hour, when the *fräulein* came running up and told us they had him in the house.

They brought him in on a litter looking like he'd been dug out of a coal mine, with both feet blown off at the ankles and even his dog tags blackened.

When they got him onto the table he was still conscious and spoke to the doc, looking down at where his feet had been. "Well," I heard him say, "I can still sleep with the *fräuleins* anyhow."

He might still have been able to manage that, at that, except that he'd been left lying across that path too long.

It was rough enough, but it wasn't too bad because when the chaplain arrived in his jeep, to hold services, he was stone sober, and he brought a T/5 and a Pfc to help him and they were sober too, and when the First Soldier showed up he was sober as anybody, and everybody was really sober.

All, that is, but the colonel. He was still conducting Orientation up in the nurses' quarters and was putting in for a Purple Heart. He thought he'd been wounded when a champagne cork had popped into the wall above his head.

so help me

Now perhaps you will think that I am just lying to you, and maybe you will even think that Fort really wanted to get rid of the Jew kid so's we would oney have two ways to split instead of three, but you know, Mr. Breckenridge, guys like me can't never get away with bull like that to big-league lawyers like yourself, so you can just taken my word for it Fort didn't really mean to hurt the Jew kid a-tall, and that's the truth so help me.

I seen this Jew high-school kid first in New Orleans on the Desire Street wharf luggin' a bran'-new leathern suitcase almost as big as hisself. He come up to me and axes where can he find the shipping steward please, so I judged he was lookin' for a job, and figgerin' to save him trouble I told him they ain't no use lookin' for work around here Bub. You think he taken my word for it, Mr. Breckenridge? No, he has to go off and see the steward for hisself. Well, soon's he find out he comes back and sets down on the wharf and commences lookin' scared-like into the fog over the river. I pulls over to him, figgerin' that any bird with rags as dressy as hisn might have a little extra cash handy, so I axed him for a handout, and he look at me like he never seen me befo', and then hand me a dime and look out into the fog over the river again.

I had a hunch I could wrangle a meal out of him if I just hung on a minute, so I settled down again easy-like and ax him has he worked on the big boats befo', though I seen he ain't. He just says no, and don't seem anxious to get acquainted a-tall. That made me stubborn so I just set still, and in a couple of minutes it begin to drizzle and he picks up his suitcase to go, so I got up too and went with him, makin' small talk all the while just to see where he was a-stayin' at. He walked down Tchoupitoulas and turned on Poeyfarre until we got to the Circle, and there he flop down on a bench, and I seen he did not know where to go, even though he had money in his pocket. We just set there a space under a tree lookin' up at Lee with water runnin' down his back.

A dollar-woman come by and give us the eye, and the Jew kid turn to me and axes do I know the lady, and I says no o' course not. Then he axes why did she look at you so funny then, and now perhaps you will think that I am just lyin' to you, Mr. Breckenridge, but that Jew didn't know what that chip wanted a-tall. I explained, gentle-like, on account him bein' so young and all, but do you think I could get him to believe he coulda bought that girl? Not him—he hadda see for hisself. So I taken him through the district and he seen I wasn't just lyin' to him. He looken a little worried when we come back to the Circle. When we set down again he remarks he wouldn't never spend no dollar of his that way, and I tol' him he could get most of them for six bits if he jewed them a little. He gimme a look when I says to jew them, but he didn't let on he was one, so how was I to know? O' course I wouldn't never have picked up with him if I'd knowed.

We got a mite friendly then, and I tol' him I was goin' down to the Rio Grande Valley, 'cause it come into my head just then how nice and warm it was in the Valley while we was settin' shiverin' in the rain in the Circle. He ax me what I am goin' to do in the Valley, and I thought quick and says

I am going to pick oranges and make three-four dollars a
day doing so, and I looked at him sideways to see would he
swaller that, and he did, hook, line, and sinker. So I tol' him
some more about the Valley. Then I waited a minute and says
casual-like maybe you would like to come along, and he say
yes he would. So we shaken hands on it and he let me sleep on
the floor of his room that night and in the morning I got
breakfast off him also. After breakfast we walken down to
the Soup line yards to wait for a freight through to Houston,
and they was about twenty fellas and some niggras there
already. All the while we was waitin' the Jew kid kep' throwin'
out hints how it might be better we should hitchhike it, so I
seen he was a mite scared, and ax him ain't he never rid a
freight befo' though I seen he ain't. He says no he hasn't
never. So I says well I ain't never hitchhiked and ain't aimin'
to start now, so that left the gate wide open for him to blow,
but he just set still and get that scared look all over his mush
again. Right then I surmised he musta somewhere got the idea
they was somethin' to see in the Valley.

Some of the fellas was cookin' somethin' by the side o' the
track, an' I walked over casual-like to see was it mulligan,
when who do my eyes light on but Luther Morgan what I
palled with on the state farm at Wetumpka. I yelled how
are you Fort old pal, on account Luther was in Fort Myers
so long, and he was glad to see me too. I called the kid over
and axed him to shake hands with my old pal Fort Morgan, so
they shook hands and Fort had a bottle of Dr. Bud's bay rum
and he give me a shot but didn't offer the kid none 'cause
he oney had a mite left for hisself. I don't think the Jew kid
wanted one anyhow. It begin to gimme a pain just to look at
that weasly-lookin' puss o' his. I like a boy with guts.

Well, Fort finished the bay and tried to bum two bits from
the kid for another bottle, but the kid said no and walked away
from him. Fort went off a little after that, and he musta gone
clean back to Canal Street, 'cause he was gone a couple hours

and when he come back he had five cans of Sterno in his pockets and another bottle of Dr. Bud's. He was pretty wobbly and when he seen the kid right away he wants to roll him, and pick up a rock as big as your head to do it with. If ever I seen a scared sheeny in my life it was that Jew kid settin' on his shiny new leathern suitcase shakin' all over like a leaf. He was so scared that even the niggras over to the side laugh a little. I got Luther quieted down a bit, and he pull out a whole handful of silver and heave it all over the yards. I oney got a Canadian dime out of it, but the Jew kid didn't get nothin' a-tall.

We heard the freight whistlin' just then and the fellas began to pick theirselves up—all exceptin' Fort. Fort has made up his mind he ain't goin' to hop nothin' but blind baggage on a silk manifest, and I couldn't convince him that there weren't no manifest due on the Soup line before November anyhow, and even that one would be goin' the other way. But all he would say was I will wait here till November then and if it is going the other way I will go the other way too. There isn't any reasoning with Luther when he is in that frame of mind, so I took two of the cans of Sterno and eighteen cents he still had in his watch pocket, and dragged him over to the side out of the way of the brakeman.

Then the freight pull up about a hundred yards down the track and the kid says hurry let's get on, like he thought they wouldn't be no seats left if we was late, so I says what's the rush—why go way down there when it will certainly come up here? It'll save you draggin' that suitcase which I surmise is pretty heavy. So we waited till it drag up to hop it.

Now perhaps you will think I am just lyin' to you, Mr. Breckenridge, but so help me it's the truth—it musta been about 2 A.M. and we was crossin' some river—musta been the Atchafalay'—when the Jew kid sit up straight real suddent and yell, "We're cut apart!—cut apart!—cut apart!" just like that. Well, just for a second he give me 'n awful turn 'cause I thought we was really cut in two and running wild, but soon's

I got myself together I knew we wasn't, and I tol' him to lay down and quit yellin' like he was nuts. I seen guys in the Army get excited in their sleep, but this Jew was the worst thing ever —he jump up and head straight for the open door. Now the Atchafalay' may not be so wide as the Mississippi but it's just as deep, and I set him down befo' he got hisself all wet. In the morning he don't remember nothin' of what he say the night befo'. I woulda tol' him to go back home, that I had decided to go to Salt Lake City instead; only I kep' wonderin' about that leathern suitcase of his.

When we got to Houston we had a chance to catch a hot-shot clear down to the Valley, though we had to walk two miles out of town to hop it—but what do you think that rookie done when it pull up and I was shovin' him into the blind, suitcase and all? He back out quick like a crawfish and say he thought he'd rather hop a freight. I says O.K. meet me by the depot in San Juan. And the train pulls out. I never expected to see him again.

I got down to San Juan just as it was gettin' light, and I guess that Sterno didn't do me no good 'cause I got off on the depot side and the brakeman called me a son-of-a-bitch and I yelled back, you yellow Mexican bastard you, oney I said it in Mex, and he run after me and give me one on the side of the head that did not even sting on account I got so much Sterno in me.

I walked downtown and seen a young punk in puttees lookin' for guys to pick oranges, and I thought hell with that noise. I tried it oncet in Florida and worked all day and oney made thirty-nine cents, and so I said none o' that for me I come down here to keep warm not to work.

Well, I'd been in San Juan almost two days and had clean forgot all about the Jew kid, Mr. Breckenridge, and was settin' on the packin'-shed platform sunnin' myself, thinkin' maybe Fort would drag in, when I seen the Jew kid.

He was settin' top of a refrigerator car pert as you please, with his hat smashed in and his clothes all over spots, but the suitcase shiny as ever. He weren't downhearted a-tall though—happiest I'd ever saw him, and wants to go to work right away pickin' oranges and make three-four dollars a day. So I tol' him the oranges wasn't ripe quite yet, and he begin to look worried again. Then he ax me where was I stayin' and I says I guess maybe I will rent myself a tourist cabin and if you wish to stay with me I shall pleased to have you and will surely get you a job three-four dollars a day. He agrees, so we start for the tourist camp and on the way I tell him, casual-like, I got no ready cash but can get forty-five, fifty dollars from my brother Bryan what is in Apalachicola on Tuesday, so he can put up his wrist watch for security I will speak to the landlady at the camp just to give it to me, but he back up quick like a crawfish at that and say no not on your life the wrist watch is a gift from his girl in Cincinnati so I said tell me all about it, because I needed time to think how am I going to get this wrist watch.

So we set down on the curb in front of the gas station and that was when he told me he was a Jew and he had a girl in Cincinnati where he come from who wasn't no Jew a-tall. He had sewed her up but his pa wouldn't let him marry her on account she ain't no Jew and her folks is very poor on top of it. Her pa said the kid must marry her or pay him a lot o' dough or go to jail, but the girl herself she wasn't even sore at him, and he liked her a lot also and woulda married her but he didn't have no money to marry on and was still in high school. So he was just about nuts not knowin' what should he do, 'cause his old man won't help him. He decides he must quit school and get hisself a job immediately so's he could get married before the baby was born, but he couldn't find no job in Cincinnati nowhere, and then he read in the paper they was men needed in Las Vegas to work on the Boulder Dam. So he tol' the girl he would go there and get a job and he would send for her, and that made them both very happy, oney when he got to Las Vegas he learns there is oney eight jobs left and there is 4,500 other fellas what had snuck in in front of him. Then he was ashamed to go home and say he can't find no job so he hitchhiked to New Orleans to try to ship out, and that was how I met up with him.

Just as he finished tellin' me I thought of a good idea, and I says come down to the telegraph office with me, David, I wish to send a telegram to my brother Bryan in Apalachicola, so he went down and I axed Bryan for forty dollars and gave it to the kid to read, and had the charges reversed. I knew Bryan would pay for the telegram since he would not know from who it was before he opened it. He would cuss me out when he read it o' course, and would tear it up immediately and would wonder was I nuts or what. We hung around the office until we found out it was accepted, and the Jew kid was convinced I was not just lying to him that I had a brother Bryan in Apalachicola. He give the woman the wrist watch, and we taken a cabin and also get some groceries off her. I had not slept on a mattress for quite some time, and so before we turned in I said to myself, Homer tonight at least you shall sleep better than you have since you was sprung from Wetumpka.

Now maybe you will think I am just lying to you, Mr. Breckenridge, but do you know I did not get scarcely twenty minutes rest that night? First I laid awake a long time wonderin' it is certainly very peculiar that this Jew should not even open his suitcase to see what is inside it, and I do not approve of wiliness in any of its many forms. He was breathin' deep, and I got to thinkin' maybe should I open it myself, when all of a suddent he give one unholy shriek, sit straight up, grabs tight hold of the side of the bed, and begins that nut line about bein' cut apart again. "Cut apart!" he yells. "Cut in two! Thy blood is not my blood! We're cut apart!" and the moonlight was on his face like I seen it on the dead faces at Cantigny, and his eyes was bright and staring straight ahead. My hair, if I had any, woulda stood up then, 'cause he begin to get up slow, wavin' those skinny arms like they was white snakes, like he was tryin' to push somethin' away from in front o' him, and didn't have no strength to do it. I got my hooks in him then and set him down hard, and he went back to sleep arguin' somethin' fierce with somebody. So I couldn't sleep much after that, bein' afraid he might get up again and decide to do a little cuttin' apart on his own.

By the time it is morning I had decided to shake him, suitcase or no suitcase, but Fort showed up that day, and that made me change my mind.

I got a job for the kid pickin' oranges with a gang of Mexicans, but did not go along myself on account I wish to see what is it inside the suitcase. I dived for it soon's he was gone, but do you know what, Mr. Breckenridge? He'd locken it and taken the key with him! Naturally I was pretty sore at such suspicious tactics behind my back as it were, because I am a proud man by nature and a direct descendent of Edmund Ruffin on my mother's side. I went off to the freight depot feeling bad, and set down just to sun myself a bit, and reflected when ever would my luck change.

It was about noon when Fort come in. I was still settin' on the depot platform, and the noise of the engine waken me, and when I sat up, the first thing I seen was Fort. I kidded him a bit about waitin' for the silk manifest and we had a good laugh together over it, and I commenced to feel better. I tol' him I was stayin' with the Jew kid until he would get wise about the telegram, so Fort axes me what have I been doin' for groceries and I tol' him I have been gettin' those on credit also. Then he remarks that he is hungry and is in great need of tobacco, so we strolled over to the camp, and Fort waiten outside, and the woman still thought it was my watch, so she give me two packs of tobacco and a bag of stale tortillas.

About six-thirty I seen the kid comin' down the road and walked down to meet him, on account I want to tell him Fort is sleepin' on his cot. His shirt was tore almost in two and the backs of his hands was all scratches and he has a scratch on the side of his neck which one look tol' me is goin' to come a tropical sore very shortly. He was all streaked with dried sweat, but was not appearing worried, so I ax him how much has he earned, and he says seventy-six cents, at which I supposed he was just lyin' to me, Mr. Breckenridge, because only a Mexican can earn that much in a day. I woulda done it myself if I'd oney knowed they was payin' that much. Then I remarked, casual-like, that Fort was inside and might as well stay with us until I got my money, which would prob'ly be tomorrow. I seen he didn't like that, but then I figgered what can he do about it if he says anything to hurt my feelings again I shall simply refuse to redeem his watch.

At first Fort and the kid did not have very much to say to each other, but after supper Luther showen him the place back of his ear where he was shot at Cantigny and let him feel the steel plate there and that broke the ice and Fort showen him the marks on his left leg too which he got in a job upstate, but which he tells the kid he got also at Cantigny.

Fort made out on the floor that night, and the kid didn't raise no rumpus, and I didn't say nothin' to Fort 'cause I thought maybe the boy is ashamed of it so I will not antagonize him by telling Luther. I can see now all right I shoulda give Fort a hint, but how was I to know?

In the morning early the Jew goes off to pick some more oranges but Fort and me didn't get up in time and I took to reflectin' it would certainy be a fine thing when the boy got paid on Saturday night because the woman in the store was already actin' very independent, as though she was becoming reluctant to extend our credit much further and was not after all a person who had a firm faith in human nature. Then I went down to the store and learned my reflectin' was just about correct, because she gave me what I axed for and then said I couldn't never have any more until I paid up. We sat around smokin' awhile after that and Fort thought that the kid must have tellen her it was not my watch at all but his watch which was a present to him from somebody in Cincinnati. If I'd thought Luther was right I would certainly have kicked that suitcase open then and there, oney I wasn't sure, and they was Saturday night to look forwards to. The kid come back just as it was getting dark out, and reports he had earned sixty-nine cents more, so now we have $1.45 coming from the Magic Valley Fruit Exchange.

Well, it was oney Friday morning, and our credit weren't no good, and all we had left was old bread and coffee. The kid tried to get them to advance his $1.45, but they wouldn't do it and he went off to work looking worried again. But they wasn't really nothin' to worry about.

Fort tried to panhandle a few nickels. in the afternoon, but all the places tol' him he would have to go to the relief station in Alamo or starve. So I copped a half dozen grapefruit seconds from the packing house, and that was all we had for supper, and by morning we have all three of us decide we would go to Alamo to the relief station there. Now I suppose you will think that I am just lyin' to you, Mr. Breckenridge, but do you know that when we got to the station that kid would not go inside? He backed out quick like a crawfish. Of course we couldn't bring nothin' out to him, so I guess he musta been pretty hungry when we got back to San Juan. I didn't ax him. But he went to bed lookin' kinda white soon's we got home, and laid with his face to the wall. He give me a pain just to look at him. I like a boy with guts.

Fort and me went to Alamo again in the afternoon an' when we come back he was still in bed and axes me will I go down to the Exchange and collect his money for him and buy some groceries on the way back. I didn't want Fort along on account Fort is very avaricious, but he come anyhow, and we got the $1.45, and right away he wanted to buy mescal, but I put my foot down on that. I came straight out for tequila or nothing at all. We got a big pint for $1.00 and give the Mex girl who

fetched it two bits because she had to go clear to the other end
of town to get it. After we killed it we still had twenty cents left
but I got to thinkin' of the kid how maybe he was gettin' sick
and all, and I stopped in the Jitney Jungle and bought a quart
of milk. After all it was his money even if he was a Jew. When
I was buyin' the milk I seen Fort starin' at the cash register,
and when we got outside he says, tryin' to be casual-like, let us
walk about a bit, Homer, that tequila has given me a headache. I guessed what was on his mind and says perhaps we
should better take the milk home first and then walk about a
bit, I believe our baby is hungry; but Fort says no we should
first walk about a bit.

So when we got a ways out of town he propositions me we
should heist the Jitney Jungle and I axes him where can we
get a couple rods, and he says we oney need one, Homer, and
I got that, and he pull a roscoe off his hip. That surprised me
somewhat because I had been completely unaware Fort was
packin' a rod on his person, but nevertheless it does not convince me and I says it is all very well for you to say one roscoe
is enough when you are carryin' it but what about me? So then
he says I can have the roscoe if I wish to be selfish, but he will
get a long cut short for hisself. I says perhaps you already have
the long cut short? And he says no, but he knows where he can
get one at for three dollars any time. I says that is very encour-
aging but where is this place where for three dollars you can
get a long cut short any time? And he told me it is the same
place where at we bought the tequila.

I ax him what he is going to use for money to get the short,
and where he is going to get a car, and several other things he
could not answer right off. I reminded him he could never get
out of the Valley without a good car, and he got peeved and
says he will pull the job alone if I have lost my guts. I told him
not to get sore, because I was with him the same as always, and
I axed him who will grab the oday? And Luther answer that
one so quick I seen he musta been thinkin' about the heist for

a couple days at least. The Jew will grab the oday he says like it is all settled.

Then we was back in town, almost to the camp, and we shut up.

Now will you believe me, Mr. Breckenridge, but we hadn't no sooner turned the corner into the camp when I stumbled against a old hitching post and dropped that milk right out of my hand and busted it? That was very strong tequila, Homer, Fort says, and then we was inside the cabin. He was still in bed, but he was curled up double, and all the bedclothes was messed up and when he seen me his eyes look like a wolf's, and then he seen I got no groceries, and he moans and turns his face to the wall. I says do not take it so hard, kid, they would not give me the money and Fort and I been arguin' with them ever since, and now it is too late to get it, the cashier has went home. Sometimes I think pretty fast so now I said let me take your suitcase down to the pawnshop, David, and I will get enough groceries for to last us until I get my money from Bryan, my brother in Apalachicola. He says I do not believe you have a brother anywhere, but take the suitcase and get me something to eat with it and come back right away I am very hungry. Fort tried to come with me again, but I stopped him in time. He has very deceptive ways sometimes.

I taken the suitcase to the pawnshop and they was two gray suits in it, almost new, a pair of shoes, some shirts and b.v.d.s, and a heavy blue wool sweater with a large white "B" sewed on the front of it. I got three dollars for the clothes and three for the suitcase and I spent two dollars for groceries in the Jitney Jungle just like I tol' the kid I would, and I got a pint of mescal for seventy-five cents which I drunk right away, and then I held out three for the short and took to reflectin' how it was oney two days ago that I was thinking my luck wasn't going to change. On my way back I seen a new Chrysler I knowed belong to the druggist on the corner, and in front of it a big elephant ears was standin'. It was almost nine I guess when I got back, and the kid was lookin' so scared it give me a turn just to look at him—more scared than hungry now, and I knowed somethin' had been goin' on. It was in the air. Fort was sittin' nex' to him on the bed when I come in, but got up quick and sat down at the table when I come in. I didn't say nothin'. I just fixed us up some stew, and the kid dragged his-self out o' bed in his dirty underwear, but didn't eat much a-tall. Nobody said much until we finished eatin' and then Fort cough a little and announces to me that the kid wanted to come in with us on the heist real bad, and I was a little sur-prised I did not know Fort was going to proposition him so quick, so I figger to myself he musta squeezed the Jew.

After that the ice was broke and the oney important ques-tion left was when to pull it. Fort musta forgot about that tele-gram I have sent because he suggests nex' Saturday night, which is a full week away, and I says no to that right away, and when I said it the mescal in me bubbled a little, and I began to hope Fort would argue about it. So I says real em-phatic Tuesday or Wednesday. I was thinkin', too, that we had to have the kid, and if we waited a week he would certainy crawfish. Fort says to me, Homer I am surprised at you, you know very well Saturday night is the only night, you should know that. So I says tonight is Saturday night, and Fort got up an' put on his coat, an' the kid set up a howl about his wrist watch, an' Fort give him a look, an' he shut up like a oyster.

We all three of us went down to the Mex bootlegger an' give him three bucks for the short, an' I took it an' beat it down the alley to the garage back of the drugstore, an' the druggist was just puttin' the Chrysler up for the night, an' I hopped in with him and give him directions, an' he seen I meant business an' was scared as the devil, but he got me in front of the Jitney Jungle without hittin' nothin'. Fort an' the kid was waitin' in front, an' I made the druggist change places with me easy-like. Then Fort an' the Jew went inside, I heard Fort start barkin', an' I seen him shove the kid. Then the kid grab about half the

money, whirls an' tears for the door droppin' bills all over the
place, an' Fort give him the shoulder, an' he went back an'
taken it all then. I'd thought he'd break his neck comin' out,
he came so fast, but Fort back out slow until he got through
the door. Then he turn so quick he even surprised me, and in
two leaps he was inside the car and we was goin' fast. Fort
threw the druggist out when I turned the corner into the highway to McAllen, an' about a minute after they got started
behind us an' I give her everything she got.

I never seen Fort so nervous befo' in all my life. He wanted
to stick to the main road right through McAllen an' shoot it
out if they was waitin' for us there, but I didn't say nothin'
'cause I know it don't pay to argue with Fort when he is nervous and has liquor inside him on top of it. I just turned up the
first side road I seen, run twenty feet into a orange grove, an'
lit out for the tracks. They come right behind me, the Jew
breathin' hard, an' we wasn't a minute too soon. The bulls
from McAllen come by a-tearin' an' turn up the orange-grove
road an' Fort started cussin' out the warden at Wetumpka
under his breath. If they'd gone forty feet further they woulda
seen the Chrysler, but they didn't, an' went back to the highway and tear out for San Juan again.

We waiten there by the tracks real quiet-like, an' it musta
been about eleven-thirty a string of empties headed for San
Anton' come along, an' we hoppen it. Fort was sure that they
was goin' to stop us in McAllen an' search for us, an' wouldn't
quit fingerin' the trigger of that long for a minute. The Jew
kid don't say nothin' but look so almighty goddam scared I
didn't know whether to laugh or kick his ugly little face in with
my heel. I like a boy with guts.

They didn't look for us in McAllen, an' we got through
Falfurrias O.K. I figgered we was out of the Valley then an'
didn't have to worry no more so long as we got out of sight
before we hit San Anton'. But Fort kep' mumblin' he ain't
goin' back to breakin' rock again no matter what happen, an'

I dozed off a-listenin' to his blabberin', an' so I wasn't wide awake when it started, Mr. Breckenridge, an' it was all over in a second, an' so I cannot say rightly just what did happen. I heard that yell from the corner, "We're cut apart!—cut apart!" an' he then jump up an' say, "Thy blood is not my blood!" an' make straight for Fort. Well now you-all can't blame Luther in a way. He was jumpy in the first place, an' him an' the kid hadn't never clicked much anyhow, an' maybe he'd squeezed the kid a mite to make him come along, an' o' course he didn't know the Jew was asleep. He jes' heard that yell an' seen him comin', an' the long was in his hand.

I guess that Jew never knew what hit him. He jes' doubled up, stretched out, made a gurgly sound in his neck, an' that was all. O' course we had to clear then, but even then they'd never gotten me if Luther hadn't pointed, an' on top of that tryin' to make you-all believe it was me had the long all the time.

Now maybe you will think that I am just lying to you, and maybe you will even think we really wanted to get rid of the Jew kid so's we could split oney two ways instead of three, but you know guys like me can't never get away with bull like that to big-league lawyers like yourself, Mr. Breckenridge. So you can just taken my word for it didn't nobody mean to really hurt the Jew.

So help me.

afterword
by studs terkel

The remarkable thing about *The Neon Wilderness* is how well it holds up after nearly forty years. When I first read it I was knocked out and the funny thing is, as I re-read it I was KO'd again. That's the thing: Nelson's stories are part of our lasting literature. They don't fade away.

Look at the stories themselves. Think of the girl and the Mexican fighter in "Depend on Aunt Elly": how they survive in their crazy way, their personalities flawed but somehow intact, their souls battered and bruised. Remember, nobody—and this is something that a couple of writers, who follow the pugs, Jimmy Breslin and Pete Hamill, have said—nobody ever wrote about prize fighters the way Nelson did; no one ever touched him; no one ever came close. So you have the girl and her Mexican with his sense of respectability and it's his respectability that is being hurt. The ache, more than a slight ache, of him and of her. It's what kids I know, street kids, call "the hurts," a way of poeticizing, of making lyric, of holding onto a note in music.

Take "Stickman's Laughter," the story of Banty—and it's somehow the Bantys the world over—the guy you see who gambles and who has expectations; beyond gambling it's that wanting something, knowing you're never going to get it. The interesting thing in the story is that Banty, at the table the loser, doesn't really lose at the end.

Read "The Captain Has Bad Dreams." The whole world, the whole human comedy, or tragedy, or tragicomedy is there and this captain is not only an observer, he's caught in the middle of it too; he's another Miss Lonelyhearts. He's on the other side, the side of authority, yet he's caught. He has bad dreams. If he were just this cold guy dispensing harsh justice, meting out harsh punishment, whatever it might be, there'd be no story. He's not. He's a vulnerable man. He's the most vulnerable of the bunch. Nelson makes him human and funny and tragic. He makes the police uniform human. The captain is just as funny as those pathetic guys in front of him who are appearing in the line-up. This is what we're talking about; Nelson has a way of capturing it; the word, again, is "the hurts."

Or think about the legless man, Shorty, in "The Face on the Barroom Floor." Here's a guy with a handicap, who ordinarily is the one you look upon as lost when you toss a dime in his cup. Instead, he's strong as hell. He's the guy most up against it, who turns out to be the strongest. He can't wear boots and he can't run but, by God, he's sure got arms and he's a tough rough boy. And in the end he becomes an innocent too.

Of course, the people in Nelson's fiction are a combination of many things. He met many prototypes. No character is based on any single person, and perhaps no single person is as funny as some of his characters. He has met general prototypes, be it the hooker or the guy who steals, but he's not recreating them. The characters are his. That's why they're poetic. He goes behind the billboards and he finds—and it's not romanticizing, it's true—he finds a crazy kind of glow there, not pathos, but this goofy kind of glow. His characters are clowns in a kind of circus, white-face clowns, tragic clowns, that speak to you about what it means to be human. Nelson himself was like that.

There's a Samuel Beckett touch to the stories in *The Neon Wilderness*, without Nelson having read Beckett yet at this time. The very nature of the life, the circumstance itself, becomes poignant in that way, like Lost Ball Stahouska, or like the guy who sticks his hand in the cash register in "The Captain Has Bad Dreams," saying he just leaned there and it opened, just like that.

We live in a clownish time. We live in a clownish world. When you have a guy like Reagan, who may be the funniest guy in the world except for the fact that people take him seriously, how can anybody be serious unless he clowns as well? Very much like Lear's fool who can say the truth in his own way, Nelson is the great clown who deep deep down is very serious in his comments about our world, and his reflections about his time. He teaches us about failures, and it's the failures that turn out to be more exciting than successes. He's the funniest man around and can therefore be the most serious.

All of this is what makes these stories as moving now as when I first read them. Nelson walks his reader on the wild side of life, to use the title from one of his books, the side the reader is afraid of, the last place the reader would choose to go, the unsafe side. Nelson is speaking for those who have no defense. He isn't looking at them through a microscope, nor living in a cork-lined room. He becomes one of them. Maybe the guy who described it best was Ross McDonald, when he said that Nelson Algren could talk about hell in such a way that he touched heaven.

Once, in 1956, Nelson accompanied me to see Billie Holiday. He was, at the time, wearing glasses. Billie's voice was shot, though the gardenia in her hair was as fresh as usual. Ben Webster, for so long big man on tenor, was backing her. He was having it rough, too. Yet they transcended. There were perhaps fifteen, twenty patrons in the house. At most. Awful sad. Still, when Lady sang "Fine and Mellow," you felt that way. And when she went into "Willow, Weep for Me," you wept. You looked about and saw that the few other customers were also crying in their beer and shot glasses. Nor were they that drunk. Something was still there, that something that distinguishes an artist from a performer: the revealing of self. Here I be. Not for long, but here I be. In sensing her mortality, we sensed our own.

After her performance, Nelson and I shambled into her dressing room. Dressing room, did I say? It was a storeroom: whiskey cases stacked against the walls, cartons of paper napkins, piles of plastic utensils strewn about, this, that, and the other. It didn't matter. She was there, with the gardenia in her hair. Lady, in the gracious manner of a lady, bade us be seated. Algren slouched into a chair against the far wall, in the semi-darkness. He appeared a character out of one of his works: Bruno or Frankie or Sparrow or Dove.

Patiently, she answered questions that I'm sure had been put to her too many times before. About the white stoops of Baltimore, of the others for whom she scrubbed, about Miss Bessie, about her grandmother, about club owners, the honest and the venal. When there was trouble remembering, her eyes half-shut as in a slow blues, her hands poised in midair. If, by chance, I hit upon the right name, her fingers snapped. That's it, baby. No words were needed; the gesture said it.

And when the conversation ended, as casually as it had begun, and the waiter had brought her a tumbler of gin— "Lemon peel, baby"—she indicated the man in the shadows, Nelson Algren. She had been aware of his presence from the beginning; there had been mumbled introductions. Now she murmured inquiringly, "Who's that man?" Nelson explained that she and he had the same publisher. *The Man with the Golden*

Arm and *Lady Sings the Blues* had both been put out by Double-day.

"You're all right," she said to him.

"How do you know?" he asked.

"You're wearin' glasses."

He laughed softly. "I know some people with glasses who got dollar signs for eyes."

"You're kind."

"How can you tell?" he persisted. How could she tell? He was half-hidden in the shadows.

"Your glasses." She was persistent, too.

Nelson Algren no longer wears glasses, but he's still a funny man. At a time when pimpery, licksplittlery, and picking the public's pocket are the order of the day—indeed, officially proclaimed as virtue—the poet must play the madcap to keep his balance. And ours.

Unlike Father William, Nelson does not stand on his head. He just shuffles along. His appearance is that of a horse player, who, this moment, got the news: he had bet her across the board and she came in a strong fourth. Yet, strangely, his is not a mournful mien. He's chuckling to himself. You'd think he was the blue-eyed winner rather than the brown-eyed loser. That's what's so funny about him. He *has* won. A hunch: his writings may be read long after acclaimed works of Academe's darlings, yellowed on coffee tables, will be replaced by acclaimed works of other Academe's darlings. To call on a Lillian Hellman phrase, he is not "the kid of the moment." For in the spirit of a Zola or a Dreiser, he has captured a piece of that life behind the billboards. Some comic, that man.

At a time when our values are unprecedentedly upside-down—when Bob Hope, a humorless multimillionaire whom I call the mechanical mouth, is regarded as a funny man and a genuinely funny man is regarded as our President—Algren is something of a Gavroche

"The hard necessity of bringing the judge on the bench down into the dock has been the peculiar responsibility of the writer in all ages of man." It was something Nelson wrote in 1961, as an added preface to his prose-poem, *Chicago: City on the Make*. The original work had been composed a decade earlier. It's a responsibility to which he has been obstinately faithful.

About two years ago, in the streets of London, I ran into a voluble Welshman. On learning I was an American—let alone a Chicagoan—he bought me a whiskey. I had no idea Americans were so popular with the people from Rhondda Valley. But it wasn't that at all. He could hardly wait to blurt out, "You're an American, you must know of Nelson Algren." He proceeded to rattle off, in mellifluous tongue, all the titles of Nelson's novels and short stories. On discovering that I actually knew the man, he bought drink after drink after drink. And on miner's pay, at that. How I got back to the hotel shall forever remain a mystery to me.

In New York, an old freight elevator man, a small battered Irishman, whose one claim to immortality was an encounter with Fiorello LaGuardia, asked me, between floors, if I'd ever heard of a writer named Algren. He had read *The Neon Wilderness*. As far as I know, he owned no coffee table.

Recently, in a conversation with a woman on welfare, his name came up. It was she, not I, who introduced it. She had been reading one of his paperbacks and saw herself in it. She had also been having her troubles with the Welfare Department and neighborhood cops. As far as I know, she owned no coffee table.

By the way, who wins in poker generally? Pretty dull people. The accountant types, the bookkeepers. Who are the ones who lose? Those who always chance the wild shots, who play on the wild side. Nelson invariably lost in poker.

Maybe Nelson Algren's horses usually run out of the money.

Maybe his luck at the poker table is not that good. Maybe he'll never be endowed by a university; nor be earnestly regarded by literary makers and shakers. But he has good reason to just shuffle along like a laughing winner. And he may be the funniest man around.

—STUDS TERKEL
Chicago, May 1985

(Portions of this text were reprinted from **Talking to Myself** *by Studs Terkel, Pantheon: 1984)*

an interview with nelson algren

INTERVIEWERS: Do you write in drafts?

ALGREN: Yes, but each draft gets a little longer. I don't try to write the whole thing in one draft.

INTERVIEWERS: How much do you usually write before you begin to rewrite?

ALGREN: Very little, I dunno, maybe five pages. I've always figured the only way I could finish a book and get a plot was just to keep making it longer and longer until something happens—you know, until it finds its own plot—because you can't outline and then fit the thing into it. I suppose it's a slow way of working.

INTERVIEWERS: Do you think of any particular writers as having influenced your style, or approach?

ALGREN: Well, I used to like Stephen Crane a lot and, it goes without saying, Dostoevski—that's the only Russian I've ever reread. No, that ain't all, there's Kuprin.

INTERVIEWERS: How about American writers?

ALGREN: Well, Hemingway is pretty hard not to write like.

INTERVIEWERS: Do you think you write like that?

ALGREN: No, but you get the feeling from it—the feeling of economy.

INTERVIEWERS: How about Farrell?

ALGREN: Well, I don't feel he's a good writer. Since *Studs Lonigan*, I don't know of anything of his that's new or fresh or well written. Frankly, I just don't see him. I *missed* Farrell, let's put it that way.

INTERVIEWERS: Some of the reviews have linked you and Farrell.

ALGREN: I don't think he's a writer, really. He's too journalistic for my taste. I don't get anything besides a social study, and not always well told, either. He has the same lack that much lesser-known writers have. He hits me the same way as, say . . . a guy like Hal Ellson. Do you know him? Well, he's a New York writer who does this gang stuff. He's written some very good books, but they're just straight case studies, you know what I mean?

INTERVIEWERS: How about Horace McCoy?

ALGREN: No, no. I didn't mean to put Farrell down there. No, Farrell, I think, is a real earnest guy—but I mention this Ellson because Ellson does the same thing. But, I mean, there's something awfully big left out. It isn't enough to do just a case study, something stenographic. Farrell is stenographic, and he isn't even a real good stenographer. He's too sloppy. In his essays he compares himself with Dreiser, but I don't think he's in Dreiser's league. He's as *bad* a writer as Dreiser—but he doesn't have the compassion that makes Dreiser's bad writing important.

INTERVIEWERS: Do you have a feeling of camaraderie, or solidarity, with any contemporary writers?

ALGREN: No, I couldn't say so. I don't know many writers.

INTERVIEWERS: How do you avoid it?

ALGREN: Well, I dunno, but I do have the feeling that other writers can't help you with writing. I've gone to writers' conferences and writers' sessions and writers' clinics, and the more I see of them, the more I'm sure it's the wrong direction. It isn't the place where you learn to write. I've always felt strongly that a writer shouldn't be engaged with other writers, or with people who make books, or even with people who read them. I think the farther away you get from the literary traffic, the closer you are to sources. I mean, a writer doesn't really *live*, he observes.

INTERVIEWERS: Didn't Simone de Beauvoir dedicate a book to you?

ALGREN: Yeah, I showed her around Chicago. I showed her the electric chair and everything.

INTERVIEWERS: Do you vote? Locally, there around Gary?

ALGREN: No. No, I don't.

INTERVIEWERS: Still you do frequently get involved in these issues, like the Rosenbergs, and so on.

ALGREN: Yes, that's true.

INTERVIEWERS: What do your publishers think of that?

ALGREN: Well, they don't exactly give me any medals for caution.

INTERVIEWERS: Do you think there's been any sort of tradition of isolation of the writer in America, as compared to Europe?

ALGREN: We don't have any tradition at *all* that I know of. I don't think the isolation of the American writer is a tradition; it's more that geographically he just *is* isolated, unless he happens to live in New York City. But I don't suppose there's a small town around the country that doesn't have a writer. The thing is that here you get to be a writer differently. I mean, a writer like Sartre *decides*, like any professional man, when he's fifteen, sixteen years old, that instead of being a doctor he's going to be a writer. And he absorbs the French tradition and proceeds from there. Well, here you get to be a writer when there's absolutely nothing else you can do. I mean, I don't know of any writers here who just started out to be writers, and then became writers. They just happen to fall into it.

INTERVIEWERS: How did you fall into it?

ALGREN: Well, I fell into it when I got out of a school of journalism in '31 in the middle of the depression. I had a little card that entitled me to a job because I'd gone to this school of journalism, you see. I was just supposed to present this card to the editor. I didn't know whether I wanted to be a sports columnist, a foreign correspondent, or what; I was willing to take what was open. Only, of course, it wasn't. Things were pretty tight. Small towns would send you to big cities, and big cities would send you to small towns; it was a big hitchhiking time, so I wound up in New Orleans selling coffee—one of these door-to-door deals—and one of the guys on this crew said we ought to get out of there because he had a packing shed in the Rio Grande Valley. So we bummed down to the Rio Grande. Well, he didn't have a packing shed, he *knew* somebody who had one—one of those things, you know—but what he did do, he promoted a Sinclair gasoline station down there. It was a farce, of course, it was an abandoned station in the middle of nowhere; I mean, there was no chance of selling gas or anything like that, but I suppose it looked good for the Sinclair agent to write up to Dallas and say he had a couple guys rehabilitating the place. There was nothing to the station, it didn't even have any windows. But we had to dig pits for the gas, and then one day the Sinclair guy comes up with a hundred gallons of gas and wanted somebody to take legal responsibility for it. So my partner hands me the pencil and says, "Well, you can write better than I can, you been to school," and I was sort of proud of that, so I signed for it.

Then my partner had the idea that I should stay there and take care of the station, just keep up a front, you know, in case the Sinclair guy came around, and he'd go out—he had an old Studebaker—and buy up produce from the Mexican farmers very cheap, and bring it back and we'd sell it at the station—turn the station into a produce stand. I mean, we were so far

out on this highway that the agent couldn't really check on us—
we were way out; there were deer and wild hogs and everything
out there—and in three weeks we'd be rich. That was *his* idea.
But the only thing he brought back was black-eyed peas. He
paid about two dollars for a load of black-eyed peas—well, that
was like buying a load of cactus—but he wouldn't admit he'd
make a mistake. So, he went around to the big Piggly-Wiggly
store and they said they'd take *some* of the peas if they were
shelled. So he set me to shelling the peas. I shelled those damn
peas till I was nearly blind. In the meantime, he'd left town, out
to promote something else.

Then one day he showed up with another guy, in a much
better-looking car—he'd left the old Studebaker there at the
station—and I saw them out there by the pit fooling around
with some sort of contraption, but it didn't dawn on me, and
then it turned out they were siphoning the gas into this guy's
car. Well, they left town before I knew what was happening.
When I caught on I was being swindled, of course, I was very
indignant about it, and I wrote letters that took in the whole
South. I gave the whole Confederacy hell. Oh, it was nowhere,
just nowhere, nowhere. So I wrote a couple letters like that—
and I was very serious at the time, and some of that got into the
letters. Ultimately, I got out of there. I poured a lot of water
into the empty tank, but I felt like a fugitive because I didn't
account to the Sinclair guy. It was a terrible farce, but later
when I got home—I don't know how much later—I read the
letters again, and there was a story in them all right. So I
rewrote it and *Story Magazine* published it, and I was off. But
that's what I mean by "falling into it." Because I was really
trying to become a big oil man.

INTERVIEWERS: Have you consciously tried to develop a
style?

ALGREN: Well, I haven't consciously tried to develop it. The
only thing I've consciously tried to do was put myself in a

position to hear the people I wanted to hear talk talk. I used the police line-up for I don't know how many years. But that was accidental too, like that junky deal—you don't exactly seek it out, you're there and it dawns on you. I got a newspaper man to loan me his card, but that was only good for one night. But then I finally got rolled. I didn't get myself deliberately rolled; I was just over on the South Side and got rolled. But they gave me a card, you know, to look for the guys in the line-up, and I used that card for something like seven years. They finally stopped me—the card got ragged as hell, pasted here and there, you couldn't read it—the detective at the door stopped me and said, "What happened, you mean you're still looking for the guy?" This was like seven years later, and I said, "Hell yes, I lost fourteen dollars," so he let me go ahead.

INTERVIEWERS: Do you think, then, that you're more interested in idiom, than in idea? And isn't that generally characteristic of American writers?

ALGREN: That's cutting it pretty close, all right. I think of a tragic example: Dick Wright. I think he made . . . a very bad mistake. I mean, he writes out of passion, out of his belly; but he won't admit this, you see. He's trying to write as an intellectual, which he isn't basically; but he's trying his best to write like a Frenchman. Of course, it isn't strictly an American-European distinction, the belly and the head; you find the same distinction here. A book like Ralph Ellison's, for example, or Peter Matthiessen's, stays better with me than the opposite thing, a book like Saul Bellow's. Bellow's is a book done with great skill and great control, but there isn't much fire. I depend more on the stomach. I always think of writing as a *physical* thing. I'm not trying to generalize, it just happens to be that way with me.

INTERVIEWERS: Can you relate *The Man with the Golden Arm* to an idea?

ALGREN: No, unless a feeling can be an idea. I just had an over-all *feeling*, I didn't have any particular theory about what I ought to do. Living in a very dense area, you're conscious of how the people underneath live, and you have a certain feeling toward them—so much so that you'd rather live among them than with the business classes. In a historical sense, it might be related to an idea, but you write out of—well, I wouldn't call it indignation, but a kind of *irritability* that these people on top should be so contented, so absolutely unaware of these other people, and so sure that their values are the right ones. I mean, there's a certain satisfaction in recording the people underneath, whose values are as sound as theirs, and a lot funnier, and a lot truer in a way. There's a certain over-all satisfaction in kind of scooping up a shovelful of these people and dumping them in somebody's parlor.

INTERVIEWERS: Were you trying to dramatize a social problem?

ALGREN: Well, there's always something wrong in any society. I think it would be a mistake to aim at any solution, you know; I mean, the most you can do is—well, if any writer can catch the *routine lives* of people just *living* in that kind of ring of fire to show how you can't go out of a certain neighborhood if you're addicted, or for other reasons, that you can't be legitimate, but that within the limitation you can succeed in making a life that is routine—with human values that seem to be a little more real, a little more intense, and human, than with people who are freer to come and go—if somebody could write a book about the routine of these circumscribed people, just their everyday life, without any big scenes, without any violence, or cops breaking in, and so on, just day-to-day life—like maybe the woman is hustling and makes a few bucks, and they get a little H just to keep from getting sick, and go to bed, and get up—just an absolutely prosaic life without any particular drama to it in their eyes—if you could just do that straight, without anybody getting arrested—there's always a little danger of that, of course—but to have it just the way these thousands of people live, very quiet, commonplace routine . . . well, you'd have an awfully good book.

INTERVIEWERS: On the point of style again, you seem to favor phrases, almost more than sentences.

ALGREN: I always thought my sentences were pretty good. But I do depend on phrases quite a bit.

INTERVIEWERS: Do you try to write a poetic prose?

ALGREN: No. No, I'm not writing it, but so many people say things poetically, they say it for you in a way you never could. Some guy just coming out of jail might say, "I did it from bell to bell," or like the seventeen-year-old junkie, when the judge asked him what he did all day, he said, "Well, I find myself a doorway to lean against, and I take a fix, and then I lean, I just lean and dream." They always say things like that.

INTERVIEWERS: What do you think of Faulkner?

ALGREN: Well, I can get lost in him awful easy. But he's powerful.

INTERVIEWERS: It's interesting that Hemingway once said that Faulkner and you were the two best writers in America.

ALGREN: Yeah, I remember when he said that. He said, "After Faulkner . . ." I was very hurt.

INTERVIEWERS: You said that the plot of *The Man with the Golden Arm* was "creaky." How much emphasis are you going to put on plot in your future writing?

ALGREN: Well, you have to prop the book up somehow. You've got to frame it, or otherwise it becomes just a series of episodes.

INTERVIEWERS: You gave more attention to plot in this book you've just finished.

ALGREN: This one I plotted a great deal more than any other. In the first place because it's more of a contrived book. I'm trying to write a reader's book, more than my own book. When you're writing your own book, you don't have to plot; it's just when you write for the reader. And since I'm dealing with the past, the thirties, I have to contrive, whereas, with a living situation, I wouldn't have to.

INTERVIEWERS: Do you think that this one came off as well as *The Man with the Golden Arm*?

ALGREN: Mechanically and, I think, technically, it's done more carefully, and probably reads better than previous books.

INTERVIEWERS: You make this distinction between a "reader's book" and a book for yourself. What do you think the difference is?

ALGREN: It's the difference between writing by yourself and writing on a stage. I mean, if the book were your own, you'd be satisfied just to have the guy walk down the sidewalk and fall on his head. In a reader's book, you'd have him turn a double somersault. You're more inclined to clown, I think, in a reader's book. You've got one ear to the audience for yaks. It's just an obligation you have to fulfill.

INTERVIEWERS: Obligation to whom?

ALGREN: Well, you're talking economics now. I mean, the way I've operated with publishers is that I live on the future. I take as much money as I can get for as long as I can get it, you know, a year or two years, and by the end of that time your credit begins to have holes in it, and—well, you have to come up. After all, they're businessmen. Of course, you can get diverted from a book you *want* to write. I've got a book about Chicago on the West Side—I did a hundred pages in a year, and I still figure I need three years on it—but I was under contract for this other one, so it took precedence. I didn't want to contract for the first one, because I just wanted to go along as far as I could on it without having any pressure on me. The one I contracted for is the one I finished, and now I'm going back to the one I want to do.

INTERVIEWERS: Did you enjoy writing *The Man with the Golden Arm* more than you did this last one?

ALGREN: Well, it seemed more important. I wouldn't say I

enjoyed it.more, because in a way this was a much easier book to do. The lumber is all cut for you. The timber and the dimensions are all there, you know you're going to write a four-hundred-page book; and in that way your problems are solved, you're limited. Whereas, with a book like that *Man with the Golden Arm*, you cut your own timber, and you don't know where you're building, you don't have any plan or anything.

INTERVIEWERS: Do you find that you take more care with a thing like that?

ALGREN: No, I always take great care. I think I'm very careful, maybe too careful. You can get too fussy. I do find myself getting bogged down wondering whether I should use a colon or a semicolon, and so on, and I keep trying each one out. I guess you can overdo that.

INTERVIEWERS: Do you think that writing a book out of economic obligation could affect your other work?

ALGREN: No, it won't have anything to do with that at all. One is a matter of *living* and reacting from day to day, whereas the book I just finished could be written anywhere there's a typewriter.

INTERVIEWERS: Do you think your writing improves?

ALGREN: I think technically it does. I reread my first book, and found it—oh, you know, "poetic," in the worst sense.

INTERVIEWERS: Do you feel that any critics have influenced your work?

ALGREN: None could have, because I don't read them. I doubt anyone does, except other critics. It seems like a sealed-off field with its own lieutenants, pretty much preoccupied with its own intrigues. I got a glimpse into the uses of a certain kind of criticism this past summer at a writers' conference—into how the avocation of assessing the failures of better men can be turned into a comfortable livelihood, providing you back it up with a Ph.D. I saw how it was possible to gain a chair of literature on no qualification other than persistence in nipping the heels of Hemingway, Faulkner, and Steinbeck. I know, of course, that there are true critics, one or two. For the rest all I can say is, "Deal around me."

INTERVIEWERS: How about this movie, *The Man with the Golden Arm?*

ALGREN: Yeah.

INTERVIEWERS: Did you have anything to do with the script?

ALGREN: No. No, I didn't last long. I went out there for a thousand a week, and I worked Monday, and I got fired Wednesday. The guy that hired me was out of town Tuesday.

ALSTON ANDERSON
TERRY SOUTHERN
New York, 1955

Reprinted from The Paris Review